The Entanglement

Your Love Is Mine

B. Commodity

© 2023 by B. Commodity

Published by Major Key Publishing, LLC

www.majorkeypublishing.com

ALL RIGHTS RESERVED.

Any unauthorized reprint or use of the material is prohibited. No part of this book may be reproduced or transmitted in any form or by any means, electronic, or mechanical, including photocopying, recording, or by any information storage without express permission by the publisher.

This is an original work of fiction. Names, characters, places, and incidents are either products of the author's imagination or are used fictitiously, and any resemblance to actual persons, living or dead, is entirely coincidental.

Contains explicit language & adult themes suitable for ages 16+

To submit a manuscript for our review, email us at submissions@ majorkeypublishing.com

Synopsis

Ever since she could remember, Sydney's life had been a series of bad luck and pure struggles. Sydney had no idea how to live her life without having to fight to earn everything she had, which sadly didn't amount to much.

After finally kicking her cheating boyfriend to the curb–for what seemed to be the millionth time, Sydney decides to take control of her life in the form of a self-help book. She quickly becomes fascinated with not only the book but the author as well, who Sydney is fortunate enough to meet in person at a book signing.

Once she meets her idol, her world is quickly turned from drab to fab and Sydney is introduced into a new world of class, money and new lovers. It seems that Sydney's misfortunes are finally over once she is taken in by her lover and her lover's husband. In a blink of an eye, her polyamorous adventures take the forefront in her life, and everyone has an opinion on her entanglement. But none of that matters because Sydney has found the love of her life with one of her lovers. Now all she has to do is fight for it...

Dear readers,

Thank you for your continued support in purchasing and reading my novels! To share some of the crazy stories that come across this imaginative mind of mine, and to have people actually enjoy them, is still an indescribable feeling. I wanted to introduce you to some new characters and a new story in this book that causes you to ask yourself, what if? I enjoy writing stories about different kinds of women so that my readers are able to relate or be challenged by them. I, myself, find traits of my own in some of my characters; for better or worse. We, as women, are complex beings and I love to be able to explore that through my stories.

With that being said, this book may introduce some of you into the world of polyamory. Please note that this book does not represent the polyamory, or poly, community. Nor my opinion on the lifestyle. Poly life has always seemed like an interesting and taboo topic to me. That was until I began to learn more about the lifestyle and meet more people of the poly community. This book is a mere story of one fictional character fumbling her way through life in an attempt to find herself. In this story, the young woman is not only being introduced into poly life, but yet another taboo topic; dating outside of her race. Take a journey with me through Sydney's story of getting herself in too deep. Thank you to all my LGBTQ and poly friends who helped me when curating this book to make it as authentic as possible.

Enjoy!

Prologue

"Fuck," Sydney cried to herself as she painfully began to tear at the wired screen window in front of her with her bare hands, desperate to get out to safety. After what felt like an eternity, the screen began to bend and tear apart as her bloody, shredded hands shook while she tried to rip it quietly.

"G, no!"

Sydney heard the rupture of a bullet in the air and froze in terror.

Asher, she thought to herself, feeling the hairs on her arms raise at the shrill sound that came from the other side of the door. She came back to her senses once she saw the gun that lay beside her on the dresser. She instantly tossed it through the open window and on-to the wet yard outside. The rain poured down harder than it had on their way over there only a hour or so ago. The storm was picking up and Sydney imagined it was at its worse.

Sydney stuck both arms out of the window and pulled her sore body through the small opening. She bit her lip in pain as she felt the wild wire cut through the flesh on her side and thighs as she crawled out on her elbows.

"Ugh," Sydney groaned as she turned onto her back and pulled herself out the rest of the way. "I made it, I made it," she said reassuring herself as she grabbed the gun and tried to stand barefoot on the wet grass.

Sydney got her bearings together just in time to hear another gunshot from inside the cabin. Her heart sank.

I should go back, he may need help, Sydney thought to herself as she looked down at the gun in her hand.

Just as she began to raise the gun and head into the now quiet cabin, Sydney heard the sound of another shot, this time through the bedroom door.

"Sydney!" Genevieve screamed wildly as she began kicking and beating on the door.

Sydney took off running south. She knew that Asher was dead and as much as it killed her, she had to leave him. There was no point in waiting. She must do what he told her to do.

NOW

"Get out. Now!" Sydney screamed through tears as she poured a pot of ice-cold water onto Shawn in his sleep.

"What the fuck, Sydney!" Shawn yelled as he scrambled out of the bed and flopped on the floor like a fish out of water.

Sydney tossed the empty pot to the side as she leaped over the bed and lunged at Shawn. She balled up her fists and began to deliver blows to whatever she could reach. She attacked his back, his side and his head furiously with her fists.

"I hate you," she said through tears as she began to tire out. "You're lucky that water wasn't boiling!"

"Sydney, why are you bugging?!" he yelled as he laid cowardly in the fetal position on the floor.

She climbed off of him and reached for the cellphone she

stole earlier while he was asleep. Clumsily she entered the password and threw the phone hard at Shawn's face, causing the force of his phone to bust his lip.

"Your dumbass still ain't learn from last time I see," she yelled through snot and tears. "Who the fuck is Tia and why is she saying that the 'baby is yours'?"

"Syd... babe," he said holding his lip and walking over to her, "it's not like that—"

"Get the fuck away from me," she said pushing him away. "Get out!"

She wiped her face with the back of her hand as she looked over at Shawn. He was dumbfounded and caught just like a kid with their hand in the cookie jar.

"Get out!" she repeated as she pointed to the door.

"I'm not going nowhere," Shawn said, now raising his voice and clenching his jaw.

He held his lip and looked around the room desperately for something to stop the bleeding.

"You are buggin' you need to calm down! You fuckin' busted my lip!" he yelled, getting angrier as he placed an old t-shirt from the floor to his bloody mouth.

This wasn't the couple's first time at this rodeo. Over the years, Shawn would always tend to slip up and have Sydney discover a new girl he had on the side. To this day she still felt the pain from the first time he cheated on her. He was untrustworthy. And Sydney was more upset at herself for allowing it to go on this long.

"We are gonna talk about this. Can you get me something for my lip, please!?" he pleaded, sitting back down on the dry side of the bed.

"Fuck your lip Shawn! There is nothing left to talk about. I'm sick of this shit and it's over. I should've kicked your ass out last time when you slept with Casey! Now get the fuck out! Why am I repeating myself?!"

Her heart was racing so hard that she could hear it in her ears. She knew mentioning Casey, a mutual college friend of theirs, would trigger her even more. But she was too far gone to care.

Sydney went to the closet and grabbed the nearest gym bag of his that she could find. She stormed across the cramped studio apartment to the dresser where Shawn kept his clothes.

"Syd... babe!" Shawn said walking over to Sydney as she threw clothes in the bag, "We decided to leave the Casey thing in the past. Besides, college was years ago...what the fuck are you doing Syd, stop touching my shit!"

She ignored him and continued on her rampage. She loudly threw everything of Shawn's into the duffle bag and sobbed while doing it.

"Syd, please calm down; they gonna call the cops. It's two in the morning," he said, trying to soothe her as the neighbors banged on the paper-thin walls.

"Good, I hope they do. Your ass ain't on the lease! I'll tell them that your ass is trespassing," she said as she zipped the bag up and threw it at his head.

"Syd, in this climate right now, you know that shit ain't even funny. They'll kill me before they even reach the door," he said, clenching his jaw and taking off his wet beater and boxers.

"You're right, it's nothing to play with so I suggest you leave," she said, folding her arms across her chest. "Go over that bitch Tia's house and go play family with her. This shit is over. I mean it," she said with exasperation.

"You know, you real fucked up for this Sydney," Shawn said as he picked up dry clothes from the floor and put them on.

"You wanna know what's really fucked up Shawn?" she asked as she pulled her waist- length box braids up to sit on the top of her head in a messy bun.

"Yea, what's that?" he asked sarcastically as he threw the duffle bag over his shoulder.

"Your baby mother once she realized she's stuck with your triflin' ass for life. I almost feel sorry for her," she said through gritted teeth. "Get out of my apartment. NOW!"

Shawn clenched his jaw again. He looked as if he had something to say, but then changed his mind and turned away. They both knew she was right, and by the look on Shawn's face, Sydney could tell the baby was his.

"I've wasted five years of my life with you. Five fuckin years of this abuse," Sydney said as tears continued to roll down her face.

"Then if it's like that, give me my fuckin jersey then since you so 'abused'," he spat back at her.

Sydney frowned and looked down and realized that she was in Shawn's high school basketball jersey. She walked to the front of their small and junky apartment and opened the door. She wasn't surprised to see her nosey neighbors all hanging in their open doorways from the hallway, enjoying the show. Some of them ducked behind their doors when they heard her open the door, but most continued to watch for the next scene.

"Nigga this ain't ATL and you ain't T.I," she said as she pulled the jersey over top her head and stood there naked in the doorway.

She threw the jersey in his face and switched her weight to the other hip. Shawn looked around irritated at the show she was putting on. A few of their nosey neighbors had made it outside to the hallway to get in better earshot of the fight. Now they got a peepshow, too.

"Bye nigga!" Sydney yelled after him as he stormed out past her down the hallway.

Sydney slammed her door shut and locked it, being extra sure to lock the deadbolt as well. At that moment she was grateful that she had enough sense to not give him a key to the apartment they shared. She headed towards her bed and laid down, being careful to avoid the soaked wet spot from Shawn's unexpected bath.

She took a deep sigh and stared up at the ceiling as she heard her neighbors one by one suck their teeth and talk shit before going back to their respective homes.

The tears rolled down the side of her face and left little puddles in both of her ears, and she couldn't do anything but just lay there. She was numb. She had kicked Shawn out numerous times in the past, only to take him back a few days later. But this time was different; she finally felt free of him. She sat up and wiped her face as she looked at the state that her raggedy apartment was left in. It was normally a junky,cluttered mess of clothes, books, and empty take-out containers. But now, post-war, it was a total disaster-zone. Everything was drenched in water, and there was blood on the carpet from Shawn's lip.

"Bitch, now what?" she asked herself, looking around the room.

Chapter 1

Thursday, September 17th

"Ugh," Sydney moaned as she felt a sharp pain on the left side of her head. She sat up and swung her feet over the side of the bed as she drowsily roamed around her studio trying to find her phone that beeped loudly somewhere in the distance.

Forget it, she thought to herself after she got tired of looking for it after a few seconds. She was too groggy to find it.

She walked to her refrigerator and poured herself a glass of cold water. She was hungover from last night. It had been eight miserable days since she kicked Shawn out. She spent last night, like most of the nights that week, alone with a large pizza and bottle of Moscato to the face.

The water felt like heaven as she greedily downed it, enjoying the crispness of it down her throat. Now that she had woken up, she realized the beeping noise was the alarm on her phone. She was certain it was her 7:45 a.m. alarm, signifying that it was time to get ready for work. Until she looked at the microwave and realized it was actually 8:49 a.m .

"What the fuck?" Sydney squealed as she ripped her night clothes off and ran into the shower.

Sydney washed and got dressed as fast as she could. She scrambled to get herself ready as well as look for her phone, which was later found under the empty pizza box. She wondered to herself how she could sleep through her alarm. A few minutes? Sure. But an hour was unheard of for her. And she was the laziest person she knew.

Sydney knew that she was spiraling and that her life was a mess. All she could do lately was stuff her face with food, drink cheap wine and cry. There was no need in going to her friends or family for support because all they would do is tell her good riddance and ask what took her so damn long to leave him in the first place.

Only eight days in, and this had been the longest breakup of their whole relationship. She was mourning the loss of her relationship. She wondered where he was sleeping every night since he wasn't allowed to stay at his mama's. The thought of him shacking up with another woman always sent her stomach into knots. She had to admit, a part of her was ready to throw in the towel and take him back.

Sydney tripped down the stairs of her apartment building that was nestled in the heart of the city. Since she was already late for work, she had to bite the bullet and order an Uber, though she could barely afford it. She walked out just as her Uber arrived and she jumped in the back of the white Altima.

"Hey, I'm running super late for work... so if you don't mind— "

"I'll do the best I can do. Safety first," Mary, her driver, said, cutting her off without even looking back at her.

Sydney sighed and sat back. She was already late for work and she knew a few minutes wouldn't spare her from the wrath of her manager. She shook her head at herself and wondered why she could never get herself together.

"Hello, Earth to Sydney," Angel said, snapping his fingers rudely in Sydney's face a few hours later.

"I swear," he said, putting his hands on his hips in annoyance, "You would think that you would step it up and actually work today considering that you were already twenty minutes late."

"Relax Angel, would you?" Sydney said, waving him away as she turned back to her pile of unfolded clothes.

Sydney had known Angel since high school. The two actually graduated in the same year and were gym partners their junior year. She, the chunky weird black girl and him, the skinny white gay kid, were naturally picked last in gym and then forced to stick with one another. The two had always managed to keep it cordial. Growing up in a small inner-city town in Boston will do that to you. Even years after they graduated from high school, the two were paired up again when they both got a summer job at Lilian's, a retail store in the mall that was basically a knock off of Macy's.

"How about you finish up these clothes,girl, so then we all can relax?" he asked, rolling his eyes and walking away.

Angel had been on his high horse ever since he was promoted to manager a year ago. Secretly, Sydney was annoyed that the two were hired at the same time, yet she wasn't even considered for the newly opened position.

"How about you finish up these clothes, girl," Sydney mocked under her breath as she pulled out the folding board to fold the pile of sheer-white shirts. "If his ass calls me 'girl' one more time..."

"What was that?" Angel yelled over his shoulder at the front of the store.

"Nothing!" Sydney said quickly back.

It was four hours into her shift and Sydney was already over it. She leaned on the store's counter and played with a loose braid as she watched a woman try different perfumes while her daughter played on her tablet at her feet. The little girl looked up and caught Sydney looking at her. She smiled and waved hard at Sydney and Sydney couldn't help but to do it back. She hadn't realized until this very moment how much she needed to see a friendly face, even if it was from a three-year-old stranger.

It had been relatively quiet that day at work, and she was ready to get off soon so that she could get to her second job on time. Just as she started plotting the story that she would tell Angel so that he would let her go a few minutes early, she saw India come into the store and spot her. Sydney smiled and waved her best friend over and indicated for her to be quiet since Angel was not too far away.

Sydney and India had been best friends since high school. They were the only black girls in their AP English class and quickly created a deep bond when the class was forced to read *Uncle Tom's Cabin.* Between the numerous questions about how the book made them feel and the constant mix up of their names, they became friends fast.

"Hey girl hey," India said as she made her way to Sydney's register and tossed her heavy bag on the counter.

"Damn girl, what you got in there, a body?" Sydney joked.

"Girl, I just walked out of that place and quit. Took my shit too," India said, rolling her eyes.

India had worked in one of the hair salons in the mall for only a few weeks. She was just as bad, if not worse, than Sydney when it came to keeping a job. So, it didn't surprise Sydney that she had walked out.

"Girl, what happened now?" Sydney asked, leaning in on the counter.

"Man forget all of that," India said, waving her off and looking around to make sure that no one could hear. "What is going on with you? I only called your ass about five times since yesterday. Where the fuck you been at girl?"

"Shh," Sydney said as she grabbed India's arm and pulled her to the back of the store.

"Um excuse me, Sydney your shift is not over for another forty minutes," Angel called out from behind them.

"Angel, I'm just taking a quick break; I do believe I am owed that by law," Sydney said over her shoulder as she continued to pull India to the back of the store.

"You got ten minutes, Sydney and I mean it!" he shrieked.

Once safely in the back alley of the store the two looked at each other and began to laugh.

"Angel is just as miserable as he was in high school. Damn, don't that queen got a man yet?" India said as she rummaged through her purse.

"Girl, I don't know. I wish he found one, his ass is so damn miserable," Sydney said as she leaned against the brick wall. "Well I guess I can't talk. And are you allowed to say that?"

"Say what? *Queen?* Girl I am just as fruity as that boy is, I can say it, but your ass better not," India said as she pulled out her black and mild and lit it. "So, the rumors are true?"

"Rumors?"

"Yea girl, rumors. Imagine my surprise when I gotta hear from your cousin Neicey that your ass finally kicked his ass out. I mean don't get me wrong— a bitch is happy you came to your senses, but damn I gotta hear it from the streets?"

"The streets though, India?" Sydney said, rolling her eyes and fanning the smoke from India's black out of her face.

"Yea hoe, the streets! I've only been waiting for this day for what feels like my whole life! So, tell me, what happened? And make it quick before Angel comes out here and I have to shove my foot up his narrow behind."

Sydney sighed and reluctantly told India the story of how she went through Shawn's phone after the two had made love and he fell asleep. She told her about the message from the girl

"Tia" and how she kicked him out, but not before showing her bare ass to all her neighbors.

"Wow, you're speaking metaphorically when you said you showed your ass in front of your neighbors though, right girl?" India said as she put the rest of her black out.

"Unfortunately, no," Sydney said as she put her face in her hands out of embarrassment, "I've been trying to avoid them ever since. The trash has needed to go out for days now but I can't show my face after—"

"Showing that ass," India said, trying to cover her laugh and broad smile with her manicured hand.

"Shut up India! I don't know what to do. And I wasn't going to bother telling you because I knew what you would say. Hell, I only told my mom because I was forced to. I can't afford to live there without Shawn's help. We were barely getting by already," Sydney whined.

"Damn girl, how bad is it?"

"Bad," Sydney said, looking her in the eye.

She wasn't lying. She had barely enough money to afford rent next month, let alone money for food, the bus or necessities. Without Shawn's extra income from his little side gigs, she didn't know what to do.

"And then this nigga here is trippin'," she continued, referring to Angel. "He's waiting to fire me for anything. I gotta really make sure I hold onto that job at Flamingo's."

"Speaking of... India girl," Sydney said, letting a sweet smile spread across her face as she skipped over and hugged her best friend.

"Oh, girl, what?" India asked stiffly, trying to push her away.

"Girl, do my hair over again for me, pleaseeee?" she asked, batting her eyelashes.

"Sure, you got $100?" India asked.

"Bitch, I just told you I'm broke," Sydney said, pulling away from India with an attitude.

"Girl, I'm joking. I was waiting for you to ask. That new growth looks crazy," India laughed. "You know you can't show up to them white people with your hair looking like that."

A few hours later Sydney was at her second job at Flamingo's. She had managed to get to work only twenty minutes late and was able to sneak in the back undetected. She had only worked at this job for a few months and was desperate to make this one stick.

"Hello, welcome to Flamingo's, we are so glad you decided to dine with us tonight on this lovely Thursday. Do you have a reservation?" Sydney said pleasantly as she welcomed a pair of older women.

"Hello dear, yes we have reservations under the name Muriel Coates. Anyway Dawn, you just have to read this book! I swear it is changing my life," Muriel said to her friend as Sydney ushered them to their table.

"Here you are ladies, please have a seat. Have you dined—"

"Oh, isn't that the same book that was on Reese Witherspoon's book club?" Dawn said, cutting Sydney off.

Sydney took a subtle deep breath and continued to ready the table for the women. She was used to being overlooked and talked down here at this restaurant, unfortunately it was the lay of the land. Flamingo's was a very pricey Italian restaurant located in the financial district in Boston. Many of the patrons came in for business meetings and barely spoke two words to Sydney or the rest of the waiting staff. In fact, the only time Sydney ever really got someone to say more than two words to her was when there was a rowdy businessman and his entourage who came in on their afternoon break; they were only interested in stuffing their face and "emptying their balls" as India would say. Often their service would end with an invitation to join them for an afternoon romp at the Four Seasons across the street.

Sydney poured the women glasses of fresh water and went to fetch their menus.

"Oh, let me see, let me see," Dawn said, putting on her purple reading glasses.

"Dawn, I swear this book has opened up my eyes! You know how down I've been since the kids went off to school. And with Don across the country working all the time... I just don't know what to do with myself anymore! This book has really shown me the light... I just feel different, you know. Umm, excuse me, hun you can do better than this," Muriel said holding up her glass to Sydney.

"Ma'am?" Sydney asked, confused as she laid the menus on the tables.

She was desperate to get away from these women as fast as she could and get back to her hostess podium. She could already tell how rude they were going to be.

"I said, *you can do better than this,*" Muriel repeated, drawing out her words. "This glass is filthy and has your fingerprints all over it. Please get me a new one."

"Sure thing," Sydney said, turning her back to her and retrieving another glass.

"Here you go," she said, placing the fresh glass down and removing the old one before walking away. "Bitch," she said to herself.

Sydney didn't bother going over the specials with the women. She was already too through with their rudeness and could feel the racism bouncing off of them.

"All yours girl," Sydney said to Cai, her co-worker, as she breezed into the kitchen with the dirty glasses.

"Yikes, that good huh?" Cai asked as she stood up and flattened her apron.

Cai was Asian and therefore the only other minority that worked at Flamingo's with Sydney.

"They already complained about my fingerprints, as if my blackness was gonna ooze into their water and contaminate them," she sighed, shaking her head.

Sydney was starving and realized that nearly half the day was gone and she hadn't eaten anything. She knew she had no money to buy food and catch a bus home. She quickly regretted coming into the kitchen for solace with all the smells of fresh Italian food being made. Unlike most restaurants, Flamingo's had a strict policy about their staff eating their food for free.

"I told my Ma about your breakup and she made this for you," Cai said, reaching into her shoulder bag and handing Sydney a Tupperware container.

Sydney eagerly snatched it out of Cai's hands and whipped the top off as she took in a deep breath of the savory smells of chicken and soy sauce.

"I would say you didn't have to, but damn, I am so glad you did," Sydney said as she grabbed a fork and sat down on a stool to eat. It was as if Cai read her mind.

Sydney had only met Cai's mom a few times since working there, but she quickly won her over. All Sydney had to do was mention how Japanese was one of her favorites and the woman had been feeding her ever since.

"Don't you even wanna know what it is?" Cai said laughing as she checked her reflection in the mirror that hung on the wall.

"It's good, that's all I need to know," she said, smacking her lips, "Tell 'Ma' I said thank you. Or how do you say it in Japanese?"

Cai smiled and said a bunch of Japanese words before turning to Sydney and giving her a wink.

"Yea, tell her I said that," Sydney teased, "Beware, those

women are so fascinated with some damn book I haven't even told them the specials for the night."

"Great, glad you warmed them up for me Syd," Cai said sarcastically as she sanitized her hands and headed out of the kitchen.

"Anytime!" Sydney yelled out to her as she grabbed her phone from out of her apron.

She had been screening her calls ever since her breakup. Shawn's number and his mama's number had both been blocked from her phone days ago. Still, she would find numerous missed calls daily from a blocked phone number that were usually accompanied by a pathetic voicemail from him.

Right on cue, she saw that she had not only missed a few calls from an unknown number but had a new voicemail as well. Sydney sighed and cradled the phone with her ear and shoulder as she listened to the message and ate her food.

"Syd... it's me, Shawn. You know it's real fucked up you blocking my calls like this. You got me out here at work asking coworkers to borrow their phones and shit. Anyway... look I know I fucked up, but bae please hear me out. I miss you... I love you. We invested too much time for you to let this break us. Now, I know I fucked up; I know that Syd! But remember when we said nothing could tear us apart—"

Sydney hung up the call and deleted the message before she listened to any more. She knew what he was going to say, and she didn't want to hear it. He always manipulated her like this and reminded her of better times when the two were deeply in love and felt like nothing could tear them apart. Shawn had abused Sydney's loyalty for years.

She put the lid on the container and decided to save the rest for later. She knew she didn't have anything at home to eat except for some ramen noodles. And tonight, she would pretend to feast with a cheap glass of wine and some of Cai's mom's good cooking.

The rest of her shift passed by relatively smoothly. Sydney had made about fifty dollars in tips which was good considering that she was just hostessing tonight. She cleaned her station and checked with the rest of the waitstaff to see if they needed any more help shutting down shop before she left, though she knew that she only had about five minutes to spare before the next bus.

"I got you something," Cai said, putting her puffer coat on.

"Oh yeah? Other than food? You're spoiling me," Sydney said as she put her own jean jacket on.

"Those bitches from earlier? They left that book they kept talking about. All lunch those two talked about this," Cai said, shaking her head and pulling the book out of her bag.

"Oh my God Cai, you really took it?" Sydney gasped, surprised as she snatched the book out of Cai's hand and gave it a once-over.

The book was heavy and had a black cover with the words, *The Elite: Steps to Change Your Life* across the cover in silver font. Sydney turned the book over and saw a picture of a smiling and polished black woman.

"Genevieve Cross," Sydney said as she traced her fingers on the author's raised name on the cover and read it aloud.

The woman seemed so statuesque and confident. She had a look that was both welcoming and as if she would bite your head off at the same time.

"I know right, I'm surprised she's African-American too. Something tells me those bitches didn't care much for anyone that was at least one shade darker than them," Cai said, wrapping her scarf tight around her neck.

"Cai, for the millionth time, girl, *please* say black," Sydney said, rolling her eyes and tossing the book in the bag.

"Well read it, I don't know, maybe it will help you to forget about that bum Sam," Cai said.

"His name is Shawn, but you knew that," Sydney laughed

as she walked out with her, "How much did they tip you anyway?"

"Phish," Cai said waving at Sydney as if she were muttering nonsense, "Those bitches only tipped me $3 and I'm sure that was only because they wanted to make their bill an even $200."

Sydney laughed and shook her head, not surprised in the slightest as she headed out the door.

"You need a ride Syd?" Cai asked as they both stepped outside into the brisk Boston fall night.

"Nah, thanks I'm good. I'll see you tomorrow, thanks again for the food!"

Sydney began to walk briskly to her bus stop that was a block away. There was actually a bus stop right in front of the restaurant where she worked, but due to her pride, she refused to let anyone see her getting onto it.

She made the bus with only a few seconds to spare and plopped down in the nearest empty seat that she could find.

It was nine at night and the bus was fairly packed with people who all looked as miserable as Sydney felt. She was exhausted from her day and cringed at the thought of the early shift she had at Lilian's tomorrow morning with her favorite, Angel. Sydney had a long thirty-minute ride home and decided to kill her time productively.

"The Elite: Steps to Change Your Life," she whispered to herself as she reread the cover and opened the book.

Chapter 2

Friday, September 25th

"Okay, okay, okay... now what is this book about again?" India asked as she parted some of Sydney's thick hair and prepared it for another box braid.

"If I have to tell you one more time..." Sydney began, not bothering to look up from the book that sat in her lap.

"Alright girl, I'm listening for real, now what is it about?" India asked, holding in a giggle.

Sydney was finally getting her hair braided. India had done Sydney's hair hundreds of times since the two met in high school. She actually had India to thank for her signature look of long box braids that flowed down to the nape of her back. India was the hood's stylist and everyone came to her when they needed their head done right for the low.

"Oh my God!" Sydney began, "Okay so this book is about self-fulfillment. It's about learning how to create your own happiness and setting yourself apart from everyone else," Sydney said, finally putting the book down a moment to gush over it.

She had become just as obsessed with the book as those women at the restaurant had last week. She had barely put it down since she started it a few days ago. She had only bothered to read the author's five page dedication while on the bus the other day. Admittedly, at first she wasn't pressed and didn't want to hear the gloats of her and her Ivy League education. She closed the book immediately.

She finally gave in late one night and read a few chapters in hopes that it would help her to fall asleep. To her surprise, she was completely drawn in after the first chapter and stayed up late reading it. She hated to admit it, but she was even a little sad that she was nearing the end of the book already.

"I can't with those self-help books. They're all the same to me. *Think positively and manifest your success* or *write down your feelings*. Or they tell you to go take walks and shit," India said, popping the gum in her mouth, "I don't know girl, sound like a bunch of bull to me. I'm glad you didn't pay for it."

"Well it's not bull India," Sydney said, spinning her head around and looking back at her, "It's actually helping me out; if you haven't noticed a bitch is going through some things, okay?"

"Damn bitch, my bad," India said, turning Sydney's head back around. "All I am saying is that if you're Qlooking for advice, your ass should've just asked me," she teased, before seeing Sydney's irritability. "Okay, tell me more. How do you think this book is going to help you?"

Sydney sat and thought about it for a minute. She had to admit, before reading this book she didn't think self-help books were really useful either. But over the last few days she had noticed a change in herself and felt more hopeful about her situation and the future. More importantly, those weak moments of wanting to reach out to Shawn had subsided as well.

"It's teaching me to be more confident in myself... I mean I don't know, maybe I feel like it applies to me so well because of my breakup. But it's just teaching me how to value my uniqueness and how to use that as my strength to separate myself from...*them*."

"Mhmm, okay..." India said, keeping her opinion to herself.

"Shut up India," Sydney said as she playfully swatted at her and the two laughed.

"Aye, Aye, what's good Syd?" said India's girlfriend Khadijah, as she walked into their apartment.

"Hey babe," India squealed as she swung her leg over top of Sydney's head and pranced over to Dij.

India melted in her girlfriend's arms. Dij, who was almost a foot taller than India, picked her up and pushed her into the door and they began passionately kissing one another as if no one else was there. The two acted as if they hadn't seen each other in months, when it had only been a few hours.

"Oh, don't mind me. Heartbroken girl over here just sitting here watching y'all love each other down, no biggie," Sydney said, rolling her eyes and opening the book back up.

Unfortunately, Sydney was used to seeing the two of them all over each other like love-struck teenagers.

"My bad Syd," Dij chuckled as she broke away from India and slapped her butt before placing her back down. "What's tea girl?" Dij asked as she sat down with them in the living room.

"Shit," Syd said back to Dij as she stood up for something out of the kitchen.

"Syd in here fangirling to some dumbass book she found at work," India said, sitting down on Dij's lap and playing in her dreads.

"I'm not 'fangirling'... but this book is good. You're just a hater," Sydney said, helping herself to a cold slice of veggie pizza from their fridge. "We all can't find our way in life from IG models turned spiritual guides overnight, India."

"Girl say what you want, them bitches be getting paid and I

am trying to head to where the money resides, you feel me?" India said, causing everyone to laugh.

"Ohh, that's by that Genevieve chick?" Dij said, eyeing the book that laid on the floor. "I heard about that shit."

"You what?" India said, shocked as she smiled down at Dij.

"See!" Sydney squealed.

"My boy Dirk was talking about it the other day. He said that book motivated him to get out of his mama's house or something like that," Dij said, reaching in her pocket and casually pulling out a wad of cash. "Now that nigga starting his own edible company. Guess it worked."

Dij was a hustler. She never had a legit job, but always stayed paid. She did it all from scamming, "managing" some girls who danced in the clubs, and even sold drugs here and there. India once told Syd that Dij promised she would stop selling once India finished up getting her Physical Therapy degree.

"Again," Sydney said, now screaming in India's face, "See! This shit works."

"Yeah, yeah, well holla at me when you make your first million girl. I gotta pee. Give me a minute and then I'm back to finishing that head," India said, lightly kissing Dij on her lips before standing up and switching her way slowly back to the bathroom.

"That shit looking right Mama!" Dij yelled after her as she watched India's large ass jiggle to the bathroom.

Sydney plopped down on the couch and began to flip through the channels on TV. She decided she would finish the book once she got back home, so that she could have some peace and quiet.

"Yo, this her right here, right?" Dij asked, tossing Sydney her phone.

Sydney looked down and saw pictures of the author Genevieve all on her Instagram page.

"She's cute... don't tell India I said that shit, you know how your girl is," Dij joked as she walked away.

Sydney was too distracted to even speak. She never thought to look the author up herself. Mainly because she avoided social media like the plague. Sydney was one of those rare twenty-somethings who prided herself on barely looking at or posting on social media. Secretly, she always felt it made her look more mature and she judged people her age who couldn't go a day without posting their food, lover or workout. The only time her Instagram account got any real use was when she used to stalk Shawn to see if he was up to no good.

Wow, Sydney thought to herself as she continued to scroll through the page.

She was excited to finally get a glimpse into the life of the woman whose words had engulfed her. Whose book had already made an impact on her by helping her get out of the deep depression she was in. Sydney was in the process of decluttering her life. First, by boxing up Shawn's stuff and tucking it away in the closet until she could drop it off to him. Being sure to not give him any access or need to return back to their home. For her second step, she would focus on decluttering her body and focusing back on her body and health.

Sydney's eyes fell on a photo of Genevieve laying on a towel on the beach. She wore a revealing black string bikini and a sun hat so large that it covered most of her face.

"Damn," Dij whispered over Sydney's shoulder as she looked at the picture too.

"I know, right?" Sydney said back as they both turned their heads to the side to get a better look.

Sydney could never pull off such a brave look like that. Genevieve was half naked in the middle of a crowded beach in Ibiza. All of her body parts were *just* covered with the thin string, keeping her from being fully nude. She had a mischievous and flirty smirk on her face, the only part of her face that was showing. She looked carefree and happy. Most importantly, she looked hot. Sydney both admired and envied her at the same time.

"India told me you been struggling since you kicked old boy out— kudos to you on that, by the way."

"Thanks," Sydney said half listening to her as she continued to scroll and boggle over the Instagram. She had scrolled over to a picture of her speaking to a packed auditorium at Cornell. She looked so calm, cool and collected.

"Here," Dij said as she peeled off a few hundreds of her cash and handed it to Sydney.

"Dij, I— " Sydney said, finally looking up and objecting.

"Take it Syd, it ain't nothin'," she said, still holding the cash out. "Just do me a favor and promise not to go back to that nigga, aight?"

"Aight," Sydney said as she took it, feeling somewhat embarrassed.

In any other circumstance, she would deny the cash. But times were tough right now and Sydney was already on her last straw at Lilian's. She made a mental note to pay Dij back the $400 as soon as she had it.

"Thanks Dij," Sydney whispered to Dij as she finally gave her back her phone and redownloaded Instagram on her own.

She was grateful that Dij saved her the embarrassment of giving her the money in front of India. India would be sure to hold that over Sydney's head until she paid her back fully. India didn't play about two things— her money or her woman.

"Anytime sis."

"Anytime what?" India asked, coming back in the room and climbing behind Sydney to continue her hair.

"Mind ya business with ya nosey sexy ass," Dij teased.

Later that night Sydney paced around her studio in deep thought with a glass of wine. Once she got off the bus and walked the half block to her home, she made two quick stops.

The first to the liquor store to get a $12 bottle of wine, and then the next to her downstairs neighbor to cop some weed.

Sydney knew that she wasn't exactly killin' it right now in the responsibility department. But fuck it, she deserved some relaxation. She thought back on the chapter in *The Elite,* when the author wrote about carving out "you time." In this time, you were supposed to do whatever brought you joy and something that was purely about you, for you only. In the book, Genevieve advised that her favorite thing to do when she needed to destress was either a shopping spree or a relaxing day at the spa.

Thus, here Sydney was pacing around her cramped studio and pouring herself her third glass of wine. Oblivious on what to do with herself.

Well ain't this some shit, she thought to herself.

Without Shawn around, she didn't know what fun looked like. They spent most of their free time together over the last few years. Anything fun they did was something that Shawn loved to do like going to basketball games or hanging at his cousin's house. Oh, and of course when he was really feeling fancy, going to Dave and Busters to beat little kids in arcade games. Sydney had no idea what *she* actually liked to do for fun.

"Ugh," she grunted to herself as she looked around the apartment, realizing she had no one to vent to.

She put down her glass of wine on her makeshift coffee/dining room table and lit her just-rolled blunt as she laid down on her bed and picked up her phone.

She opened up her phone again. It was still on the recently downloaded Instagram app. After logging back in, she scrolled through her feed for a little bit before she landed on a picture of Shawn with some Spanish looking chick... Tia.

Sydney rolled her eyes at her own stupidity as she began to choke on smoke from the weed. She hadn't even thought of her needing to detach Shawn from her social media too. He probably never thought she would see this because the last time she had been on Instagram was when she posted a pic from her mom's 55th birthday dinner, two years ago.

She went onto Shawn's page and saw a few more new pics of him and the new "love of his life", his words. She felt like an idiot as she realized that one of the pics dated back to the week she actually kicked him out. He had been out there embarrassing her the entire time.

"Fuck nigga," she cussed under her breath as she tried to go onto Tia's page to see that she was blocked.

Guess the bitch has some sense, she thought to herself as she followed suit and blocked Shawn.

"Genevieve Cross," she said drunkenly aloud as she typed out the first name that came to mind into the search bar.

After hitting the follow button, Sydney began to scroll down her Instagram page. She quickly noticed that there was a new post that wasn't there earlier when she stalked her page at India's house.

It was a flier for a book signing Genevieve was doing in Boston, in just two days.

Sydney shot up and continued to read to find out where and when it was happening. She had to go; clearly this was a sign.

As soon as she took another hit of her blunt, a thought occurred to her. "Fuck!" she yelled, frustrated when she remembered she was scheduled to work at Lilian's. She knew it would be nearly impossible to convince Angel to give her a day off.

"Do what makes you happy. Every time. Never put another's happiness over yours."

The line from *The Elite* appeared in Sydney's mind. It wasn't a coincidence that she found this book and a week later found out that the author would be in her hometown. She knew what she had to do.

Two days later...

"I have nothing to wear," Sydney whined.

"All them clothes, and you don't have nothin'?!" India said with her nose deep in her Physics book.

"Nothin'," Sydney continued to whine as she stood there in just her towel. "Indiaaa, come help me."

Sydney had successfully called out of work for the book signing. Well, as successful as one could be when calling out for a stomach bug. She called the store and told them that she had been shitting for 24 hours straight.

"Ew, girl keep that shit to yourself. LITERALLY," Angel had said to her on the phone before hanging up.

India got up and stomped over to Sydney's closet as she tried to search for something for Sydney.

"What if I told you that there were other places where you could go to get clothes from that were NOT from the Goodwill?"

"Hush and leave me alone." She was used to India coming at her wardrobe. Fashion was never at the forefront of Sydney's mind.

Sydney grabbed her small makeup bag and decided to make an attempt at putting some on. She rarely wore much makeup but considered this a special occasion. She was going to meet the author who was helping to change her life and she needed to look her best.

"I still can't believe she is actually here for a signing, what are the chances of that?" India asked as she pulled out a thick gray turtleneck dress and gave it the once-over. "I guess this will do."

"Fate," Sydney said as she rubbed dark brown eyeshadow

on her finger and dabbed her eyelids. "Thanks again for the ride girl."

"No problem, can't have you riding up there on a bus," she said, tossing the dress on the bed. "Though I hope ya ass is getting an Uber back. I am not coming back out tonight," India said sternly.

Sydney stepped out of her towel and pulled the dress over her head, not even bothering to put a bra on.

"Must be nice to be a part of the itty-bitty titty committee," India said, returning back to her book.

"I guess," Sydney said as she slid on her Dr. Martens boots and thrift store leather jacket. "How do I look?" she asked, spinning around to model her look for India.

"Cute girl, add some lipstick and let's go," India said with a tube of something red already in her hand.

In usual Sydney fashion, Sydney arrived late to the signing. The signing was taking place at a small museum just twenty-five minutes away from Sydney's apartment. However, Boston traffic had other things in mind as it took her an additional twenty minutes for them to get there.

Sydney stumbled in trying to catch her breath as she handed the attendant her ticket. The museum was beautiful, grand and busy as people viewed the various pieces of artwork and paintings. Sydney had always wanted to visit this museum. She was grateful that Dij gave her some extra money just in time for her to get this ticket and pay the difference of what was still owed for her rent. The magic of how everything perfectly lined up for her to be here this evening was not lost on her. She was ushered down the hall into a large room where she could hear someone already on stage beginning the event.

"Shit," Sydney said as she walked into the room and dropped her phone, book and purse all at once causing the whole room to turn and stare at her and her loud arrival.

Sydney was mortified and scrambled to pick her things up

and avoid the eyes of everyone in the room as she tried to find a seat near the back. She could feel her heart beating in her chest as she walked through aisles of people who all still watched her, annoyed, as she stumbled to find a seat in the crowded room. Once she finally found a vacant one and got her things settled, she bravely lifted up her head. She felt like she was back in college.

Sydney instantly locked eyes with the speaker who stood on stage. Genevieve looked at Sydney and gave her a small reassuring smile and wink as she raised her microphone back to her mouth. Not until this moment did Sydney realize that she waited for her to find a seat before she would speak. Sydney was mortified.

"As I was saying... Thank you so much Anna for having me here this evening. This event is lovely, and the people?" she said, eyeing the crowd and shaking her head in approval, "The people are beautiful as well. Everyone please give Anna, the coordinator of this evening, a hand first and foremost."

The room lit it up in soft claps as Genevieve stood at the podium and clapped to the woman sitting down to the right of her. Anna sat beaming, obviously pleased to be hearing the accolades coming from the guest speaker of the night.

Sydney was sweating and slowly took off her jacket to get comfortable. Between rushing in here and then causing a scene, she was a wreck. A frail man who sat next to her offered her a napkin and a weak smile.

"Thank you," Sydney whispered to him as she took it and dabbed at the nervous sweat that she felt growing at her temples.

Genevieve was even more drop-dead gorgeous in person. Luckily for Sydney, she found a seat that wasn't too far from the stage. She could see Genevieve perfectly. She wore a lilac chiffon sleeveless pant suit that complimented her tawny brown skin tone perfectly. Her black hair laid neatly in a healthy bob that landed just on her shoulders and was tucked perfectly behind her left ear to show off her oval-shaped diamond studs. She looked classy and sexy at the same time; and her powerful energy could be felt all throughout the room.

"I must say I am really amazed and honored about the success of my fourth book, *The Elite: Steps to Change Your Life.* As a matter of fact, if I may toot my own horn, I just found out this morning that I made the New York Times bestseller list for the *third* week in a row!" Genevieve exclaimed as everyone in the audience began to clap for her.

Genevieve continued talking to her fans and engaging them in conversation about her thought process when curating the book. The whole time, Sydney marveled at Genevieve's grace as she floated across the stage in her very tall and, Sydney was sure, very expensive six-inch nude pumps.

"So, let's talk about it!" Genevieve said after finishing reading some highlighted excerpts from her book. "I want to open up the floor and talk to my readors. Please, anybody have any questions for me?" she asked as she finally took a seat and turned her gaze to Sydney.

Is she looking at me? Sydney asked herself as she began to fidget in her seat.

She hadn't moved an inch since she sat down. She was too mesmerized to move, to mesmeized by Genevieve to say the least. When she made eye contact with her for the second time, she felt as if she were caught drooling. She quickly tucked her loose braids behind her ear and looked down at her feet.

"Come everyone, please. There is a mic in the middle of the room; we are taking a few questions and then we will have the signing," Anna said as she waved everyone over to the mic in the center of the room.

A few people eagerly got up and made their way to the microphone, beginning to form a small line. Sydney both envied and hated them. Being a self-diagnosed introvert,

Sydney was used to having mini anxiety attacks whenever she was forced into public situations. She hated going to public events and would always much rather stay in than go out. The idea of public speaking brought instant butterflies to her stomach, and she felt herself instantly get uncomfortable as she began to tug at her turtleneck.

She herself had a few questions to ask the author. For starters, she wanted to know how Genevieve became so confident in herself and how she decided to take that leap of faith in life. But Sydney's anxiety was currently getting the best of her as she continued to keep her gaze down on her tapping boot.

Sydney looked up and tried to play off the fact that she was sure Genevieve was looking back her way. Only now, Genevieve rested her head on her hand as if she were intrigued by Sydney and as if she were the show she came here to see. Sydney felt as if she were losing her mind. The room was filled with at least 100 people. Surely, she wasn't looking at her and this was her anxiety playing tricks on her.

Shit, Sydney thought to herself as she awkwardly looked around and remembered the scene she made when clumsily came into the room. She probably was waiting for Sydney to get up and tumble her way all the way over to the microphone.

"Okay, I think we have our first reader ready. Hey friend," Anna said giddily into the mic from the stage, "What one question, and I do mean one, do you have for our author?"

Sydney took a sigh of relief as Genevieve, as well as everyone else in the room, turned their attention to the man at the microphone. Sydney took this opportunity to gather her stuff and quietly exit out of the room.

When she stepped into the hallway she took a deep breath to try to steady her nerves. She was a nervous wreck. She also began to regret the fact that she hadn't read any of Genevieve's earlier books. Maybe she would think her questions were dumb anyway and she would tell on herself with her ignorance.

What is wrong with me? she wondered as she spotted a waiter setting flutes on his tray.

"Free?" Sydney asked as she rolled up on the man.

"Uh, yes, yes ma'am. It's champagne," the waiter said, handing her a flute.

"Thanks," she said, downing half the glass in one gulp.

A part of her wanted to leave right then and there. There was no way in hell she was getting in that line to speak, and she knew that. But on the other hand, she did want her book signed and to at least see Genevieve up close. She made it this far; she at least owed herself that.

She shook her head at herself as she thought of the irony of her being afraid at the very book signing for the novel that taught her how to be fearless. She decided to put her big girl panties on and get in line to at least get her book signed.

Sydney walked over to the slow-building line where she was to stand to get her book signed. She kept herself preoccupied while she waited in line by helping herself to another glass of champagne as she reread some of her favorite quotes from the book.

Finally, the Q&A session had wrapped up and a swarm of people came out to stand in line for the signing. After a few minutes the line began to move, and before Sydney knew it, it was her turn. She walked slowly up to the table that was filled with spare books, business cards, a few bottles of water and the author, Genevieve Cross.

"Well, hello there," she said, greeting Sydney warmly.

Sydney felt star-struck seeing her this up-close. Genevieve was beautiful, she exuded strong masculine energy that was all wrapped up in a dainty feminine package.

"Now, aren't you the one who came in late to my signing and caused a scene?" Genevieve said to Sydney, already knowing the answer.

Sydney dropped her mouth open, shocked and embarrassed at the memory. Genevieve in return giggled and leaned back in her chair and gave Sydney an inquisitive look as she placed her pen in her mouth.

"Unfortunately," Sydney said, finally finding her voice and answering her question, "My mother always told me I had two left feet."

"Come," Genevieve laughed while waving Sydney over closer to the table.

Sydney listened and walked up to the table and handed Genevieve her book as she tried to steady her shaking hand. Even her two glasses of champagne couldn't compete against her nerves.

"What's your name, hun?"

"Sydney... with two y's," she said routinely, hoping that she wouldn't have her name misspelled in her own book.

"You know I was a bit disappointed to not hear you speak up at the end," Genevieve said as she slowly opened the front cover of the book and thumbed a few pages in.

"Oh," Sydney said, caught off guard. She couldn't believe she was getting called out right now.

"I'm just curious to hear what your favorite part of the book was," she said as she slowly signed her name in the book before writing a few more words.

"Well," Sydney said, trying to buy herself some time.

How didn't she have an answer? What did she plan to say once she got to her? How could she not think of one damn question to ask? Suddenly, she felt dizzy and anxious as her champagne finally began to hit.

"All of it," she said honestly. "To be honest I found your book at a time in my life where I was just so lost— am, I am lost."

Sydney could feel her eyes begin to water as she reflected on all the struggles she had had recently.

"I was so depressed that it was too hard for me to leave my

bed, let alone my apartment. I mean, I'm still kinda lost now I guess. But it's different, you know— "

"Excuse me," Anna said, cutting in, "Ms. Cross has only about forty more minutes to spare, and there are about thirty more people waiting in line to see her," she said while gently placing an assertive hand on the table.

"Oh, right, I'm sorry," Sydney began to apologize as she felt her face become hot.

Sydney was happy that she was deep caramel or else she would be as red as an apple right now. Here she was babbling like an idiot while the author was probably just being polite. Sydney reached for her signed book, just to have Genevieve place her dainty manicured hand on the top of Sydney's.

"Don't you dare apologize," Genevieve said sternly to her.

She looked at Sydney with the same intensity as she had when she was on stage.

"You don't apologize when you aren't wrong, not ever," she said while squeezing Sydney's hand before swinging her head quickly back to Anna.

"Anna, did I *tell* you that I would only sign for an allotted time?"

"No Ms. Cross, you did not, but—"

"So why are you telling me to rush my time with my fans? As a matter of fact, the only one wasting time here is you."

Genevieve gave Anna an ice-cold stare that looked as if she could drill holes through her skull. Sydney felt second-hand embarrassment as she began to fidget uncomfortably for her. Every fiber of her being was telling her to take a step back to let them squabble it out in private. But she couldn't move, especially not with Genevieve's soft hand still on top of hers.

"Yes ma'am," Anna said, obviously embarrassed, "I'll go... do something else," she said, scurrying away before turning back around. "Are we still on for dinner? Our reservation is in an hour..."

Genevieve's full lips morphed into a stern line as she turned her attention back to her, "Anna, we will discuss that later. Please go busy yourself somewhere else."

"Oh, okay..." Anna said, hurt as she walked away.

Something made Sydney feel bad as she could sense her presence was the reason for Genevieve's cold responses to Anna.

"I'm so sorry, I didn't mean to cause any problems," Sydney said.

"Oh hush, what did I tell you about apologizing? It's hard to find good help nowadays, you know what I mean?" Genevieve asked, finally removing her hand from on top of Sydney's. "You were saying?" Genevieve asked as if nothing had happened.

"You've changed my entire life," Sydney said without missing a beat. "Before, everything was just in a box for me, my life that is," she gushed, "I thought that this was it for me. This was all that I was going to get and all that I was going to ever be..."

Genevieve sat back, clearly captivated with what she was hearing from Sydney.

"And?" she asked, allowing a smile to creep across her face exposing a small gap in between her two front teeth.

"And now I realize that there is so much more to me, to life... to everything. I am the one in control of my life, not anyone else. I have a separate path from my peers and I have to find it, I can't just follow along in hopes that it finds me. Or think that I can just... tag along to someone else's. You know?"

"That's right," Genevieve said, leaning in and reaching her hands out for Sydney's. "Thank you for sharing that with me Sydney," she said, gripping her hands tightly around hers.

"No, thank you Ms. Cross."

"Call me Genevieve, please," she said with a wink. "How about you stick around and look at the art? I heard it's lovely," she said, finally releasing her hands and handing her back her book.

"Yeah, I think I will," Sydney said, knowing that she was lying.

Sydney had only fifteen minutes to get an Uber before the late-night rate spike.

"Great, I'll find you then," Genevieve said.

Chapter 3

Monday, October 5th

Sydney held on to the clothing rack and slowly stretched out her calves. This morning she had decided it was time to fill up her free time with one of her old favorite hobbies— running. She hadn't run since her sophomore year of college, her last year on the track team. The same year she met Shawn and opted to skip practices to roll around in bed with him instead.

Sydney used to run and race with her brothers growing up. Being determined to not lose to her brothers who thought of her as weak since she was the baby, and only girl. Because of her stubbornness, this led her to being fast in high school where she seemed to move flawlessly on the track, despite her normal clumsy behavior. In highschool, she was a star and captain of the track team. All was well until her second year in college when she met Shawn and consequently lost her scholarship. Her family was livid with her and she was mortified when she and her mom had to take out a huge loan for her to finish school. A loan they were still paying on today.

Sydney smiled to herself as she heard Genevieve's voice in her head, reciting the words about finding "joy" in things that could be once seen as a daunting task.

Sydney felt the burning sensation rip through her sore calves as she slowed down to use a nearby rack to steady herself as she stretched her hamstrings. This part of getting her body back in shape would be a bitch, but it would be worth it. Sydney was excited to get back to one of her favorite pastimes, despite feeling like an elderly woman currently.

Needless to say, Sydney's little 45-minute run around her neighborhood left her body in pain and made her realize just how out of shape she was. She straightened out her sore limbs and fixed the clothes on the rack that she had shifted. She smiled at a nearby girl who looked to be 16 years old, who aimlessly thumbed through racks of sweaters while humming along to her headphones.

Sydney walked to the dressing room to get a quick moment alone and to check her phone since the store was so quiet today. She stepped into one of the stalls and pulled the curtain shut as she pulled out her phone to check for any missed notifications. It had been a week since the book signing and she still had Genevieve on her mind.

Washed, she thought to herself as she looked at her reflection in the mirror.

She wore a tattered old black sweater that she found in a Goodwill in New Jersey years ago. Her hair hung wildly in her face, and she pulled it back by tucking a few loose braids behind her left ear. The same way Genevieve had worn her hair a few days ago.

Sydney scrutinized herself further and decided that she did not like what she saw. She looked disheveled and a mess.

No wonder he cheated, she thought to herself as she looked down at her soft thighs and wide hips.

Sydney had never been a skinny girl, but she never really

been considered "thick" either. She still had her thick legs from being a runner and her overall physique still appeared slim. But lately, her average body size had softened and fluffed up more than usual. She was letting herself go. Or had she always been like this?

She pulled out her phone again and opened up her Instagram as she sat down on the small wooden chair in the dressing room. She had become very familiar with using this app ever since she found Genevieve's page. Sydney went to the search tab and typed in the handle out of memory and pulled up Genevieve's page.

Bleep! Bleep! Bleep!

The store's alarms were going off, signifying that someone was currently shoplifting. Angel had decided to invest in the expensive alarm after the store had a spike in stolen merchandise a few months back.

"Oh shit," Sydney gasped as she dropped her phone to the floor just as Angel snatched open the curtain to the room.

He glared down at her, and Sydney instantly knew that her ass was grass. She should've been on the floor watching the customers. The last place she needed to be was in the dressing room alone with her phone.

Twenty minutes later, Sydney was giving the description of the 16-year-old shoplifter to the mall cop. As she was describing the girl, she realized the red flag she missed of having an unaccompanied minor in the store during a school day. She could feel Angel's beady little eyes drilling her the entire time that she stood there, awkwardly describing how she left the girl alone on the floor to go to the back. Once the mall cop was through with her, Sydney took a deep breath and slowly turned around to face Angel.

"Listen, I know I fucked up. And I don't wanna play the victim here, but I'm sure you heard about my breakup and honestly...I've been going through it," she began to plead as she took small steps towards him.

"Save it, we all have issues, Sydney," he said, raising his hand and putting it inches away from Sydney's face.

"I've been really nice, but at this point this is beyond ridiculous," Angel huffed as his voice began to get higher. "I'm doing you a favor by not firing you right now; you're lucky!"

Oh, thank God Sydney thought to herself.

"But I will be docking your pay to how I see fit."

"By how much?" she asked, screwing up her face, no longer liking what she was hearing.

"Hmph, oh I don't know. The shoplifter had five whole minutes of stealing some top-line items thanks to you," he said, dragging it out and picking at his fingernails. "I think a three-day dock of your pay will be equal to the amount of merchandise we lost."

"Three days? Are you crazy?" Sydney yelled.

"Did I stutter? You should feel lucky I'm doing your ass a favor—-"

"That is not doing me a favor," Sydney said, cutting him off. "You know I need that money, Angel. I have bills to pay. I'll pick up extra shifts, but I cannot lose three days out of my check. Also, there isn't anything in here worth that much and you know it!"

Sydney was furious. She knew she had fucked up, but not three days' loss of pay worthy. When they ran back the camera, they saw the girl only got away with a few shirts and Ugg slides.

Angel began to laugh in Sydney's face as if she had said a joke.

"You really think you have a choice in this matter huh?

Wake up Sydney, *I am* the boss. Take it or leave it, girl, and we both know you need this job," he said, turning his back to her and walking towards the back.

Sydney had had enough. She was tired of people treating her as if she were a child. As if she had no say on what happened in her own life. She was sick of being treated like a doormat by everyone from Shawn to Angel. She was tired of men period. She felt her heartbeat begin to speed up as she walked swiftly behind Angel.

"Hey Angel!" she yelled to his back as she walked quickly over to him.

Just as Angel turned around to answer her, he was met in the face with her name badge that hit him square in the eye.

"Ahh," he shrilled, as he looked back up at Sydney with one good eye as his hand covered the other.

"Fuck you and fuck this job!" Sydney said gleefully as she reached behind the counter and grabbed her coat and bag. "You think I need this shit? I don't need this shit! Your ass think you doing something making your measly $19 an hour," she yelled as she walked back over to Angel as he cowered away from her.

"You are a sad, pathetic, excuse of a bully who preys on other people to make you feel better about yourself. You're sick!" she yelled, pointing hard at his arm. "You know what your problem is? You still have a chip on your shoulder from high school. Classic case of the bullied becoming the bullier. But not today!"

She felt electrified as she saw the words from Genevieve's chapter on *"Giving your problem a name"* come to mind.

"You are the problem here, not me!" she yelled in between jabs to his frail arm. "You, ANGEL! You got the right one today!"

She was on a roll and getting a high from seeing Angel's terrified face.

"I'm calling security!" he wailed as he ran to the store phone that sat near the register.

As if waking up from a dream, Sydney came to her senses and pulled her coat on and walked swiftly out of the store, laughing all the way to the bus stop before the guards could get there.

....

Sydney was working her waitressing shift at Flamingo's while telling Cai about the dramatic quitting she had done earlier in the day.

"Oh my God, Sydney," Cai said as she took a big bite out of her granny green apple, "So you're really like done done?"

"Looks like it. Kinda too late to go back and grovel after I physically assaulted the store manager," she said as she reached up for the hot plates. "This one is supposed to have a side of green beans Hector, not the mashed potatoes," she yelled back into the kitchen as she placed the plate back down.

"Wow, good for you, that was really brave," Cai said, shaking her head in amazement.

"It was dumb, that's what it was. I wasn't even thinking straight. I went from losing three days of pay to losing a whole other income," Sydney said, folding her arms.

The reality of the situation finally hit her once she was seated on the crowded bus.

"Yeah, very dumb," Cai slipped and said before catching herself. "I'm sorry Syd, well something tells me that you have something bigger and better coming," Cai said chipperly as she playfully slapped Sydney on her arm.

"Oh yeah? Well, I hope you're right. Because only a miracle is going to save me," Sydney said with a dry laugh.

"Don't worry, it will," Cai said, reaching for the plates. "I'll wait for the green beans and bring them to your table for you.

You have a patron at table five that should be ready for you. You need that tip money right now, girl."

"Thanks Cai," Sydney sighed as she sulked out of the kitchen.

She couldn't think of another time when she felt this dumb — not including the times she repeatedly took Shawn back after catching him cheating. Or the time she took him back in just before finding out that he gave her a STD. She really made a fool out of herself in Lilian's and only realized it once it was too late. She had no back up plan, no rainy-day fund and definitely could not ask her mother for money again. She knew it would be only a matter of weeks before she was out on her ass.

"Hello, welcome to Flamingo's. My name is—"

"Sydney," Genevieve said, finishing off her sentence.

Sydney shot her head up from her order book to look at her patron for the first time. She was so busy pouting, she didn't even bother to look at the person who sat at the table.

"Umm... wow, hi," Sydney said, stuttering as she locked eyes with Genevieve's killer stare.

Genevieve sat at the table alone, though it was set for two people. She wore a simple cream dress that matched perfectly with the fur jacket that hung loosely on her shoulders. Sydney eyed the coat and wondered how much something like that could cost. Though it wasn't cold enough to wear it yet to Sydney, she instantly drooled over its regalness. She was left speechless at Genevieve's presence.

"Well hello there," Genevieve said with a light laugh.

"Ms. Cross, what a small world," Sydney said nervously as she played with her stray braid that lay on her shoulder.

"Please Sydney, call me Genevieve," she said smiling and leaning in on her elbows. "I'm actually here to meet with my realtor. We decided to meet for lunch to sign some additional closing docs on my new home I just brought in Weston."

"Oh wow, congratulations. Life must be good, that's where

all the rich folks play," she said awkwardly, regretting it as soon as it left her mouth.

Genevieve must've thought that she was an idiot. She always turned into a bumbling fool whenever she was around.

"Well, I guess you could say that," Genevieve laughed as she sipped on her water while still watching Sydney.

"So, what can I get you?" Sydney asked, remembering that she was at work.

"How about a nice bottle of your best champagne to start off with until my realtor gets here?"

"I'll get you a bottle out in a second," Sydney said before stopping herself from leaving. "It's really nice to see you again, Genevieve."

"You too Sydney," she said, giving her a small wink.

"Hector! Let me get some of those clams and French onion soup, pronto! We have a special guest in the house," she yelled once back in the kitchen.

"Gotchu mami!" Hector said as he disappeared quickly.

Sydney raced over to the freezer and walked in to grab the most expensive bottle of Brut that she could find.

"Whoa, whoa, whoa! What's the rush?" Cai asked as she walked back in the kitchen.

"Guess who is here?" Sydney said, jumping up and down like an excited child.

"Who?"

"Genevieve Cross! The author of *The Elite: Steps to Change Your Life*!"

Sydney was racing around the kitchen like a maniac trying to set her tray to bring back out to Genevieve's table.

"Oh yeah, that lady did ask if you were working today," Cai replied back nonchalantly.

"Wait, what?" Sydney asked, freezing in her tracks. "Someone came in here asking for me and you didn't tell me?"

"Sorry girl, it honestly slipped my mind once you started

telling me about you quitting your job," Cai said, putting one hand on her hip as she used the other to massage her sore neck.

"Yeah, she came in here all fancy wearing fur. What's wrong with that lady? It is only 60 degrees outside," Cai said.

Like Sydney, Cai was a true New Englander and only thought a heavy coat was needed when it was below zero.

"Ugh, focus Cai," Sydney said waving her hands to get more information out of her friend.

"Yea, she came in here and was asking if you were working today and I told her yes. Didn't think much of it, it's nothing new for a customer to ask for the same waiter that they had before."

This was true. Sydney did have a few patrons who would always request her when they came in to eat. But she never served Genevieve. Now that she thought about it, she never told her where she worked either.

"Oh, so that's your girl crush, eh?" Cai teased as she peeped out the door to Genevieve who was now accompanied by a middle-aged black man.

"It's not a crush," Sydney said as she shamelessly checked her reflection before picking up her tray.

"Uh, huh," Cai said, holding the door open for her.

Genevieve enjoyed an exquisite three-course lunch thanks to Sydney that day. Sydney took it upon herself to order for the table once Genevieve asked her to order her the best off the menu. For the table she ordered her favorite lobster pasta salad, pan-seared lamb with the truffle mac and cheese, and the honey duck over pasta with crème brulee for dessert.

She did her best waiting on the table and making sure to hang back a little longer each time she visited the table.

"So how was everything?" Sydney asked, already knowing the answer. She and Cai were cleaning the table off from its last round of food.

"Everything was wonderful Sydney, thank you," Genevieve

said, batting her eyes at Sydney as she gently placed a hand on her stomach to indicate she was full.

"No room for coffee?" Sydney asked, not ready to give them their check.

"No ma'am, you will have to roll me out of here if I have another bite," her realtor said who looked like he was seconds away from busting out of his vest.

"Sydney, I cannot afford to gain any more weight, trust me," Genevieve said, reapplying lipstick with the compact mirror she got out of her purse.

"Oh, trust me, you are perfect," Sydney said, laying the check gently on the table.

Sydney could hear Cai scoff at her comment from behind her. She suddenly felt embarrassed and wondered if she was fangirling just a little too hard.

"You are far too kind," Genevieve said as she gently placed a hand on top of Sydney's, causing instant flashbacks to the last time they touched.

"Thank you so much for the wonderful lunch, it was a pleasure seeing you again," she said, giving Sydney's hand a tight squeeze.

"It was a pleasure seeing you again too!" Sydney said, before walking away on Jello legs, with a tray full of dishes.

"Is she gay?" Cai blurted as soon as they were in the back and lowering the trays down on the counter to be washed.

"What?" Sydney said, letting out a dry laugh, "I don't know. Why do you ask, you interested?"

"No, strictly dickly over here my friend," Cai said, placing glasses on the counter. "But I think you are. You two were so extra, Sydney!" Cai said with her thick accent.

"Extra how?" Sydney asked, acting oblivious as she cleaned off her tray with a towel.

"'*Oh Genevieve, you so perfect*'," Cai said in a singsong voice.

"Shut up Cai," Sydney laughed as she swatted her with the towel.

"And then here she goes, "*Sydney it was so nice seeing you again*'," Cai placed her finger in her mouth and pretended to gag.

Sydney continued to laugh at Cai as she peeped out the door to see Genevieve leaving out the front door.

"I still can't believe she asked for me," she said out loud. "How did she even know I worked here?"

"I don't know but that's creepy. I don't like her; she got those crazy eyes."

"What are crazy eyes, Cai?"

"You know, when you got those crazy eyes! Her eyes are too extreme, like she looks through you, not at you," Cai said, shaking from a random chill. "Be careful of her, she gives me the creeps."

Sydney rolled her eyes and shook her head at Cai as she walked back to the table to collect the bill. She opened up the folder to find eight crisp $100 bills. Four of those were left for the meal, while the remaining were left as a tip. Sydney gasped and looked around to see if someone was pulling some sick joke.

She pulled the receipt out of the folder and turned it over to see a note written in Genevieve's handwriting. Sydney knew it was her handwriting because she still looked at the signature on her signed book every day. Hell, she had even traced it with her fingers when she thought back on the moment from the signing.

"Sydney, I didn't forget about how we got cut short at the signing. My apologies on how it ended. You are a brilliant girl who I have recently learned has exquisite taste as well. I must pick your brain some more! In the meantime, I remember you told me that you were going through some tough times. I hope

this helps. Let's meet up for dinner, my treat. Give me a call. Genevieve."

Below her message was a phone number. Sydney smiled and placed the receipt against her chest. With this extra money and a few extra shifts at the restaurant, she could pay rent next month. Maybe Cai was right, things were beginning to look up.

Chapter 4

Monday, October 12th

"R*eal ass bitch give a fuck 'bout a nigga!*" India and Sydney sang at the top of their lungs in unison as they sang along with the radio.

The two were cruising the I-90 in Dij's CL white Mercedes-Benz. They were leaving from an interview India had set up for Sydney through her cousin, for a front desk representative at a three-star hotel.

"Girl, let me turn this shit up. You know it's my shit!" India yelled as she cranked the volume up to the max.

Sydney laughed at her friend as she took off her seatbelt and carefully removed her blazer before neatly folding it on her lap and sliding it back into a plastic bag. She was going to return this blazer first thing tomorrow and hadn't even bothered to take the tags off. The blazer served its purpose and could now go back home to Marshalls. A splurge for Sydney.

A few days had passed since Genevieve gave Sydney her phone number and she had not heard back from her. After a few hours of playing it cool, Sydney finally gave in and sent Genevieve a quick text of gratitude.

Sydney: Hi Genevieve it's Sydney. Thank you so much for your generous tip! You do not know how much I appreciate it.

Unfortunately, she had not heard back from her yet and she felt bummed out about it.

"*Act up, you can get snatched up*!" India sang as if she were the third member of the City Girls. "Come on bitch, don't leave me hanging!"

India swatted at Sydney's leg, trying to get her attention back. She laughed as Sydney rolled her eyes once she saw India trying to twerk in her seat.

"Girl, we gonna end up in the back of someone's car if you don't relax!" Sydney yelled as they sped off at an exit.

"Chill boo, I got this," India said, waving Sydney off. "So how was the interview?"

"It was okay," Sydney said dryly as she slid her old blue college sweatshirt back on over her head.

"'*Okay*'? Girl you gotta give me more than that, my cousin Mookie pulled a lot of strings for this interview. You know you got the exclusive call; the job hasn't even been posted online yet. You're welcome by the way," India said, rolling her neck for emphasis. "I thought a hotel job would always be fun! You get to see people sneaking in there trying to get a room to be all nasty in," she giggled.

"Don't get me wrong, I think it went well. I got stuck on that damn question again though," Sydney replied as she took a long sigh.

"The '*where do you see yourself in five years*' question," India said, already knowing, "I don't get why you can't just lie like the rest of us."

"I know, I know, I had a whole pre-planned narrative to say that I got from the book," Sydney said shaking her head, "I just froze up. My bad, girl, I hope I didn't fuck up."

"Oh," India said curtly.

Sydney turned her head to look at India who had now stiffened up and had a frown on her face.

"Now India, I know you ain't got an attitude over that? You know I would never intentionally fuck up an interview, especially not when your family helped me."

"It's not that. I know your broke ass would never mess up you getting a job. I'm just tired of hearing about that damn book."

Sydney let out a small laugh that she instantly regretted once she saw India cutting her eyes at her.

"India, you cannot seriously be jealous of a book. You do understand that this," she said pulling the book out of her tote, "is a *book,* it's a tool."

"I get that Sydney," she replied as she stopped at a red light. "You are just so obsessed with that book and that woman!"

"I am not obsessed!" Sydney said defensively as she shoved it back in her bag.

"I tell you all the time to come to me with tips and tricks to woo these clowns in the interview and you never come to me. You know I keep me a new job— "

"You quit them just as much too," Sydney spat back.

"Bitch, and?" India said, snapping her neck at her. "Listen, I can do what I please. I have a girlfriend who takes care of house and home while I get these degrees. Any job that I do in my precious spare time is just for spare cash. Mainly to help your ass out."

"Bitch, and your point?" Sydney said folding her arms and holding in a laugh because she knew that it was true.

"My point is, come to me hoe! Not that damn bitch; that lady is weird, yo! It's annoying you would rather listen to her and not your best friend."

The two pulled into the long car line to get their garage ticket to go into their favorite restaurant, Red Lobster. Going to Red Lobster after an interview was always a ritual of theirs that started with their first job together at 15 at the movie theater.

"Has she even texted your ass back? Who does that? Drop money like that then not reply back to someone."

"Nope, she hasn't," Sydney said sadly as she began to wipe her makeup off with a napkin. "Maybe she was just paying it forward. You know, do good and good will come back to you and all that shit."

"Also, next time you're deciding what to wear to an interview, ask me. That blazer looked like it belonged on someone's mother," India laughed.

"Bitch my shit was cute. Who claimed you were the best dressed anyway?"

"Bitch, the world!" India said swiftly as she pulled into a parking space.

"I see Dij got you all gassed up per usual," Sydney said snidely.

"Speaking of which, we're doing a drive by later. I need all of her niggas and fans to see what she got at home, hell I'ma remind her ass too."

Sydney laughed as they climbed out the car and she watched India slowly switch to the elevator. She wore fitted high-waisted skinny jeans that laid perfectly in her four-inch thigh-high boots. On top, she wore a burgundy crop top sweater that exposed her tattoo of Dij's name that she proudly had on her left breast.

India was always one of the best dressed in high school; unlike Sydney, she had a taste for fashion. India was short and shapely and always managed to find the best outfits that accentuated her body and curves. Fashion was her passion and no one could ever quite match her style. India was actually the one who got Sydney into thrifting; unfortunately Sydney never fully grasped the concept of mixing and matching labels with thrift finds.

"I'm sick of being used and abused," Sydney said behind her as she pulled her hair up into a ponytail, preparing for her feast. "Can't you take one of your other friends to go spy on your boo?"

The two stepped into the elevator and Sydney shook her head at India and contemplated objecting. She knew that India was only doing a drive-by to see what girls were hanging around Dij. India had always been insanely jealous and territorial with all of her relationships, but when it came down to Dij, she really didn't play.

"Now she's *'used and abused',"* India sighed while shaking her head. "Bitch, tell that to my pockets," India said as she patted her small Chanel purse. "This is my treat tonight. Even though I'm sure you have some money still from your suga mama."

"Oh girl," Sydney began but then decided to stop.

Instead, she bent down slightly and kissed India on her cheek, resting her head on her best friend's shoulder.

"Thank you, India," she whispered as they rode the elevator up.

"You're welcome Syd, just be mindful girl. You know it's easy for you to get wrapped up in things fast. Like Shawn and that year you tried keto, remember how your ass landed in the hospital?" India and Sydney laughed at the memory together.

"Just come to me sometime too, I know you better than... a book," India said, softening her tone as they reached their destination.

Sydney shook her head in agreement and kept her mouth closed. She knew it was more of an issue with Genevieve than the book that really got underneath India's skin. Like she thought to herself earlier, India was extremely territorial.

....

The next morning, Sydney decided to get up and go for a quick run. As soon as she set outside of her building she felt the sharp, cool whip of the fall air rip through her thin yoga pants.

"Ugh," Sydney grunted as she pushed back against every instinct she had to run back inside and to get back in bed.

Thanks to Genevieve's generosity, Sydney's bills were covered next month, and she was even able to semi-stock her refrigerator. She was grateful for the safety net she had this month, but she was still stressed about finding another job to support herself. She had lied to India last night, she had straight bombed her interview and she was positive that she was not getting a call back.

No matter how hard she tried, Sydney could not connect with the interviewer during her interview. All of Sydney's answers were mundane and meek. To be honest, she didn't want the job, but she knew she was in no position to turn down the money. During the whole interview she kept questioning herself on why she was even there. She had a Communications degree for God's sake.

Sydney pulled out her earphones and placed a bud into each ear before turning on some trap music, her favorite thing to work out to. She spent some time stretching before she began to slowly jog on her routine route. She was grateful that there were not too many people out walking around since it was only 8 a.m. Sydney crossed the street and jogged by her favorite bodega on the corner. Once she passed the store, she would jog up a few more blocks past the school bus stop, before finally turning left and jogging through the old park near her home that typically housed more junkies than children nowadays.

These early morning run sessions were becoming bittersweet for Sydney. Though she hated to get up and work out, it was always therapeutic for her to see her neighborhood and the different residents who lived there. Sydney loved her hood, she loved her neighbors, the shop owners, the little kids and even some of the junkies were decent.

After thirty minutes she successfully completed her loop around the block and ended back at the front steps to her apartment building. She grudgingly climbed the three flights of stairs and unlocked her front door. Sydney kicked off her shoes and stripped out of her sweaty clothes. Not until she removed the buds from her ears did she hear her own heavy panting from her run.

She shook her head and grabbed a water bottle out of her fridge and stood naked in the middle of her apartment guzzling it down. She was nowhere near the shape that she used to be in college. A few years ago, she would easily eat up a three mile run, but now she couldn't handle much more than two miles before her legs started giving out. Still, she was making progress.

She was caught off guard hearing her phone ringing from the bed. No one called her anymore except for her mother or a bill collector. Even Shawn had finally stopped calling. And there was no way in hell that that was the job calling her back for another interview.

She picked up her phone and dropped it right back down on the bed when she saw who the caller was. The caller ID read: Genevieve Cross.

"Shit," Sydney hissed to herself, suddenly terrified to answer the phone.

She began to nervously bite on her cuticles as she debated on picking up the call or not. She had been waiting to hear back from her for days; why was she nervous now?

"Hello," Sydney said a little too coolly when she finally answered on the last ring.

"Sydney, hi, it's Genevieve Cross," Genevieve said on the other line.

Yeah... caller ID, Sydney thought to herself. "Genevieve, hi! How are you?" Sydney said, sitting down on her bed.

"I'm doing well Sydney, and yourself? I hadn't heard from you so I thought I would give you a quick call to check in," she said, not bothering to wait on an answer.

"Oh, no! I sent you a text a few days ago thanking you for the generous tip! I— I guess you didn't get it?" Sydney stuttered.

"Of course, I got it," Genevieve said. "How else would I have your number, hun?"

"Oh," Sydney said, caught off guard as she changed her posture and sat up straight. *She sure had no problem in finding where she worked,* Sydney thought.

She wasn't sure how to respond back to that. She couldn't tell if this was a friendly call or not by the tone of Genevieve's voice. She suddenly felt too insecure to speak, scared she may say the wrong thing.

"I do believe I told you to give me a call, not a text Sydney," Genevieve said sharply into the phone. "We call, we do not text."

"Noted?" Sydney said with it being more of a question than a statement.

"Anyway, let's grab dinner, how does tonight sound? I'm meeting a few friends at the Menton tonight around 8 p.m. and I would love for you to be my date."

"The Menton?" Sydney gawked.

The Menton was one of the most expensive restaurants in the state. Sydney and her friends would always joke around about being too poor to even step foot in there.

"Yes, have you heard of it? My friends tell me it's all the rave," she continued, sounding distracted. "Anyway once I heard it was an Italian restaurant I naturally thought of you with your superb taste."

"It's a fusion actually between Italian and French," Sydney said in a daze.

She was already mentally destroying her closet and knowing that she would have nothing to wear. She wouldn't dare ask India for help though, she knew that she would tell her to not go.

"Oh, see that's why I keep you around," Genevieve giggled. "Listen, I am just pulling up to my breakfast meeting. What's your address? I'll come get you around six or so we can grab drinks first."

"Oh, I don't know, I think I can meet—"

"Address, Sydney, I want to have some time alone with you before I subject you to my friends," she teased with a light chuckle.

Sydney sighed and closed her mouth. There was no need in fighting Genevieve. She could tell that the woman was rarely told no. She told her her address and secretly cringed to herself as she wondered what Genevieve would think once she saw where she lived. Sydney was not ashamed of her neighborhood, but she knew to many this was considered a rough part of town. She winced at the visual of Genevieve pulling up to her apartment building and hitting the lock button on her car door at her first sight of the random group of men that always remained sitting on the front steps.

It took Sydney nearly two hours to get dressed. Mostly because she decided that she had nothing to wear to this dinner and was afraid that she would stick out like a sore thumb. After trying on just about every evening dress that she owned, she finally settled on an old little black dress that she had gotten from India.

"You can never go wrong with a LBD," India once told her.

This was a very old dress that eventually became Sydney's once the Freshman 15 hit India and caused her breasts and butt to swell.

She was unsure if this evening would be more casual than business, so she thought this dress would be the perfect combination of both. The fitted dress hugged Sydney's hips and had a deep V-neck that showed off her humble chest. The dress fell just to the top of her knees and was just conservative enough that she thought she could pull it off.

Genevieve arrived at Sydney's house at 6 p.m. on the dot. Thankfully, Sydney was on time and hopped quickly into Genevieve's white Rolls-Royce before she had a chance to really take in her surroundings. The two went to a bar near the Menton and relaxed with some glasses of chilled champagne.

Their conversation was light and warm. Sydney learned that Genevieve was originally from Maryland and left the state the first chance she had to go away to boarding school and then Spelman College. She knew that she wanted to be an author ever since she was a teenager and spent most of her younger years to herself with her nose in a book. After she graduated college, she attended Yale where she graduated with her masters. She moved around a bit after that and lived in about seven different states before finally deciding to live in Los Angeles for the last five years. And now, she was looking forward to starting over and settling down in Boston for a life more "off the grid."

After an hour of Genevieve talking, now tipsy and loose, the two headed across the street to dinner.

"Sydney, I want to introduce you to a few of my friends," Genevieve said as the two arrived at the restaurant and sat down at the table.

Sydney made the right call on her dress that night. It seemed all of Genevieve's friends, though very polished, were dressed in risqué outfits. Sydney wondered where they all were going to after dinner as this looked to be the pre-game to a costume party.

"So, this is Melissa and her partner Tom," Genevieve said,

nodding her head to the middle-aged white couple that sat to the left of her.

"And over there is my dear friend Vicky... and... and," Genevieve lingered, clearly at a loss of words on her friend's date's name.

"It's nice to meet you all," Sydney said, swooping in trying to save Genevieve.

Genevieve smiled at Sydney for the save and gave her knee a quick squeeze of gratitude under the table.

"Oh, the pleasure is ours darling," Vicky said, dragging out her words, clearly a few drinks in already. "And this is Jeremy," she said, playfully grabbing the younger man's face in her hand.

"Don't worry Genevieve, I honestly don't expect you to keep up with my freak of the week," Vicky said, causing everyone at the table to laugh but Sydney.

Vicky looked to be in her early 40s and reminded Sydney of one of those cougars she would see in the mall all the time with their play toy. Sydney instantly noted that Genevieve referred to her as a dear friend and wondered if they were around the same age. From this lady's attire and demeanor, she couldn't imagine Genevieve being friends with her. Vicky seemed loud and coarse. She wore a leopard print short dress that Sydney was positive doubled as a nightie.

"Thanks for getting our friend out of the house, Sydney, since she's got in town we have only seen her once!" Melissa said as she tossed her long blonde hair off her shoulder.

"Oh, stop it you guys, you know how it is! Busy, busy, busy!" Genevieve said as she sipped on her wine and smiled slyly.

Like Sydney, she opted to wear a simple black dress tonight that complemented her petite frame. On her feet however, she rocked a pair of killer Louboutin's and Sydney instantly felt insecure about the heels she wore on her feet that she had gotten from Target years ago.

"I'm just teasing G," Melissa said as she gently placed her hand on Genevieve's arm and let it linger there as she began to rub it gently.

Sydney noticed the interaction between the two and was caught off guard. Once she noticed Melissa catching her stare she grabbed for her wine glass quickly, spilling it all over the table.

"Shit! Sorry, I am so sorry. I'm such a klutz," Sydney said, trying to pat the spill up with her cloth napkin.

"Here, let me get it," Jeremy said as he grabbed Sydney's napkin out of her hand and used his own to quickly clean up her mess.

"He's a waiter," Vicky said, drooling over him as if he were a plate of food. "We met at The Cheesecake Factory, isn't that a riot?"

Vicky began to cackle, laughing at her own joke before grabbing Jeremy's face and kissing him deeply. The two began to make out loudly at the table and Sydney saw a boner slowly growing in Jeremy's tight leather pants just as he grabbed a handful of Vicky's dreads and yanked her head back to lightly suck on her neck.

Sydney thought the two were going to start having sex at the table. She looked around at the others who all seemed unphased by the scene in front of them as they reviewed the menu and chatted about what to order. Genevieve slid Sydney her glass of wine and nodded her head to drink, as if she sensed how awkward Sydney felt.

"Vicky what in the world were you doing at the... Cheesecake Factory?" Genevieve said, not trying to hide her disgust at the thought of the place.

"Sampling the goods darling, sampling the goods," Vicky growled as she yanked Jeremy's head back up to continue to make out.

"So, Sydney, tell me how you two met?" Melissa asked a moment later after the waiter left the table with their orders.

"Oh," Sydney said, caught off guard just as she was downing the rest of Genevieve's wine and was finally beginning to feel the effects.

"We met at my Boston book signing a few weeks ago," Genevieve answered for her.

"Oh," Melissa said as she and Tom shared a look between one another, "Well it must be nice to get to connect with one another."

"Sydney said my book has—is helping her through some tough times. Out of all the people there, she and I connected the most," Genevieve said beaming and looking over at Sydney.

"In what way has the book helped you Sydney?" Tom asked.

"Honestly, it's helping me get my shit together," Sydney blurted out and instantly regretted. "Sorry for my language!"

"No need to apologize at all," Vicky said, finally coming up for air from Jeremy's mouth, "We're all adults here, ain't that right baby?" she asked Jeremy as she wiped her saliva off of his chin.

"Welcome back," Genevieve said to Vicky, who playfully waved her off in return.

"Where did you all meet? Was it in school?" Sydney asked as she grabbed a breadstick and began to break it off into little pieces.

She knew that it would be highly unlikely that Genevieve met Michelle at an HBCU, but she was desperate to get the attention off of her. Sydney never felt comfortable with being the center of attention. India however thrived on it, hence why the two got along so well. Sydney suddenly wished India was there to be her shield and felt a twinge of guilt.

The table fell silent from Sydney's question, and everyone turned their gaze to Genevieve as they waited for her response.

Genevieve picked up her glass and smiled as if she were pondering what to say.

"We're all part of an exclusive club. I met Michelle and Tom nearly fifteen years ago once I joined the club and we all became fast friends. I was even the maid of honor at their second wedding!" Genevieve shared. "And as far as that character over there, I've known Vicky since Spelman. We were freshman roommates together."

Their dinner continued on with Genevieve and her friends catching each other up on each other's lives and work. Sydney managed to get through the rest of the evening by only saying a few words and sharing funny waitressing stories with Jeremy, who she was sure was on at least three different types of drugs.

"I hope you had fun tonight Sydney," Genevieve said as they pulled in front of Sydney's building. "It's nearly midnight and these fools are still out here?" Genevieve asked as she gawked at the group of men who were playing dice on the apartment's stoop.

I knew it was coming, Sydney thought to herself as Genevieve pulled her fur coat tighter around her neck and locked the car doors.

"Sydney, I would like to offer you a job if that's okay with you," Genevieve said in a tone that let Sydney know that she really wasn't asking permission.

"I'm new in this area and trying to move into a home while simultaneously being on a book tour has proven to be a much harder task than I originally thought it would be. I need an aide who I can trust and who I know will handle things for me on the backend so that I can focus on other tasks. I'm not sure if you are aware, but I am already working on my fifth book and I know this one is going to be my best one yet," Genevieve said with her face lighting up.

"Genevieve, wow I'm flattered," Sydney gushed, caught off guard. "Would I be your assistant?"

"My muse," she said not missing a beat, "But yes, there will be some mundane administration things I will need you to handle as well. You're a special girl, Sydney and I know we were not brought together by accident. I want my next book to be for you and your generation and the other people like you who are struggling to find their way," she said.

Sydney was shocked. She never expected that this night would end with a job offer. She quickly began to start a list of pros and cons on whether or not she should take it. But who was she kidding? She needed the money.

"Don't worry about answering tonight, you can give me an answer by tomorrow. Please know that I will require you full time, so you must quit that waitressing job. You're too good for that place anyway," she said, changing to a softer voice.

Genevieve reached over to Sydney and moved a stray braid out of her face and tucked it behind her ear.

"You are so beautiful, Sydney, why do you hide that face behind all of this hair?"

She allowed her hand to slowly graze Sydney's face as she lowered it from her. Sydney felt her skin grow warm while chill bumps simultaneously prickled her skin from Genevieve's touch.

"Not that I am not honored, because I so am, but can I have more than a day to sort all of this out? I still have bills to pay and can't leave my job hanging—"

"No, one day is enough," Genevieve said shortly. "You cannot dwell on new opportunities like this. What do I say in the book?"

"*'Embrace change— no scratch that, become madly in love with change. Run towards it as fearlessly as you can. Be so in love with accepting new opportunities of growth that the word 'no' appalls you,'*" Sydney said quickly. She remembered that quote word for word. It was one of her favorites from the book.

"That's right," Genevieve said, pleased with her answer as

she grabbed Sydney's left hand and held it gently in hers. "Don't worry about the bills, give me a number and I will pay them for the next three months for you. Consider it your starter fee. As my employee you will be paid generously and taken care of. You cannot grow into the person you are destined to be, Sydney, by bussing tables," she said.

"Okay," Sydney said, taking a moment to ponder over it, "I guess I'll give you an answer tomorrow."

"You guess?"

"You will get your answer tomorrow Genevieve, for sure," she said confidently as she sat up straight. "Now get out of here before these fools strip your rims with us in the car."

Genevieve laughed and squeezed Sydney's hand tighter, "There's my girl."

Chapter 5

Tuesday, October 13th

"So just like that?" Cai asked as she folded her arms.

"Just like that," Sydney said as she folded her apron and handed it to Cai. "Here, it's not much, but consider it as a parting gift," she said with a weak smile.

Sydney had just quit her job at Flamingo's. It was not an easy decision. She knew the risk that she was taking by dropping her waitressing job— her only source of income. Be that as it may, she desperately needed a chance to grow and could not pass up a once-in-a-lifetime opportunity. That's what she told the store manager anyway before heading out of their back office.

"A lot of people would want this job, Sydney, are you sure?" Cai asked, confused. "That lady is kinda crazy."

"I'm not sure Cai," Sydney sighed, "But what else do I have to lose?"

"Uh, girl everything!" Cai yelled with her accent sneaking through, which let Sydney know that she was serious.

"You met this lady a week ago and already you are running

off to work for her. You're moving too fast. Why can't you work with her for a few days here and there?"

"Because it doesn't work like that, Cai. Damn, you sound just like my mother this morning. I wish you two would both relax, I am an adult," Sydney said trying to laugh it off, "I got this."

Sydney was no fool, she knew that if things went south with Genevieve she would be left with nothing. But she couldn't keep living the way she was. She was sick and tired of living handout out to handout. She was also tired of the same tiresome life. At this rate, it would be only a matter of time before she would end up back with Shawn, playing step-mommy to his kid.

"Life's too short," Sydney said, opening her arms, going in for a hug.

"I don't want my last memory of here to be me arguing with my best work friend," she said as she bent down and wrapped Cai into a warm hug. "I'm going to miss working with you," she said genuinely.

....

Sydney laid on her back in her bed while watching the old wooden ceiling fan slowly spin. It was one of those random warm days in fall that you only experience for a day or two tops before the weather drops again drastically. Sydney had her window open and felt the cool breeze from outside slowly glide into her apartment bringing the sounds of outside in. She pulled on the last of her roach that she found when digging in her purse for her keys earlier. She laid there and listened to the people outside talking and laughing with one another while walking down the street. She could also hear old Hondas racing and rumbling down the bumpy road as they blasted Reggaetón from their scratchy speakers.

Sydney laid there and let her mind drift and rest as she enjoyed the peace of the moment. Quitting earlier today had really stressed her out. She knew her manager wanted to lay into her ass for quitting so abruptly, but it had to be done.

Sydney put the rest of the roach out in her ash tray and closed her eyes for a quick nap. That was until she thought about India and the fact that she had been dodging her calls the last two days. Sydney knew that she had to sit down and break the news to India sooner or later. Especially because Sydney had told her mother and she knew it would only be a matter of time before word made its way back around to India.

Sydney felt her phone ringing in her bag beside her and dug it out to see that it was a call from Genevieve.

"Hello, Genevieve."

She had figured that Genevieve would call for her answer later on tonight around 10 p.m. at least; to give her 24 hours. Yet it was only five in the evening, and she had already rung her.

"Hi Sydney, how are you?"

"I'm well Genevieve," Sydney said, sitting straight up in the bed as if she could see her. "And you?"

"I'm well Sydney, thanks for asking," Genevieve breathed into the phone. "So let's have it. Have you made your decision?"

"Yes... yes I have. I...uh well I quit my job today," Sydney said into the phone proudly.

"And?"

Sydney could hear horns beeping in the background and imagined that Genevieve was caught in rush hour on her way home from yet another meeting.

"And, I've decided to take you up on your offer, I'm all yours," Sydney said, smiling into the phone.

"Good girl!" she squealed.

Sydney was excited to hear her excitement and she stood up and walked over to her bedroom's window.

"So, when do I start, boss?" Sydney joked.

"Right now. I am about thirty minutes away as long as this God-awful traffic allows me," Genevieve said as she laid on the horn and yelled at the driver for cutting her off.

"Wait, thirty minutes?" Sydney asked, surprised.

"Yes, thirty minutes. Please pack a bag for about two to three days' worth of clothes. We are going to Connecticut tonight."

"Connecticut?"

"Sydney, why are you repeating everything I say? It's like hearing a delayed echo," Genevieve said agitated.

"Pack business clothes and heels. We'll go over logistics in the car... is this going to be a problem Sydney? I did tell you I will need you on call at all times..."

"No, no problem at all. I am all yours," Sydney said as she placed eyedrops in her eyes.

"See you soon," Genevieve said before hanging up.

Sydney rolled out her old pink zebra print Betsey Johnson luggage and quickly decided that Genevieve would not approve. She then raced to the closet and pulled out Shawn's old Burberry rollway that housed some of his clothes. She unzipped the bag and let all of its contents fall on the floor. Like a wild woman, she tossed the bag on her bed and walked over to her closet.

She didn't have many "business clothes" so she settled for pulling some of her old work clothes from Lilian's, which mostly consisted of black dressy shirts, leggings and the occasional slacks.

After pulling three work outfits and some clothes for any "down time" that she had, Sydney threw in some toiletries, make up and undergarments before hurrying to go brush her teeth and change her clothes. The last thing she wanted to do was to show up to her first workday high— even though she was. Times like this she needed India the most to be her personal stylist and to alleviate any nerves that she may have.

Forty minutes later, Genevieve called to say that she was outside. Sydney struggled with her suitcase and her tote bag all the way to the car, even though there was a group of men who sat merely a few feet away from her who stood aimlessly smoking and talking. They all seemed too distracted by Genevieve and her ride as she sat parked in front of the building. Genevieve looked up just as Sydney got closer and quickly took her seatbelt off and hopped out of the car.

"Do you have a driver's license?" Genevieve asked as she popped her trunk door open with her keys.

Sydney could hear the men talking in low voices as they snickered with one another. She knew that they were looking at Genevieve and she instantly became agitated.

"Yes, I do," Sydney answered as she clumsily loaded her luggage and shoulder bag into the trunk.

Sydney had only gotten her license two years ago after India forced her to. India refused to let Sydney borrow her car and drive it around without a license — though she had been doing it for years prior.

"Great, you're driving," Genevieve said lightly, tossing her the keys. "My driver is off for he next few days, but we can manage, right?"

"Oh Genevieve, I uh..."

"Come, Sydney, we already have some monstrous traffic ahead of us. Let's get going," Genevieve said, climbing into the passenger side and closing the door behind her.

The ride to Connecticut went fairly smoothly. On the outside, Sydney was cool, calm and collected as she navigated Genevieve's Rolls-Royce down the interstate. On the inside though, she was a ball of nerves. During the four-hour car ride to New Haven, Genevieve spent most of her time working on her laptop and making miscellaneous calls. From what Sydney could gather from the overheard conversations, Genevieve was asked last minute to speak on an all women's panel about the topic of feminism for today's black woman. After a few hours on the phone, Genevieve finally turned her attention to Sydney.

"So, Sydney, tell me about yourself," she said.

Sydney found it easy to talk to Genevieve during their ride into New Haven. Maybe it was because she was trapped in a car with nothing else better to do, or maybe it was due to the fact that she felt like she could let her guard down with Genevieve in that moment. Sydney told Genevieve about her family and how she was the youngest, with two older brothers who were both enlisted in the army straight out of high school. Sydney told her about her mom who was forced to raise three kids alone once Sydney's father passed away when she was only three years old. Sydney shared with Genevieve about her struggles of "fitting in" and how alone she felt in life until she met India in high school. She even shared with her about her breakup with Shawn and how it still affected her to this day.

By the time that they pulled into the Omni Hotel, Sydney felt exhausted from talking so much. Sharing about herself, her family and friends, to an unbiased ear, made Sydney feel good. She also noted how Genevieve was sure to turn off all electronics before turning to Sydney, giving her full and undivided attention when Sydney told her about herself. Genevieve barely said two words during Sydney's rambling and listened attentively as if she would be quizzed on it later.

"We have a busy day tomorrow, Sydney. We will start early at 8 a.m. with breakfast in my room. I made all the arrangements, but going forward you will be the one to take over. How does that sound?" Genevieve asked as if she already had the answer.

Sydney was a little bummed once she realized that the

evening was over and that the two were to separate to their individual rooms that night. She also had to admit she felt a little slighted that Genevieve was eager to wrap their night up so quickly.

Secretly, Sydney hoped to make sense of the night before with Genevieve. She had been so affectionate and fun when they were out with her friends. She even remembered how she felt after feeling Genevieve's fingers lingering on her skin. Sydney wondered if that part of their budding friendship was now over since she had decided to work for her.

She quickly realized that she did have a little girl-crush on Genevieve. Though Sydney had never really been with a woman, she wasn't so quick to cast out the idea. She liked to consider herself pretty fluid when it came to her sexuality. Though she had always preferred and been in the company of men, she was not opposed to being with a woman. Sydney found some women to be drop-dead gorgeous. With their intellect mixed with divine femininity, energy and sex appeal, she viewed women to be straight up goddesses. And Genevieve was no exception.

What am I thinking? Sydney snapped back to reality when she realized how she was lowkey lusting now over her now boss.

While just standing in this hotel lobby late at night in travel clothes, Genevieve still had every man in the room watching her. She was gorgeous— and her energy electrifying. Didn't hurt that she had a both perfectly toned and curvy body as well. The valet guys almost fought over who would be the ones to come and serve them when they had first pulled up and Genevieve jumped out of the car.

Genevieve and Sydney said their goodnights and headed in their separate directions to their rooms. It was Sydney's first time staying alone in a hotel room. She made sure to take the hottest and longest shower when she arrived, being sure to fill up the entire bathroom with steam. Next, she harassed room service for some late night desserts to curb her sweet tooth. She wrapped up the evening watching Family Guy and eating cheesecake while lounging snuggly in her complimentary white robe. Sydney slept hard as a rock that night.

The next morning, Sydney made sure to get up on time for her official first day of work. Per Genevieve, today was a "down day." Sydney threw on her favorite mom jeans and Hillman sweater before placing her wild braids into a loose bun on the top of her head. She smiled at her reflection in the mirror, happy at what she saw. Already she felt like she could see a glow on her face from this much-needed change and distraction. Sydney hadn't stalked Shawn or his baby mama in days and was proud that she had found a healthy vice to get over him.

Sydney knocked on Genevieve's hotel door at 7:59 a.m. She beamed to herself at her punctuality and hoped that Genevieve would take note too.

"Sydney, right on time," Genevieve said, opening the door before ushering Sydney inside her room.

Unlike Sydney's room, Genevieve's room was a massive suite and had a modern mini living room that was decked out in all black decor.

"Wow," Sydney said with her mouth open as she walked aimlessly around Genevieve's suite.

"Nice room, huh?" Genevieve asked, taking a seat on an overstuffed chair. "Come sit with me Sydney."

Genevieve was wearing a long silk pink robe that Sydney imagined she brought from home. Even with it being eight in the morning, Genevieve looked beautiful, elegant and rested. She wore her hair up in a high ponytail and the only jewelry she wore was a pair of simple pearls that sat in her ears. Her bare skin glowed and Sydney could even see a trail of freckles that sat on top of her nose.

Sydney did as she was told and made her way over to Genevieve, taking note of the two silver carts that sat with them in the room. Sydney assumed they were food and instantly felt her stomach growl.

"This suite is gorgeous, Genevieve, and so was my room," Sydney added before reaching into her shoulder bag and pulling out a notebook. "Thank you so much for the accommodations. You know, I've never been to New Haven."

"Really?" Genevieve asked, raising an eyebrow. "It's so close to Boston I am surprised. I went to Yale for grad school."

Sydney of course remembered this already but assumed this was something that Genevieve rarely missed the opportunity to brag about. Can you blame her?

"Wow, what did you study?" Sydney asked, being sure to sound very impressed.

"Psychology," she said with a slight smile. "Maybe later I can take you to a few of the museums and one of my old favorite restaurants for a bite to eat," she said, slowly sipping on her coffee while maintaining eye contact with Sydney.

The two sat in silence staring at one another for a few more moments before Sydney looked down at her notebook, unable to stay in the competition. Genevieve had a way of looking through you that made her feel so naked and seen. And being in such close proximity together only intensified the butterflies she felt in her stomach already.

"Before we go any further... I need you to sign a few documents for me," Genevieve said, gently placing her coffee down and standing up to walk into the bedroom.

"Please help yourself to some coffee, Sydney," she yelled from the other room.

"Thank you, but I don't drink coffee," Sydney yelled over her shoulder, noting that Genevieve had not invited her to eat any actual food.

"Wow, really? What are you, a unicorn?" Genevieve asked, gliding back into the room.

She sat down again across from Sydney and handed her a black folder.

"This is for you," Genevieve said.

"Oh, what is it like tax documents and stuff?" Sydney asked as she opened the folder and thumbed through the pages.

She hated this part when starting a new job. All these documents did was confuse her and she would often rely on her mother or India to fill them out for her. The thought of India made Sydney's stomach turn with remorse and she felt a frown spread on her face.

"Yes, there are some documents in there. Also, there is an NDA, do you know what that is, Sydney?"

Genevieve asked Sydney the question in the same tone you would ask a child what their favorite color was. She sat with her legs crossed and straightened out her robe before slowly picking her cup of coffee back up and raising it to her mouth.

"Isn't it like a gag order that celebrities make people sign when they're scared of people knowing they're really freaks?" Sydney asked while laughing lightly.

Despite Sydney's ill-timed joke, Genevieve sat there like a statue and burned a hole into Sydney's face with her ice-cold stare. She stared at Sydney as if she were waiting for her to finish performing a scene.

"A non-disclosure agreement," she started, acting as if Sydney hadn't said anything, "is an agreement that keeps all parties protected. Though you may not consider me a ...*celebrity*. There are many who do. I have quite the following, Sydney, and I am often hounded by paparazzi and fans," Genevieve said, puffing her chest out.

"Oh, Genevieve I didn't mean to insinuate—"

"No need for that Sydney," she said, raising her hand to

stop her, "You said what you said and meant what you meant. It is fine. Trust me, you will see for yourself soon enough."

Sydney felt like an idiot and sat there, silent. She had her foot so far up her own mouth she didn't know how to get herself out of this one. She couldn't tell if Genevieve was insulted or challenged. Regardless, she instantly hated herself and decided to stop being so careless with her words.

"I want you to read over that carefully before you sign. I will not be offended if you want a lawyer to look over that. You know, seeing as I am not a *real* celebrity..."

"Nonsense," Sydney said, removing the cap off her pen with her mouth and signing her name on every line she saw.

The last thing she wanted to do was to offend her anymore.

"Aren't you going to read it?" Genevieve asked, screwing up her face.

"There's no need Genevieve, I trust you," Sydney said, looking up and giving her a small smile.

"Well thank you Sydney, but honestly, I would prefer you read it. It may be something that surprises you in —"

"Done," Sydney said, signing the last page and handing it over to her. "I'm ready for whatever. Your secrets are safe with me Genevieve."

"Excellent," Genevieve said, taking the folder with her face lighting up. "How about we celebrate then?" Genevieve continued as she stood up and whipped off both of the lids and exposed a platter of fruits, yogurts and something that Sydney assumed were to be pancakes.

"Oh... what's all of this?"

"I am on a very strict diet regime. I eat a preplanned breakfast and lunch every day. I have sent you the calendar of my meals to your email. Today we got a little spicy and I've added pumpkin protein pancakes to the lineup to jazz up our Greek yogurt and fruit," she said as she grabbed two plates.

"Yum," Sydney said dryly as she took a plate from Genevieve's hand.

Sydney herself was more of a meat and potatoes girl. When Genevieve told her that they would be having breakfast in her room, she was prepared to have a spread of bacon, cheesy eggs and buttery fluffy pancakes. Not this pale, sugar-free mess.

"Oh! That reminds me," Genevieve said as she scurried off again to the bedroom.

Sydney took the moment to poke the yogurt with her spoon. It barely budged an inch. She wondered how far the nearest McDonalds was from the hotel.

Genevieve returned from the room with a big white bag and a smile. She took a seat on the loveseat and patted the cushion next to her again.

"I got you a little something," Genevieve said.

"Aww," Sydney said as she raced over to sit next to her.

Sydney reached into the bag and pulled back the layers of thick white tissue paper to see a white MacBook Pro in the bottom of the bag.

"Genevieve!" she gasped as she snatched it out of the bag and opened it.

"You deserve the best! I have already set up your Apple account and email and— Oh, there is more!"

Genevieve's face lit up in excitement as she pulled out two additional bags and watched Sydney open her gifts. Sydney smiled at Genevieve, who looked like a little kid on Christmas. She didn't think she had ever seen her smile this hard and wondered how sore her cheeks would be later. If this all came from gifting Sydney, she could surely get used to it.

Sydney reached back into the bag and pulled out a white iPhone Pro Max.

"Oh my God!" Sydney yelled, unable to contain her excitement.

Sydney was still walking around with a barely functioning iPhone 6 that was being held together by duct tape and prayer.

"Yes! You have a new number and a few contacts stored in there," Genevieve said beaming. "I thought we could go shopping later too for an outfit for you for tomorrow."

"Oh my God thank you so much Genevieve," Sydney said, lunging in and giving her a hug before thinking about it.

Genevieve sat as stiff as a board, but after a few seconds, she scooted in closer and wrapped her arms tightly around Sydney's waist.

Sydney released Genevieve out of the hug to only feel her arms close tighter around her waist. Sydney was surprised at how warm and vulnerable Genevieve felt during the hug. It was a pleasant surprise.

"Thanks for all of this but a shopping spree isn't needed on top of this," Sydney said laughing as the two finally separated.

"Hun... it is. There is a certain caliber of dressing that I will require from you, too. Tonight, you should look through the rest of the folder," Genevieve said, returning to business.

"And what's wrong with the way I dress?" Sydney said, laughing while putting her hands on her hips.

This, of course, was something that she was used to being told.

"Let's just say, though you looked lovely the other night, I would have preferred to see that dress in the trash rather than sitting next to me at dinner," Genevieve said bluntly.

Sydney's mouth dropped open and she let out a single laugh. That dress was India's. No one ever criticized India's fashion.

"And how do we feel about this hair?" Genevieve asked with her index finger to her chin as she looked up wearily at Sydney's messy bun.

...

"A few more feet, come on Sydney girl, you can do it," Genevieve chuckled as she retrieved her hotel card and unlocked her hotel door.

The two were returning from the panel discussion at Yale. It had been a packed event and Sydney was sure that every feminist in the tri-state area made their way to Connecticut to hear the women speak. Sydney reached Genevieve's doorway and quickly kicked off her four-inch heels that she had been running around in all day.

"I don't know how Beyoncé does it!" Sydney said exasperatedly, as she collapsed on the couch with her bags in tow.

Genevieve laughed and shook her head at Sydney, "Trust me you will get used to it. I bet it feels a lot different than those boots you stomp around in."

"My precious Docs," Sydney said with a devilish grin as she placed her right foot in her hand and began to massage it.

She was exhausted. Despite being ready to pass out, she had thoroughly enjoyed the panel and loved watching Genevieve on stage captivating an audience again. The panel discussion was only for a few hours and ended promptly at nine, but the planning for the panel was the real bitch. Sydney found herself sore and ready for bed after a day of running behind Genevieve, helping her to prepare for her last-minute gig. Genevieve had the pleasure of joining other authors and a few professors on a heavy open-panel discussion about the injustices of womanhood in post-Trump's America.

"Drink?" Genevieve asked as she headed to her mini bar.

"Please," Sydney said as she ran her hand through her hair just to be reminded that it wasn't there.

Yesterday, Genevieve suggested that Sydney "upgrade" her look by losing her braids and cutting her hair into a short pixie cut. When Sydney attempted to object, pleading that braids were her signature look, Genevieve responded with three words: "change and growth."

So here she was. Sitting here feeling as bald and bare as a 1990s Halle Berry. She didn't love her new look, but after spending a few hours last night staring at herself in the mirror she didn't hate it either. It made her feel sleeker and more polished. It even, dare she say it, made her feel bold and maybe even a little sexy.

"What will you have?" Genevieve asked as she pulled out two glass cups and placed ice in each.

"Surprise me," Sydney said as she leaned back deeper into the couch with her eyes closed.

"How about a vodka gimlet...I think we have all of the ingredients here," she said as she rummaged between the bar and mini fridge that was adjacent to it.

The noise of the bottles and ice clinking together made Sydney open one of her eyes to see what was going on.

"A what?" Sydney asked.

"A vodka gimlet," Genevieve said matter of factly with her back to Sydney as she busied herself with the drinks. "I must be aging myself here. All you need is ice, lime juice, some sugar... and vodka of course," she said as she spun around with the two drinks in hand.

"Wow, sugar? I'm surprised; that's not on the calendar for tonight," Sydney teased as she accepted her drink from Genevieve's hand.

"Hush you," Genevieve said as she playfully swatted at Sydney before sitting down next to her.

Sydney took a long sip of her tart drink and smiled. It was actually really good. She never drank anything outside of cheap wine and maybe beers. This was the perfect nightcap.

"It was really amazing to see you up there today Genevieve. You are so comfortable and confident on stage. How do you do that? I would be a nervous wreck," Sydney said, leaning back into the couch feeling relaxed.

"Why thank you Sydney," Genevieve said as she began to

finally take off her own heels before crawling up onto the couch into a tiny little ball.

"I do believe most of those people were there to hear me speak," she said as she smiled to herself, "What do you think?"

"I think you're right. I thought we were going to be stuck there for hours, I saw so many people with copies of your books," Sydney said, reflecting on the evening while suppressing a yawn.

"Did I work you too hard already?" Genevieve laughed as she reached over to grab Sydney's face and turn it towards her.

"Today was perfect, thank you again Genevieve for this opportunity," Sydney said sincerely as she gently placed her hand on top of Genevieve's. "You truly don't know how much I appreciate you. I feel so lucky to even be here. Thank you for... seeing something in me. For seeing *me*."

Despite her throbbing feet, achy back and bald scalp, Sydney was thoroughly enjoying herself. She couldn't remember the last time she felt this excited about... anything. It felt good to be included in something bigger than her own little bubble of misery. Watching Genevieve on stage was so inspiring and left her with a buzz that she couldn't shake or quite put into words. If this was only the beginning, she couldn't wait to see what was next.

Genevieve looked over at Sydney intensely as if she were lost in thought.

"You really mean that. Don't you?" she asked.

"I do," Sydney said quickly as she sipped more of her drink.

She was beginning to feel the warmth of the liquor creep all over her body. Genevieve seemed to be enjoying her drink as well as she visibly became more relaxed. She joked with Sydney and made any excuse to lay her hand on or to touch Sydney in some way. By the time the evening dwindled down the pair were two drinks in and were giggling like old friends.

"Ugh," Sydney moaned, looking at her phone and noticing

it was almost one in the morning, "We have an early day, we should probably go to bed."

Sydney sat up and yawned as she reluctantly got up to walk to the front door with her shoes in hand. She was not ready to leave, but knew it would be best for her to leave now.

"Sydney?" Genevieve called her as she pulled on her arm.

Sydney turned around to see Genevieve standing directly behind her. She had to look down at Genevieve who was almost three inches shorter than her without her heels. It was funny to Sydney how such a petite woman had the power to feel like the biggest person in the room.

Genevieve grabbed Sydney's face with both of her hands and pulled it towards her own. The warmth of Genevieve's hands on her face made Sydney melt as she allowed her to guide her face towards her own. She knew what Genevieve intended to do and her heart began to race. The light, playful banter and hand grazes had all led up to this. Yet, a part of Sydney was still afraid that she was misconstruing Genevieve's true intentions for her.

Being this close to her, Sydney could smell her expensive perfume mixed with the blunt aroma of vodka and lime that came from her lips. Genevieve looked Sydney square in her eyes as if asking for permission, even though it was clear what she intended to do. Sydney could feel her pulse quicken as she hovered her face merely inches away from Genevieve's, waiting for her to make the first move.

Genevieve paused, and for the first time since they met, broke her stare with Sydney. She dropped her eyes to the ground and began to lower her hands from Sydney's face to Sydney's disapproval. Swiftly, Sydney grabbed Genevieve's face and kissed her on her mouth gently for no more than a few seconds before pulling away. Her lips were soft and full and felt like pillows against Sydney's, nothing like Shawn's hard lips that always seemed dry and rough.

At first, the curious peck on the lips seemed harmless. A light moment shared between two friends that came consequently after one or two many drinks. This light kiss could be laughed off the next morning between the women over breakfast. They could easily agree to never mention it again, and to continue like nothing happened.

Sydney rested her forehead on top of Genevieve's after the kiss, digesting what just happened and trying to decide if this was something they would be capable of laughing off.

Did I fuck up? Did I take it too far? Sydney asked herself as she stood there with her.

Sydney didn't want to stop but was unable to tell what was going through Genevieve's mind. Just as she began to craft an excuse to run out the room, Genevieve grabbed the back of Sydney's head and kissed her back passionately. Sydney was only shocked for a moment before she began to fully kiss Genevieve back, allowing her tongue to explore her mouth.

She threw her shoes to the ground so that she could free her hands to hold onto Genevieve who was pushing her hard against the door. Once her hands were free, Sydney attempted to grab Genevieve's face again, but was stopped once her arms were pinned behind her to the door. Leaving her trapped between the door and Genevieve's soft and warm body. Sydney felt heat spread all over her as she softly bit Genevieve's lip.

Chapter 6

Saturday Morning, October 17th

It was early in the morning and Sydney laid in bed knocked out asleep. She had had a long week with Genevieve that ended with a big payout. After their make out-session in New Haven that night, Genevieve finally broke away and decided to call it a night. Reluctantly, Sydney listened and went to her room where she laid awake for most of the night thinking about what had transpired. The next morning the two acted as if nothing happened and traveled back home while keeping the conversation light. Sydney felt so confused as to why Genevieve seemed to be backpedaling but didn't want to push it.

When Genevieve dropped Sydney back at home she told her she had the next few days off and to check her bank account. When Sydney finally dragged her luggage up the stairs and checked her account, she saw that Genevieve had paid her $3,000.

"Oh shit," Sydney had muttered under her breath while she tried to rationalize it.

She made $3,000 in just two days with Genevieve. She

would be lucky to make that same amount in a month with her two old jobs combined.

Just as Sydney got deeper into her dream about sharing a yacht with Omarion and the rest of B2K, she was awakened by a faint knock on her door. She closed her eyes tighter and nuzzled deeper into bed and hoped it was someone at her neighbor's door.

"Syd, open the damn door!" she heard India yell as she continued to knock more ferociously this time.

"What the actual fuck," Sydney muttered as she tossed her comforter off and dragged herself to the front door.

"Rise and shine bitch," India said gleefully, before she froze and bulged her eyes at Sydney's head. "Oh my God. Where is your hair?!" she said as she barged in past Sydney.

"India, what time is it?" Sydney asked, yawning as she closed the door behind them.

India showed up with bagels and two to-go mugs in hand. After she placed them down on Sydney's kitchen counter she spun around quickly to grill Sydney.

"It's 9 a.m. Syd and where the hell have you been? And where is your hair? Take that damn scarf off and let me see," India said with her hand on her hip.

Sydney was in no mood for India's antics that morning, even though she knew her drop-in was long overdue. She snatched off her own head scarf and gave India a weak smile and spin before brushing past her and going into her bathroom, where she plopped down on the toilet to pee.

"If it wasn't for your mother, I would have sworn you were dead. Imagine my surprise when I called her and she told me that you have been busy with your 'new job'," India said, now leaning in Sydney's bathroom doorway watching her pee.

Sydney wasn't surprised that her mother told India the news before she could. She also wasn't surprised how her friend was invading her space at that very moment. Sydney finished using the bathroom without saying a word to India. For days she imagined this very moment and what she would say, but now that it was here – she was speechless. She finished using the bathroom and went to the sink to wash her hands and then her face before pulling out her toothbrush.

"And I was like, 'nah Mrs. Mack you gotta be mistaken. *Sydney*? A new job and she didn't tell me, her *bestest* friend in the world. Clearly she was wrong... right Syd?"

Sydney continued to brush her teeth with her back turned to India. She knew that she was better off letting her friend go off now than to interrupt her. Especially because she knew that she was the one who was wrong in this situation. Sydney finally finished brushing her teeth and returned her toothbrush in its cup on the sink and turned to face her friend.

"It's true. I got a new job. I quit Flamingo's a few days ago and have been busy with work these last few days. My bad girl; I swear I had plans on telling you today," she said while looking at the ground without making eye contact.

"Nope, that's not good enough," India said, switching her weight to her other hip while sipping her coffee that smelled like pumpkin spice. "What are you not telling me? Who are you working for because I know you didn't get that hotel job. And who the fuck told you to cut your hair? You really let someone else do your hair, and you let them *cut it*?"

She stared at Sydney and looked her up and down as if examining her would help her to find her answers.

"Did you get the lemon in my tea like I like girl? You know it don't hit unless it's sour like I like," Sydney laughed as she attempted to walk out the room before being blocked by India.

"Alright," Sydney sighed as she raised her arms in the air, defeated. "I'm working for Genevieve! There, now move so I can drink my tea!"

"You got to be shittin' me," India said, with her mouth dropping open.

"Nope, and look," Sydney said walking past her and to her phone, "I got paid already girl," she said, holding her phone up for India to see the money that was just deposited into her account.

"Bitch," India said, snatching the phone out of Sydney's hand to get a closer look. "What the hell did that lady have you do to get money like this after only a week? I know you not out here selling booty."

"Try a few days," Sydney chuckled as she blew on her tea and noticed the extra lemon slices that floated in it.

"A few days? Girl... is this legal?" India whispered, with worry etching her face.

"India, yes!'" Sydney said, laughing as she plopped down onto her worn loveseat that Shawn's dad had loaned them when they first moved in.

"Spill it. And I mean everything," India demanded. "Because right now this is givin' very much escort vibes, and I don't like it!"

Sydney did as she was told. Starting from the day when Genevieve popped up at her job with her realtor all the way to the kiss they shared their last night on the trip. That last part was harder to share, and Sydney delivered the update with uncertainty.

"Girl, is she even gay? Because you ain't. What the hell is going on?" India belted, letting out a long laugh as she bit into a bagel.

"I don't know, maybe? And you don't know about my sexual preference India, I can be bi—"

"Syd, kissing a girl freshman year at a party when you were drunk off of Dubra does not make you gay. Straight girls always want to pull that card like that means something," she said, rolling her eyes, "Trust me, I'm a lesbian and your best friend... I know."

Sydney rolled her eyes in return and took a big bite out of

her bagel. There was no point in arguing with India, especially not when she is right. Sydney loved men and knew she wasn't gay, likeley not even bi-sexual. But she did feel something for Genevieve, that was real. And she was attracted to her. In fact, she felt flushed the whole time that she talked to India about her.

"Don't play with that woman, Syd. It's nothing worse than a girl trying to figure out her sexuality with a woman who knows it for sure," India continued as she pulled out her phone.

"Also, woman or not, this is now your boss... are you okay with this? It sounds to me like she's taking advantage of you. Kissing your boss, Syd? That's a slippery slope—"

"And this is why I've been avoiding you because I knew you would take it there."

"Can you blame me? I mean let's talk facts here. You've met this woman a week ago—"

"It's been like three weeks," Sydney said exasperatedly as she threw her head back, annoyed.

"Okay it's been *three weeks*," India said dragging out the last words for emphasis, "and this woman has popped up randomly at your job, taken you out to meet her nut ass friends — that you met in *my* dress might I add— she's paid your bills off for the next few months, she buys you a new laptop and phone and then she hires you for a job and makes out with you! Oh," she said, jumping up from her chair, "Let's not forget the fact that she made you sign a contract to keep quiet that your dumb ass didn't even read through!"

"What's your point India?"

"My point? Syd in what fuckin' world does this make sense? This is not normal."

"Says who?" Sydney said, finally agitated and over this conversation. "This may not be normal in your world, but hell it clearly is in mine now. Just be happy for me India, damn! Finally, something good is happening for me, you would think of all people you would be happy for me. Now I don't have to ask you for money."

"I am happy for you, I'm happy you're making money. I just want to make sure this is safe. You know how you get Syd..."

"What does that mean?" Sydney shot back.

India opened her mouth to say something and closed it quickly before returning her attention to her phone.

Sydney was tired of being patient with India and trying to make her get it. She felt like she was dragging this out and she was ready to move on. "And what are you looking up on your phone?"

"I'm looking your new boss up," she said with her eyes glued to her screen. "I Googled her and the only thing that comes up are her books. It's so weird."

"She's an author," Sydney said, uninterested in the conversation. "How is that weird?"

"Because nothing else comes up. No information on her personal life, if she's married, or even anything about her past..."

Sydney thought about how Genevieve warned her how she was a celebrity and how important it was to keep her discretion. The fact that nothing could be found online about her did not surprise her in the slightest. Genevieve did not play about her privacy.

"If she has you signing a contract that tells you to shut the fuck up, that means she has some shit to hide Syd. Something about this just seems fishy to me. Just be careful, please."

"I will, now can we drop this?"

"Sure girl," India said, locking her phone and tossing it onto the table, "But let's read over that contract first."

"No, I'm pretty sure that goes against the whole point of me signing the thing in the first place India," she said, "Look I'll read over it again today. For real."

"Well girl you done told me everything now!" India yelled, causing them both to bust out in laugher.

"Fine," India said, unconvincingly. ."Promise me you'll read over it or have someone professional look it over?"

"Promise. For all I know that could've been a one-off thing anyway. We were just tired and buzzed, that's all," Sydney said, barely believing the lie herself.

Sydney sighed and wandered to her bed to pull her comforter off while she wrapped it around her body and plopped down next to India. She knew India and knew that this would not be the last time that she would voice her concerns about Genevieve. She also knew that her friend would keep digging to find dirt on her. Sydney always teased India and told her how she should moonlight as a private investigator. Speaking of PI's, she decided to change the conversation to one of India's favorite topics.

"So, what have I missed these past few days? How's Dij?"

Saturday night...

Sydney sat in the back of the truck staring at the back of Raphael, her driver's, balding head. She tugged at her headscarf and checked her reflection in her phone for the fourth time. She was still getting used to rocking her new short cut and was unsure how to style her short pixie cut that seemed flat. Last minute she decided to throw the colorful scarf on her head before heading out the door.

A few hours ago, Genevieve asked Sydney if she would join her for a late dinner at her home. Sydney, who was lying in bed binging *Dear White People*, eagerly accepted and got dressed. She hadn't read the contract yet like she had promised India, but she had time. She would look it over as soon as she came back home.

She wasn't sure what to wear tonight. Sure, Genevieve had

taken her on a mini shopping spree when the two were in Connecticut, but that was mostly for work clothes. And though she hadn't specified, Sydney didn't think that this was a work dinner.

She found herself nervous while sitting in the back of the private car that Genevieve had sent for her. She was excited to see Genevieve and to be invited to her home. She wondered if they would talk about what happened at the end of their trip or if that was truly a one-off. She also wondered and hoped that something similar would happen again tonight.

After forty minutes, the truck pulled up to a gated community and Sydney couldn't help but feel her stomach flip as she gawked at all of the beautiful million-dollar homes she saw. Even though it was nighttime and relatively dark, the homes were lit up beautifully and Sydney marveled at the manicured lawns and expensive cars that sat in the driveways. The truck had gone up a long windy road before driving up a steep driveway that led to a gorgeous mansion on a hill.

"Wow," Sydney whispered to herself as they pulled up to Genevieve's home.

The home was beautiful. It looked to be three stories tall, and the walls were covered with windows that made it look like a house made of glass. The glass house was sleek and classy, just like Genevieve.

Raphael parked the car in front of the house and hopped out of the driver's seat. He rebuttoned his blazer and straightened out his suit before opening Sydney's car door and offering her a hand to help her out.

"Thank you," she said nervously as she tugged her leather jacket tighter around her.

"Ms. Cross told me to have you go right inside," Raphael said with a gentle smile as he nodded his head in the direction of the front door.

"Just like that?" Sydney asked, confused.

"Just like that," Raphael repeated with a light chuckle as he stood there patiently.

"Just open the door and walk in? With no knock?" Sydney was stalling and Raphael knew it.

He laughed again and extended his hand once again to Sydney.

"How about I walk you to the door and open it for you?" he asked as Sydney placed her hand in his and did as she was told.

She felt weird about walking into Genevieve's house unannounced, but didn't want to get her or Raphael in trouble for not following directions.

Slowly, Raphael walked Sydney to the massive wooden front door. With his other hand, he pulled open the door before ushering Sydney inside.

"You sure you don't want to join me?" Sydney chuckled nervously as she walked in.

"Not tonight Miss Mack," he said, chuckling as he released her hand. "Enjoy your evening and your dinner. I will see you later on," he said, closing the front door in front of him.

Sydney was left alone. She turned around to see that she stood in a massive room that had a sunken living room and fireplace in the middle of the room. She took a few steps into the home as she looked around cautiously for Genevieve. Sydney took off her jacket and laid it on a nearby chaise and tiptoed down the three short stairs to the living room. The house appeared to be just as beautiful inside as it was on the outside. In the background, Sydney could hear Sade playing and in the air she could smell dinner being made. She walked around the room and viewed the art that hung on the walls. The pieces were ...unique, and in black and white. All the pieces on the walls were of nude bodies in various shades of gray and all in different poses. They made Sydney feel uncomfortable but she couldn't stop staring at their nudity.

"Sydney, you're here. Finally," Genevieve said, standing in the doorway with two wine glasses in hand.

Per usual, Genevieve looked stunning. She was barefoot and wearing a simple long cream chiffon form-fitting dress that reached to the floor and had a slit that traveled all the way up to her thigh. She wore her hair up tonight and wore big bohemian earrings— something that looked to be more of Sydney's style than her own.

"Thank you for inviting me," Sydney said, walking to her and accepting the drink. "Your home is beautiful Genevieve," she said, kissing her lightly on the cheek, "and I love those earrings!"

"Thank you, Sydney, I just picked these beauties up today," she said, winking. "I will have to give you a tour of the house later. You can imagine the hell I gave my interior decorator to get this all done in just a few weeks. It's so good to see you," she gushed, leaning in for a hug.

Sydney happily embraced her and hugged her back as Genevieve's sweet and expensive perfume wafted into her nose.

"It's good to be seen," Sydney said as she stepped away from Genevieve and smiled.

She could tell Genevieve was in a good mood and felt how relaxed her energy was tonight. Seeing this, Sydney began to relax a little herself.

"You know Sydney, I really enjoyed our trip to New Haven. It reminded me of my old grad school days," Genevieve began while looking Sydney in the eyes.

"Really?" Sydney asked shyly.

She wondered if Genevieve made a habit of making out on doors with her coeds in between psych classes, too. Sydney sipped her wine to fight back a smile and fought the urge to turn her face up at the tart taste. Genevieve was watching.

"Really," Genevieve answered as she sipped on her wine

and watched Sydney intently. "Do you like the wine? It's one of my favorites."

"It's delicious," Sydney lied.

"I knew you would like it, Sydney."

Genevieve had a habit of always repeating Sydney's name when talking to her. To Sydney, hearing her name come out of her mouth repeatedly always gave her butterflies and made her feel like she was special to her.

The two stood in silence for a few moments before Sydney awkwardly began to look around trying to break the ice.

"Interesting art you have here," she said, walking slightly away from Genevieve and looking at the wall art.

"Thank you, the photographer is actually... an acquaintance of mine. He has a real knack, doesn't he? How he captures the beauty of a naked body."

"Mmhm," Sydney said as she looked up to view a photo of a naked man baring it all in a black and white photo while staring back seriously at the camera.

Genevieve walked over to Sydney to gain back her attention. She gently grabbed Sydney's chin and turned her head to face her as she started deeply into her eyes.

"Sydney, I have not been able to get you out of my mind, or what happened on our trip," she said softly. "Let me ask you something?"

"Anything," Sydney said quickly, immediately hating the thirst that she heard in her own voice.

"Did you really read through the contract fully?" Genevieve asked, raising an eyebrow.

"Mhm," Sydney lied. *Damn why is everyone so pressed over this contract,* she thought to herself.

"From front to back? Each page—"

"Genevieve, I read it," Sydney giggled. "It's fine. We're all good."

"Yes?" Genevieve asked, shocked.

"Yeah," Sydney said back confidently.

"I feel something for you Sydney... Something I haven't felt in years and I'm not alone, am I?" Genevieve asked curiously.

Sydney shook her head no. She was stuck and unable to speak, like a deer in headlights. During the trip, Sydney had learned to maintain eye contact with Genevieve, no matter how intimidating it was. At that moment, she felt it nearly impossible to return her stare and looked down at the floor.

"How did you feel when I kissed you, Sydney?" Genevieve whispered.

"Huh?" Sydney asked as she sipped more of her wine.

"Now you know I hate that word... it's not even a word, it's a sound. A sound effect for the dunce to save time," Genevieve sighed, looking disappointed as she sipped her wine and walked over to the front window, away from Sydney.

"It felt... right," Sydney spoke up, following behind her. "I'm not able to explain it. It just felt ... right. And I enjoyed it... I enjoyed it a lot," she blurted, wanting not to ruin the mood.

Genevieve smiled at her, happy with her response.

"So, I wasn't wrong?"

"I do believe it was me who kissed you first Genevieve," Sydney said laughing, "So no. you were definitely not wrong."

"So, what if I kissed you again right now?" Genevieve asked, with a perfectly arched eyebrow raised. "What would happen then?"

Sydney stepped in closer to her and smiled.

"How about you find out?"

Genevieve smiled, ready to take on her dare. She grabbed the wine glass out of Sydney's hand and placed both of their glasses down onto a nearby glass table. She turned around and raced back over to Sydney and grabbed her face with both of her hands. Within seconds, Genevieve's lips were kissing Sydney's. Genevieve let her hands travel down to Sydney's waist as she pulled her hard into her and Sydney wrapped her arms around Genevieve's shoulders. Sydney still wasn't 100% sure on how to kiss a woman back, like what should she do with her hands? She decided to figure it out as she went.

Sydney could feel Genevieve's hands fall from her waist and begin to wander around her body, making Sydney become hot and tingly all over. Sydney, without thinking, slid her tongue into Genevieve's mouth where she was greeted with Genevieve's warm tongue that gently caressed hers.

In the back of her mind Sydney wondered if Raphael sat in his car watching the two go at it right in the living room. Seeing how the walls were literally made of glass, she felt as if she were in a snow globe on display for the world. Sydney had the feeling that it wasn't his first time delivering someone to Genevieve. He probably sat right in the car and drooled at the sight of the two women going at it without a fear of anyone seeing them.

There was a loud noise of a glass shattering that came from somewhere in the house and it startled the pair, causing them to break apart.

Sydney laughed sheepishly as she wiped hers and Genevieve's lipstick from around her mouth. Genevieve did the same and rolled her eyes playfully at the sound.

"Sydney, please go help in the kitchen while I grab us another bottle of wine from the cellar," Genevieve said softly. "Also, what in the world is this on your head?" she asked, eyeing Sydney's headwrap suspiciously before looking at the rest of Sydney's outfit and scowling.

Sydney wore an oversized old Pepe sweatshirt that doubled as a dress. She had stolen it from Shawn. She accompanied the sweatshirt with thick white knee-high socks and of course her beloved Dr. Martens.

"You don't like it? My mom got it for me on one of her trips to Cape Verde earlier this year," she said tugging subconsciously at her head wrap.

"I do wish you would wear your hair out and wear the clothes I got you. What's wrong with your hair and why are you covering it?" she asked, folding her arms.

"Nothing is wrong Genevieve," Sydney said quickly, "I just didn't know how to style it. I guess I'm still getting used to it."

"That cut is absolutely stunning on you," she said. "When I was your age I wore the same style and it was dashing."

"Really?" Sydney asked, wondering if she could get more information from her. "And how long ago would you say that was?"

Genevieve laughed just as another shattering sound came from the kitchen that was followed by a loud, "Shit!"

"Nice try," she smiled slyly as she glided past her. "Let's say that was about five to fifteen years ago," she said with a wink.

Sydney laughed, only slightly annoyed that her question was dodged.

"The kitchen is down the hall to the left, you can't miss it," Genevieve said over her shoulder.

Sydney did as she was told and grabbed her wine glass before wandering her way to the kitchen. When Sydney stepped into the kitchen, she realized this was the source of the music and noted how it got louder. To no one's surprise, the kitchen looked straight out of a home magazine. It was completely wooden with black cabinets and a kitchen island. The stove was full of pots and pans and the room smelled rich with seafood and spices.

"Mmm, smells good," Sydney said aloud as she walked deeper into the room looking for a chef or maid.

Suddenly, a man stood up from behind the kitchen island and looked over at Sydney inquisitively with a small dustpan in hand. Sydney's first impression of the man was that he was too handsome and well-kept to be the help.

He was tall and good-looking and wore his long brown hair in a messy bun that sat on top of his head. Sydney noted his tanned skin and green eyes that seemed to pop against his light gray sweater. He had a rugged short beard and wore a pair of thick black glasses on his face.

"Hi," Sydney said awkwardly, walking closer to the man. "I'm Sydney."

"Hi," the man said as he stood frozen staring at Sydney.

He seemed to realize he was staring and dropped his eyes to the dustpan in his hands, "Glass... I uh, dropped a glass... or two," he said as he shuffled over to the trash can and threw the glass out. "Please be careful. I think I got it all up though."

Sydney noticed the man had on loose sweats and stood in the kitchen barefoot, as if he were right at home. She was more worried about his bare feet around glass than of her own that were safely in boots. Who was this man? She was so confused.

"Um, Genevieve told me to come in here to help out... but it looks like you have everything under control," she said looking around the kitchen noticing only two bowls that sat on the counter. "I'm sorry I didn't catch your name?"

"Oh, I see you two have met," Genevieve said, coming into the room with a bottle in hand.

She stopped at Sydney and gave her a kiss on the cheek as she placed the bottle on the island and went to stand by the man who had returned to the stove after washing his hands. "Of course we met, you sent her in here to the room where I was at," the man said, agitated as he sprinkled parsley into a pot.

"True, I guess that wine is hitting me harder than expected," Genevieve giggled as she rested her head on the man's arm and snaked her arm around his waist.

Sydney felt a twinge of jealousy creep up as she forced down another gulp of her wine.

Who is this dude and why are they so damn cozy? she asked herself.

"So, this is Sydney, the wonderful woman I have been

telling you about. Isn't she gorgeous?" she asked as her mahogany eyes landed on Sydney's.

"And this, this is Asher, Sydney," Genevieve said looking up at him. He stood at least a foot taller than her.

"Her husband," Asher said matter-of-factly.

Sydney choked on the wine that was currently traveling down her throat. She tried to catch her breath but felt a sharp wet pain in her throat that quickly sent her into a series of loud uncontrollable coughs.

"Oh, now look what you've done," Genevieve said as she walked over to Sydney and patted her on the back while she continued to cough. "You always ruin the fun."

Chapter 7

October 17th

Sydney gasped for air as she tried to stifle her coughs with her hand. For the life of her she could not catch her breath and the more that she tried to stop them, the harder they came out.

"Breathe, Sydney. Take it easy," Genevieve said as she continued to pat and rub her back. "Asher, get her some water."

"No...no I'm okay," Sydney said, embarrassed as she finally felt able to breathe.

"Good, can't have you dying before you taste some of Asher's wonderful cooking. He's made a seafood medley tonight; what is it called again?"

"I wish you would've told me we were having company tonight G," Asher said, clearly agitated and ignoring her question.

He turned the knobs off on the stove before turning around and getting another bowl out of the cabinet.

"Why ruin the surprise?" Genevieve asked now, moseying around the kitchen.

Asher shook his head at Genevieve and began to fix the

plates of food. Sydney stood there still stunned as the couple moved around the kitchen prepping for dinner.

What kinda twilight zone am I in right now? she thought to herself.

"Any allergies Sydney?" Asher asked, annoyed as he spooned soup into a bowl.

"No..."

"Good. I made— "

"Cioppino," Sydney said finishing his sentence. She clocked it as soon as she saw the red sauce and seafood. "I work — worked at an Italian restaurant."

Asher paused momentarily, looking up at Sydney before returning to fixing the plate and handing her one.

"Sydney, come have a seat," Genevieve said, pulling out a chair for her at the table. "I imagine you have a few questions."

"You think?" Sydney said as she took her plate and sat down, causing Genevieve to laugh.

"God, you're such a riot Sydney, I swear."

The table was fixed up beautifully. There was a bowl full of fresh bread, a huge salad, and a plate of crostini de tonno— a finger food dish of tuna and bread that was a hit at Flamingo's. The table was clearly set for two and Sydney only imagined the amount of energy that was put into this meal.

Asher took a seat across from Sydney and she could see him clenching his jaw while he sipped his wine. He clearly did not want her there and was as surprised as Sydney was at how the evening unfolded.

"More wine, Sydney?" Genevieve asked as she poured wine into her glass without waiting for an answer.

She took a seat at the head of the table, sitting in between Asher and Sydney. Genevieve smiled at the two of them and placed her hands together before taking a deep breath and picking up her spoon to eat.

"Are you Cape Verdean, Sydney?" Asher asked.

"Cape Verdean? No, just regular black," Sydney answered awkwardly, taken aback that this white man was questioning her.

"I ask because of your wrap," he said, nodding his head to her headwrap. "Those are the colors of their flag."

"Oh, that makes sense. To be honest it was a gift from my mom. She went there earlier this year," she said, touching it subconsciously.

"It's beautiful," he said matter-of-factly.

"Oh, I know, just lovely," Genevieve agreed.

Sydney scrunched up her face at her, reflecting back to just a few minutes ago when Genevieve viewed it with disgust in the living room.

"Thank you," Sydney said, taking a sip of water to soothe her now sore throat.

"So, you bring her here— and didn't even tell her, huh?" Asher asked as he talked to Genevieve as if Sydney wasn't even there.

Genevieve ignored his question and turned her attention to Sydney.

"So, Sydney, yes, this is Asher, and he is my husband of the last seven years," she said, reaching out and grabbing his arm.

"Genevieve... you never mentioned a husband," Sydney said meekly.

Her head was spinning, and she suppressed the feeling of wanting to run out of the room.

"I know Sydney. You see, most people do not know that I am married, well most of the public that is," she said, reaching for the tongs and putting salad on to her plate before passing the bowl to Asher.

"Don't get me wrong, Asher is no secret... but we do have an unconventional marriage. Our marriage is not really accepted by most people, and we choose to keep what's special to us... to ourselves."

"Unconventional?" Sydney questioned.

"We're polyamorous," Genevieve said calmly as she stared at Sydney, trying to see her reaction.

"Genevieve is polyamorous ... I myself do not practice the polyamory lifestyle," Asher corrected her as he got out some salad and passed the bowl to Sydney.

Sydney slowly spooned salad onto her plate before placing the bowl down as she tried to digest what she was hearing.

"So...you're swingers?" she asked, confused.

"Oh, hun no," Genevieve laughed as she began to eat her salad. "Though it's a common misconception, there is a difference. Polyamory is the practice of having more than one loving partner. It's like consensual anti-monogamy. We, as a couple, do not 'hook-up' with other couples as swingers do. Instead, we believe that it is possible to have more than one romantic relationship at a time. Asher and I do not limit ourselves to just one another."

Sydney reached for a piece of warm bread and broke a piece off before placing it in her mouth. If she were being honest, she had lost her appetite completely. But she didn't know what else to do to avoid sitting there looking dumb.

"Polyamory is about a deeper connection. It goes beyond the physical, it's about an intimate, emotional connection. Like the one that I feel with you," Genevieve said, reaching across the table and rubbing Sydney's arm. "I believe that we as human beings have an innate need to connect with one another. And that doesn't end just because you are married. We should not limit ourselves to just one person; it's unfair to think that only one person is capable of loving you at a time."

"Unfortunately, as you can imagine, society does not take too kindly to a marriage like ours. Sure, there are those token celebs who flaunt it around, but it's a little bit more tricky for us. I mean it's bad enough that we are already an interracial couple," she paused and chuckled, "Once you add a few extra lovers to the mix... well, let's just say the media would throw a frenzy if they ever found out."

Asher rolled his eyes and continued to eat his soup. He sat and ate in silence as he listened to Genevieve break everything down for Sydney.

"Do you see why I had you sign the NDA? It's important that you understand how private and personal this is to me. I cannot risk this getting out; unfortunately society is not ready to learn how common this actually is. Sydney, eat your soup before it gets cold," Genevieve said, eyeing Sydney's bowl even though she had barely touched her own.

Sydney did as she was told and spooned a mouthful of soup into her mouth. The soup was absolutely delicious, and the flavors instantly burst in her mouth. Flamingo's had nothing on Asher's soup. She eagerly spooned more soup into her mouth, being sure to add a shrimp this time. She peeked up just in time to see Asher smirking at her enjoying her food before turning his gaze back to his own.

"How is it?" Genevieve asked as she finally began to eat her own food.

"It's delicious," Sydney said, dipping the bread into the soup.

"No surprise there, Asher is a phenomenal chef. Which is perfect because I can't even fry an egg," she laughed again.

"Ash, do you remember that time I tried to make us breakfast and nearly burned our apartment down?"

"How can I forget? From that day on I told you to never touch a stove again," he said looking at Genevieve, smiling while reaching for her hand. "And you haven't since then, have you?"

"You're still alive aren't you?"

"Barely...a boiled egg almost ended my life."

The two laughed together as they reminisced on their past. Sydney eyed the two and noticed how Asher's eyes sparkled when he looked at Genevieve. He seemed to be so grim only a few seconds ago, but now seemed to light up when reflecting on their past.

"How long have you two been together?" Sydney asked, still feeling slightly uneasy seeing them be affectionate with one another.

"Fifteen years, married for seven," Asher said while still looking Genevieve in the eyes.

"Oh hush, now she's going to know our age," Genevieve said, swatting at him.

"How old are you Sydney?" Asher asked, turning his attention to her.

"Twenty-four... I'll be twenty-five next month. And you?"

Asher raised an eyebrow and looked over at Genevieve. "She's a little young for you, no?" he asked as he removed his hand from her and shook his head in disapproval.

"I'm forty-two," he answered.

Genevieve scowled at Asher.

"I have to be honest... this is all very... very *new* for me," Sydney began nervously, "And excuse me for being blunt. But why am I here? Am I expected to be in a relationship with the both of you?"

Asher scoffed and grabbed his wine glass.

"As stated before, G practices the lifestyle, not me. Though I respect her views, I am good with just her. I don't *need* anyone else's love. I don't need you Sydney," he said bluntly.

Sydney was taken aback and glared at Asher while trying to bite her tongue.

"Well that works for me, because trust me, I'm not interested," she said, throwing her napkin down as she wondered if Raphael was still outside with the car.

The nerve of this man to come at me that way. Who did he think he was? she asked herself.

"Sydney, excuse him. Asher is just a little protective..."

Genevieve said. "Please, eat. Let me continue to explain. After you hear me out, you can decide what you want. No hard feelings, okay?"

"Okay," Sydney said reluctantly as she continued to eat.

"Okay," Genevieve sighed as she looked at Asher and rolled her eyes, "Asher and I met at Yale. He was there getting his master's in architecture while I was there, as you know, getting my masters in psychology."

"We met one day at a bar and were instantly smitten with one another. We were inseparable; it was disgusting!" she joked.

"Anyway, we knew we were soulmates and quickly decided to spend our lives together. However, a few years after we graduated I felt that something was missing. Don't get me wrong, Asher is the most amazing man that I have ever known. He is smart, gorgeous, hilarious, a great cook, a phenomenal lover and despite how he is acting tonight, one of the kindest souls that I know."

Sydney looked over at him as he sat twiddling his wedding ring on his finger while he listened to her. It suddenly dawned on Sydney that she had never spotted a ring on Genevieve's hand, not until tonight. Sydney looked at the beautiful stone that sat on Genevieve's left ring finger. How had she missed that earlier?

"Hence, how I know Michelle and Tom. Michelle and I worked together in New York at my first job post-grad. She knew how in love I was with Asher but understood how I felt. You know, like something was missing? She told me that she and Tom had gone through the same thing. One night, she invited us out with them. Little did we know, the invite was to a party— a swingers party," she said, pausing to drink some more wine.

"Needless to say, after that night my life was changed. We decided to try it out. At this time we were five years in and we needed a pick-me-up. I wasn't ready for marriage, but I also wasn't ready to leave our relationship. We both started meeting people through the parties. It worked out for me a few times, but for Asher, he couldn't really accept it. Despite this, we decided to stay together and make it work. We agreed that the swinger lifestyle wass too reckless for us; so we compromised. I was then allowed to carry out, discreetly of course, as many polyamorous relationships as I wanted. As long as they were with people who were special to me and who were properly vetted prior of course."

Asher rose up from the table and began to clear out the dishes.

"And now here we are today. Sure, I've had my fun dating around while maintaining my relationship with my husband. I've also had some failed relationships too that hit me hard..." she said trailing off as if caught in a memory.

Asher returned to the table with small bowls of crème brulée with a single scoop of vanilla ice cream.

"Thanks babe," Genevieve said, smiling up at him as she gave him a wink. "He knows this is my favorite. Anyway, let's fast-forward to today. We are still very happy in love. Our marriage is as strong as it has ever been. Our careers are thriving, we're healthy and wealthy. Yet, there is still something missing. And I believe that is you, Sydney."

"Me?" Sydney asked, shocked, with her mouth full of ice cream. She couldn't stop eating whatever this man sat in front of her. She was like a pig being led to slaughter.

"Sydney, don't talk with your mouth full, but yes, you. I've known since the first moment I saw you. Sydney, I think you are what's missing in my life. You are not only a muse for me... you are so much more. I want to be in a relationship with you. I want to take care of you, have you take care of me in return and to eventually...fall in love with you."

Sydney was speechless. She slowly digested the words.

"Fate brought us together Sydney, I mean what are the odds that we would meet and be here where we are? If you agree, and you want to be with me, I want to move you in. I need you near me, Sydney, at all times. We have a guesthouse in the back; it's yours if you just give me the word. However, if you want to keep it strictly platonic, if this is too much for you, I will understand. You would not be the first to turn me down," Genevieve said sadly.

"Regardless of what you decide, you will remain employed with me either way. But the decision is yours. So, what do you say?"

Chapter 8

Monday, October 19th

"Soooo..." Sydney said after an excruciating one-sided conversation with India, "I said yes."

"Wow," she said flatly.

The two were in Sydney's apartment surrounded by open suitcases and bags. They were surrounded by piles of messy, folded clothes and shopping bags with some of the new outfits Sydney got on the trip and a few days ago.

Sydney had decided to move out and move in with Genevieve. It didn't take her long to make her decision; not as long as she thought it should, to be honest. She saw the risks, she knew the chances she was taking, but she also knew that she couldn't continue to live in the same rut that she was in.

She had made up her mind to live in the moment. This was her chance to not cower for once at the thought of stepping out into the unknown. She was venturing out to do something for herself and only herself for the first time in her life. She was tired of playing it safe.

"So, what's really tea?" India asked suspiciously.

She stood in the middle of Sydney's crowded living room

with her hands on her hips. She had a stone-cold face, making it impossible to read her mind.

"Girl, what you mean?" Sydney asked, turning around to pack her Uggs away.

"Syd, you and she kissed and now you're moving in?" she asked ,walking over to her and tugging Sydney's arm. "I know you haven't been with a *woman* and not told me."

Sydney laughed and waved her hand as if India was speaking nonsense.

"Girl, no! That isn't what is happening here. She is my boss, she offered to give me a whole guesthouse for the next few months," Sydney said with agitated haste. "Listen, we talked about the kiss. It was just a drunken slip-up, it's actually funny now. We laughed about it."

"Mhm," India said, folding her arms, not convinced.

Sydney moved past her and opened her panty drawer and began to grab some of everything, from thongs to granny draws. She hoped that India would drop this and drop it fast. She was a horrible liar and knew it, but she knew she already shared too much with India. For now, she will honor the NDA and not tell her friend about what else was discussed the other night.

Sydney kept trying to rationalize with herself. She wasn't *actually* lying. She hadn't slept with Genevieve, at least not yet. She also couldn't help but to think of the nagging memory of the NDA she signed. The same NDA she still hadn't read over. She made a mental note to review the copy that was emailed to her tonight, once she was settled in. Her plan was to move fast and avoid her friend's glare at all costs.

She was just about to close her drawer shut when she noticed one of her old faithful friends tucked in the back corner.

"Look what I found!" she shouted, spinning around with a silver vibrator in her hand.

Sydney waved it around and danced with it all the way

over to India who swatted it away laughing. She was glad to see her trick of distracting her working.

"Remember when you got me this India?" she laughed as she tapped it playfully on India's thigh.

"Girll that thang better be clean!" She squealed. "How do you still have that? I got that for you back in our junior year of college. After you and Shawn's third break up I believe," she giggled as she moved past Sydney and plopped on her bed.

"It barely got used. I had a man, remember?" Sydney said, tossing it in her bag.

"And don't you have a woman now? What you packing it for?" India teased.

"Girl," Sydney sighed annoyed.

"Aight, truce, girl," India said looking distracted.

"Just like that? You letting it go that fast?" She was shocked.

"Yea, you gonna do what you want anyway, that's that Scorpio shit. For the moment, I am happy for you. Just please be smart Syd, that's all I ask," India said, looking sincere. "I don't believe that y'all just kissed randomly out of nowhere and that it's not going to happen again. Just don't be a dummy bitch," India smiled. "Deal?"

"Deal," Sydney said, walking over to her friend.

"So, what's up with you girl?" Sydney could sense the shift in energy coming from India. They'd been friends for over a decade, and she knew when something was wrong. Sydney knew India just as well as India knew her.

"Psh," India said, sucking her teeth and moving her faux locs to the side, "I don't know. Same shit... but your girl Dij has been actin' really funny."

"What you mean?" Sydney asked, confused.

"It's this bitch named Tiffany— "

"Tiffany?!" Sydney yelled, already not liking where the story was going. "Who the fuck is Tiffany?"

"The bitch that's been hanging around her. And then I saw her number in her phone. No texts though," she said, letting out an agitated sigh. "She thinks she is slick and deleted it. Like I'm dumb. Girl, she so late. I was doing that in high school."

"You went through her phone?"

"Don't judge me Sydney, not right now," she snapped.

Sydney let it go. "Did you say something to her?"

"Umm, have you met me?" India asked, standing up and walking away as if she could escape her problems. "I said something, which led us into this big ass argument," India said, talking fast with her hands. "Of course she's denying it and saying the girl been hanging because she wants to be put on, but I don't believe it. We haven't had sex in two days and now we aren't talking. She been out later too these last few nights. I don't know Syd, but I know I don't like it."

Sydney bit her bottom lip and shook her head in disbelief. She couldn't believe what she was hearing and she hoped that it wasn't true. She knew how much India loved Dij and she also knew how much Dij loved India. She had never seen India fall this hard for anyone before.

"Well what you want to do girl? Usually, I would say you are buggin' but I can tell how much this is eating you up. But bitch are you sure you're not overreacting, just a tad? It's only been a few days since y'all had sex," Sydney said gently.

"Bitch we can't go more than a few hours. I know something is up, don't play with me," she said, rolling her eyes. "And oh, don't worry, you already know I'm plotting on getting some answers. I'm gonna drop by to say hello when I know that Tiffany bitch is around. And you are going to help me."

"Oh, I am?" Sydney was caught off guard.

"Yup, don't worry girl I will keep you posted," she said with a devilish wink. "Why are you packing up? I thought you said that she paid your rent up to the end of your lease?"

"She has. I have a few keepsakes and clothes I want to bring with me."

"Keepsakes? I hope it ain't none of bum ass Shawn's shit," India teased.

"Hush. Well since you are using my services to mess with Dij, how about you do me a solid?"

"What?" India asked, raising an eyebrow.

"Girl help me with my hair," she fake cried as she whipped her headscarf off her head, revealing her messy hair.

"That's what your ass get for letting some other bitch cut your hair! I've been waiting for this moment," India said, switching over to get a better look at the matted mess on top of Sydney's head.

"You're lucky I can't have you out here looking crazy. Get me a comb, brush and flat iron. I am about to teach you how to style this."

Sydney eagerly ran towards her bathroom following India's direction, just as she heard her phone ringing in her bag.

"Damn," India said judgmentally as she watched Sydney trip and stumble over to the running phone.

Ever since Sydney started working for Genevieve, she worked on being more responsible with her phone. Keeping it charged, ringer on and nearby just in case Genevieve were to call or need something.

"Shut up," Sydney whispered under her breath just as she slid it unlocked.

It was Genevieve.

"Genevieve, hi," Sydney said, cautious of making her voice sound both light and professional so she wouldn't tip India off.

"Come outside," she said curtly.

"Huh— I mean, I'm sorry?"

"I said... come outside," she repeated before hanging up the phone.

"Was that your majesty?" India asked, smacking her gum.

Sydney rolled her eyes and slid her Uggs on her feet.

"Where you going?"

"Something is downstairs for me. I'll be right back," she said as she threw on a jacket.

"Nope, I'm coming too," India said on her heels as they headed out the door and down the three flights of stairs.

"This feel like some *The Devil Wears Prada* shit," India said laughing to herself.

"Hush, it's nothing like that. She probably just has to drop off—"

Sydney gasped as she opened the heavy front door to the building and saw a white Audi with a red bow on top of it.

"Shut up!" India gasped in disbelief from behind her.

Genevieve popped out from the driver's side with a huge smile on her face as she made her way over to Sydney.

"Surprise!" she yelled as she strutted over in her pumps.

Genevieve looked gorgeous with a full face of make-up and her hair pinned up into a simple bun. Despite it being nearly 40 degrees out, she got out of the car wearing a navy-blue sleeveless dress that had a deep V-neck to accentuate her full breasts.

Genevieve walked over to Sydney and gave her a light kiss on her cheek while grabbing her hand into her perfectly dainty one.

"I'll take your silence as gratitude," she giggled as she examined Sydney's face.

"This... this is mine? Genevieve you shouldn't have... I can't accept this," Sydney started to say, finally coming back down to Earth.

She had never been gifted anything this extravagant. She was both honored and slightly uncomfortable with her grand gift. She could never afford to give Genevieve anything like this.

"Nonsense, of course I should have and of course you can.

You *will*. You're my muse and you deserve the best," she said with a twinkle in her eye.

"Damn Syd, this has buttercream seats too!" India said, running past her and opening the passenger door to get a better look inside.

"Who— who is your...friend?" Genevieve asked locking her eyes on India who was currently taking a TikTok video of herself in the new car.

"That's my best friend... India!" Sydney yelled, waving her back over.

"Genevieve this is my best friend India, India this is Genevieve."

"Nice to finally meet you. I feel like I know you already by the way Syd can't stop talking about you," India said, heading back over with her hand extended.

"Charmed... I'm sure," Genevieve said dryly as the smile disappeared from her face as she gave India a once over and didn't attempt to shake her hand.

Sydney could feel the tension between the two which let her know that India did too. She wanted to diffuse the situation as soon as possible before India said something damaging.

"Genevieve, thank you so much... I'm at a loss for words," Sydney said, positioning her body in between the two women so that India's waiting hand didn't seem so obvious.

"No worries, you can thank me later," she said, patting the back of Sydney's hand before finally letting it go. "I have to go; as you know I am meeting some friends at the opera tonight. I just wanted to drop your gift off to you. Oh, Raphael says hello," she said nodding her head behind them to Raphael who sat waving in the truck behind Sydney's new car.

Sydney gave him a wave and a smile back.

"Thank you so much," Sydney said, suppressing the urge to give Genevieve a thank you kiss and hug, "I'll see you tomorrow?"

"See you at home," she said, giving Sydney a wink.

"India," Genevieve said stiffly as she nodded her head at her and began to walk down the steps in her six-inch heels.

"Genevieve," India said, snapping her neck.

Chapter 9

Tuesday, October 20th

Sydney scrolled through Genevieve's agenda for the day to make sure that there wasn't anything she missed. Sydney noted that she had about two hours of free time before she was due for a zoom meeting with Genevieve and decided to take advantage of that time to be productive.

Do what you love. Find the time; there is always time! she recited the words from Genevieve's book in her head as she threw on some leggings, a thick fleece pullover and put on her Nikes. She skipped down the stairs two at a time and smiled at the sight of her new home.

Genevieve had flown out to Texas for a book signing and allowed Sydney to hang back to unpack and get comfortable in her new home. The guesthouse was beautiful, almost as beautiful as the main house. Sydney's new space came with a loft, a full bathroom, a living room equipped with a 70-inch flat screen and a small office for her to work. The house had Genevieve written all over it with its minimalist décor down to the white furniture and cream accents. The house was perfect and the only thing it missed was a kitchen.

Sydney did find it strange but blew it off once Genevieve informed her that she would have full access to the staff as well as the kitchen at any time. So Sydney didn't let it bother her too much; she was sure she would quickly adapt to having others cook and clean for her.

Sydney stepped outside of the guesthouse and cut across the yard, being careful to walk around the grand pool that had been emptied for the winter. She couldn't wait for summer to come so that she could take some swims at any time in the day. Sydney had never had a pool growing up. Money was always tight in her household and her mom made do the best she could as a single parent. They lived in a tight two bedroom apartment for most of Sydney's childhood until her mom was able to purchase a condo for her family that was nestled outside of Boston. Sydney's mother still lived there to this day.

She made it to the front of the house and put her air pods in just as she began her stretches. Genevieve's house was in a very hilly neighborhood and Sydney was excited to push herself to run all the way around her new neighborhood. Just as she finished her stretches and turned on her favorite trap playlist, she felt a tap on her shoulder and spun around. It was Asher. She did her best to refrain from rolling her eyes.

Asher had been less than pleased when he saw Sydney rolling in the house with her new car full of bags. It seems that he and Genevieve had had a heated discussion after dinner the other night and he expressed how he did not want Sydney moving in with them. Despite his best efforts of trying to convince Genevieve to not move her new toy in, she did anyway.

He was pissed. This was Sydney's first time seeing him since she had been fully moved in. At this point, she had met all of the staff and gotten a real tour of their home. She imagined that this whole time he sat cooped up in his office sulking at her mere presence.

And now here he was today, in shorts, sneakers and a Under Armour long-sleeved shirt. Sydney looked him up and down and instantly realized what he was out there to do.

"You run?" he asked, surprised as he began to bend over and stretch.

"Yeah... well I'm trying to get back into it," Sydney admitted, feeling uneasy talking to him without Genevieve. "I used to run track in high school and a little in college."

"Yeah, me too," Asher said dryly, as he removed his air pods from his ears.

"Nice..." she said, eager to get away.

Sydney turned and began to lightly jog down the driveway. She didn't feel the need to stay any longer to chat with Asher than she had to. She knew that he didn't like her nor did he want her there, and the feeling was mutual. Sydney was still trying to wrap her head around the fact that the two of them were going to share Genevieve. She was also still reeling from Genevieve setting up a doctor's appointment for Sydney with her personal OB/GYN. Genevieve tried to say it nicely, but how nice could one be when asking their new partner to get screened for STDs? Deep down Sydney felt that that was really a request of Asher's and not from her.

"Wait, hold up Sydney," Asher said, jogging behind her just as she made it to the gate that was opened at the end of their curved driveway.

"How about we run together? I can show you the ropes. It would be nice to run with someone for once."

Sydney stopped in her tracks and looked up at Asher, who towered over her 5'8" height.

"You sure?"

"Definitely. Besides, it can get a little dicey in some areas. We've only been here a little over a month and I've already been chased by three dogs," he said chuckling.

Sydney laughed as well at the visual of him running terrified from dogs. It was what he got for being so rude to her.

"Genevieve doesn't run?" she asked as the two began to jog in a slow steady pace beside one another.

"Nope. Genevieve had a bad accident as a teen and her left knee got all messed up from it. The same accident that killed her mom. She's had to have about four surgeries on it since I've known her."

"Oh my God," Sydney said, quickening her pace to keep up with Asher, "I didn't know her mother died."

"You've known her for a few weeks... there's a lot you don't know about her," he said matter-of-factly.

Sydney felt a twinge of irritability but decided to let it go. Something she was beginning to get really good at doing.

She was having a harder time than she liked keeping up with Asher as the two ran through the neighborhood. They passed a few lavish homes that had expensive cars that Sydney had only seen in rap videos. She passed the grand homes and wondered about the inhabitants inside. She had never seen a neighborhood like this ever. Each unique yet commonly-themed home reminded her of the movie, *The Stepford Wives.* She and India had done some snooping online a few days ago and found out a few members of the Patriots lived out here as well.

After thirty minutes in, Sydney couldn't feel anything but fire in her legs and lungs and she stopped running to bend over and try to catch her breath. This route had nothing on the one she took in her old neighborhood.

"You okay?" Asher asked, coming over to her and jogging in place.

"I...I need water," Sydney panted as she felt sweat drip from her pixie cut down her neck and onto her back.

"Come on, the community lounge is right over there,"

Asher said, pointing across the street to a random building that sat back on a half-acre of land.

The two made it into the building and Sydney collapsed onto the nearest seat she could find, which lucky for her was a plush loveseat. The community lounge was gorgeous and looked like a mini spa inside, equipped with a small bistro. After a few minutes Asher returned with two water bottles and a smile. He tossed the water bottle at her and took a seat beside her as they both cracked open the bottles and drank.

"Some community lounge," Sydney said as she finally caught her breath and looked around.

There were a few people in there, mostly elderly white people who all stopped and stared at Sydney and Asher.

"Tell me about it," Asher said back to her absentmindedly. "This community wasn't my choice, trust me."

"Was it Genevieve's?" she asked, already knowing the answer.

"Yup," he sighed as she shook his head and stared back at an elderly white woman who stared at the two blatantly without trying to hide it.

"People don't take too kindly to an interracial couple out here I bet," Sydney said, turning her attention to the woman. "I heard the stories, but damn."

"It's ridiculous; this is Massachusetts for God's sake. Not Alabama in the 50s."

"This is New England," Sydney corrected him, "There's a lot more racist shit out here than people care to admit."

"It's fuckin' ridiculous! This is the third time I've been looked at like this since we have been here, yet Genevieve is set on living here...in MAGA land," Asher scoffed.

Welcome to my black ass life, Sydney said to herself. "Can't say I blame her," she said instead, "You think Genevieve is going to let some old racists dictate her life?"

The two looked at each other and smirked, both knowing the answer.

They looked back up at the elderly woman who still glared from across the room. People were now bumping into her as they tried to walk by. The old broad had no shame and stood mere feet away staring at them. Asher shook his head in disgust and took another gulp of water before asking loudly, "Can I fuckin' help you with something?" He shook his head in disgust and watched as the old woman snapped out of her daze and ran directly into a magazine rack in her haste to leave the building. Sydney laughed out loud.

"Genevieve always gets what she wants," he said, guzzling more water and returning to their conversation as if they hadn't just caused a scene.

"Like me moving in..." Sydney said sheepishly.

"Exactly."

"I guess you're not really on board with her having me as a side lover huh? I don't get it, she's done this in the past, why do you have beef with me?" Sydney wondered out loud.

The fact that Asher wasn't welcoming to her bothered her more than she cared to admit. She never thought she would have the chance to have a conversation like this with him and wanted to take advantage of the opportunity. Besides, he was the only one who she could legally talk to about this, other than Genevieve. And he was also probably one of the only few people on this planet who knew how she felt about all of this.

"It's not you per se," he began with a sigh, "G and I have been together for fifteen years. Neither one of us are in our 20s anymore. At some point I just thought this would phase out, ya' know? We are in our 40s, we moved across the country, and I really thought we were leaving all of *that* behind us. I think we're heading in one direction and the next thing I know she's moving you in. With absolutely no regard for me or my feelings. I should've known she had ulterior motives when she insisted on finding a home with a pool house or in-law suite."

Asher looked defeated talking about this and for a second, Sydney began to feel guilty.

"I'm sorry Asher—"

"Don't apologize. Listen, I'm sorry I've been such an ass to you. I know how it is being with G. She's magnetic, she's beautiful, smart as hell and has the power to make you agree to do anything as long as it means you get to be around her," he snickered.

"Look at me, I'm 15 years deep and still can't tell that woman no," he said, loosening the bun on his head and letting his brown hair fall to his shoulders. "I just felt a bit ambushed, you know? Here I am thinking we were starting a new journey and here she goes doing the same old shit."

"Trust me, I know," Sydney said as she reflected on her inability to tell her no. "How about we start from scratch?" Sydney asked, turning her body to face Asher.

"Sure. Hi, I'm Asher, the ball-less man hopelessly in love with the dynamic woman who has dragged him around the country and life for nearly twenty years," he said with a slight smile as he extended his hand.

"Hi Asher, I am Sydney. The dumb 20-something who fell under her spell and doesn't know what the hell she is getting herself into," she said, shaking his hand. "But I sure am excited."

The two shared a laugh with one another.

Chapter 10

Saturday, October 24th

Genevieve and Sydney were on their way home from a very dry and late dinner meeting with Genevieve's publisher. It had been a tense dinner that consisted mostly of Sydney sitting there in silence as Genevieve went back and forth with her publisher. Genevieve and her publisher, a rep named Danica who had a scary glare, debated all dinner about when the deadline was for her fifth book. Genevieve was persistent that she needed more time and Danica refused to budge. Needless to say, Genevieve lost the fight and agreed to move the deadline up to mid-November.

Sydney didn't understand why Genevieve fought so hard against her publisher; she had boasted for weeks how she was almost finished with writing it. Though Sydney herself hadn't seen the book or even seen Genevieve actually writing it, she was excited to get her hands on it and to see the masterpiece that she helped to inspire.

By the time the two went to their car, Genevieve was riled up and could not stop ranting.

"I should really just go independent. I'm sick of this shit!

You cannot rush perfection, and I will not be rushed!" Genevieve huffed to no one in particular as they sat in the back of her SUV.

Sydney pulled out her phone and began to review Genevieve's calendar to see if she could spot an opening for her in the next few days to focus on her writing.

"You have a few hours of open time on Monday and nothing at all for tomorrow. How about we pencil in some time for you to write then?"

"Absolutely not," Genevieve said curtly. "I am a brilliant writer. I cannot just write on cue; it doesn't work like that. I have to be moved to do it Sydney; you wouldn't understand, you haven't created anything of this magnitude before," she said brushing her off. "The moment has not happened yet where I am struck with it, and with this deadline looming over me, I fear it may stunt my creative process altogether," she said, straightening her dress and cracking her window, despite it being frigid outside.

"You simply wouldn't understand, no one can," she said again as she sighed and watched the snow falling from outside.

"Well, I have never written a book, that is true," Sydney said cautiously as she shivered from the cold air filtering in, "But you have started writing this one already and it's not like it's your first book ever. You say all the time that it's almost finished. Can't you just send the first few chapters to appease them?"

"There are no chapters."

Sydney screwed her face in confusion and was grateful that it was dark so that Genevieve couldn't see her facial expression. She was so lost. Genevieve boasted all the time how this book was nearly finished.

"But Genevieve you say all the time the book is nearly finished—"

"Nearly finished up here Sydney," she said, tapping her

French manicured finger to her temple. "This is my process. I have it written in my mind; I just haven't transferred it to paper yet."

"Oh," Sydney said quietly.

She wasn't sure what else to say to something like that. To her, it sounded like Miss Perfect had a real procrastination problem. Who knew? Sydney reached for Genevieve's hand in the dark and scooted in a little closer to her, careful to not let Raphael see from the front.

Genevieve held her hand tighter and allowed a smile to creep on her face as she turned her attention to Sydney.

"Well I am your muse, right?" Sydney whispered to her.

"Yes, yes you are," Genevieve said, kissing the back of Sydney's hand. "How about we take the rest of the evening for ourselves? I'll grab a bottle of wine and join you in the guesthouse."

"Sounds...sounds like a plan," Sydney said nervously.

She switched her gaze to her window and viewed the traffic as the SUV creeped through the snow with the rest of the cars on the highway; trying to hide her anxious face. She knew tonight would finally be the night. She hated to admit it, but Sydney was terrified to sleep with Genevieve. She had never been with a woman in that way and feared that she would disappoint her.

It killed her that she wasn't able to talk to India about this. She literally had the lesbian guru in her back pocket and was unable to use her. In her replacement, Sydney had spent the last few days watching lesbian porn when she had time away from Genevieve, which honestly hadn't been as much time as she thought. She knew it was only a matter of time before this would happen, especially since she received her clean STD results back a few days ago.

"Did I tell you how gorgeous you look tonight?" Genevieve asked, interrupting her thoughts.

She scooted in closer to Sydney as she placed her hand on her knee and began to draw small circles with her thumb.

"I think Armani really suits you, and black is definitely your color," Genevieve said.

"Thanks, I have a great stylist," Sydney joked.

Genevieve placed her hand up to Sydney's head and pulled her in close to whisper into her ear, "Tell me, are your undergarments black too? Or are you going to make me wait until later to find out?"

Sydney felt herself flush just as Genevieve attempted to kiss her. Sydney pulled back slightly, looking up at Raphael, who kept his eyes focused on the road. She was hesitant to show affection to Genevieve whenever they were out and had even become slightly trained not to do so.

"Sydney, everyone under my employment is under an NDA. Kiss me," Genevieve demanded. "Kiss me now," she said as she pulled her face toward hers.

Sydney could taste the red wine that Genevieve had had for dinner on her lips as she kissed her back. She slid her tongue into Genevieve's warm mouth and allowed her hands to roam over Genevieve's beaded dress, feeling her toned thighs and round hips underneath. She was a pro at kissing Genevieve now. Mainly because that was all that the two had done over the last few weeks— running around to make out every time they were left alone. But after tonight that would all change.

Genevieve quickly slid her hand underneath Sydney's short dress and allowed her fingers to trace her white lace underwear underneath, causing Sydney to instinctively close her legs tighter around her hand.

"Open up," Genevieve said in Sydney's ear just as she tugged on her lobe with her teeth.

Shit, Sydney thought to herself as she did what she was told. *This is hot.*

Genevieve then used her fingers to massage Sydney's clit

from the outside of her panties. Sydney felt herself begin to get wet from the gentle touch. She suppressed the urge to moan and decided to kiss Genevieve back harder, nearly ready to pull her on top of her.

"We should be home shortly ladies," Raphael said from the front of the G-wagon just as Genevieve pulled her hand from under Sydney's dress.

Sydney whimpered, not wanting her to stop.

"Soon," Genevieve whispered with a devilish grin as she fixed her hair and slid back to her side of the truck.

Twenty minutes later, the pair finally made it home. After Raphael got the ladies safely in the house, Genevieve did as she promised and grabbed a bottle of wine before meeting Sydney in the guest house.

"It's freezing out there," Genevieve said, coming through the front door and removing her fur coat that was covered in fresh snow just from her short walk from the main house to the guest house.

"You wanted to live in New England," Sydney teased as she took the bottle away from her. "Speaking of New England, is Asher home?"

"Now why does that make you think of Asher?" Genevieve asked.

"You know.. old, white and stuffy," Sydney teased as she smiled to herself. Truth be told, Asher wasn't so bad afterall. After their adventure the other day, Sydney had hoped that they may actually get along.

Sydney had already taken off her shoes and coat. She still wore the Armani dress and was in desperate need of some liquid courage to get through this evening. As excited as she was to finally be with Genevieve, a small part of her hoped thatAsher was home so that they would put this off for one more night.

"No, he is not. He went to Rhode Island for a few days. I

think his sister is having a baby shower or some nonsense like that," she said waving the thought off. "It's just you and me if that is okay with you Miss Sydney," Genevieve said, shaking the snowflakes out of her hair.

"Well, more wine for us," Sydney said, raising the bottle in the air.

"Well... pop it open then!" Genevieve squealed as she stepped out of her own heels and dimmed the lights.

"Sure; one problem, we don't have any glasses!" Sydney giggled.

"No glasses? How are there no glasses in this whole house?"

"There are no glasses because some brilliant woman decided to design this house without a kitchen," Sydney giggled as she grabbed the wine opener and opened the bottle.

"Oh, yes, yes," Genevieve said as she sat gently on the couch and folded her legs underneath her. "Well...I am brilliant."

The two laughed at the comment. On the outside, Sydney felt that she appeared cool, calm and collected, but on the inside; Sydney was a nervous wreck. She took the bottle of wine and took it to the head before even looking to see what kind of wine it was. After she was done, she wiped her mouth with the back of her hand and looked over at Genevieve, only slightly embarrassed at her barbaric actions.

Genevieve let out a light laugh and got up and walked over to Sydney. She snatched the bottle out of her hands and took it back the same way Sydney had, even using the back of her hand to wipe off any excess that threatened to fall on her designer dress.

"Well damn," Sydney said, shocked at what she was seeing.

She was sure that this was the first time that Genevieve drank wine that was not in a wine glass.

Genevieve finished her gulp and handed Sydney the bottle again before letting out a burp.

"Drink," she ordered.

"Yes ma'am," Sydney laughed, enjoying seeing this looser side of Genevieve.

It seemed that all of the drama from dinner had evaporated, and Genevieve was relaxed and happy. Sydney lifted the bottle back to her lips as she felt heat creep all over her body. She wasn't sure if it was from the sweet warmth that was hitting her system from this bottle or if ti came from the heat that radiated off of Genevieve's body.

Genevieve pressed herself against Sydney as Sydney began to put the bottle down.

"Nuh, uh," she said, tilting the bottle back up for Sydney to drink. "Drink some more."

Genevieve began to run her hands all over Sydney's body as if she were discovering it for the first time. She traced Sydney's collarbone with her index finger, sending shivers all over her in return. Sydney had a hard time focusing on holding the bottle of wine to her lips as she was getting felt up, but she knew better than to disobey her.

Genevieve removed the bottle from Sydney's hand and took another gulp before sitting it on the floor by their bare feet. She stood back up and grabbed Sydney's breasts as she placed her face in between them and began to kiss them softly while fondling them.

Sydney moaned at her light touch, feeling like her skin was on fire. Genevieve then used her tongue to draw circles on Sydney's cleavage before trailing her tongue up Sydney's neck and reaching behind her to pull down her zipper; causing Sydney's dress to fall to the floor and leaving her standing there in just her lacy underwear.

Genevieve took a step back and admired Sydney. Her eyes wandered over every inch and curve, and she smiled to herself.

Sydney stood and watched Genevieve as she then began to take off her own dress and let it fall dramatically to the ground exposing her completely nude body underneath. Sydney's eyes wandered over Genevieve; she was beautiful. Her body was tight and fit for a woman her age and her breasts sat perky on her chest. Genevieve's stomach was flat and toned and had a light trail of freckles that trailed down in between her legs to her bare vagina.

"Let's go upstairs," Genevieve said, grabbing the bottle of wine and leading the way up the stairs.

The two reached the bedroom and Sydney sat down on the bed, inching her body back slowly. She felt like a virgin all over again.

"Genevieve, I've never done this," she whispered to her in the dark.

"You've never done what Sydney?" she asked as she took Sydney's hand and began to kiss the inside of her palm gently.

"I've never been with a woman."

"Never?" Genevieve asked with a raised eyebrow.

"Never, I'm sorry..."

"Never apologize," she whispered as she placed Sydney's hand on her left breast. "Don't worry. I will take care of you."

Sydney froze for a moment before beginning to massage and fondle Genevieve's hard nipple that was under her palm. She touched Genevieve in the way she liked to be touched. The way that she wished Shawn would have touched her.

Genevieve moaned and rolled her eyes back as Sydney began to play with her nipple with her fingers before eventually moving in closer to her and placing one of her breasts into her mouth. Sydney could hear Genevieve's breathing become heavier. She saw the way she aroused her while she played with Genevieve's hard nipple in her mouth. She surprised herself with how turned on she felt by giving Genevieve pleasure, something that she didn't know was possible until now. Shawn always made foreplay feel like a dull chore. Something he couldn't wait to be done with so he could get to the "real" intercourse. Sydney tried to stop thinking about him as she focused on Genevieve and wondered what would come next.

Genevieve then climbed onto Sydney's lap and straddled her as she kissed her hard, forcing her tongue into Sydney's mouth. Sydney kissed her back with just as much passion as she allowed her hands to grab onto Genevieve's soft ass that slowly grinded in her lap.

Genevieve pushed her down and began to kiss her from her neck, her breasts, and then to her navel. Sydney could feel her legs shaking with excitement as she laid back and let Genevieve work her magic.

"Do you have a vibrator?" Genevieve asked, causing Sydney to open her eyes in shock.

"Huh?"

"Sydney..." Genevieve scolded, "you know i dislike when you— "

"Top drawer on the left," she said, sitting halfway up and pointing to the white dresser that sat across the room with her foot.

Genevieve ran over to the dresser and dug around the drawer a few seconds before pulling out the silver vibrator. She turned it on to speed one and the sound of the little vibrating machine filled the room. Sydney laughed as she watched Genevieve jump from the shock of it.

"Oh my, we're going to have some fun. Take off your panties."

Sydney did as she was told and awkwardly lifted herself up enough to remove them, exposing her pussy and thin line of pubic hair.

"Beautiful, Sydney," Genevieve said, laying on top of her and kissing her deeply again, "I've been waiting for this for so long," she moaned in her ear.

"Me too," Sydney breathed.

"Lay still. Tonight, I will take your lesbian virginity. Do you trust me Sydney?" Genevieve asked, looking her straight in the eyes.

"Lesbian virginity?" Sydney asked laughingly as she tried covering her mouth.

Clearly something that corny had to be a joke.

She stopped laughing once she realized she was the only one. "Yes, I trust you completely Genevieve."

Genevieve smiled and leapt off of Sydney and ripped her legs apart. She took Sydney's pulsating vibrator and slid it slowly in and out of her mouth, making sure that it was moist and warm. The sight of her doing that in return made Sydney wet and caused her to reach down to touch herself.

"Now don't make me get the handcuffs. Keep those hands up there, this is all me. Do you understand?" she demanded while swatting her hands away.

Sydney obeyed and raised her arms over her head behind her and relaxed as much as she could. Genevieve slowly inserted the vibrator, causing Sydney to shiver as she felt all six inches enter her. Sydney grabbed the sheets behind her as she felt herself delightfully fill up with the foreign object. Down below, Genevieve got to her knees and kissed Sydney's inner thighs gently with her mouth. She savored each kiss she planted on Sydney as she let Sydney's body jerk and move from pleasure. Genevieve then turned the vibrator up one more level as she moved the toy slowly in and out of her, causing her legs to tremble even more.

"Mmm," Sydney gasped and arched her back.

"Sydney, you've been such a good girl. Let me make you cum, okay?" Genevieve asked in between kissing Sydney's inner thigh.

"Mmhm," Sydney shook her head eagerly as she reached down to grab Genevieve.

"What did I say about those hands Sydney? Keep. Them. Up. There."

She felt herself already on the verge and threw her arms back obediently. She was liable to agree to anything at this moment.

Genevieve turned the vibrator up another notch; this made Sydney jump and grab the white sheets tighter around her. She felt the sweet, warm, tingling sensation that began to creep all over her body. Sydney knew she was seconds away from her guaranteed burst of ecstasy. Sydney had not orgasmed in so long, she almost forgot how sweet it felts... and she was so, so close. She felt Genevieve's soft tongue separating her lips below. Genevieve slurped and made love to Sydney's pussy to the point that she felt tears come to her eyes as she was hit with a full body orgasm, sending her body into uncontrollable shakes as it ripped through her entirely.

Sydney screamed so loud that she was sure that the neighbors could hear all the way down the hill. Sydney's body still writhed and twisted into her sheets as Genevieve continued to massage her throbbing clitoris with her expert tongue. She showed no mercy on Sydney as she watched her orgasm again only seconds after her last one.

Once Sydney's breathing regulated back to normal, Genevieve came up for air as she slowly took the vibrator out of her and tossed it to the side. She crawled up to Sydney with a Cheshire smile across her face.

"I knew you would taste like heaven," she said as she kissed her deep on her mouth and lifted one of Sydney's legs in the air as she mounted her.

Chapter 11

Thursday, November 12th

"Okay, so what am I saying again?" Sydney asked, putting her car into park and turning to look at an agitated India.

The two sat in Sydney's Audi around the corner from a pool hall that was about twenty minutes from India and Dij's apartment.

"Aight, so remember how I told you that you could pay me back? This is it."

India was referring to Sydney owing her one after keeping mum on the whole 'move-in with Genevieve' thing.

"Uh-huh," Sydney said, irritated.

She already didn't like where this was going. She signed up for a day with her best friend catching up on some much-needed girl time after being away with Geneviever. Sydney had just come back that morning from a two-day trip to DC with Genevieve. It had been her first time in the Chocolate City, and she had spent most of her time wrapped in the sheets with her.

"Well it's time to make us even. We gonna go in there all

casual and act surprised to see them there," India said as she checked her makeup in the mirror.

"We're gonna act surprised to see her at a spot that she hangs out at every day?" Sydney asked, hoping that her sarcasm didn't go over India's head.

Sydney knew something was up when India requested a quick stop home to change before they went for dinner and drinks at some new Peruvian spot downtown. After twenty minutes of waiting, India had walked out of her bedroom in an Adidas bodysuit that hugged all of her thickness. She even had the nerve to accompany her bodysuit with open-toe YSL heels and a full face of makeup.

"What?" she had asked when Sydney rolled her eyes.

"So, you're gonna go in there and pay her back that money you owe her," she said, playing with her right mink eyelash.

"What money?" Sydney snapped, surprised that she knew about that.

"Syd, you know her ass gave you some money when you kicked Shawn's ass out. You know it, I know it, Jesus knows it, hush," she said.

"I don't have any cash on me," Sydney said, rolling her eyes and shaking her head. India really did know everything.

"I know. That's why you're gonna take your time and go to the ATM while I hang back and talk to that *Tiffany* girl," she said, saying her name like it was a joke.

"Bitch," Sydney exasperated at hearing the nonsense scheme.

"Syd, you're already dressed and we here, so chill. Besides, who are you supposed to be tonight? You're dressed like Michelle Obama," she laughed as she put lip gloss on before getting out of the car.

"What's wrong with Michelle?" Sydney said, stepping out into the brisk cold air as the two walked to the hall.

She wore a simple black silk sleeveless top that had a high

neckline. She accompanied the top with black pants and four-inch knee boots. On her shoulders sat a black leather jacket.

"Ain't nothing wrong with the queen, but you're not the First Lady," India said laughing as she folded her arms to warm herself.

"You don't like? Genevieve brought it for me," Sydney chuckled.

She hated herself once she realized she mentioned a gift from Genevieve.

"Damn, Masta' still divvying out gifts?"

"Bitch shut up and hurry up, it's cold."

Sydney sighed and braced herself as they reached the front door and walked into the building. They sauntered into the crowded pool room that was filled with thick smoke that smelled of weed, liquor and body heat. The room was mostly filled with men, which was normal for a Thursday night. On these nights, the place was packed with all the hood niggas getting together to play pool, stunt with one another, and shoot their shit.

Sydney would have never agreed to go here if she knew this was on the itinerary for tonight. She felt like a piece of meat as the two walked through the crowd and to the bar.

"Don't worry, this is on the way to the restaurant. Let's just stick to the plan and then we can be out here within an hour," India said over the music. "Look, there is Dij right there. Let's say hi."

Dij looked up and saw them just as India pointed in her direction. As if she already knew what was headed her way, the smile instantly wiped off of her face and she tapped her man to move aside.

"Hey babe, surprise," India said, reaching over to Dij and pulling her into a hug before kissing her deeply.

Per usual, Dij was deep with a group of her friends. Only this time she wasn't the only girl in the group. All the men muttered to themselves and looked lustily at India before turning their heads away respectfully. Sydney always knew that Dij's friends envied the fact that she pulled a girl like India. India was every hood nigga's dream, and she could care less because she only wanted Dij.

"What up Syd? Look at you! Ain't see you in a minute girl, come here," Dij said, raising an arm so that Syd was able to give her a quick side hug.

"Nothing much, been busy working. Wanted to spend some time with my girl since I had a free moment," Sydney said, taking off her leather jacket and folding it on her arms as she stood awkwardly.

"I hear that... so India," Dij said, turning her head quickly down, "What you doing here? You ain't tell me you were coming tonight," she continued.

"We wanted to grab drinks before dinner and Sydney told me she wanted to give you something," she said softly as she gently wiped her lip gloss off of Dij's bottom lip. "So I thought: two birds, one stone. Smart, right Khadijah?"

"What you got?" Dij asked, turning her attention back to Sydney.

"Huh? Oh yes," Sydney said, turning on her heels, "Be right back!"

She darted off to go to the ATM, secretly glad to be away from that awkward situation. From behind her she could hear the word "Tiffany" leave Dij's lips and she prayed India didn't lose it. She turned and looked at the girl who she suspected was Tiffany. She was a tall Spanish girl who had thick, long black hair that laid on her back. She was curvy and looked beautiful and strong. For a moment, Sydney wondered what a girl like her was doing hanging with Dij and her crew. But then she remembered that looks could be deceiving.The girl had a tattoo on the corner of her face for God's sake. Sydney hoped India knew what she was doing as she watched Tiffany look Dij's and India's way at the sound of her name.

Sydney had two people ahead of her at the ATM. She took the time to check her work emails and to see if she had missed any calls from Genevieve.

She suspected that she wouldn't see any as she remembered seeing a date night with her and Asher on the calendar for tonight. The two had gone out for dinner and were going to some museum opening somewhere deep in North Massachusetts. She supposed they would be out all night.

She smirked to herself as she reached the ATM and slid her VISA in. In the past she would think it would've been ludicrous to have to calendar time and dates in to meet with her lover. But now, she didn't bat an eye at the fact that she shared her lover with another. Once the two became intimate, she shockingly didn't care anymore. She felt very close to Genevieve and believed that the two had deep connection with one another, one that couldn't be matched with anyone else.

Just as Sydney retrieved the money and tucked it in her purse, she turned around to see India lunging for Tiffany as Dij tried to hold her back.

A sudden gasp and "oh shit" ripped through the room and Sydney bolted to the scene.

"You stupid bitch! You think you cute, I'll fuck your ass up!" India screamed while beating Tiffany's head with her left fist as her right hand had a handful of Tiffany's thick hair.

"Yo, India what are you doing? Syd! Get your girl!" Dij screamed as she pulled India off of Tiffany and onto her feet as she carried her out.

"India!" Sydney yelled because she didn't know what else to do as she followed them outside.

Forty-five minutes later India and Sydney sat on hard wooden stools at the bar in Red Lobster. Sydney and India sat in silence as they drank their classic margarita with their cheddar biscuits on the side.

India and Dij had a screaming and shoving match in front of the hall as they entertained the small crowd that nosily followed them outside. After a few minutes Dij had had enough of telling India to keep her hands to herself.

"India just go! You wildin' right now! Syd, get your girl and go!"

"India, come on let's just go!" Sydney cried out, embarrassed for her friend while trying to hold her back from delivering blows to Dij's face.

"Damn Dij your bitch fuckin' you up," someone had snickered from the crowd.

"What even happened?" Sydney finally asked as she came back to the present.

Last minute she had decided it would be best to nix the Peruvian restaurant and to take India further away from Dij than just a few blocks. She had hoped that a trip to their favorite restaurant would help lighten India's mood.

"Dij is lying, that's what happened. I know she is fuckin' that girl Syd," India said wiping her free-falling tears from off of her round cheeks.

India was beginning to slur her words, which was no surprise to Sydney since India was already on her second margarita and had always been a lightweight.

She wouldn't stand a chance drinking with Genevieve, Sydney thought to herself as she refrained from smiling at the thought of her.

"She fuckin' that bitch girl," she continued, cradling her glass and looking down at the half-eaten biscuit in front of her. "Ask me how I know?"

"How do you know?"

"The way she said her name, '*Tiffany*'," she said while snarling her upper lip.

"So, I asked that bitch myself, right when she came over to us! I asked, 'you fuckin' my girl?'"

"Oh my God India, this was not a part of the plan," Sydney said, shaking her head in disbelief.

"You don't get it Syd... no offense, but when you found out about Shawn all you did was break up with him and kick him out. That's all you did each time you caught him cheating actually. I'm sorry but that ain't enough for me. That bitch gotta get it too!"

India had downed the rest of her drink and waved over the bartender.

Sydney finished her drink too and thought about what India said. A part of her was offended and felt that her best friend was covertly calling her a punk. But the other part of her knew she was right. Short of stalking the girl from watching her Instagram, Sydney had no real interest in seeking vengeance on Tia or even Shawn for that matter.

"So, get to the part where you ended up beating the girl upside her head," Sydney said.

"So, I asked her if she fuckin' Dij and you know what that bitch said?"

"What she say?"

"She said, 'where you hear that from?'" India said with disgust etching all over her face.

Their orders of food arrived with their shots of tequila that India had requested. Once the waiter was out of earshot Sydney turned to her friend, once again in shock.

"So, you fought the girl over that? I thought she owned up to it," Sydney said, popping a crunchy fried shrimp in her mouth.

She hadn't had any fried foods in weeks because of Genevieve's diet that had become her own as well.

"No, I fought her because she laughed while she said it.

Like it was a joke, like I was a joke!" India yelled, picking up the shots and handing one to Sydney.

"Here, take this with me. I'm blacking out tonight bitch."

"No, one of us has to drive your ass home. I'll pass," Sydney said, putting up her hand.

"Fine. More for me. I need to smoke too," India took back her shot and without hesitation, tossed Sydney's back as well.

"Girl, no you don't. Don't you have a drug test you need to pass for that new job?"

"Man fuck that job. Also, I'm not going home tonight. I don't want to see Dij," India said loudly as she began to dig into her pasta.

"So, where you going?"

Two hours later the two stumbled into Sydney's guesthouse. India had one arm thrown across Sydney's shoulder as Sydney slowly pulled her into the house. India was tore down and Sydney was forced to cut her off after her fourth margarita. She had never seen India drink that much and she was mad at herself for letting her get this bad.

Sydney walked India slowly up her stairs to the bed which she let her fall drunkenly onto. Sydney ran into her bathroom and came back with a small trash can and a glass of water.

"Syd... I'm so fucked up," India mumbled as she sat on Sydney's bed in a drunken stupor.

"I know, girl, I know. Don't worry. We're home," Sydney said as she took off India's heels.

"Home? This ain't my home— Syd!" India screamed, bulging her eyes and looking around.

"Is this your new place? Girl! Let me go take a tour, I wanna see how the rich and siddity live," India said, trying to stand up only to be too drunk and fall right back down on the bed.

India laid back down on the bed and started laughing at herself.

"How about I give you a tour in the morning, India? It's late, and girl you are too drunk for me," Sydney said shaking her head.

She took the moment to step out of her own boots and to take off her jacket. She was exhausted and ready to go to sleep after such a long day.

"Syd?"

"Yeah girl?" Sydney said over her shoulder as she looked for one of Shawn's old t-shirts to give India to sleep in.

"How long you been fuckin' her and why you ain't tell me yet?"

Sydney turned around quickly to see India sitting up looking at Sydney.

"I...I..."

"Syd, I just found out the love of my life is possibly a lying and cheating whore. Please don't you lie to me too," India said, beginning to strip out of her clothes clumsily.

Sydney sighed and walked over to India to help her. She was so drunk and pathetic right now, Sydney didn't have it in her to fight with her. Besides, India was so far gone that she likely wouldn't remember this conversation anyway.

"India, I couldn't tell you because I signed a non-disclosure agreement."

"You signed an NDA?"

"Yes— "

"And your ass ain't tell me?! Your best friend?"

"I think that's the whole point of the NDA, India," Sydney said, smirking." And we had a whole conversation about this already back at my apartment. Now will you drink some water and go to bed? Your ass is drunk"

"So, I'm right, you are fuckin' her?" India said, ignoring Sydney's demands.

"Yes India, you're right. But it's more than that... I'm with Genevieve," Sydney said timidly.

She helped bring India to her feet as she sloppily stepped out of her one-piece and plopped back down on the bed in just a bra and panties.

"If you are with her, why you all the way out here? Why you not in the big house?" India asked while raising her arms over her head for Sydney to put the shirt on her.

"What you think, I'm a slave?" Sydney laughed as she peeled back some covers for India. "Some 'big house'."

India laughed too and got in bed. "Bitch you know I'm drunk. And she is massa'..."

"Nah girl," Sydney sighed as she tucked India in bed and sat down beside her, "Genevieve is married. She and her husband, Asher, live in the main house."

"She's married?!" India said with her eyes bulging. "Asher? I know that is not a brotha's name."

Sydney laughed at her friend again. Ironically, it was easier than she thought it would be to tell her this news. She had been avoiding her for weeks, scared of accidentally slipping up and giving India some clue that would confirm her suspicions. And if Sydney was being honest, she felt as if a weight had been instantly lifted off of her shoulders.

Sydney gave India a rundown on the last few weeks of her life. She started with her signing the contract, the kiss in New Haven, meeting Asher and of course her first time with Genevieve.

After a while, Sydney looked up and out of her bedroom window to see the sun rising. When she looked back down to India, she noticed that her eyes had finally closed and that she was asleep. Sydney tiptoed downstairs to grab ibuprofen for the hangovers that were sure to come once they woke up. She climbed back up the stairs and threw off her clothes before slipping into an old t-shirt and climbing into bed with India.

Just as she felt herself dozing off to a sweet, serene sleep after an extremely long day Sydney heard from behind her, "So a bitch lost her lesbian virginity and wasn't gonna tell me," India giggled in her sleep. "Did you eat it?"

......

"Sydney...Sydney..."

Sydney was in the middle of a deep sleep. She was dreaming of herself sitting in an empty classroom looking at a blank chalkboard. In her dream, she looked to her left and then her right, but no one else was in the room with her. Sydney felt a moment of panic as she suddenly felt a severe case of FOMO wondering where her classmates and teacher were.

"Sydney...Sydney..."

Again, Sydney looked around and saw that there wasn't anyone else in the room. She tried to stand up from her desk and realized that she was stuck and unable to move. Sydney began to become frantic as she realized that she couldn't move her hands either. She could feel her heart beating hard in her chest and felt tears beginning to burn her eyes.

"Sydney!"

The sound of Genevieve's voice made Sydney jolt up in her sleep. She opened her eyes to see Genevieve standing over her with anger etched all over her beautiful face.

"What is going on here?" Genevieve asked, folding her arms.

"What are you talking about?" she asked while rubbing the cold out of her eyes, confused.

"I am talking about the half-naked woman in your bed... in my home, at ten in the morning," she said while moving her stone-cold glare to across Sydney's bed.

Sydney turned around to see India lying beside her, beginning to stir out of her sleep. One of India's breasts had popped out of her bra in her sleep, and she laid there looking disheveled and crazy with mascara tears dried and stained on her face.

The shirt Sydney had given her last night lay beside her on the bed.

"Syd..." India whined weakly.

Sydney knew what that meant and hurriedly reached over India and pulled the trashcan closer to her.

"It's right here girl," Sydney said just as India lurched to the side and threw up in the trash can.

Sydney looked back up to Genevieve and knew she had fucked up.

"Sydney, meet me in the kitchen in five minutes. And it will be in your best interest to get your guest ready to leave as soon as possible."

Five minutes later, Sydney had managed to brush her teeth and wash her face before throwing on some sweats to meet her fate. She opened the back door to the house and took off her Uggs at the door, careful to not drag any snow water onto the pristine floors. She slowly walked to the kitchen where she could hear pots and pans being taken out and imagined Asher was beginning to make their breakfast.

"Good morning," she said timidly, entering the kitchen to find Asher and Genevieve.

They both looked refreshed and happy as they were in their weekly Friday morning routine of making breakfast while in their Pjs.

"Morning Syd," Asher said as he whistled happily and stirred some eggs in a ceramic bowl, "How do you want your omelet?"

"Good morning, no eggs for me today, I may barf," Sydney said, walking closer to Genevieve who sat at the kitchen island sipping coffee and reading the newspaper.

"Whoa," Asher said looking up at Sydney, "Fun night 'eh? You look like you need some pancakes to soak it up," he laughed.

"You have no idea. Do you mind?"

"No, I got you," he said, glancing at Genevieve who still sat silently reading.

Asher looked back to Sydney and mouthed a silent, "What happened?"

"Hey Genevieve, sorry about India. She had a rough night and couldn't go home— "

"Sydney, on what planet is it okay for me to find you in bed with another woman? A woman that I don't know, might I add," she said calmly while keeping her eyes down on the newspaper.

"Genevieve you know India, that is my best friend. You met her a few weeks ago at my place," Sydney said, hopeful that the clarification would ease the tension.

"Oh, the loud girl that was fawning all over your car," she said back, uninterested.

"Yes...her. Listen, she and her girlfriend got into a big fight last night and I didn't think it would be a big deal to bring her here," Sydney said quickly.

"Oh, so she's a lesbian. That makes it even better," Genevieve said, folding up her paper and laying it on the counter. "I guess you don't remember the clause in your contract that said you are not to date anyone outside of *us*," she stressed.

Sydney bit her tongue to suppress the need to say, "huh?"

Why would a clause like that be added to an NDA? Why would Genevieve feel the need to add who Sydney could and couldn't date if they were poly? Also, she couldn't understand why Genevieve was tripping like this. She had met India before, and Sydney was sure she'd told her about her being a lesbian before.

Across the kitchen, Asher had eased himself to the farthest counter away from them as possible. It was evident he didn't want any part of it, and Sydney couldn't blame him. He turned up the speaker that was currently playing India Arie's song, *I am not my hair*.

"Genevieve, I am sorry if you feel disrespected, but India is my best friend. That is it; nothing has ever happened between us and never will," Sydney couldn't believe that she even had to say this.

Sydney reached for Genevieve's hand, trying to remedy the situation.

"Uh-huh," Genevieve said, snatching her hand away from Sydney and folding the newspaper back up before hopping off of her stool.

"You just make sure that you get your *friend* out of my house within the next hour, Sydney. I think that is more than enough time for her to empty her bowels and clean herself up."

Genevieve walked over to Asher and placed a hand on his shoulder to pull him down for a quick kiss on his cheek.

"Thanks for breakfast babe, but my appetite is gone. I'm heading out for the day to clear my head," she said, sashaying her way out of the kitchen.

"Genevieve!" Sydney said, jumping out of her seat and grabbing her arm to stop her, "I'm sorry. I didn't mean to offend you. Can we talk about this?"

"Sydney, remove your hand from me," Genevieve said coldly.

Sydney, hurt, did as she was told as she bit her bottom lip.

"Hun... I think it is best that you review the contract. Clearly there are some things you need a ...refresher on. Clear my calendar for the week. I am taking the next few days off, so you will have plenty of time to get your shit together then," she said storming out of the kitchen.

Sydney stood dumbfounded, not quite sure of what had just happened. From behind her, she heard Asher angrily throw the bowl of eggs into the sink, causing Sydney to turn around at the noise.

Asher stood there bent over the sink clenching his jaw and shaking his head.

"Why do I feel like I just fucked up, royally?" Sydney asked him.

"Because you did," he said dryly, walking out of the kitchen in the opposite direction of Genevieve.

Chapter 12

Sunday, November 15th

It had been a few days since Genevieve began giving Sydney the cold shoulder after finding India in her bed. Sydney had tried repeatedly to make it up to Genevieve by getting back on her good side but had had no luck.

Today, she decided to surprise Genevieve with an impromptu massage and facial at one of Genevieve's favorite spots in town. Sydney had been very meticulous with planning this surprise for her and even put down a generous deposit just to make sure that the two were able to be squeezed in today.

Sydney closed the door behind her to the main house and began to make her way up the stairs to Genevieve's office when she stopped dead in her tracks at the sight of a young man sitting on the couch playing on his phone.

"Umm... hi," Sydney said, confused and stopping herself from walking up the stairs.

She turned around and slowly walked over to the man, confused about who he was and why he was there. As she made her way over to him she noticed Genevieve's Fendi luggage sitting neatly next to him.

"Hi, I'm Sydney," Sydney said, extending her hand to the stranger.

"Oh... the infamous Sydney, nice to meet you," the man said standing up and shaking Sydney's hand.

Sydney gave the man a quizzical look and couldn't help but to shake the feeling that she saw him before. He was tanned and handsome with a sharp square jaw and short bristled beard.

"And you are..." Sydney said, taking her hands back and tucking them into her back pocket as she looked up at the tall handsome stranger.

"Oh... I'm Finn," he said, chuckling as if Sydney had missed the joke.

"Finn?"

"Yea... you know Finn, Genevieve's friend...?" Finn said, sounding less confident the more he spoke.

Sydney scrunched up her face and immediately caught an attitude as she tried to connect the dots. She managed and inputted everything in Genevieve's detailed planner. She knew what Genevieve's day-to-day looked like because she mapped it out and studied it as if it were her bible.

"Wow... this is embarrassing," he said, letting out a dry laugh as he scratched the back of his head, "I guess you don't pay much attention to the artwork around here much, huh?" he asked as he looked over his shoulder to the picture that hung on the wall behind him.

Suddenly, Sydney realized where she knew the man from. He was the man that hung in the living room butt naked on a beach with his semi-erect penis resting freely on his thigh. Genevieve had said that she knew the photographer, but never mentioned anything about actually knowing the model too.

"Sydney! Perfect, you saved me a trip to the guest house," Genevieve said, walking down the stairs with a huge smile on her face.

She looked gorgeous in her mink fur that hung loosely on her bare shoulders. Genevieve wore huge Dior glasses and wore her hair in loose pin curls all over her head. She looked like she walked out of an ad for the 1950s Negro woman.

"I see you met Finn. Finn, this is my Sydney," she said, reaching the landing and kissing Sydney lightly on her cheek before walking over to Finn and planting a kiss on his lips.

Finn swooped her up in his arms and began to kiss her deeply, being sure to grab a handful of her ass in the process. They made out and felt on each other as if Sydney wasn't even there.

"Whoa, whoa, whoa," she said, wiping her cherry red lipstick off of his lips, "Save that for Punta Cana."

"Punta Cana?" Sydney felt heat flush all over her body.

"Yes, we're leaving now," Genevieve said nonchalantly while still looking at Finn, "Finn, bring the bags to the car while I wrap up here. Tell Raphael I'll be out shortly."

Finn did as he was told and gathered her bags with a small smirk on his face as if he had proved a point.

"Sydney," he said, nodding his head to say goodbye as he walked the bags out.

"I wish I knew that you were leaving... I had a special surprise planned for you," Sydney said, hurt as she looked down.

"The spa?" Genevieve asked.

"Yes, how did you know?" she asked, surprised.

"Hun... you used my credit card," Genevieve said with a light snicker as she began to roll leather gloves over her right hand.

Sydney felt like an idiot. She forgot that she used her "run around" credit card that Genevieve gave her for miscellaneous things to book the session.

"Oh, before I forget, here. Be a doll and bring this upstairs for me and lock it away," she said slowly, removing her wedding ring off of her finger before placing it gently in Sydney's palm. "And beware, Asher is up there pouting like a child."

Sydney didn't blame him. What man would be happy with his wife going away for an island rendezvous with the likes of Finn? And minus her wedding ring?

"When will you be back?" Sydney asked, playing with the ring in her hand.

She couldn't believe that she was leaving this easily while the two of them were in the midst of a fight, their first fight at that. If she could leave this easy to go with one of her old toys, did this mean that she was done with Sydney?

"Oh Sydney, now you look just like Asher," she said walking over to Sydney and kissing her warmly on the lips. "Chin up. I will be home in a few days," she said, sashaying to the front door.

"I'll call you all once we land. Goodbye Sydney," she said, walking out the door.

Sydney turned around and raced up the stairs two at a time. She was furious. For days she dealt with Genevieve icing her out and ignoring her, just to have her up and leave with *Finn.* Sydney walked the hallway to Genevieve's wardrobe room to drop her ring off in her safe. On her way back downstairs, she stopped in front of the open master bedroom door where she saw Asher standing, looking out of the window.

Sydney gave the door a soft knock.

"Come in," he said with his back still turned towards her.

His hair was down by his bare shoulders, and he stood in just pajama bottoms that hung loosely on his hips, despite it being almost two in the afternoon.

Sydney walked into the grand and dark bedroom and walked straight over to him to see what he was looking at. Below, she could see Raphael loading the bags into the SUV before closing the trunk and climbing into the driver's seat. The two watched as Raphael slowly drove down the steep driveway towards the airport.

Sydney felt lost and hurt. She fought the urge to cry even though she felt the burning sensation behind her eyes. She didn't know what this meant for her and Genevieve and wondered if she had reached her expiration date already.

"What do you have planned for the day?" she asked while still watching the SUV as it became smaller and smaller.

"You're looking at it," Asher mumbled solemnly.

"Wanna go spend Genevieve's money at the spa and then pig out?" she asked him.

......

"And what the fuck is a '*Finn*' anyway?" Sydney yelled before knocking back the rest of her beer and waving for the waitress to bring her another one.

Asher laughed as he took a chicken flat, placed it in his mouth and inhaled the meat straight off the bone all within seconds.

"Impressive," Sydney said, raising an eyebrow.

"One thing you must learn about me, Syd... I do not play about my chicken," Asher said as he took back a shot of whiskey.

The two were enjoying a binge session at Hooters after the spa. After an afternoon of pampering that consisted of a full body deep-tissue massage, a facial and a clay bath, the two decided to continue their 'Genevieve free day' the best way they could by indulging in cheap, greasy food and beer.

"You know, you are nothing like what I expected," she said, stealing one of his wings and biting into it.

"What did you expect?" he asked, leaning back in his chair with a smirk as he sipped his beer.

"I don't know," Sydney said thinking about it, "You give me

'I gotta clap when the plane lands' kind of vibe," she said laughing cautiously.

"Ouch, that bad huh?" he asked, grabbing one of her onion rings.

"What can I say? You are married to Genevieve."

"And you think Genevieve would be married to a white guy from Rhode Island who rocks a bun? Come on Syd, give me some credit, damn."

"True," Sydney said as she took back her shot and screwed her face up to the bitter taste.

"Ya' know, despite what you may think I try hard not to be her personal robot; you should try it sometime," Asher said with a sly smile.

"Shade!" Sydney yelled, fake hurt even though she knew he was right.

"I'm just saying... you think G approves of my man bun? I only grew my hair out to spite her. She *hates* it," he laughed as he reached for another one of Sydney's onion rings.

"Ah, ah,'" she said, swatting at his hand and shielding her rings for her life. "You're braver than me, when she told me to cut it, I cut it."

"Happens to the best of us, Syd. Look at Finn, he once had dreads. Another shot? Fuck it, we're Ubering tonight," he said waiving the waitress back over.

"That nigga had dreads?" Sydney squealed as she covered her mouth, realizing she was well inebriated.

"Fuck is a *Finn* anyway?," she asked again. "When I saw him today and realized who he was, my stomach dropped. He's so corny, he's so pretentious, he's so—"

"G's type," he said finishing her sentence. "That's why she keeps him around. Every time she needs her kicks and giggles or wants to piss me off... and evidently you too, she calls him. I call him her little fuck boy. He has been on call for her for years. Last I heard he was modeling in Europe."

"Ugh," Sydney groaned, feeling herself become irritated again. "I don't know how you do it, Ash. I mean, I know I came in and stepped all on your turf... but this is not for the faint of heart."

"You know you're her first woman that she took on," he said as he removed the shots off of the waitress's tray.

In the background the men in the bar began to whoop and cheer as the Patriots made a touchdown against the New York Giants on TV.

"I am sure that's not true; I am not her first woman," Sydney laughed thinking about the last session the two had had in their hotel shower in DC earlier in the week.

"I know that," Asher exasperated as he handed Sydney her shot. "But you are the first woman she's wanted a relationship with. Don't get me wrong, G is truly bisexual, fluid or whatever you kids call it nowadays. Hell, my wife has had more pussy than me," he stopped and laughed.

"Thanks, that makes me feel so much better Ash."

"I say all that to say... she said it was something about you that she just couldn't miss out on. Don't stress it Syd, she's not getting rid of you. She just needs to blow off some steam."

Sydney felt herself blush and felt butterflies. It was reassuring to hear that come from Asher; it was as if he read her mind. She had tried to play it cool, but she was secretly shitting bricks at the thought of being kicked out of Genevieve's life forever.

"Let's cheers," he said, raising his shot in the air. "Let's cheers to Genevieve and her toxic possessiveness that leaves us whipped and stupid."

"Here's to the woman that can have anyone and everyone that she wants, but refuses to share her lovers with another soul," she added as they cheered and took their shots back.

......

. . .

Sydney woke up the next morning in her bed. It was the first morning in a while that she woke up on her own and not by a deafening alarm clock signifying that it was time to get up and go to work. With Genevieve somewhere gallivanting in the Caribbean with Finn, Sydney saw no need to make herself get up early. Hell, she was on vacation too.

She peeked her head out from underneath her comforter and reached for her phone on the nightstand. She had a few missed texts.

Cai: Hey girl, long time no speak! How are you and how is life with the dragon lady?

India: Bitch call me when you wake up!! You are not gonna believe what I got planned for your birthday!

Sydney grunted and nuzzled herself back under her warm covers. With everything that had been going on with Genevieve over the last few days, she had honestly forgotten that her birthday was coming up. She had been less than enthused to be over the mid- twenties mark and shuddered to think how close she was to her thirties.

She also hadn't talked to Cai in weeks and felt bad for going MIA on her. She honestly couldn't remember the last conversation the two had and she missed her work friend. Sydney made a mental note to reach back out to her later that day and plan a lunch date.

And as far as India, the two hadn't really spoken much about the other night. Sydney felt like India was embarrassed by her actions and didn't want to relive that night. Simultaneously, neither did Sydney. She still wasn't sure if India remembered her confession to her that night, but she really hoped she hadn't.

She felt her stomach growl and decided to head to the main house to see if she could scrounge something up in the kitchen.

After she freshened up and threw on some comfy and warm clothes, she sprinted quickly into the back of the main house and made her way to the kitchen.

Maybe some French toast? Sydney thought to herself after she pulled out some eggs, vanilla and brown sugar.

"Woof, woof!"

Sydney froze in her tracks and wondered if she was still drunk from last night. She knew what she heard wasn't a dog. Definitely not in Genevieve's pristine home.

"Woof, woof!"

This time she knew she wasn't bugging. She placed the gallon of almond milk down on the counter and quietly tiptoed towards the sound that came from the back of the house near the study. As she got closer she then heard a familiar hearty woman's laugh that made her put a pep in her step and barge into the room.

"Ma?" Sydney said, entering the room.

She couldn't believe her eyes, not only was her mother there smiling and laughing with Asher, but she was currently petting a large tan dog.

"Mommy!" Sydney squealed as she ran over to her and jumped into her arms for a warm hug.

Sydney's mom looked beautiful as always. Her chocolate skin was glowing in her white and black African garb that Sydney was sure came from her last trip to Africa with her girlfriends. Sydney's face was an exact replica of her mother's down to their almond-shaped deep brown eyes and full bottom lip.

"Hey Syd girl, look at your hair!" she said, kissing her teeth and running her fingers through Sydney's short wild hair.

"Yeah, I cut it a little way back," she said, subconsciously reaching up and touching it, "Ma what are you doing here? I didn't even know you were back in the States. How was the trip?"

"Girl, it was amazing!"

"Sydney mentioned that you were a traveler. I think that's great. I've been dying to get back out and visit some new places," Asher added.

"Oh, yes I try to go every couple of months, nothing like traveling. You know this girl hasn't left the States yet!" she said, cutting her eyes at Sydney. "I even made her get a passport and you would think she would take advantage—"

"Okay, Mommy," Sydney said, trying to cut her mother's rant short. "So what brings you out here again? I would've come to you if I knew you were back."

"Well I decided to pop in on my baby. You were so vague when telling me about your new job, so I wanted to come check it out for myself. You know I have to make sure baby girl is good," she said while rubbing her soft hand on the side of Sydney's cheek. "Girl I can't believe you cut your hair! Not sure how I feel about it yet..."

"Thanks, Mommy," Sydney said, rolling her eyes at her bluntness. "Should've known you weren't asking for my new address just to mail me a souvenir."

Sydney momentarily looked away from her mother and back to the large dog who sat panting at Asher's side.

"And you brought a... dog?"

"No, I did," Asher said proudly as he roughly rubbed the dog's head, who wagged his tail in return.

"You did not," Sydney said, shocked as she walked over to the dog who immediately jumped on his hindlegs and began to try to lick her on her face.

"Yes, yes I did. After our convo last night, I decided it was time to do something for me. Meet Max or Jake...haven't decided on a name yet," Asher said with glee as he pulled the dog down off of Sydney. "He's a three-year-old Chow and Labrador mix. I picked him up from the shelter the first thing this morning. I've been visiting him there the last few weeks; decided to take him home today."

"She is going to kill you," Sydney said to him, shocked.

Genevieve hated dogs. She would often rant on how they were loud, how they stunk and how they were a waste of space. And this came from just spotting them on the street. Imagine her reaction once she saw this dog prancing around in her home.

"Fuck it," he said looking her squarely in her eyes. "Excuse me Mrs. Mack! I'm from Rhode Island, we have no filter," he said apologetically, turning toward Sydney's mother.

"No need Ash, this is your home, and please, call me Leah."

"Ash?" Sydney said, sitting down on the couch and patting the cushion next to her for her mother. "When did y'all become so friendly?"

"Since I came up this man's driveway and knocked on his door," Leah chuckled as she plopped down next to Sydney. "He opened the door and that dog just came flying out! He was chasing him like a madman until I was able to lure the dog back with one of my granola bars from my purse," Leah said.

"Yea, we definitely have a running partner on our hands, Syd," Asher said as he patted the dog who stood there wagging his tail, excited to be getting all of this attention.

"Oh, you're back running?" Leah asked Sydney with a smile. "You know my Sydney is really good with animals too. When she was a little girl she would volunteer at the local vet near our home. They called my Sydney the 'dog whisperer'; she just has a way with them you know? I told her she would be a veterinarian one day."

"Wow, I forgot about that," Sydney said thinking of her old days hanging out at the vet's office and playing with the animals. She would hang there sometimes all day during the summer to avoid the fact that she didn't have any real friends. So, the animals became her friends.

"I sure didn't," she continued reaching over and lightly patting Sydney's hand. "I'm sure she can help you train that dog."

"Well, let me let you two catch up. It's a pleasure meeting you, Leah, and thanks again. I think I better give this big boy a bath and try to work on a name."

"It was a pleasure meeting you too, Ash. Hopefully I can meet your lovely wife sometime soon," Leah said in a tone that subtly threw shade. A tone that only Sydney would be able to catch.

Asher put the leash on the dog and guided him out of the room leaving Sydney alone in the study with her mother.

"Baby, you did not tell me you were living like this! This house is beautiful," she gasped as she looked around the study that doubled as a library with hundreds of books spread around the room.

"Isn't it? Want to see my house? It's in the back."

"Yes, of course, but first... tell me what is really going on here," her mother said, raising an eyebrow at Sydney.

"What do you mean Mommy?" Sydney asked, playing dumb.

Her mother's intuition was uncanny. Sydney's mother was able to see through a lie the way a fish was able to breathe underwater. As a kid Sydney and her brothers struggled to hide anything from her.

"I mean, how do you go from living in a studio with Shawn, working two jobs to maintain, to living in a guesthouse and being an assistant to a millionaire? Something funky is going on here," Leah said as she shifted her full body in her seat.

As much as Sydney wanted to be honest with her mother, she knew that she couldn't. She could not possibly understand, let alone would she support it. Her mother was very old school and believed in old-fashioned values. She didn't talk to Sydney for a week when she decided to let Shawn move in with her. In high school, she was surprised when her mother was supportive when India decided to come out to her first before she came out to her own mother. Her mother believed in no sex before marriage, no shacking up, and believed that the man should be the head of the household. All beliefs that were for sure not being practiced in this household.

Sydney wasn't up for a fight today, so she decided to put on her best Genevieve impersonation and gave her mother the PG version on why she was there. Explaining how she met Genevieve after the breakup, how Genevieve believed that she could be a mentor for Sydney, and ultimately how she had leveled her up.

"Mommy even if this doesn't work out, she is setting me up and helping me improve my resume. Who knows, I can even be an assistant to Michelle Obama at this point!" Sydney boasted, trying to use her mother's favorite as an example.

"Well that is good Syd, and I am glad that you are happy—"

"But?" Sydney asked.

"But, I don't want you to get too comfortable, baby. I didn't send you off to school to be someone's assistant for the rest of your life. What happened to your dreams? Your goals? You are helping this woman achieve her goals, but I do not want you to lose sight of your own."

"I'm not," Sydney said, trying her best to hide her annoyance, "I'm just figuring it all out still. I don't have the answers yet on who I want to be or become. But she is helping me to find out. And honestly Mommy, I think it is a hell of a lot better than moping around in that apartment and being depressed about Shawn."

"I hear you, but just be smart. Don't get wrapped up too deep in this woman and if you are giving her any ideas for her books make sure you get your cut, you hear me?"

"Yes, Mommy," Sydney giggled. "Come on, let me show

you the house and then let me take you out for brunch in my new ride. All on me!"

"Alright now, now that is what I like to hear!" Leah said, standing to her feet and tossing her bag over her shoulder.

"Syd?"

"Yes, Mommy?"

"What kind of freak nasty mess are these people into with all those nude photos in their living room?" she whispered under her breath.

Sydney laughed at her mother as they walked through the house.

"I better not hear you mixed up in none of that, you hear me?"

"Yes, ma'am."

Chapter 13

Friday, November 20th

Sydney stood behind a thick black curtain as she clutched her clipboard tightly to her chest. They were at the end of Genevieve's three-day press tour that concluded with an interview on *The Breakfast Club* where Genevieve was there to talk about her current book and to promote book number five. Book five still didn't have a name yet, and Sydney still hadn't seen Genevieve writing or working on anything. She started to wonder if this book even existed. She also didn't know how Genevieve convinced her publisher to push back the deadline for her first draft, but by some miracle she had been granted more time.

Things were still tense between the two and Sydney was borderline over it. She had slowly become accustomed to Genevieve's icing her out and decided that it would be best for her to keep her head down and work both quietly and efficiently. Once Sydney had to whip out her vibrator to use it on herself, she figured that their relationship part of this deal was over.

Sydney fidgeted on her feet as she looked at Genevieve,

who sat coolly talking to DJ Envy before gracefully turning to her left to laugh at a joke from Charlamagne. She looked graceful and calm and not a bit nervous to be talking to them while a whole room sat and watched. She didn't look at all like Sydney, who sat silently on the opposite side of the glass with butterflies in her stomach.

Sydney had been anxious ever since Genevieve's publicist sent over the invite for the interview. Sydney couldn't imagine Genevieve sitting there being interviewed by Charlamagne for too long before he would say something controversial to tick her off. But to Sydney's surprise, the interview was light and funny. Genevieve was able to put on her usual charm and get some good promotion in for her projects.

Sydney decided to head back to the dressing room to watch the rest of the filmed show while she packed up the room and cooled down. It was so cool to Sydney that Genevieve was about to be streamed on people's radios and television screens. Genevieve had a tight schedule today that Sydney wanted to make sure she upheld . Once in the room Sydney grabbed her phone from out of her purse and saw a text from India who was for sure texting her about the birthday plans they had tonight.

India: Girl I ain't saying too much but be sure to bring your cash in ones and cute pj'sssssss

Sydney laughed gently to herself. She could always tell when India was drinking by the way she added extra letters.

Syd: slow down girl, it ain't even 1pm yet!! And I'm not even in Mass. See you in a few hours hoe!

Sydney was looking forward to whatever India had in store for her tonight. She had been dead tired ever since Genevieve got back a few days ago. Genevieve had been working Sydney like a dog from sunup to sundown. Sydney couldn't believe she was saying it, but she actually couldn't wait to get away from Genevieve for a few days. She now understood why Asher was so quick to make runs to see his family every few weeks.

Sydney diligently packed Genevieve's makeup away in its black leather bag just as she watched Genevieve hug the hosts goodbye on the dressing room's television screen. She banked that once Genevieve left the stage she would shake a few hands backstage before autographing a few books. Sydney knew that meant she only had a few minutes to be prepared for their departure.

Sydney noted the time and they were right on time for Genevieve's lunch. She quickly grabbed a complimentary ice-cold water bottle and sat it down on the coffee table near Genevieve's phone and the pecan salad she laid out for her. On the floor next to that sat Genevieve's pink slippers for her to slide her feet into as soon as she came in. Sydney reviewed the set up and found no flaws. Sydney had to make sure everything was perfect, especially after having Genevieve yell at her a few times about something not being right or out of place.

Sydney was fastening the strap down on Genevieve's roll-away when she heard her come bursting through the door with a devilish grin on her face.

"I've got an idea," Genevieve said with her back against the closed door.

She wore a modest black dress with a skirt that fanned out and twirled as she walked. Between her skirt and smile Genevieve looked like a giddy schoolgirl.

"What's that?" Sydney asked, surprised at Genevieve's sudden playful energy.

"Somebody has a birthday coming up in a few hours," she said, tiptoeing over to Sydney with her eyes burning the side of Sydney's face.

"Oh... I'm surprised you remembered," Sydney mumbled as she rolled Genevieve's luggage to the door. "Raphael should be here in twenty... looks like we overestimated time," she said looking down at her old watch that once belonged to her father.

"Sydney... hey," Genevieve said, lowering her tone and

walking over slowly to Sydney, "I know I've been a real bitch these last few days...let me make it up."

Sydney was shocked to hear this. Deep down, she felt a flutter in her stomach, but she didn't want to give in so easily. She wanted to play it cool.

"I laid out your lunch and slippers. I know you are probably eager to get out of those heels," Sydney said as she attempted to brush past her.

Genevieve grabbed her arm and yanked Sydney back to her before grabbing both of Sydney's hands into her own. Genevieve took a step in and placed her forehead gently against Sydney's. In her pumps she stood just as tall as Sydney, who had opted to wear flats today.

"Sydney... this isn't easy for me," she began, "I know I can be a jealous, raging bitch sometimes, but I just feel so deeply for you..."

"So, what are you saying, Genevieve?" Sydney asked. She wanted to hear the words come out of Genevieve's mouth before she got her hopes up. She needed to hear it.

"I'm... I'm..." she struggled to let the words leave her mouth, as if the concept of apologizing was foreign to her, "I'm sorry Sydney. I am so sorry."

Sydney stood there shocked, not believing her own ears. Before she had time to think about her next words, they came spilling out of her.

"Genevieve, please understand that India is just a friend—my best friend. There is nothing going on between us. She is my family— "

"Understood Sydney," she said, cutting her off with puppy dog eyes. "There will be no more issues on my end. I promise."

Genevieve looked up into Sydney's eyes and placed her hands on her face and kissed her deeply. Sydney instantly pulled Genevieve in closer to her by the waist and melted in her embrace. It had been so long since she felt her touch, and she greedily relished in the moment.

A few minutes later they sat in the back of Genevieve's SUV as Genevieve told Raphael about her time on the show.

"Are they short in real life, Genevieve?" Raphael asked, taking a second to peak in the backseat from the rearview mirror. "They always say those TV people are shorter in person," he chuckled.

"Raph, it's a radio show," Sydney giggled. " They're sitting down for most if not all of the show."

"It's true though Sydney," Genevieve laughed. "That Charlamagne looked like he was my height in person! I just hope I looked good up there."

"You looked great. It was a really great segment, Genevieve," Sydney said as she squeezed Genevieve's hand tighter.

She was thrilled to be back in her good graces and anxious to see what she had in store for her once they got home. Sydney just hoped that the two would have enough time to properly make up in bed before she had to leave for the evening for her birthday plans with India.

Sydney rested her head on Genevieve's shoulder as she resisted the urge to kiss her again. Though she knew that Raphael would turn a blind eye to the two's affection, she didn't want to lay it on too thick for Genevieve. Sydney was still a bit taken aback on how easy it was for Genevieve to treat her like she was nothing.

"Hey, didn't I tell you I had a great idea earlier? Your tongue was so far down my throat I didn't even have a chance to share it with you," she teased Sydney.

"My tongue?" Sydney asked, sitting up and looking Genevieve bravely in the face. "I do believe you were the one who kissed me, ma'am."

"Touché. Well, do you want to hear it or not?"

"All your ideas are brilliant babe, but lay it on me," Sydney said, still holding her hand.

"I think we all deserve a nice little getaway, wouldn't you say? Between the crazy work days we had over the last few days, to Asher having that damn mutt run rampant all over my pristine house— it's time to get away."

When Genevieve came home to find Maverick, the hyper-friendly and affectionate dog running amuck in her house, she was less than enthused. In fact, Sydney remembered being able to hear the shouting match between her and Asher all the way in the guesthouse. By the grace of God, Maverick was still in the house. Sydney figured that Asher had won that battle and she secretly cheered him on from the inside.

"Really? Where did you have in mind?" Sydney said, with her interest piqued and excitement in her voice.

"Tulum... tonight," Genevieve said, kissing Sydney's hand lightly and smiling.

"Tulum?! As in Mexico?"

"The one and only my dear," she laughed. "As soon as we get home we pack our bags and head out on our *private jet* at about ten tonight. Me, you and Asher will spend the next few days having fun in the sun while I wine and dine my girl on her special birthday."

"There's nothing special about turning twenty-five," Sydney said aloud before coming back down to Earth. "Genevieve I don't know what to say!"

"Don't worry, this trip does not require much talking," she said as she grabbed Sydney's face and began to kiss her on her mouth before planting kisses gently on her neck. "And this birthday is special. It's special because you get to spend it with me and I am going to make sure you enjoy every minute."

"Genevieve," Sydney whispered as she felt her getting closer to her "spot" on her neck.

"Shit," Sydney suddenly hissed.

"Wow, I'm not used to hearing that until a little bit later, but I guess we are a little backed up, huh?" Genevieve teased as she stopped kissing her on her neck.

"Genevieve, is it possible that we can push this trip back just one day? India had plans for me tonight... I don't want to cancel on her so last minute."

Genevieve's body immediately tensed up at the sound of India's name.

"It's just that she has been going through a really tough time and had been planning this night for weeks. To be honest, tonight is not just about me, but is for her too..."

"Sydney, I know we just agreed on me not interfering with your friendship. But this is the part where you need to decide what is best for you," she said calmly while looking straight ahead out of the truck's windshield.

"You and I have some mending to do to our relationship, and honestly, I miss you Sydney. I need you right now just as bad as I can tell that you need me," she said, turning toward Sydney and resting her hand on her thigh while she pleaded her case.

"The decision is totally yours, but please know that if we cannot leave tonight, we will not be going, period. How about I give you the car ride home to think about it?" she asked rhetorically as she slid away from Sydney and moved over to the other side.

Feeling Genevieve's hands and heat leave her body sent Sydney's mind into overdrive and she instantly knew what her choice was.

Four hours later, the two arrived home. Sydney had decided to head to Tulum tonight with Asher and Genevieve and made a beeline for the guest house so that she could pull together some clothes. Genevieve had graciously supplied her with a new wardrobe for winter but she did not have many pieces for this trip. The weather was guaranteed to be hot and sunny, and Genevieve already promised Sydney a shopping spree tomorrow morning.

Sydney waited until the clock turned five before finally telling India that the plans for tonight were off.

Syd: Girl, don't hate me...

India: What?

Syd: We have to reschedule tonight, girl

As soon as Sydney typed those words she felt her phone vibrate in her hand.

"Hey, girl," Sydney said, nervously picking up the call.

"What the fuck Syd? How you gonna cancel on me like this? I'm at VIP right now picking up some stuff for tonight!"

Sydney sighed and plopped down backwards onto her bed. India sounded pissed, just as Sydney knew she would be.

"India, I am so sorry, girl, but I can't miss this opportunity. Please don't hate me, I promise we can get up as soon as we get back."

"Wow, Syd," India said as she got quiet on the phone.

Hearing India *not* voice how she felt was always a bad sign. Sydney felt her stomach turn.

"I guess you and your girl made up huh?" India asked dryly.

"Yeah something like that," she said shamefully. "She rented a private jet for me and all, India. We fly out tonight. I can't say no to that, you get that, right?"

"Damn a PJ? That sure beats a night here at some raggedy strip club with me," India said into the phone.

"Stop it, nothing beats time spent with you," Sydney said genuinely.

"Shut your cheesy ass up. Aight girl, I guess I'll tell the strippers to sit on ice until you get your ass back here. Where you going?"

"Tulum."

"Have fun, let me know when you land," India said quietly.

"I will girl... and I am sorry again. I love you," Sydney said meekly.

"Love you too."

Sydney hung up and laid on her back for a few more seconds wondering if she made a mistake. It hadn't been too long since Dij and India broke up and Sydney was worried that leaving her alone was the wrong decision. She didn't have much time to think about it before she heard a knock on her front door. She got up and tiptoed down the stairs knowing that it was likely Asher; Genevieve never knocked.

"Hey," Sydney said, opening the door to see Asher and Maverick on the steps.

Maverick immediately ran in and charged at Sydney, jumping up on his hindlegs to hug and lick her.

"Hi to you too, Maverick," she said, hugging him back and scratching the top of his head.

"I was wondering if you could do me a few favors before we leave tonight," Asher said, walking in and closing the door behind him as he watched Sydney and Maverick play.

"What's up?"

"One, can you take Maverick with me to the dog hotel? You know how skittish he gets around new people, and he only seems to listen to you," he sighed as he plopped down on Sydney's couch.

"Maverick, down," Sydney commanded as Maverick got down off of her still panting and wagging his tail. "Maverick sit."

He complied and sat down.

"Oh, you mean like that?" Sydney asked as she walked over to Asher.

"You can be a real show off sometimes you know that?" Asher asked with a half smirk on his face that immediately left once Maverick jumped on the couch with him and began to lick him, sending Asher's glasses to fly off of his face.

"Well, we still have some work to do," Sydney laughed as she retrieved his glasses and handed them back to him. "What's the other favor?"

"I don't want you to take this the wrong way...I fully understand how bad this is going to sound, before it even comes out of my mouth," Asher said, cleaning off his thick black-rimmed glasses with his shirt before placing them back on his face.

"Asher, what?" Sydney asked.

"Do you know where I can get some weed? I want some for the trip," he said, diverting his eyes from Sydney.

"Wow... Asher Cross the pothead, who knew?"

"Alright, Syd, a simple yes or no would suffice," he said, rolling his eyes.

"And you come to little ole me to be your supplier? What do I look like, some *drug dealer*? It's because I'm black, huh?" Sydney asked, folding her arms and trying to hold back a smile.

"Syd, will you stop being a jackass?" he smiled, though he tried to hold it back. "And no, you honestly would be the worst drug dealer in history. Too... jumpy and clumsy," he teased as he threw a throw pillow at her head.

"Ass," Sydney laughed, knowing that he wasn't wrong. "Does she know about this plan of yours?"

"G does not know, so let's keep this between us. She thinks weed is a 'poor man's drug'." Every time I smoked she would lecture me."

"What would she prefer, you become a cokehead?" Sydney scoffed.

"At least then I would have something in common with her friends," Asher slid in smoothly.

"I'm not opposed to bringing Mary on this trip with us," Sydney said with her wheels beginning to turn. "You sure we can have that on the plane?"

"Perks of flying on a PJ," Asher grinned as he petted Maverick on his head who was now dozing off on Asher's lap.

"To be honest, I only know of one person we can get it from... and I'm not sure it's a good idea," she said hesitantly.

"Why not? We gotta head to Boston anyway to drop him off. They're on the way, yeah?"

"Yeah... but it's India's ex-girlfriend, Dij."

"Okay, and?" he asked, confused, "That's good then; we can maybe get a family discount, yeah?"

"Just me talking to her is violating a whole bunch of girl code rules, and she's already mad at me. You wouldn't get it," Sydney sighed.

"Why, because I got a dick?" Asher asked as he and Maverick stood up.

"No, because you are one," Sydney said, reaching for her leather trench coat and phone.

"Well you owe me anyway. Come on, let's go now before G gets hip. I have cash," he said, putting Maverick's leash on him.

"How do I owe you?"

"I told G about your mom saying you've never left the country. I also reminded her that your birthday was tomorrow, a small detail I learned from your mother the other day."

"Of course," Sydney said, rolling her eyes. "Wow so this trip was your idea?"

"Yeah, I figured you could use a break. G's been riding you like crazy lately. And I'm sure not in the way you would like," he winked at her as they walked briskly to the garage.

The trio arrived in Tulum at about three in the morning. For the most part, Sydney had enjoyed her first trip on a plane. She tried her best to play it cool and as if she weren't a newbie flying through the air, but she gave herself away once she felt her first hit of turbulence. Sydney was so terrified that she got sick and immediately ran to the bathroom. She spent the rest of the flight clinging to Genevieve terrified, with her head in her lap.

The place that they were staying at was beautiful. It was a

villa, nestled an hour away from the airport, in the middle of the ocean. To reach the villa, guests walked a long narrow stone path from the mainland and over the ocean to the hut-style villas. Once inside, Sydney was amazed to see that their villa consisted of three bedrooms, three and a half bathrooms, a grand eat-in kitchen, a bohemian-themed living room and of course an outdoor pool. *An outdoor pool, in the middle of the ocean!*

Sydney couldn't believe she was ringing her birthday in at such a beautiful resort and was beyond grateful for Genevieve and Asher. They all were exhausted after the fight, especially Sydney, so they all crashed in their respective rooms: Asher and Genevieve in the master bedroom and Sydney in the bedroom that sat on the opposite end in the villa.

Chapter 14

Saturday, November 21sh

Later that morning Sydney enjoyed a snooze in as she drifted in and out of her slumber. Her bed was amazing and even more comfortable than the one she had already in the guesthouse. Sydney jerked awake once her eyes focused on the blurry figure in front of her and saw that it was Genevieve's eyes that were set on her, as if she came out of thin air. At some point in between consciousness Genevieve had slipped into the room with a serving tray of food and a small gift.

"Whoa there," she giggled as she placed a gentle hand on Sydney's arm. "Didn't mean to scare you. I just wanted to be the first to wish you a happy birthday, beautiful," she cooed as she bent down and gave Sydney a gentle peck on her lips.

Sydney sat up and smiled as she pulled the hanging scarf off her head and tossed it to the other side of the bed.

"Thank you, Genevieve. This is beautiful," she said, hoping that they were in the period of their relationship when morning breath wasn't offensive.

Sydney's eyes wandered over the beautiful spread that

Genevieve laid out in front of her that came equipped with a sea of beautiful orange lilies that laid all over her white comforter. She gasped as she took it all in before her eyes landed on a coral box to the side that Sydney knew had to be jewelry.

"Babe," Sydney said gently as she felt tears coming to her eyes. She had never had someone show this much effort and love before and she was taken aback.

"You deserve it all baby. Here," Genevieve said, grabbing the box and handing it to her, "open your gift."

"Gift? Like this wasn't enough," Sydney said waving her arms to the view outside of her bedroom window of the beautiful clear water and palm trees.

"Open it," Genevieve demanded, smiling.

Sydney smiled hard and did as she was told as she opened the box to a white and gold watch. Sydney gasped as she read the box that said *Audemars Piguet.*

"You got me an AP?!" Sydney squealed as she gawked at the watch, almost afraid to touch it. She had never seen one in one in real life.

"Relax, I got it for a bargain actually. Here let's put it on," Genevieve said as she eagerly took off the old watch on Sydney's arm and replaced it with the AP. "See, I can't have you walking around with that raggedy thing on you... not when you're mine. There, look at it, it's perfect!"

Sydney felt a sting at Genevieve referring to her watch as "raggedy." The old watch that she wore had sentimental value to Sydney as it was the only thing of her father's that she owned. She had been wearing that watch ever since she was about 15 years old and found it once rummaging through some old boxes.

"Genevieve, I don't know what to say..."

Sydney held her arm up in the air as she watched the sun hit the watch causing the mini diamonds to shine and glisten.

The watch felt both heavy and expensive on her and she hated to admit it, but it looked a lot better on her than her dad's worn leather black watch. She honestly wasn't even sure who her father's watch was made by, something she never worried about until this very moment.

"Sydney," Genevieve said trying to gain back Sydney's attention, "I just wanted to give you something special that you can look at every day and think of me."

"Thanks babe, but believe me, you are always on my mind," Sydney said, gently grabbing Genevieve's hand before taking it in her own.

"Well believe me you are always on mine too. Sydney... I love you. I know it has only been a short period of time, but it's the truth! I really, really do Sydney. And if you do not feel the same way, please do not feel compelled to say— "

"I love you too," Sydney blurted out. It was the truth, she felt that way for a while, but it was solidified last night once Genevieve catered and soothed her on the PJ. She felt so safe and terrified at the same time while laying in her arms.

"Do you?" Genevieve asked with a smile etched on her face and a twinkle in her eye.

"Yes, I have for a while now," Sydney began. "Why me Genevieve? Asher told me you've never been with another woman, why am I so special?"

Sydney had been wondering this for a while. Genevieve was sophisticated, sexy and one of the smartest people that she had ever met. She couldn't fathom why Genevieve wanted her out of all the other women and men she could have.

"Don't you ever let me hear you ask such a foolish question like that again," Genevieve said gently kissing Sydney's lips and placing a nurturing hand to her face."I love you for you Sydney. You wake something up inside of me that I have never felt before. I knew it since the first day you came falling into my book signing," she said giggling.

"I did not fall," Sydney laughed, feeling the tears well in her eyes.

In the back of her mind, she wondered what people would say if they knew how much her life drastically changed all within a few months. She went from a toxic relationship with a man she dated for most of her dating life to a thriving relationship with a married woman. She still couldn't believe it herself. This was her new life.

Genevieve laughed with her and rubbed her face. She had a twinkle in her eye and looked the most at ease that Sydney had ever seen her.

"Say it again," she whispered to Sydney.

"I love you Genevieve."

"Mmm," Genevieve hummed, "I love how that sounds. I love you too, Sydney."

Sydney turned her attention back to the tray of food on her bed and placed it on the nightstand before turning back to Genevieve and pulling the covers down beside her.

"Join me?" Sydney asked deviously.

Later on that day Sydney lounged about the pool soaking in as many rays as she could. After she and Genevieve had made love, yes, they made love now that it was established that they were in love, the duo slept away the rest of the morning until Asher came knocking on the door to announce that lunch had arrived. The two cleaned up and threw on their bikinis and headed outside to the lanai where the hotel's staff had laid out a beautiful lunch for them.

Genevieve and Sydney were both too lazy after their morning session to go shopping. Instead, Genevieve hired them a personal shopper who picked out a few pieces for them both for their trip. Sydney feared that the black string bikini that the stylist came back with exposed way too much of her naked body and felt as if she needed to be covered in a one-piece instead.

"Sydney, look at yourself! You are a knockout, and you deserve to show that beautiful figure of yours off. Besides, dieting with me has done your body good, look at you!" Genevieve had persuaded as the two looked at their reflection in Sydney's bathroom mirror.

She was right. Dieting with Genevieve by only eating the rabbit food that she ate had given Sydney a flatter stomach and smaller waist. She turned to the side to get a better view of her back and noticed that her small rolls that were once there, were now gone. Her already rounded hips seemed to have turned into toned ones that stood out. Sydney was still bottom heavy but had muscles bulging in her thighs which she could attribute to her runs with Asher three times a week. She almost didn't recognize herself. She was hot! She tucked one of the orange lilies from that morning behind her ear and did something she never did, snapped a shot for Instagram.

After a few hours in the sun, Genevieve had retreated back to her bedroom saying that she was feeling inspired and wanted to write a few pages for the book. She left Asher and Sydney outside as the two lounged and soaked up some rays while sipping on their mojitos. Genevieve was barely in the villa before Asher darted over to Sydney, lightly tapping her on her knee and holding up a rolled joint in his hand.

"You read my mind," Sydney said looking up at him while shielding her eyes.

Asher had tanned beautifully already; his white cool skin was tanned and warmed. He wore his long hair out and wild and thanks to the Tulum sun it looked as if he got some blonde highlights that ran wildly in his dark mane. Sydney never really noticed how attractive and fit Asher was, but she did now as he lit the weed and began to smoke it. She watched as his chiseled chest inhaled the smoke and she let her eyes wander down to his six pack that was so perfect it almost looked fake. Asher was fine, who knew?

"Damn," Asher said after he hit a series of coughs and tried to cover it with his fist.

Sydney laughed as she took the joint away from him and began to take a few hits herself. Dij's shit was always strong and Sydney knew she gave her something extra just because it was her birthday. Sydney took a long pull and savored it before she exhaled it.

This is the life, she thought to herself.

"Yeah, I got to get your girl's number. Haven't smoked anything like this since I was in Amsterdam earlier this year."

"You went to Amsterdam?!" she exclaimed, now turning her body to fully face him as she handed back the weed. "Be careful with that, big boy," she teased.

"Fuck you Syd," Asher smiled as he snatched it out of her hand.

"So, is this what it's like?"

"What?" Asher said, leaning back on his elbows as he blew smoke rings.

"Belonging to Genevieve. Sexing all day, receiving fancy gifts and jetting away for impromptu vacations?"

Asher let out a dry laugh as he pondered what Sydney asked.

"This life has its perks," he said carefully, "but it's important to keep your own identity. Don't get too wrapped up if you know what I mean."

"Yeah, I know what you mean," Sydney said as she glided her Christian Dior sunglasses back on her face and contemplated taking another nap.

"Do you now?" Asher asked rhetorically, eyeing her up and down.

"Yes, I do. Are you trying to say something?"

"Not at all Syd," he shook his head and laughed. "I just realized who you remind me of now with this new look."

"Who?"

"G, when she was about your age, down to the haircut," he said, shaking his head in disgust and passing her the weed to finish.

"Listen I got something booked for us, how about you get dressed and meet me in the living room."

"For just you and me?" she asked, confused as she wondered if the weed was making her hear things.

"Yup, I got some things lined up for today that I thought you would enjoy. Laying around on vacay is nice and all, but G and I have two totally different styles of vacationing. If you trust me, I would like to take you out on an adventure for your b-day. What do you say?"

"Can we bring the weed?"

"Phish," he said, waving her off and pulling his hair into a bun, "We have three joints rolled and ready, let's go on an adventure."

Chapter 15

Tuesday, December 1st

"Thanks, Ralph," Sydney said to Raphael as she tapped him on his shoulder before hopping out of the SUV.

"No problem, text me when you are paying and I will be waiting for you two in the front— "

"No Jean, I HATE that cover, that will not be the cover for my book and I do not care what the publisher wants," Genevieve yelled into her phone as she slammed the car door behind her. "Who in their everlasting mind thought that a PINK cover would fit my brand? Pink? Pink? Jean, do I really look like that kind of woman? Am I a child?"

Sydney and Raphael exchanged exasperated looks with one another. They were having quite a rough day with Genevieve today who seemed to snap at just about everyone who came into her path.

"Have a lovely lunch, ladies," he said, winking at them before driving off.

Sydney secretly wished that she could peel off with him too to avoid Genevieve, especially before going into Flamingo's.

Since the two had a few meetings today in Boston, Sydney wanted to be sure to make a reservation at her old restaurant in hopes of running into Cai. She had never called her back last month. She genuinely felt bad and missed her friend. She was no fool and knew that Cai would likely be less than enthused to see her after ghosting her. So, taking a page straight out of Genevieve's book, she decided to come with gifts from Tulum in tow. This was the beginning of her friend apology tour and India was next.

"Hi, we have reservations under Cross," Sydney said to the unfamiliar host once the two were inside. She quickly scanned the restaurant and smiled at how different the restaurant looked and felt now that she didn't work there. "Is Cai working today? Is it possible that we can sit in her section? I'm an old friend."

"No problem ma'am, would you like me to get her?" the young redheaded woman asked.

"No need, I'll surprise her."

"One moment ma'am, let me just make sure that the table is ready," the hostess said, scurrying off into the restaurant.

Sydney smiled at her replacement and could already tell that she did a hell of a better job than she had while there.

"Here Sydney," Genevieve said as she tossed her heavy black fur-lined trench coat at her to put away.

Without a word Sydney took her coat and rushed over to the coat check where she unloaded both of their coats just in time to get seated at the table. It was only a few minutes before Cai appeared at their table with a pitcher of ice-cold water. She was always a much better waitress than Sydney was.

"Hello and welcome to— SYD?!" Cai squealed mid-sentence.

"Cai!" Sydney yelled excitedly as she jumped to her feet to give Cai a hug.

"I am on the phone! Please keep it down," Genevieve said, giving the two the evil eye.

Sydney finally let Cai out of her embrace and grabbed her gift bags that sat on the floor and pulled Cai to the back of the restaurant all in one swift move. She smiled to herself as she pulled Cai through the crowded restaurant to the back where they could squeal as loud as they wanted, far, far away from Genevieve's phone call.

"Syd where you been girl, oh my God look at you! I almost didn't recognize you... where is your hair? Why you so skinny?!"

Cai had so many questions that Sydney didn't know where to start.

"Sorry girl, I know I've been a bit M.I.A. lately, life has just been so crazy!"

"Is everything okay?" Cai asked, concerned. She looked around to make sure no one saw before she plopped down next to Sydney. "You look so different. Your face is sunken in and you have no hair. What that lady do to you?"

"What... Cai... she's done nothing. I am fine. More than fine actually. I am great," Sydney said, stuttering and caught off guard. "In fact I just came back from Tulum and I brought you some gifts!" she chimed, placing the bags in Cai's lap and smiling.

Cai's face lit up as she reached into the black gift bag and pulled out a ceramic statue of a woman, a handmade woven dreamcatcher and a black and white scarf that was made by a little old woman Sydney met one day on the beach.

"Wow, thanks Syd," Cai said, smiling as she wrapped the scarf around her neck.

"No problem, and in this bag is a gift for your mother. I got her and my mom a book of popular Tulum recipes; make sure she gets that for me."

Sydney was proud of her gifts and hoped they would make up for lost time, though she knew it would be a reach that all would be forgiven with some souvenirs.

"I better get back to the table before dragon lady throws a fit," Cai said, snatching the scarf from around her neck and stuffing it back in the bag.

"Stop it, she's not that bad," Sydney lied. She knew that Genevieve was far too distracted with that phone call to even notice the two of them missing. "Besides I have the menu still memorized and I will give you both orders."

"Syd, are you really okay?"

Annoyed, Sydney now rolled her eyes and stood up.

"Cai, I am great! I've been dieting and working out a few times a week, I dropped a few pounds that is all," she said, spinning around to show her new physique and toned calves.

"It's not only that, your clothes, your hair... even how you speak now— "

"What's wrong with how I am talking?" Sydney asked, placing her hand on her hip. She heard the superiority in her voice as soon as the words left her mouth. But can you blame her? English wasn't even Cai's first language, and she should be the last person to judge someone based off how they spoke.

"That," Cai said pointing her chin at Sydney's hand clutching her hip. "You sound and look just like ... *her*. You look like you are two seconds away from calling the manager on me."

Sydney didn't like how Cai kept referring to Genevieve in a negative light, but she was not about to correct her and risk slipping and telling her about the real relationship the two shared that went way beyond work. In fact, Genevieve and Sydney were regularly sharing a bed now and Genevieve was sleeping with her way more than she did with Asher.

"You come in here with your all black and wearing *heels*.

You hate heels," Cai said, beginning to laugh,."And where is the color? The old Sydney had beautiful long braids and would always wear something funky like your boots or a bright scarf or something. Now you look... old."

Cai was never one to bite her tongue.

"Maybe you just don't like the new me, but I do," Sydney said defensively before folding her arms across her chest. She didn't like how Cai was making her feel.

"Look we better go, we will both have a skinny girl margarita, no salt or sugar. Don't bother bringing any bread out, we are not eating it this week," Sydney regretted saying it as soon as she saw Cai roll her eyes and hold back a smile.

"We will have the calamari salad, baked not fried. No appetizer either, oh and throw in the soup of the day for us both too. Please let whoever is in the back know that it's me they are cooking for so that they can throw a little extra love into it too."

"Sure Syd," Cai said, standing up and smoothing out her apron. "Thanks again for the gifts. I'm sorry for... I just worry."

"No need Cai, I'm good, girl. How about I call you later this week? I should be back up here this weekend to hang with India, how about you join us?"

"Sure. Just give me a call; I'm off this weekend."

"Sounds like a plan," Sydney said walking back to the table.

They both knew that they would not hear from one another anytime soon.

.....

Sydney glided into the perfect parking space in the garage. She climbed out of her car and rolled her hoodie over her head. To no one's surprise, it was freezing even colder than it had been the day before. Luckily for her, she had gotten a spot close to the entrance of the mall. Sydney rushed to the back of her car to pop the trunk and snatched India's gift of a dozen handmade scarves, a book on healing she picked up from the airport and a bottle of some expensive Mexican tequila. Sydney sashayed into the mall, trying to be careful to not trip over her five-inch stiletto boots that she had just bought with Genevieve the other day.

Sydney entered the mall and immediately felt like she was in a Christmas snow globe. The mall was covered in white fake snow and had just about every corner of the mall crowded with Christmas decorations. Sydney smiled to herself while looking at each storefront decorated with flashy Christmas decorations, looking as though they wanted to outdo the other. She slowly pulled her hood down off of her head while she enjoyed this bit of nostalgia and reflected back on her years of being a teenage shopper here and then eventually working here at Lilian's.

Speaking of Lilian's, she thought to herself as she took a hard right to go up the escalator. She would take the long way to India's new job to ensure that she got a good look at Lilian's. Hell, who was she kidding, she wanted a good look at Angel, and better yet she wanted him to get a good look at her. India had told her how he got demoted after everything went down with her quitting and the shoplifter incident, and Sydney couldn't wait to see it for herself.

Just as she stepped off the escalator and saw a glimpse of Angel's frosted blonde tips bopping away behind the cash register, she felt someone grab her arm to get her attention.

"Syd? Bae, I knew it was you!"

Sydney turned around to see Shawn. He was wearing a security uniform and looked about ten pounds heavier than she remembered, but it was him.

"Wow look at you," he said as his eyes wandered over her from head to toe, "I saw this girl come in here with this hood and I said to myself, 'I know that ain't Syd.'"

Sydney snatched her arm back and adjusted her purse that

was falling off her shoulder. She didn't know he worked here; India never told her that.

"I didn't know you worked here now."

"Yeah, I started about a month ago... damn Syd, I feel like it's been forever. Can we talk?"

"No," she said without hesitation. Something she had learned from Genevieve.

She glared at him to watch his face flinch as if she just punched him in it. She wanted to continue, "I have no interest in talking to you and I've been telling you that for months. Stop calling me." Sydney realized she was standing there with her hand on her hips the same way she had yesterday when talking to Cai. She immediately straightened herself up.

"Oh, I see how it is," he said, wounded as he backed away and rubbed his scruffy beard that sat in patches on his face.

"How's the baby, Shawn?" Sydney asked, enjoying this power she felt over him. She never stood up to Shawn. Well except that last time when she poured ice-cold water over him. She'd never been more confident in her life that she didn't need him. She needed him to know that too.

"Oh, you got jokes now?"

"Your girl must be about seven or eight months now. Nice to see you finally got a job. It seemed like it was damn near impossible when we were together."

"Yea, well a nigga got a little more motivation now, you feel me? It helps when you have a good woman in your corner," he said, attempting to hurt her.

Sydney laughed in his face and waved him off as if she had better places to be than sitting there talking to him outside of Lilian's.

"All that tells me is your ass can't mooch off her ass. Kudos to her, maybe she had more sense than I did taking care of your bum ass."

"And who do you think you are? You were in love with my

so-called 'bum-ass' not too long ago. Just 'cuz you got a new haircut and clothes you think you better than someone? I guess the rumors about you are true."

"Rumors?" Sydney asked, entertained.

"Yea, the rumors that you up there suckin' on clits and dicks in that big ole house you staying at."

Sydney felt her stomach twist and tried her best to not break her composure. Who did he hear that from?

"Fuck you, Shawn."

"Yeah fuck you too Syd. People talk, be careful who you call your friends out here. I'm sure that big old fancy *author* of yours don't want her business in these streets. Humble yourself, baby girl, before you back struggling like the rest of us."

Sydney felt her blood begin to boil but refused to give Shawn the satisfaction of causing a scene in the mall when it was as packed as it was. She had a lot to process and needed to get away fast.

"Moral of the story, stop calling me. I am done with your cheatin' bum ass and want nothing to do with you. Look, I got places to be," she said, picking up the gift bags, "I'm meeting with India to give her a few gifts from my latest trip to Tulum. As in Mexico. Have a nice life Shawn and congrats on your little job," she said, turning so briskly on her heels that she thought she may fall over. She briefly peeked up to see Angel standing in the storefront window with his mouth open and mannequin in hand. Sydney couldn't tell if his mouth was open from witnessing that small fight or because of the new her, but she winked at him anyway in her haste to get away.

"Some friend you are, India got fired from Jewels two weeks ago," Shawn yelled from behind her.

Sydney pretended as if she didn't hear him as she continued to walk down the busy hallway towards India's job. She whipped the corner to find out that he was right, and she wasn't there. Sydney made sure to even ask one of the employees working in the store that night and they confirmed that India had been let go a few weeks ago due to not coming in for work.

Sydney made it back to her car and dialed India's number just to find it going straight to voicemail. She was so confused about why India didn't tell her earlier. Sure, India could barely keep a job, but that was before when she had Dij to fall back on. Now, she was supporting herself while going to school and struggling to do so. And after her breakup, the loss of this job must've felt like the ultimate punch in the gut for her.

Sydney knew that the two hadn't spoken as much lately, but she didn't think she had missed that much in her life. Sydney sat in the car a few more minutes trying to decide if she would take the forty-minute car ride to India's apartment to find out what was going on. Just as she made up her mind to travel to meet India she heard her Bluetooth ring and hoped to see that India was returning her call.

"Hello?" Sydney said, answering the call while backing out of her space.

"Hi, beautiful," Genevieve breathed deeply into the phone.

"Hi babe," Sydney said, feeling a smile creep across her face from the sound of her voice. "What are you up to?"

"Well, I am sitting at home wondering what my Sydney is up to," she said calmly. Sydney could tell that she was drinking.

"I'm missing you, that's what I'm up to," Sydney said honestly as she glided her car to jump on the interstate to head to India's home.

"Come home," Genevieve said bluntly.

"Babe," Sydney began to whine, hating that she was caught out at such a horrible time, "I have to run to India's and I will be right there. I just found out she lost her job! And then I got into a horrible fight with Shawn— "

"Sydney," Genevieve said, scolding, "I do not care about those people. I am home, in your tub, naked. I am sitting up to my chin in bubbles and am on my third glass of champagne, baby come home... mama's had a long day."

Sydney took a deep sigh and eased her way back to the exit lane. She knew that India needed her, but so did Genevieve. Besides, she wasn't sure how she would be able to get into India's building if she wasn't even answering the phone.

"I got a surprise for you too... and it's waterproof," Genevieve purred.

Sydney thought it over and decided that she wouldn't be of much use to India tonight. She would check on her first thing in the morning, she swore it to herself.

.....

Sydney and Genevieve stumbled clumsily through the house and into the kitchen. It was barely nine am and the two were awake and starving. Once Sydney arrived home last night the two reheated the tub and spent the rest of their evening enjoying their new toy. They had passed out naked and wet in Sydney's bed and had only been awake for a few minutes before they decided to make their debut into the main house.

They walked into the kitchen giggling like schoolgirls, with Genevieve's arms wrapped protectively around Sydney's waist.

"Thank you for last night," Genevieve whispered in Sydney's ears before nuzzling and kissing her on the spot on Sydney's neck that always turned her on.

"And thank you for this morning," Genevieve said, gliding across the kitchen and standing on her tippy toes to lightly peck Asher on the lips. He smiled and continued to scramble the eggs on the stove.

As if on cue to annoy Genevieve, Maverick came barking and panting from the library with a toy in his mouth. He made a beeline for Sydney and tried to jump in her arms, lick her face and push the toy into her hand all at once.

"Maverick!" Sydney squealed, too delighted to scold him for forgetting all of his training.

"That damn dog," Genevieve said disgustedly as she sat down to the kitchen island where Asher had laid out her latte and morning paper.

"He loves her," Asher said, turning the stove off and transferring the eggs to the serving bowl. "Alright ladies, I'm trying out a new banana French toast recipe. As usual, please be kind and tell me what you think," Asher said, setting two plates onto the kitchen island for them.

"Asher, you spoil me. I don't know how I will ever be able to live with another man again," Sydney said, running over and plopping down to her plate.

"You never will. You're mine and I am all the man you will ever need," Genevieve cooed as she leaned in closer to Sydney.

"I forgot how annoying new couples are," Asher said, rolling his eyes at their corniness.

"That's right," Sydney said leaning in for a kiss.

"Not until you wash that dog saliva off your cheek," Genevieve said, blocking her kiss with her slender hand.

"Ouch," Asher said laughing as he escorted Maverick out. "Come on man, you know the rule. The queen is back. I'll get you after breakfast."

Maverick whined as he obeyed Asher and went back into the library with his head down. Slowly but surely, they were getting better with one another, and Sydney smiled to herself before replacing it with a frown.

"Why is your face like that? It's because of the dog isn't it? See Ash, I'm not the only one who hates him," Genevieve fake whined.

"Nice try G," he said, shaking his head and digging back into his plate. "So?"

"Perfect," Genevieve and Sydney said in unison with their mouths full.

They weren't lying either. Though, they were cheating on their diet and having bread for the first time in weeks, so anything in the carbohydrate family was likely to make them orgasm.

"Nice," Asher said, obviously pleased with himself. "So I know it's not the food; why the face?"

Sydney bit her lip and hesitated on if she should share, but she did. She told them about bringing the gifts for India to the mall just to end up arguing with Shawn.

"He said people are ... talking about me, saying how I changed and think I'm better than them. That's not true. I mean I have grown, but I'm still the same," Sydney had decided to play it safe and not mention the things he said about Genevieve and Asher. Not yet at least until she spoke to India to figure out why her ex knew so much about her personal life.

"Oh Sydney, who cares?" Genevieve said, yawning and finishing her latte.

"I care," Sydney said meekly. "And he's not the only one. Cai said it to me too the other day. It's like people don't even recognize me."

"This is what happens when you level up, not everyone is going to move to that next level with you. I say good riddance," Genevieve said, blowing it off.

"I think what my wife means to say is, maybe you have changed Sydney; is that so bad though? Isn't that what life is all about? Who wants to be stagnant? And look at who said that, your ex-boyfriend that *you* broke up with."

"Yea, you're right. Fuck him," she said, feeling more confident and sitting up straighter.

"Then again," Asher said sitting down on the stool next to her, "you have to make sure you're changing for the better. You don't want to lose sight of yourself and what makes you, *you*. Especially if a good friend like Cai told you that," he said, pausing before finishing his sentence, "I wish I would've listened."

"And what does that mean?" Genevieve asked, placing the paper down and darting her eyes swiftly to Asher. She sat on edge as if she were waiting for those words to come out of his mouth before she pounced.

Uh-oh, Sydney thought to herself as she stood up to clear the plates.

"It's just that sometimes it's easy to get wrapped up in your... significant other. It happened to me, trust me I get it," he chuckled dryly. Oblivious to the trap he was walking himself into.

"When?"

"When what?" he asked, turning to finally look her in the face.

"When did you lose these so-called *friends,* due to a significant other?"

"Pshh, started in grad school and they have been dropping like flies ever since."

Ouch, Sydney thought as she turned her back and debated running back to the guest house.

"Oh, so I am to blame for the fact that your very close and very inept group of *boys* decided they didn't want to play with you anymore once I made you a man? So that's what you're saying?"

"G," Asher said as he took his glasses off and placed his fingertips to the bridge of his nose, something that Sydney had recently learned that he did to try to calm himself down. "Cut it out will ya? Stop putting fuckin' words in my mouth. Like I said, I can relate! I know what she is going through."

"Hmph," was all Genevieve said as she slammed her paper down and walked out of the kitchen.

"And for the record you did not 'make me a man'," Asher yelled at her, losing steam by the time he finished.

"Wow," Sydney said as she began to load the dishwasher.

"How bad do you think it is?" Asher said, looking away in the direction that Genevieve walked off to.

"Well my friend," she sighed as she walked over to him and sympathetically patted his hand, "I think you might as well get a sleeping bag. Because you are about to be sleeping in that library with Maverick for the next few nights."

Chapter 16

Saturday, December 5th

After days of begging, Sydney finally succeeded in getting India to meet up with her to have a much-needed talk. India had been dodging Sydney like the plague and it had been weeks since her birthday mishap. Sydney not only wanted to make amends for ditching her, but she also wanted to get to the bottom of how Shawn knew so much about her new life. She had sat on it ever since she saw him and always came back to the same possible conclusion. India told him.

Sydney hoped she was wrong. Her suspicions that India wasn't as drunk as she thought the night began to grow the longer it took for her to get ahold of her. Sydney hoped that Shawn's intel came from him doing his own snooping versus having it come from India. But how else would he have known?

Ever since she realized that India could be talking behind her back and putting her in a legal violation of her contract, Sydney had been uneasy. Not only would her best friend's transgression of talking to an ex go against girl code, but it also would be like a direct punch in the gut for Sydney. There was no one else that she trusted as much as India. She also knew that if Genevieve found out, it would end their relationship and leave Sydney back at square one. There was too much to lose.

It was around nine at night and Sydney was glad that she had the night off to herself. Vicky was in town for the weekend, so Genevieve would be preoccupied for most of it. Sydney couldn't help but to secretly wonder if the two of them had something going on in the past. She couldn't see it, but then again, you never knew.

Sydney walked down her stairs and looked at India, who sat quietly on the couch in her one-piece black bathing suit and matching cover up. She swiped away on her phone with one hand while she used the other one to balance the faux-loc bun on top of her hair.

Sydney had finally gotten India to answer the phone earlier that day. She had to bribe her with an open crib and new jacuzzi, but it worked. After weeks of not seeing each other, the duo were back together. But things seemed strained.

"You ready, girl?" Sydney asked. The two were hanging back in the house wasting time, both afraid to brave the freezing temperature outside before getting to the just-installed jacuzzi.

"I guess," she sighed as she tightened the coat around her and grabbed the bottle of Hennessy. "We've let it warm up long enough."

"It's only been thirty minutes," Sydney joked sarcastically as they inched towards her front door and took a deep breath. "Last one there is a rotten egg!"

Sydney jetted off through the door feeling the cold air whip through her coat and causing her to squeal. She ran the small loop around the pool and could see the steamy jacuzzi just yards away.

"Move bitch!" India laughed as she pushed past Sydney

and kicked off her sneakers and coat before jumping into the jacuzzi.

Sydney's teeth chattered as she ripped away her coat and slid out of her Ugg slides before gracefully stepping into the tub.

"Bitch!" she yelled, teeth chattering.

"Here, let's take a shot," India said, taking the bottle to the head before passing it to Sydney so she could do the same.

Sydney felt the warmth instantly go to her head and handed the bottle back to India before allowing her body to fully submerge in the tub. She could finally feel her body loosen up.

"How does it feel?" she asked India.

"Marvelous," India said with her head back and eyes closed.

The two sat like that for a few minutes in awkward silence. Sydney wasn't sure how to get the conversation started and found it hard to talk to India for the first time ever in their friendship. She decided to use an ice breaker and reached behind her to pull out a blunt and lighter from her coat pocket. She inhaled deeply and prayed that it would help to calm her nerves.

"Oh bitch, are we sharing?" India said peeking up and scooting over closer to Sydney.

Sydney giggled and took another puff before passing it to India, who inhaled deeply. A little too deeply, as it led her into a series of coughs.

"Damn girl, where you get this from? Their weed is different out here in the boonies," she said passing it back to Sydney.

Sydney laughed and took another hit. This was actually the last bit of her birthday weed and she was happy to share it with India. She felt herself begin to relax.

"It shouldn't be so foreign to you; it's from Dij."

"Dij?"

Sydney knew she messed up from the high-pitch voice India used to say Dij's name.

"When did you see her?" India asked, turning her body to face Sydney.

"A few weeks ago," Sydney answered hesitantly.

India rolled her eyes and began to shake her head, "So I guess girl code just went out the window, huh?"

"India, I didn't think it would be that big of a deal. We just needed some weed before the trip."

"Syd, if I'm not talking to her that means you ain't talking to her. Then your ass had the nerve to see her the same day that you ditched me!"

"India, I have apologized a million times for my birthday. Look, we are together now; can we make the most of it? Besides we were only there a few minutes and the whole time she kept asking me about you."

India folded her arms and pouted before turning Sydney's way and questioning, "What did she ask?"

"She asked how you were, how was school and where you were working at," Sydney said, smiling and leaning in remembering how Dij's face lit up when she asked about her. "She misses you, girl. I really think you should give her another shot and hear her out— "

"Yeah well I don't remember asking for your dating advice, Syd," she said harshly as she grabbed the bottle and took another swig.

"What is up with you?" Sydney snapped.

"What you mean?" India asked, not looking at her.

"I mean you acting like this. You can't tell me who I can and cannot see India, grow up."

"I know you ain't telling someone to 'grow up'," India said cackling. "Girl, just a few months ago I was giving you money to keep your lights on. Don't play with me."

"That was low," Sydney said, hurt.

"Well..."

"You're such a hypocrite. You get all mad at me for seeing your ex, when you up there telling mine all my fuckin' business!"

There it was. Not how Sydney planned to confront her with this information. But between the hostile environment, the Hennessey and her period being on, it was time for everything to come to a head.

"What?" India said, spinning back around to Sydney with a bewildered look on her face.

"You heard me. You the one with some damn nerve. I was going to let it go but fuck it. I ran into Shawn the other day. Thanks for the heads up that he works at the mall now, by the way," Sydney said, feeling like she was on fire. "Anyway, that man sat there and told me all about *my* life. How the fuck would he know about that India? How could you?"

"Sydney, you got me all the way fucked up if you think I would ever speak to that bum ass nigga. I don't know what you're talking about, but I do know you need to calm down."

"Or what?" Sydney said, puffing out her chest and looking India square in her eyes.

"Nah," India said, standing up and walking over to the edge of the tub to get out. "This lady got you feeling yourself now. Sydney, have you ever thought that maybe he knows your life because it's all over your damn Instagram? Damn girl, I can't get up there and not see a post from your ass! Maybe people are tired of seeing you flaunting all of this lady's money with your new look, clothes, and attitude. Every time you post it's either of you chasing her ass or you spending her money."

Sydney cringed knowing that it was slightly true. After receiving all of those likes and comments on her swimsuit post, she had gone a little IG crazy and started documenting her life.

"Your dumb ass tags her every time too, like we get it.

RELAX! Every time I go on IG I see a post from you and about how you are virtually on her dick— "

"Excuse me," Genevieve said.

Her voice cut through the cold night like glass and Sydney felt herself gasp. Behind them stood Genevieve and Vicky, both draped in their mink furs.

"Sydney, what is going on?" Genevieve asked, not removing her eyes from India.

"My friend and I are having a private conversation," India said, all attitude.

"Not like this, not in my house. Listen, India, I don't know where you are from, but we do not do *ghetto* shit like this out here. I could hear your voices all the way from the driveway," Genevieve said, trying to keep a steady tone.

"Ghetto?" India yelled, zipping her coat up.

"India?" Vicky yelled. "India and Sydney? What y'all some strippers?" Vicky asked, laughing at her own joke as she playfully slapped Genevieve's arm. "I bet these hoes ain't even step out the damn country but they named some India and Sydney," Vicky cackled.

Sydney knew that this would end badly and tried to diffuse the situation quickly.

"Hey, hey Genevieve...and Vicky," Sydney said, climbing out of the jacuzzi and stepping into her shoes, "We're sorry we just got a little loud. We'll head back to the house," Sydney said.

"No. Your guest is going to leave now. We know what happens when you two drink and stay late," she said, eyeing the bottle of Hennessy that sat on the ground.

"I'm not going anywhere. I am not Sydney. You cannot dictate where I am going," India said, snapping her neck. "Damn you already hijacked my plans for her birthday. Can you please spare her for a few more hours?" she asked mockingly, pleading.

"Oh, is that right?" Genevieve asked, stepping closer to India while folding her arms. "Well you are correct. You are not Sydney, so no, I can't tell you what to do."

Sydney felt like she was just slapped in the face hearing her say that, but she stood there and continued to say nothing.

"But what I can do is call the police to get your hood rat ass out of my house. Sydney doesn't need to belittle herself to hang out with the likes of you anymore. And I will make sure of it," she said, reaching in her coat's pocket for what Sydney imagined to be her phone.

"Okay, we all need to just calm down," Sydney said, finally finding her voice and stepping in the middle of the two.

"Seriously, how about we all just get back into the jacuzzi and continue the party. The one with the dreads is cute," Vicky slurred while leaning on Genevieve's shoulder and dancing to a beat she only heard in her head.

She's drunk. Shocker, Sydney thought to herself as she began putting her coat on.

"Sydney, handle this before I do," Genevieve said, drilling her eyes into India.

Sydney turned and looked at India, who was beginning to tap her foot. Most people would think it was due to the cold temperature, but Sydney knew it was a telltale sign that India was seconds away from laying hands on someone.

"India, come on, maybe you should just go," Sydney said, defeated.

"Syd, are you serious right now?" India looked dumbfounded. "Are you fuckin' serious right now?!"

"India, look, she is going to call the cops and it's not that deep."

"We were in the middle of a fight, Sydney. Have a damn backbone for once!"

"I do believe she has asked you to leave. Please hurry, you

two do not want to catch pneumonia out here," Genevieve said matter-of-factly.

"Sydney you are wild if you let this lady tell you what to do. Don't you see she is just manipulating you? She's trying to ice you out completely from your old life. I don't even know who you are anymore," she yelled, exasperated and hurt. "It's either me or her, Syd. I'm not playing."

"Tsk, tsk , tsk," Genevieve breathed behind Sydney. "She is so jealous of you, Sydney."

Sydney's heart dropped to her stomach as she stood in the middle of this feud. She looked from India to Genevieve and bit her lip. Genevieve was right.

"India... don't make me choose," she said meekly, swatting tears from her eyes. "It's funny how now that the tables have turned, I am the one with the problem. I got it together, I make an income, and I don't need you anymore. And you *can't stand it*, can you?"

"What you tryna say, Syd?" India asked, her voice noticeably shaking.

"India... maybe you are just jealous..." Sydney whispered.

"Say no more. I see what it is. Goodbye Sydney," India said as she made her way to the front of the house with tears noticeably running down her face.

Chapter 17

Friday, December 11th

Sydney sighed as she slouched deeper into the leather couch in the home's theater room. The projection screen had just been installed earlier that day and Sydney couldn't wait to sulk her Friday night away while watching some corny Christmas movie. At her feet Maverick whined and panted as he sat watching her from the floor.

"Come on Mackie," she said, patting the seat next to her. He gladly jumped up beside her and rested his head on her lap as she petted him sadly. Sydney felt as if she were at rock-bottom ever since her fight with India. Neither of the two had reached out to one another since. And even though Genevieve assured her that she made the right decision, Sydney felt like shit. She missed her best friend, she missed her sister, and she hated how she treated her that night. India must've felt so attacked and alone.

To make matters worse, last night Sydney and Genevieve got into another fight. The two of them were at dinner going over the details of Genevieve's book. Unbeknownst to Sydney, Genevieve had been on a writing spree ever since Tulum and had actually finished it while abroad. The two of them had gone out to celebrate that night and Genevieve kept reminding Sydney that the power of their love is what motivated her to finish the book.

Somewhere in the night, in between caviar and wine, the conversation led to possible book covers for the next manuscript.

"Tell me Sydney, when you bought my book from the book store, did it just jump out at you? The publisher thinks my next book needs to be hot pink. I mean honestly, do I look like a hot pink kinda gal?" Genevieve had laughed, while she eased her hand up Sydney's skirt under the table.

"Honestly, I didn't buy your book. I guess I kind of stole it from my job."

The two had argued the whole way home. Genevieve was infuriated with her that she didn't buy her book. In her eyes, Sydney single-handedly sabotaged her sales, even though she was a bestselling author despite the fact.

By the time Sydney woke up and reported to work the next morning, she found a note from Genevieve saying she had dashed away with her favorite fuck-toy, Finn. And here she was now 24 hours later watching movies by her lonesome.

Sydney aimlessly scrolled through her Instagram feed, not not looking to see if Genevieve had posted anything. She saw a light turn on around her, and to her surprise, saw a man bun accompanied with a smile.

"Woof!" Maverick barked, excited as he jumped off of Sydney's lap to jump and dance at Asher's feet.

"Hey man, I missed you," Asher said, bending over and rough-housing Maverick.

"What are you doing back? I thought you were gone for the next few days?" Sydney asked, peeking over the couch, too lazy to get up.

Asher had been across the country at some work event in

Oregon and wasn't expected back for another few days. She was pleasantly surprised to see him home so early though.

"News travels fast. Heard that G was off with our favorite fuck-boy, so I knew that meant you two must be fighting again."

"Yup," Sydney sighed as she turned back around to face the screen. "Thanks for coming back, homie."

"Wanna talk about it?"

"Nope," Sydney said honestly.

"Cool, me neither. I came with gifts," he said in a sing-song voice as he sat down next to her.

"Oh, I love gifts!" Sydney squealed and clapped her hands.

Asher pulled his backpack off and opened it on his lap. From the bag, he pulled out mini bags of candies that Sydney could only assume were edibles, and a bottle of Gentleman Jack.

"I brought back a few of your favorite things," he said, passing them off to her.

"Hmph, I think whiskey is more of your favorite thing. But thanks, this will do," she said, opening up a bag of gummies and popping a blue one into her mouth, before handing him the bag of candy.

It took exactly forty-eight minutes before their edibles hit them. They knew because they kept count while watching *A Christmas Story*.

"Is this our thing now? Getting high and drunk together when she isn't around?" Sydney laughed as she laid her head down onto Asher's lap. The room was spinning, and she couldn't get it to stop no matter how many times she tried to stop the moving by holding on tightly to the furniture.

"Why not? It's nice to do this with someone. G won't anymore," he said with his head laid back and a boyish grin on his face.

"Genevieve used to smoke the 'reefer'?" Sydney joked, covering her mouth from her loud laughs.

"Shit, she used to be the biggest pothead," Asher said laughing. "But don't tell her I told you that. She would kill me."

"I won't," Sydney said, wiping tears from her eyes that came from laughing so hard.

"I'm serious, Syd. My ass would be grass. G focuses so much on making it look like she is perfect. Like she has the perfect life. It gets old after a while. I know you get that."

"Shit, you know I do," Sydney said, reaching her hand up to dap him in agreement.

"Ah fuck it, time for another shot! Lift up," Asher said as he sat up.

"I can't, it's so cozy here. You should try it," she hiccupped, sending them both laughing.

"I gotcha," he said mischievously as he carefully grabbed the bottle and poured some whiskey into a shot glass. "Okay I am going to lift your head up. All you have to do is sip."

"Gotcha," Sydney laughed as she felt his fingers wiggle underneath her head and gently raise it up.

The shot glass reached her lips and Asher gently turned it up as the liquor poured in her mouth and down her throat. He placed the glass down and continued to smile at her.

"Perfect," Asher said gently as his eyes roamed down to Sydney's lips.

Sydney looked back at him and returned the friendly smile. From behind her head, she could feel Asher gently rubbing her scalp with his thumb. It felt both soothing and nice and sent tingles all over her body. Before she thought about it, she felt a moan escape her mouth from the scalp massage.

"That's nice," Sydney whispered before closing her eyes.

After a few moments she opened her eyes to see Asher still peering down at her. The energy in the room had suddenly shifted. Asher seemed to sense it too as he placed the shot glass on the other side of him and moved his hand to the side of Sydney's face where he gently began to rub her cheek. His tenderness surprised Sydney, and she looked up into his eyes almost to confirm that the moment was real, and that this was him.

She reached up and removed his black-framed glasses and placed them behind her before reaching up and grabbing his face just as he pulled her in closer to him. Their first kiss was both tender and timid. Their lips touched one another softly as if afraid that they were invading the other's space. Once Sydney felt her lips on Asher's, she felt fire all over her body and pulled him in closer to her as she kissed him deeper. Sydney felt Asher's tongue ease into her mouth and slowly caress her own, sending trembles to her thighs. She then, in return, bit his bottom lip which led to a low moan escaping from somewhere deep within him.

Beneath her back Sydney could feel Asher's dick begin to swell and she imagined her panties were soaked. In the back of her mind, she kept telling herself to stop, but she couldn't. It felt so right and natural, and most importantly it felt amazing due to the vices in their system.

Asher's right hand grabbed Sydney's throat and gave it a light squeeze before he began to kiss her deeper. Sydney moaned in delight as she felt her legs begin to quiver harder. It wasn't long before Asher's hand ended up underneath her leggings and in between her thighs.

"Fuck," Asher whispered as he felt her wetness.

"Ash, wait... stop," Sydney said abruptly, pushing him off of her and sitting up. "What are we doing? This isn't right," she said.

"What's wrong with it?" Asher asked, trying to shield the massive boner peeking out from his cargos with a couch pillow.

"I think I'm going to go... yeah, I gotta go. Goodnight Ash," Sydney said, jumping over a sleeping Maverick and scurrying out of the room.

Chapter 18

Sunday, December 13th

Sydney laid in the darkness and looked up at the night sky through the skylight on her bedroom's ceiling. It was somewhere between 10 p.m. and 2 a.m. and outside it looked like it was beginning to rain. Which would mean another nasty, slush-filled day in Boston, since it had already been snowing earlier. Sydney was slightly grateful that the weather would match her mood; she was still miserable. She sat up and turned her pillow over to the other side as she lightly fluffed it.

Looks like another sleepless night, Sydney thought to herself as she tossed herself back on the pillow.

Genevieve had been gone for a few days now. Besides her sending Sydney a photo of her half-naked on the beach in a hot-pink bikini, the irony was not lost on Sydney, she had had no communication with her. Sydney felt the familiar feeling of hurt and longed for Genevieve to come home so that they could talk. She hated the power she had over her. But more importantly she dreaded how she would feel if Genevieve was really through with her for good.

A crackle of thunder and lightning made Sydney jump as her pitch-dark room lit up for a few seconds. She sighed and flipped her pillow again and balled up her fist and punched it. She flopped back down and tried to get the images of Genevieve frolicking on the beach with Finn out of her mind.

Just as she felt herself begin to doze off, Sydney felt her stomach growl loudly.

"Ugh," she moaned, not being able to catch a break tonight. Ever since she and Asher had kissed, she had been avoiding the main house. Which naturally meant that she was left starving in her kitchen-less guest house. Sydney still hadn't processed what happened with the two of them the other night. She was ashamed and embarrassed.

Asher probably thinks I'm an idiot. What if he told Genevieve? she wondered as she threw herself onto her side and tried to squeeze her eyes shut to chase sleep.

She knew that she wasn't totally to blame for the other night and reminded herself that even though she kissed him first, he kissed her back, hard. Sydney smiled to herself as she remembered how his lips felt on hers and the feel of his prickly beard growing back on his cheeks. She missed that feeling, something she hadn't realized was missing until now. The roughness of a man.

If Sydney were being completely honest with herself, she would even admit how much she enjoyed that kiss with Asher. And how much she wanted it to happen again.

What would Genevieve think? She would kill us, she pondered.

Despite Asher and Sydney both being in a polyamorous relationship, they were not in a relationship together. To most, this wouldn't be a complicated matter; it would be ideal. But for those who have been with a woman like Genevieve, you know that this is not an option. Genevieve did not like to share her toys. And to be honest, Sydney wasn't sure she could willingly share her with someone else in that capacity. To Sydney, Asher and Genevieve's marriage was something far left from what the two of them shared with one another. Sure, she'd seen sweet little romantic gestures between the two, but she'd never seen the raw passion and lust between the two like she saw in her and Genevieve's relationship.

Desperate for sleep and a break from her own thoughts, Sydney finally broke and pulled out her silver vibrator. She cozied back in bed and cranked it up to level four before hoisting up her oversized t-shirt and trailing the vibrator over her left nipple, around her navel and finally down in between her legs.

Sydney instantly gasped and arched her back as she saw Asher flash in her mind. She tried to brush away the image to only have another image of herself and him kissing as his hand traveled in between her legs. Sydney felt his lips on hers and bit hard into her own as she felt herself verging.

Suddenly she heard her bedroom door slowly open and felt her stomach drop.

Ash? she thought but didn't dare to say.

"It's me, Sydney," Genevieve whispered in the dark as she took off her hooded trench coat and tossed it on the chair.

"What are you doing here?" Sydney asked, still clamping her covers in her hands from fear. She must've been dreaming and passed out while still on the vibrator. This couldn't be real.

"Shh," Genevieve said as she slid naked out of her house robe and under the covers with Sydney.

"When did you get here?" Sydney asked, still confused as Genevieve placed a cold shaking hand on Sydney's face and yanked it towards hers.

Genevieve kissed her hard and deep before suddenly stopping and reaching under the covers to pull out the pulsating vibrator that laid at Sydney's side.

Sydney and Genevieve looked at it and then each other

before bursting out in laughter. Genevieve turned it off and tossed it over her shoulder.

"Missed me, huh?"

"You have no idea," Sydney said hungrily as she pulled Genevieve on top of her and kissed her neck before sucking on her bare breast. Sydney clawed at Genevieve as if someone was threatening to take her away. Genevieve returned the favor and yanked Sydney's t-shirt off before reaching her hand down to play with Sydney's throbbing clit.

"Babe," Sydney squealed, excited about the familiar touch. Just as she opened her eyes back up, she saw Asher standing and watching in the dark. Even in the dark, the two locked eyes. They held their gaze while Genevieve played with Sydney before easing her middle finger into her. Not until Sydney gasped did she look up and realize Sydney's eyes weren't on her.

Suddenly all three of them froze and stared at each other silently. Asher stood in the doorway with a long sleeve shirt on, soaking wet from the rain. He was just in boxers and his house-slippers, it looked as if he just ran out of the house. He had a look of guilt on his face as he looked back and forth between Sydney and Genevieve.

He told her, Sydney thought as her heart began to race and Genevieve turned around to look down at Sydney, who still laid in her arms.

"Asher... come," Genevieve said while locking eyes with Sydney before pulling the covers back and licking down Sydney's trembling body.

Asher did as he was told as he pulled his shirt over his head, tied his wild soaked hair into a bun and slipped out of his wet shoes and boxers. Within seconds he was in bed beside a naked Sydney who felt very self-conscious. She couldn't run if she wanted to. Genevieve had her pinned down as her tongue reached her navel and began to move further down south.

Asher did a deep sigh as he watched Genevieve and grabbed his dick in his hand. Sydney was eye-level to it from where she lay, and she must admit, she was impressed. She had never seen a white man naked in person, and was glad that that stereotype was just that.

Genevieve stuck up her middle finger and placed it in her mouth as she sucked loudly on it to get it wet again. She looked up at them and nodded at Asher just as she eased her finger back into Sydney, whose body began to convulse from the pleasure. Her previous shyness instantly disappeared. Following the unsaid order from Genevieve, Asher swooped down and gently grabbed Sydney's head to face him.

"You okay?" he asked gently as he rubbed his thumb on the side of her face.

Sydney shook her head knowing that this was Asher asking for her permission to join in. He kissed her first this time and placed his naked, cold and wet body as close to her as he could while he played and twirled her nipples in his hand. Sydney moaned into his mouth and grabbed Genevieve's head from below as she felt her begin to eat her out in the way that always drove her wild.

"Oh my God," Sydney yelled, breaking away from Asher's kiss to gasp in pleasure.

Asher dipped his head to Sydney's breast as he sucked and teased her hard nipple with his tongue. Sydney had never had a threesome in her life and reflected briefly on Shawn's harsh words not too long ago. Was he right?

She felt her back begin to arch as she dug herself deeper into Genevieve's wet mouth. She was near again and refused to miss this one. Sydney came so hard her whole body shook from her shoulders all the way down to her toes. She heard Genevieve laugh as she sat up and wiped her face. Seconds later, Sydney came back down from her daze and opened her eyes to see Asher entering Genevieve from behind. She had her ass poked perfectly in the air, waiting. Asher slid into Genevieve so effortlessly that there was no denying he hadn't done it thousands of times before. He roughly pulled her by the back of her hair, forcing her to her knees like he was.

"Fuck me baby," Genevieve growled as she placed Asher's hand roughly on her throat and began to tongue-kiss him.

Sydney watched the two fuck each other hard and passionately as if she didn't lie right there, spread eagle, in front of them. Sydney couldn't help but to watch their naked bodies intertwine in the way that only life-long lovers' bodies could do. The two of them were hot and she was surprised and aroused to see how aggressive Asher was in bed, and how submissive Genevieve was with him. She thought that she would feel jealousy in that moment, but to her surprise, she felt envy. She wanted a piece too.

She got up to her knees and snatched Genevieve's face roughly from Asher's. She began to kiss her hard in the same way he had. Behind Genevieve, she could hear and feel Asher pick up his speed and smack her plump ass hard, causing Genevieve to moan into Sydney's mouth. Sydney opened her eyes and smiled as Asher watched Genevieve take one of Sydney's nipples in her mouth before biting it.

"Kiss," Genevieve said, bending over more so that the two could kiss one another over top of her.

They listened and began to ravish each other's mouths hard as they panted together. Genevieve slid from under the pair and pulled Sydney back as she placed her legs in the air.

"Enter her Ash," Genevieve demanded as she stood on top of the bed and watched as if she were playing some naughty game of Barbies.

Ash listened and slid into Sydney, both gasping the deeper he went into her. Sydney immediately dug her nails into his back, not realizing how much she longed to feel a man in her again and not a dildo. Asher kissed Sydney's calves as he wrapped them around his neck and began to pound harder into her once he figured out the lay of her land.

"Fuck!" Sydney said, barely able to breathe between him and her muscular legs now pressing down on her chest. Above her she looked up to see Genevieve, who had finally sat down and found the previously tossed toy still in bed with them. She placed it in her mouth and sucked it clean while watching the show in front of her. She then turned it on and placed it directly on her puffed clit and used it until she, Sydney and Asher all climaxed together.

Sydney woke up the next morning laying perfectly still in Genevieve's arms. From behind her, she could feel Genevieve's light breath tickling the back of her neck as she slept soundly. Sydney smiled deeply to herself and nuzzled in closer to Genevieve. The room was cold and her feet felt like bricks. Under the covers she attempted to dig her feet deeper under Genevieve's to realize that the feet that instinctively covered hers were not Genevieve's, but Asher's.

Sydney slowly raised and turned her head over her left shoulder to see Asher's blue eyes looking sleepily back at her. The two of them smiled at one another as he nestled behind Genevieve with his face slightly propped on top of her head.

At some point she dozed back off and woke up to Genevieve placing gentle kisses all over her face.

"Wake up sleeping beauty," she cooed.

Sydney slowly opened one eye at a time and let out a deep yawn and stretched, "Where is Asher?"

"Well good morning to you, too," Genevieve teased while rolling her eyes. "He's gotten up to go work out. Apparently, he didn't do enough last night."

Genevieve winked at Sydney, while Sydney felt shame flash across her face.

"Oh Sydney, lighten up. It was a threesome. People do it all the time," Genevieve yawned as she threw the covers off of her and scooted out of bed.

"I never had one," Sydney said quietly. "And what does this mean now? I mean... is it okay?"

"Is it okay?" Genevieve asked with a quizzical look as she threw her robe on and ran her fingers through her wild thick hair. "Baby it is fine. Do you know how long I've waited for this very thing to happen?"

"Huh?" she asked, reaching for her t-shirt that laid at the foot of the bed.

"Sydney," Genevieve scolded as she glided over to Sydney's side of the bed, "Ask what you really want to ask."

Sydney took a moment to ponder her words. She knew exactly what she wanted to say to Genevieve but finding the courage to say the words aloud was a whole other challenge. Sydney quickly ran through the pros and cons of the situation.

"How do you feel about me and Asher? I liked last night..." she said shakily.

"Well, like I said. I've been waiting for this, to share a lover with him. Asher made it very clear years ago that he was not interested in the poly lifestyle. But then, came you," Genevieve said, reaching out and holding Sydney's hand.

"Don't overthink it. Just enjoy the moment and let's have fun. I don't want you two to get too close though," Genevieve said, squeezing her hand a little more tightly while looking her straight in her eyes, "Asher and I have agreed you two will only be together when we are all together."

Sydney tried to ease her hand away, a little uneasy about that decision being made without her approval. Genevieve patted her hand and stood back up.

"Now, let's get up, it's nearly eleven. I still have to unpack and— shit!" Genevieve yelled as she winced over in pain before plopping back to the bed.

"What is it?"

"My knee. As usual," Genevieve said, rubbing it with her hand and shaking her head.

"Sorry babe," Sydney said, jumping out of bed and getting on her knees to rub Genevieve's pained knee. This wasn't the first time she witnessed her having a random spasm, that oddly came mostly when she was out of high-heeled shoes.

She got down into her normal position and began to massage it in the way that she knew Genevieve liked."How did this happen anyway?" Sydney asked.

"It happened when I was about fourteen. I was in a really bad car accident. The car was totaled, and I was lucky enough to make it out with just this bum knee."

"Oh my God, I never knew that. Look at us finding out new things still," Sydney said, puckering up for a quick kiss that Genevieve eagerly gave her.

"Did everyone make it out of the accident okay?" Sydney asked absentmindedly as she grabbed some almond oil and rubbed it in her hands.

"No... my mother was the driver. She did not make it," Genevieve said while dropping her eyes to the floor.

"Oh babe... I'm sorry, I didn't know."

"I know."

"Were you and your mother close?" Sydney asked, now rubbing the oil deeply into Genevieve's knee.

"No, not at all. My mother hated me just as much as I hated her, I imagine. We were like oil and water," she said with her eyes beginning to well. "You're lucky Sydney, you know that? To have the mother that you do. She loves you and it's evident all over you. I lack that. It's one of the many things about you that I just adore."

"Babe," Sydney said, caught off guard, "Thank you. I don't know what to say. But you are right, I am extremely blessed for my mama."

"Yes, you are dear," Genevieve sniffed as she wiped falling tears away.

"Hey, hey, hey, none of that, not today," Sydney said, raising to her feet and wiping tears away with the back of her hands.

"Why not today? What makes it so special?" she joked while briskly wiping her face.

"Today is the first morning after a threesome that I have *ever* had. I say we get up," Sydney said, slowly and carefully pulling Genevieve up to her feet, "and go tell Asher to get off the treadmill and get his ass in the kitchen for some French toast with bacon, eggs and hell, grits too."

"Sydney today isn't a cheat day," Genevieve said disapprovingly as she slowly placed her bare feet back into her snow boots.

"But babeeeee," Sydney whined and pouted.

"Fine, but after brunch I say we repeat last night in my bed?"

"Deal," Sydney squealed.

Chapter 19

Monday, February 15th

Sydney woke up in the middle of her two lovers and smiled to herself, glad to be the first one awake for the first time. It had been a few months since the three of them first shared a bed with one another. It didn't take long before Sydney began to get used to it and looked forward to her nightly visits from the couple. Finally, Genevieve got fed up making that cold trek to the guest house and told Sydney to come visit them for a change. After a few times of bringing her overnight bag over, Sydney decided to just move into the main house and had been sharing their bed with them. After a while, it began to feel weird being intimate with Genevieve without Asher.

She cozied up to Asher, who she felt slowly stirring awake behind her. She turned around to face him gently, careful not to disturb Genevieve, who breathed heavily on the opposite side of the California king bed. Asher laid perfectly still with his wild brown wavy hair all around him. Sydney smiled to herself as she had flashbacks of the three of them last night and when she snatched his hair tie out of his head and grabbed a handful of his hair as he went down on her with Genevieve.

Sydney took her index finger and gently moved a piece of Asher's hair away from his open mouth. She smiled again as she took that finger and gently traced his lips, trying to repress the urge to wake him up. Asher slowly opened his eyes anyway from her touch and Sydney felt as if she were caught in the act. He smiled at her and grabbed her hand before gently kissing the outside of it as he pulled her in closer to him.

Sydney felt her naked body rest against Asher's under the covers and instinctively reached underneath to feel his morning wood.

"Well, good morning," Sydney whispered before looking over her shoulder to make sure Genevieve was still asleep.

It seemed to be getting harder and harder for the two of them to stay away from one another. Both of them had been following Genevieve's rules religiously and tried their hardest to stay away from one another when they were not in her presence. However, as time progressed and the two became more intimate, their friendship naturally began to turn into something more and Sydney would catch herself longing for just Asher many days. And the way she caught him staring at her when Genevieve wasn't looking— she could tell that he felt the same.

Sydney began to stroke Asher's meat slowly as she watched his eyes slowly roll to the back of his head. She debated quickly about waking Genevieve up so that she could join but decided against it once Asher reached in between her legs and began to massage her clit.

"Mmm," the sound escaped Sydney before she realized it. She bit her lip quickly and reminded herself just how brave the two were being to be doing this with Genevieve sleeping soundly beside them.

Sydney began to quicken her pace, wanting Asher to feel as

good as he was making her feel. She felt him force his hand deeper in between her legs before he eventually slid a finger into her and looked deeply into her eyes.

"Shh," he mouthed as he clenched his jaw holding back his own moan.

"Woof," Maverick barked as he pushed open the bedroom door with his nose and made his way swiftly into the room.

"Maverick, no," Asher and Sydney said in unison.

It was too late. Maverick had bombarded the trio in bed and joined them before running around in mini laps like a madman, right on top of all of them. Sydney quickly removed her hand off of Asher and tried to jump up to stop Maverick, but it was too late.

"Asher!" Genevieve screamed as she snatched her sleeping mask off of her face and stared, disoriented.

"Maverick, down!" Asher demanded as he got out of bed.

"I'm so sick of that fucking dog, Asher. Get that mutt out of here before I get rid of it myself," she snarled as she grabbed Maverick by his collar and yanked him roughly to the floor. Maverick let out a loud *yip* as his body hit the floor hard.

"Genevieve!" Sydney yelled, crawling to the foot of the bed to get to him.

"You need to fuckin' relax!" Asher yelled as Maverick got up and cowered behind him. "You're lucky he didn't bite you!"

"If he did, he would be dead!" Genevieve said through gritted teeth as she folded her arms over her bare breasts.

All three of them stood in the room butt-naked and bewildered. It was too early for all of this, and Sydney knew that Genevieve would need to cool off.

"Come on Ash, it's supposed to be warm today. Let's take him on a run," Sydney said, lightly touching Asher's arm before heading to her dresser for some clothes.

Ten minutes later, Asher, Maverick and Sydney jogged through the front gate of their house. Though it was only 40 degrees, it still felt like an unusually warm day for February. Sydney was glad to get a break away from Genevieve and her wrath. She didn't like the way she grabbed Maverick and worried that he had been hurt. She was also glad that she had a chance to run off some of last night's Valentine's dinner.

Asher made *confit de canard,* a French meal of special duck that took 36 hours for him to prepare. Asher was so pressed about this meal that he spent hours in the kitchen for the last few days and made countless trips to various stores for ingredients. Per usual, the meal was delicious, and the garlic and savory duck was succulent and well paired with the roasted potatoes and vegetables.

"Hey, you okay?" Sydney asked as she and Maverick caught up to Asher, who was jogging ahead of them. She had just realized that they had been jogging for at least ten minutes without speaking a word to one another.

"I'm sick of her shit, like did you see that back there?" Asher said, halting mid-jog.

Sydney suppressed the urge to laugh at how fast he broke his silence to talk shit about Genevieve.

"I thought she really hurt him for a second there," Sydney said, kneeling down to pet Maverick's head and to nuzzle her cold nose into his warm neck.

This morning's assault was already forgotten for Maverick who stood panting and wagging his tail, excited to be with the ones he loved the most.

"Her anger is ridiculous. If he would have bit her... what was I supposed to do?" Asher said, frustrated, with his hands on his hips. They both knew that Genevieve would make Asher get rid of Maverick, or worse, have him put down.

"Hey, we can figure it out," Sydney said, coming up from behind him and hugging him. They were safely far away from the house so Genevieve couldn't see their affection. "Maybe I can, I don't know, move back into the guesthouse and bring Maverick with me. Out of sight, out of mind."

"You're not going anywhere, Syd," Asher said, turning to her and kissing her lightly on her lips before wrapping his long arms around her shoulders. "We'll figure it out. She just has to get over it. I just get tired of living life for her. What about us?"

Sydney stood silent as her ear laid on Asher's chest listening to his rapidly beating heart. She didn't know what to say. Every time Asher went on a rant about Genevieve, which seemed to be happening more often lately, it left Sydney feeling awkward and stuck in the middle. If she agreed with him and admitted that she, too, felt smothered by her and her rules and tidbits, he may betray her and tell Genevieve. Sydney would be lying if she didn't admit that she still felt that Asher wanted Genevieve just to himself and that he was capable of anything to ensure that.

"Well?"

"Well what, Ash?" Sydney whined. "What do you want me to say? I don't want to be in the middle. Come on, Maverick," Sydney said, pushing him off of her and beginning to jog again.

"You are not in the middle. It's about having a backbone, Syd," Asher said, catching up to her and matching her pace. "Look at you right now. When was the last time you spoke to India? It's been months. And your mom? When did you last see her?"

Sydney tried to act as if his words didn't faze her as she held on tightly to the leash and jogged ahead. She hadn't thought of India for months. This was a lie— she tried to pretend that she wasn't thinking about her. It tore her up inside to miss the holidays with her. Luckily for Sydney's mother, she did get to see Sydney over the holidays. But only for a moment.

"It's happened to you too, Syd. Come out of the fuckin' sunken place."

"White people can't say that," Sydney said, rolling her eyes at his referring to the mega-hit movie *Get Out* that was based on a black man escaping from psycho-killer white people.

"Whatever. Just tell me you have my back next time she starts on him again. He is *ours,* Syd. You know it, just back me up here," he said, snatching the leash out of her hands and forcing her to stop running. "Come on, think how hard it is for me to have to ask *you* to help me get permission from *my* wife to keep my dog. This is not one of my finest moments," Asher fake begged and poked out his bottom lip, looking miserable.

"You look stupid," Sydney laughed as she walked close to him and grabbed his face and pulled it down to hers.

"Now what would the neighbors say?" Asher asked into her mouth.

"They won't know, they think we all look alike anyway," she said as she slid her tongue into his mouth. Something she had been wanting to do all morning.

Later that night, Sydney and Genevieve arrived home late after an afternoon-turned-evening of shopping. They had spent the day with Genevieve's personal stylist who put the looks together for book five's promo tour in a few weeks. She was scheduled to do a few signings in about ten cities across the states. Sydney was excited to finally get to travel again but dreaded the idea of being back on a plane.

The two dropped their bags by the door as they simultaneously kicked off their heels and tossed their coats on the nearby chaise.

"Whew, what a day babe. You want a glass of red?" Genevieve asked over her shoulder as she headed to the wine cellar.

"Yes, please," Sydney said, taking off her hat and fluffing up her pixie cut.

"Syd!? Help!" Asher yelled from what seemed to be the library.

"Ash?" Sydney asked, terrified as she ran towards him. She

reached the library just in time to see Asher lift a lifeless Maverick off of the floor and onto the couch.

"Oh my God, what happened?" Sydney screamed as she rushed over to Maverick.

"I don't know, I just found him like this. I was upstairs working and then I realized I hadn't heard from him in a while. I went to go check on him and found him like this," Asher rambled.

"Okay, call the vet, he's breathing... but barely," Sydney said, rattled. "Maverick, Mackie, come on wake up, baby," Sydney said, patting Maverick's face and trying to get him to open his eyes. She hoped to see some eye movement from him to make her feel not as helpless.

Behind her, Asher clumsily called the vet who instructed him to bring him to the Pet E.R. immediately.

"I'm coming with you. You drive," Sydney said, following behind Asher who already had Maverick in his arms. The two reached the living room just as Genevieve appeared from the downstairs cellar.

"Where are you going...? I have wine," Genevieve said, showing the two full glasses in her hand.

"There's something wrong with Maverick... I don't know, we have to go," Sydney said with her voice cracking with fear as she rubbed his head again.

"Well can't Asher take him? I don't see how that would be cause for you both to go," Genevieve asked, nostrils flared.

"You're sick, you know that?" Asher spat quickly as he glared at her with his face screwed up.

"Asher, what are you talking about?" she asked calmly as she sipped her wine and walked over to them.

Sydney was confused about why Asher was so upset with Genevieve. She couldn't believe that they were wasting time like this. They needed to go; Maverick was dying.

"You *know* what the fuck I am talking about Genevieve," he shot back.

"Not a clue, hun," she smirked before looking at Sydney. "Sydney, babe, please stay and have a glass with me, you deserve it after the day you endured with me. Asher can take his dog to the vet alone."

Asher scowled at Genevieve with his eyes narrowed, holding his sick dog who still wasn't moving. Sydney stood between the two as she looked back and forth. She didn't know what was going on but knew that it made her feel very uneasy and not safe.

"Come on Ash we have to go," Sydney said, grabbing her purse. "We'll take my car, it's out front already," she said, ushering Asher out the door and mouthing, "Sorry," to Genevieve.

A few hours later, Asher and Sydney headed out the Pet E.R. and made their way to a nearby bar to get a much-needed drink. The two were spent after rushing Maverick into the E.R. to only sit and wait while he got his stomach pumped. He pulled through and was finally stable, though the vet assured Asher that the story may have been different if they got there even a minute later. The vet decided to keep Maverick overnight to monitor him. They also decided to take some samples to figure out what made him that sick.

Sydney plopped her Celine bag onto the bar's countertop as she slid out of her coat and handed it to Asher. "Two whiskies and Cokes please," Sydney said wearily as she watched Asher neatly drape their coats over the stools next to him.

He took a seat near Sydney and let out a long sigh as he removed his glasses and pinched the bridge of his nose before returning the glasses back to his face.

"Ash...he's gonna be alright, you can breathe now," Sydney said, gently rubbing his forearm, not believing her own words.

If that were true, she wouldn't feel so uncertain about the situation.

Asher clenched his jaw and held his gaze down on the counter until the bartender returned with their drinks.

"Thanks," Asher said solemnly before knocking half the drink back.

Sydney watched silently as she sipped on her drink and rolled the straw wrapper in between her fingers. They sat quiet for a few more minutes before Sydney couldn't take it anymore.

"You know what I *really* can't stand?" Asher blurted out with his gaze still locked on the game that played on the TV above.

"What?" Sydney asked, relieved that he was the one to break the silence.

"*Hun.*"

"Huh?"

"That 'hun' shit she always says; hate that passive aggressive shit," he said.

"Oh, Genevieve," she said, catching on. "She says that to me all the time. What's the problem with that?"

"Exactly; she says it in a demeaning way. You've never noticed that? As if it's a pet name for the remedial. It is always coupled with her trying to get her way for whatever she wants."

"Damn," Sydney said aloud before taking a gulp of her drink.

He was right, she didn't say it often, but she said it often enough. She felt a queasiness in her stomach as she realized she was always a pawn for her.

"She said that holding us up tonight. As a bargaining tool for me to not take you too. She just acted like it wasn't a big deal," Asher ranted.

" '*Not a clue, hun*'," he mimicked Genevieve as he took another sip of his drink. "She couldn't care less. It's as if she didn't see him dying right in front of her. Whether you like dogs or not, you have to have a heart," he said, shaking his head slowly in disgust.

"Ash... what are we not saying right now?" Sydney asked him meekly before slowly facing him. She wasn't brave enough to say it, so she would make him do it.

"She's a psychopath, Syd."

"Ash," Sydney shook her head in disbelief and waved him off playfully, "You are just upset, and I'm sure the drinking is not helping—"

"Syd, you remember that night after we kissed?" he interjected. "When G popped back up and— "

"And you told her that we kissed?" Sydney finished smartly. "Yeah, I remember."

"Well," Asher said, raising his empty glass to the bartender, indicating he was ready for another. "I was scared, but I told her about our kiss. For better or worse she is my wife, Syd. I didn't want the situation to go unreported and then blow up to something else, like we are sneaking around behind her back," he said, locking eyes with Sydney, who immediately felt flushed.

"Well after I told her, she grabbed her stuff and stormed out. It took me a second to realize she was heading towards you... and by the time I did realize, my heart dropped. I ran after her as fast as I could."

"Ash, what did you think she was going to do?"

"Thanks man," Asher said, accepting the new drink and throwing it back just as vigorously as he did the first one. "Syd, there's something you need to know about G...something I should have told you about a while ago," Asher said, looking down at his glass.

"What is it?" Sydney's mind was going a mile a minute. She could feel the hairs on her arm stand up as if she knew what was coming her way.

"I was never able to prove it... but I am pretty sure G was

responsible for an accident that happened while we were in grad school."

"An accident?" Sydney whispered while leaning in closer to him, not wanting anyone to hear. Even when terrified of her, Sydney still felt the need to protect Genevieve's image.

"You see, I was dating this girl when I met G. Her name was Rachael. She and I had been dating for only six months or so by the time G came into the picture. One day Rachael and I were meeting up with some friends when they introduced G to us. Rachael knew it was over before I did," Asher said, letting out a dry chuckle.

"Anyway, G and I started messing around behind Rachael's back for a few months."

"Wow, Genevieve knowingly played the side chick?" Sydney asked, astonished.

"She did, for a while too. I felt like too much of a jackass to break it off with Rachael myself...or maybe I was more of a coward. I became the worst boyfriend imaginable to her just so she would be the one to end it. But she never did. Finally, G got tired of waiting for me to 'man up' and told me she was confronting Rachael herself."

"And what happened?"

"This is where the story gets weird... the two of them were both studying psych, so they had a lot of classes and study sessions together. One day she told me she was going to confront her after one of their study sessions and she would call me to give me a heads up once it was over. I waited up all night to get a call from one of them, but neither one of them ever called me or showed up to my apartment. Their sessions tended to end around 11 p.m. or midnight, so I was starting to freak out. Finally, around one in the morning, I started getting worried and started frantically calling both of them. Neither answered."

Sydney could feel herself inching to the edge of her seat

from listening to his story. Knowing Genevieve now, she imagined that she probably tore that girl down to shreds when she confronted her. Sydney felt her heart tug at the feeling Rachael must've felt knowing that she lost a good man like Ash forever.

"Around two in the morning, I left to head to the study hall where I knew their study group met at on Thursdays. As soon as I hit the corner I saw flashing red lights and saw scattered policemen everywhere. The sidewalk had been taped off and there was dried blood on the ground that was being photographed. There were a couple of passersby and students behind the yellow tape gawking at the scene. I went over and asked one what happened. I had a bad feeling in the pit of my stomach, I just knew... I knew that this scene was my fault."

"Finally, one of the guys told me that 'a girl had jumped' that night right after her study session. Just out of the blue, she met with her classmates and studied as if everything were normal and then out of the blue... she just jumped. Off of a four-story building with no warning."

"Oh my God Ash,'" Sydney gasped as she reached out to grab his hand.

"Yeah... I raced down to the hospital just as her family arrived from New York. The hospital and doctors ruled it a suicide attempt. They saw no evidence of any other foul play, and Rachael was in a coma."

"She survived?"

"If you can call being fed through a tube for the next few years survival, yeah. She eventually woke up and regained some of her motor skills back but she had no recollection of that night or why she would try to harm herself. Unfortunately, after the ...accident, our relationship ended. It was for the best. Her family hated me and though they never outright said it, they thought I was trash and to blame for the mishap. And they were right."

"No, they were not Asher, don't say that," Sydney said

sympathetically as she rubbed the back of his neck. "And Genevieve? Did you ever... confront her?"

"I tried Syd, but she always claimed she never spoke to her that night. She said she punked out last minute. I never believed her. She disappeared for about two weeks after it happened and randomly popped back up, saying she had a family emergency back home in Maryland to tend to. She acted as if she were shocked when I told her about Rachael, but a part of me always knew..."

"Ash, what are you saying?"

"I'm saying that I am tired of hiding the facts about G from everyone, including myself. I saw the signs. I know she had something to do with Rachael. I can't prove if she actually pushed her herself or if she used her words—but I know she is to blame for why Rachael is not even fifty yet and lives in an Assisted Care facility. It's all my fault Syd," he said with his voice beginning to crack from guilt and grief. "She's sick, Syd. That night I came running into your room? I thought ... I thought..."

Sydney took a deep gulp as she tried to fight down the tears she felt coming up in her throat. Seeing Asher this upset broke her heart.

"I thought she was going to hurt you, too. And I cannot... I will not let that happen to you."

"Asher..." Sydney began to rebut but stopped short once she remembered how bewildered he looked when he appeared in her room that night. She never fully understood what made him run over to her house like that, but now she did.

"Do you think she did something to Maverick?"

"All I am saying is whatever G wants, she gets. She hates Maverick; the fact that he just almost died and she couldn't care less... once these results are back in and it proves me right, that's it."

"That's it?"

"I'm doing what I should've done nearly twenty years ago. I am leaving her for good. She is nuts. I know she tried to kill him, just like how she tried to kill Rachael, and just like how— "Asher cut himself short and began to re-clench his jaw. Whatever he was about to say, he decided against it and decided it would be better to finish off his drink instead.

"What time is it?" he asked.

Sydney reached for her phone and saw that she had a missed call and a text message from Genevieve.

Genevieve: I miss you, where are you?

Sydney: We are still at the E.R. We should be wrapping up soon

Genevieve hated texting, so Sydney knew she was desperate for her attention. Sydney didn't even feel guilty about lying to her. She needed time to process everything that Asher was saying. Despite him being consumed with grief, she knew that he had a point. Genevieve's possessiveness, how controlling she was and how she couldn't seem to function without having one of her lovers chasing after her— it all added up.

"What's wrong?" Asher asked, scrunching up his face with concern as he rubbed Sydney's knee.

"Nothing," she lied, "It's a little after midnight. Should we head home now?"

"Are you in a rush to get back to her?"

"Honestly... no," Sydney said truthfully.

"Promise me you won't say anything to her, Syd," Asher asked wearily.

"I promise. Just promise me that your next moves will be smart ones. We have to figure this out together and if what you are saying is true... we both are in danger. Especially now," Sydney said, grabbing his hand and placing her hand in it.

"I agree," Asher said, kissing Sydney's hand and holding it to his face.

The two of them didn't need to say it, but they both knew. They were in love, the real love that develops slowly from a friendship and a common bond. No one could have foreseen this.

They made a quick pit stop before heading home. The two ducked off to an empty parking lot they found not too far from the bar. In her car, the two made passionate love in her backseat that left them both breathless and sweaty. Sydney knew that this was just a Band-Aid to try to cure all of their shared revelations of the night. She knew that making each other pant and claw at each other before achieving an orgasm was not going to make all of their problems with Genevieve go away. But for the moment, she enjoyed the time the two shared with each other and basked in the love.

Chapter 20

Tuesday, February 16th

Asher and Sydney finally walked in the house at nearly two a.m. As soon as she stepped foot through their front door she felt a chill in her spine and that familiar uneasiness begin to creep all over. It was also weird for her to walk into a quiet house without Maverick running sloppily over to her from the living room ready to drown her in licks.

"I don't want to sleep in the same bed, let alone the same room as her tonight," Sydney whispered to Asher who she found in the kitchen drinking a glass of water.

"I know," he said solemnly as he placed his glass down on the counter and sighed, "I'm killing time myself. I'm so nervous about tomorrow, Syd."

Sydney knew he was referring to getting the results back from the vet. She was nervous too, despite what the results may be, she knew in the pit of her stomach that everything was about to change.

"Come on, we're both procrastinating," Sydney sighed. "I think it would be suspicious if we both take a shower, so how about you take one in the guestroom tonight? Make sure to get your neck extra good. You have lipstick on your collar," she said, smiling at him weakly.

Sydney went to give him a final kiss and placed her hand gently on his face to pull it down to hers.

"Syd... you're shaking," Asher said, taking both of her hands into his and looking down with concern. "Listen, I'll take the hit tonight and will go upstairs to her and keep up the charade. How about you cool off in the guesthouse tonight? I'll tell her you didn't feel well or something."

"Are you sure?" Sydney felt an instant relief at the thought of not having to sleep next to Genevieve after finding out she tried to kill someone... twice.

"Positive. Take the night, get your mind right. We'll regroup tomorrow when we pick up Maverick, okay?"

"Okay," Sydney said solemnly, throwing her arms around his waist and hugging him tight. She wished he could join her in the guesthouse.

"Don't worry, we got this. I promise," he whispered into her hair before kissing her on the top of her head.

Surprisingly, Sydney was able to sleep hard that night despite her not having two bodies on either side of her. She had wild dreams that night of Maverick, India, Genevieve and even Shawn. She woke up the next morning and laid in bed for about twenty minutes trying to figure out what the dreams meant. She also used the time to think about her failed friendship with India and how Asher was right. Sydney had isolated herself in this relationship. She no longer had ties with the outside world, and when she did, she was only allowed to be with her mother.

Sydney jumped in the shower in hopes of calming her skittish nerves as she did a deep dive into her own psyche over the last few months. It was ironic; she started this journey with Genevieve to find herself and ended up even more lost than when they had begun. Her world was no longer her own, but Genevieve's. So many people tried to warn her on the way, and she cast them to the side, including Cai and India.

Sydney stepped out of the shower naked and realized she had no fresh towels to dry off with since she hadn't been living in the house for months. As she stepped out of the bathroom and into the hallway she ran right into Genevieve who was making her way up her stairs. Genevieve was completely dressed in vintage Chanel from head to toe. She looked like she stepped out of *Breakfast at Tiffany's* and looked perfect in her pink tweed outfit.

"Well... good morning," Genevieve said, reaching the top of the stairs and examining Sydney's naked body.

"Good morning," Sydney mumbled, not prepared as she ran to the linen closet and grabbed the first towel she saw. She was not prepared to see Genevieve yet. She tried to avoid eye contact with her as if she could tell that she and Asher were intimate alone last night.

"You two got in pretty late last night..." Genevieve said with her eyes finally locking in on Sydney's.

Here we go, Sydney thought to herself as she walked back into the bedroom. She wished that Asher had given her a warning she was on her way to her. She also hoped that he was okay himself.

"Yea... we were at the vet all night; it was pretty touch-and-go there," Sydney said with her back to her.

"So Asher tells me," Genevieve said as she glided in behind her and took a seat on Sydney's bed.

Good... he's alive, Sydney thought as she began to grab her lotions and act as if everything was normal.

"So, what made you sleep here last night? We missed you in bed."

"I just needed a moment to myself. Seeing Maverick like that... was terrifying."

"Oh," Genevieve said unenthused. "You know we have a busy day today and have already missed our breakfast meeting."

"Shit," Sydney said aloud as she remembered what day it was. "Sorry Genevieve, I'll be ready in twenty minutes. I'll call Raphael so he can drive us today, it totally slipped my— "

"Your mind? Yeah, I've noticed, hun," she said curtly.

There it was. Asher was right. Sydney was in no mood for Genevieve's condescending tone this morning.

"Well excuse me, my dog almost died last night," Sydney snapped. "He's doing better. They have pumped his stomach and we will find out what got him sick later today, thanks for asking," Sydney snapped, almost not believing the words came out of her own mouth.

"He's a dog," Genevieve said, rolling her eyes, "And he's not yours, he's Asher's. Besides, whatever almost killed him is bound to leave some psychological damage. He'll never be the same again, you guys may not even want him— "

"He's ours. We want him," Sydney said, cutting her off and regretting it instantly.

"I see," Genevieve said quietly. "Sydney, help me figure out something here."

"Okay," Sydney said timidly as she pulled her black wool dress over her head, opting to go braless today.

"The animal E.R. where *you and Asher's dog* is has a waiting room that closes around midnight. I imagine they have this set in place so that they don't have people hanging around all night milling around and crying over their pets. So how is it possible that you and Asher both told me that you were there for an hour and a half longer than what is allowed? It takes about twenty to thirty minutes to get here from there... so to my calculations, you both should have been home around 12:30 at the latest after visiting with 'your' dog."

Sydney stood frozen, unable to break the stare that Genevieve had locked her into.

"Funny, Ash had the same look on his face when I asked him this as well," Genevieve said with a light chuckle as she got off of the bed, straightened her skirt and slithered over to Sydney. She reached her and rubbed her face gently and tenderly with one hand. They stood like that for a few more seconds before she went in for the kill.

"You both neglected to mention the dive bar, Eddy's, that you spent time at last night as well. Or that random parking lot where your car was parked for twenty-five minutes," she said calmly.

Sydney felt her heart sink to her stomach and her mouth open. How could Genevieve know any of that? Did Asher tell her? Would he do that?

"Genevieve, I— "

"Shh," Genevieve said, placing her index finger gently on Sydney's parted lips. "Don't even waste your time lying, Sydney, you have been caught. The both of you." With that Genevieve's eyes became even darker and her hand fell and went underneath Sydney's dress and pried open her legs.

"What are you doing?" Sydney yelled, trying to push her away.

"Confirming what I already know. You and Asher are fucking behind my back. Open your legs Syd, let me feel now!" she yelled as she dived for Sydney.

Sydney began to run around the room trying to get Genevieve off of her and stop her from further violating her.

"Are you fuckin' crazy?" Sydney finally yelled, slightly winded from fighting her off.

"No, but you must be to think you can lie and fuck behind my back. How many times Sydney? Answer me that! How many times have you allowed my husband to fuck you behind my back? Do you think I'm an idiot? You two went to that sleazy bar before taking the party to the back of your car, like the fucking whore you are."

That's it, the car, Sydney thought to herself as she stopped dead in her tracks.

"Do you have nothing to say for yourself?" Genevieve asked with her arms folded. "Prove me wrong then. Lay on this bed and open your legs Sydney. I know what your pussy feels like when it is freshly fucked."

"You are sick," Sydney said, feeling her terror now turn into pure anger. "You have a tracker on my car, don't you?"

Genevieve stood stone-faced as if Sydney hadn't just called her out. Sydney's words didn't register to her at all.

"Hello!? Do you have nothing to say? Genevieve, why are you tracking me?"

Seeing Genevieve's expressionless face was the final straw.

"That is it, I am done. Now you are chasing me around this room trying to shove your fingers in my pussy— and not in the way I want!" Sydney yelled as she pulled out a duffle bag from her closet.

"You are fuckin' sick in the head. I did not sign up for this, Genevieve! How long have you been tracking me, huh? What more do you want from me? I have given you so much."

"You've given *me* so much?!" Genevieve exclaimed as her face contorted with anger. "Little girl, I've given you the world! Including my home, my money, my car and MY husband! I only ask what I gave you back in return. I want everything from you Sydney, everything. What are you doing?" she asked at the sight of Sydney packing her bags.

"I'm leaving. I do not belong to you Genevieve. I am not a toy; you cannot control my life. Everyone was right! You have me perfectly isolated in your sick little world; I don't even know who I am anymore. I have given up everything for you and blindly followed you like an idiot! No more, this is over."

"Sydney, you have signed a contract," Genevieve said with

a small smile as she walked closer to her. "You cannot leave me that easily. Besides, I am willing to overlook last night. I think it would be best for you to stay out here for now on. No more sleepovers with Asher and me in our bed. Please... stop packing, let's discuss this."

"Genevieve, fuck your contract," Sydney said through gritted teeth as she snatched the dress over her head and threw on some old ripped up jeans, a college sweatshirt and her boots. She not only wanted to feel like herself again, but she knew she had a long traveling journey in front of her. She would stand on the corner in the cold and wait for an Uber before she got back in that car Genevieve bought her ever again.

"Sydney! Sydney come back here right fucking now. Sydney... please!"

Sydney was already out the front door and securing the order for her Uber to Cai's house— the only place she knew that Genevieve wouldn't be able to find her. She just hoped that once she arrived there Cai would be home and would forgive her. She would send for the rest of her things eventually. Everything that truly mattered to her was already in her duffle bag.

Sydney began to jog down the driveway once she reached the front of the house, panicked that Genevieve was following her. She turned back for a second and saw Asher standing in their bedroom window looking down and watching her from the second floor. He watched her with sadness in his eyes and she wondered what his fate would be.

It wasn't too late, he could join her and she hoped he would. Her bag fell to her feet as she looked up at him, the two having a million conversations within just a few seconds of stares. Then, she saw Genevieve's arms wrap around his waist from behind and saw Genevieve appear next to him with her notorious smile on her face. Sydney felt her heart break as she saw Asher place a loving kiss on the top of Genevieve's head the same way he had done to her only hours before.

She felt the hot tears running down her face before she realized she was crying. She roughly wiped them away from her face as she picked up her bag and turned around to see her Uber at the bottom of the driveway. With one final glance up at the couple in the window she took the phone she had in hand and smashed it to the ground, before sticking up her middle finger to the both of them. Making sure to cut off any connection they thought they had to her.

Chapter 21

Tuesday, March 2nd

It had been a long two weeks since Sydney moved out of Genevieve's mansion. Within fourteen days every single thing about Sydney's life had changed. After running down the driveway, Sydney caught a ride to Cai's house. To her relief, she was welcomed with open arms by both Cai and her mother. Sydney spent a few days after that moping on Cai's couch. Cai's mother's cooking couldn't even shake her out of her deep funk, no matter how much she was fed. Eventually, in true Cai fashion, Cai was able to get Sydney somewhat out of her slump with tough love and constant reminders about how lucky she was to escape the "dragon lady" while still alive.

"I always told you that lady was nuts, but does anyone listen to Cai? Nope!" she said, answering her own question.

The two were back at work at the Flamingo's. It was Sydney's first day back and sadly, it was a struggle for her. It seemed that her now perfectly manicured hands were incapable of doing hard labor and Sydney spent most of her shift dropping trays, food and even spilling a hot latte on herself.

She was currently in the kitchen, hiding out and wiping away her tears, frustrated at her own self.

"And stop that crying. It has been two weeks now Syd! Plus, you're making me look bad," Cai whispered as she handed Sydney some napkins for her face.

"I'm sorry Cai... it's just hard. And everyone here hates me now," Sydney sniffled as she patted her face dry. "It's like I'm useless now; I can't even hold a tray."

"Everyone does hate you now..." Cai agreed.

"Remind me to teach you what 'sugar-coating' is later," Sydney said, rolling her eyes.

"Syd, you know I keep it real, it is the Japanese way! A lot of people thought you were full of yourself to quit the way you did. You didn't make it any better when you came in here with that bitch looking like one of *them*."

Sydney knew the "them" Cai was referring to were the patrons who frequented the restaurant. Flamingo's always attracted a certain kind of upper-echelon crowd. This crowd was known to look down on the staff, insult their intelligence and barely make eye contact with them. The only plus to the situation is that most people would leave a hefty tip as compensation for their rudeness.

"I think it's been long enough, Syd. Come on, no more tears man," Cai said, exasperated as she pulled out her tip book and peeled out a few bills before handing them to Syd. "Here take some of my tips, because I know you couldn't have gotten much today."

"Cai..." Sydney began to protest, knowing that she didn't have a dime to her name.

"Hush," Cai said, putting her hand up, "You'll need some money later tonight and I don't want people to think I'm your man or something when I have to keep paying for you," Cai said chuckling.

"Tonight?" Sydney asked, confused as she stuffed the money into her apron, not bothering to count it.

"Yes Syd, we're going out tonight. It's time you continue to right your wrongs. India and I exchanged numbers a while ago and I called her—"

"You did what?" Sydney yelled.

"I called her. I got her number last summer when she invited us to that block party. Listen, I love you but you need more help than my couch can give. Besides, you are eating all our food and have no money to replace it. I called her and told her what happened. We agreed to all go out for drinks tonight."

"Cai, it would have been fuckin' nice if you asked me instead of going behind my back," Sydney felt flustered and felt her heart beating hard in her chest. She was upset at Cai for telling her business, but mostly she was nervous to face India.

"Syd, we don't have time for this," Cai said, waving her off. "Besides, you need your best friend in more ways than one," Cai said, standing to her feet and brushing the wrinkles out of her starched and perfect work slacks.

"Yeah, well, how so?" Sydney asked, defeated and folding her arms across her chest.

"Well, first of all your hair is a fuckin' mess. It will probably help your tips if she can do that head of yours. I don't know much about black hair, but I know that...that is not it," she said winking at Sydney as she headed out the door laughing .

Later that night, Sydney and Cai arrived at the pool hall in Cai's old Honda Accord. Sydney gasped once she saw where they were headed for the night.

"Let me guess, India picked this place?"

"Yup," Cai said while applying some baby pink colored lip-gloss. "Come, while you two talk, I'll find me a man."

The two hopped out of the car and briskly walked to the entrance of the hall. Sydney felt out of place immediately as they entered. She wore a headscarf that she that night and a simple long black dress she got years ago from H&M under her faded leather jacket that sat on her shoulders. She still felt naked without her designer labels.

"Oh, there she is," Cai said, scanning the crowd before dragging Sydney across the room.

The two of them reached the bar to see India sitting by herself cradling a drink. As soon as Sydney's eyes landed on her, she felt rushed with a flood of emotions and found herself speechless.

"Hey," Cai said, sitting down at a stool and patting the one in the middle for Sydney to sit.

"Hey," India greeted back.

Sydney took a seat in the middle of the two, unable to look India in the eyes yet. She suppressed the urge to run away and decided to look down at her chipped nail polish instead.

"Can you not speak?" India asked with a tinge of attitude.

Sydney finally looked up at her best friend. India looked good. Per usual, she was the best dressed one in there that night in her Fendi sweat suit. She wore her natural hair out in a twist out and her makeup was subtle but flawless.

"Go ahead Syd, tell her what happened. I'll order drinks," Cai said, getting up from her seat and walking towards the opposite end of the bar to the bartender.

Sydney took a deep breath, "You were right."

"I fuckin' knew it," India said rolling her eyes and shaking her head. "What happened? Tell me everything."

Forty-five minutes later, Sydney finally finished telling her girls the story about her horrible breakup from her throuple relationship. She picked up from the night Genevieve and India got into the fight, the first time she made love with Asher and Genevieve, the incident with Maverick and finally finding out she was being tracked.

"Bitch..." India said, shocked at all that had transpired.

"I know. And now I am here. Stuck and dumb— oh and

back broke. What's worst of all is that I haven't heard anything yet from Genevieve about this contract and I'm scared of the repercussions that I may face. I also... I miss Asher, like a lot."

"And he hasn't reached out, like at all?" India asked.

"Nope. He wouldn't know how to get to me anyway. They don't know where Cai lives, and I no longer have a phone..."

"I was wondering why I hadn't seen your thirsty ass on the 'Gram lately," India said, still babysitting her drink. "Weren't you on your mom's plan anyway?"

Sydney sighed and shook her head as she stared off into the distance. Like most of her fellow Gen Z population, she was still on her mother's phone plan. And she had no interest in explaining to her mother why she was out of a phone, a job and a place to stay.

"He's pussy anyway, Syd. The fact he knows that bitch is crazy and still chose her over you, that says a lot. Fuck him!" Cai added.

"Right, fuck that nigga. The nerve of him to gas you up only to be pussy whipped once the daytime hits," India agreed. "We should go key his car!"

"It's not that easy y'all. I get it, it's hard to explain, but that woman puts you under a spell. I just want to talk to him one more time; it hurts not talking to him. I honestly thought that by now I would have heard from him... or even Genevieve."

"I think he owes you an explanation. I say we run up on him at his work and demand answers. His ass owes you that at least!" India yelled getting riled up.

Sydney felt herself smile at hearing India getting rowdy about her. It made her feel like their relationship wasn't completely lost, despite all the damage that had been done.

"I don't know about that, I say you let it be. Consider yourself off the hook! You never told me about this contract Syd," Cai said, cradling her beer, "What exactly does it say? What happens now that you broke it?"

Sydney sighed and placed her face into her hands. As much as she tried to forget about it, this contract haunted her. Especially since she hadn't really sat to read through it until she left Genevieve.

"Well, according to the contract, since she fronted me money and paid off my rent, I am responsible for back pay plus interest."

"Interest?!" Cai and India squealed in unison.

"Yup. I'm looking at a $50,000 debt at minimum from the money she put into me, my attire and lodging. I even tried to go back to my apartment and they wouldn't let me in there. I added Genevieve onto the lease once she convinced me to. She told me that since she was paying the bills, she wanted to be sure to have her name on it as well. At the time, I thought nothing of it, but when I went there a week ago the locks were changed. And the landlord refused to 'get involved in a domestic dispute.'"

"She paid his ass off," India said, shaking her head.

"Yup. All my shit is still in there or at least I hope it is."

"Nah, we rolling up on that nigga tomorrow morning at work. The fuck do they think this is?" India said, talking with her hands.

"That's not even the worst part," Sydneyed sighed. "Genevieve knew that I hadn't read the contract, even though I lied to her and told her I had. She gave me that contract and let me sign it without reading it and finding out myself that I was signing off to a relationship with her exclusively. Also, she made sure to add that I would receive zero profits back from the book she wrote damn near for me! By time I stepped foot in that house that woman knew she had me trapped. I get nothing..."

"We are getting you answers. You were dumb and caught up, but this is not okay. We go home tonight, sleep and plan for what you will say. Then tomorrow we go there, you talk to Asher, and you get your shit back."

"Do you think he will help you, Syd?" Cai asked.

"He's my best bet. But I am honestly not sure. I'm scared to face him, to be honest. Like he hurt me too, you know? Maybe even more than Genevieve."

"You love him don't you, Syd?" India asked.

Sydney nodded her head yes. She refused to let the words leave her mouth.

"I am sorry this is happening to you. You are a good person and you don't deserve this," India said, grabbing Sydney's hand and giving it a squeeze.

"So, does this mean I am forgiven?" Sydney asked sheepishly. She knew she didn't deserve to be forgiven this easily after all the damage was done, but she also knew how much she needed India.

"Yeah hoe, we are good. I missed your ass like crazy and despite how fucked up you were in that relationship... we all have been there. Hell, I was stuck on stupid with Dij."

"No, not me. Three people in a relationship is too much for me. I'm strictly dickly too," Cai said, tossing the rest of her beer back.

They all laughed together and for the first time in weeks, Sydney felt a glimmer of hope.

Chapter 22

Wednesday March 3rd

The next day India and Sydney got up bright and early to make it all the way to Worcester. After last night, it was made very clear that Cai was ready to give Sydney the boot from her apartment. She didn't even try to hide her excitement once Sydney told her she was going back with Cai only to pick up her things before heading to India's.

Sydney checked her reflection in the mirror once again. She felt like a mess and felt so awkward in India's clothes. She wanted to look "nice" when seeing Asher and unfortunately, the only thing "nice" that she owned was still at the mansion and she was sure that those clothes had been thrown out.

"Here, put on some lipstick in my purse— the red one," India barked as she took a wild left turn at a street light and glided her car into the garage of Asher's job.

"India... I'm nervous, what do I say?" Sydney asked, trying her best to keep a steady hand.

"Tell him you want your shit back and out of that dumbass contract!" she yelled while accepting the garage ticket from the startled attendant. "Listen, if anything, just tell him how you feel and see where his head is at."

Sydney sighed and lazily applied the crimson-colored lipstick across her lips. She was a ball of nerves and kept having to rub her sweaty hands on her bouncing leg.

India pulled into a parking spot and turned the car off before looking at Sydney.

"Syd, you look great. Don't worry girl, you got this. Come on, let's go."

"You're coming too?" Sydney asked surprised. She didn't want to be rude, but she was sure that Asher's place of business was no place for India's loud antics.

"Girl..." Sydney began.

"Hush, I will sit quiet as a mouse in the waiting room," she said, hopping out the car behind Sydney. "Ain't no way in hell I'm letting you in there alone with that crazy woman on the loose."

"What you gonna do if you see her?" Sydney asked jokingly.

"Just know we have glockiana on our side," she said gently patting her purse before pushing the button for the elevator.

"Asher. Asher Cross please. Can you let him know that... Sydney is here?" Sydney said timidly once they reached the front desk on the fifth floor.

"Sydney who?" the perky blonde asked as she grabbed her phone.

"Sydney Mack," Sydney said, hearing her voice tremble.

After a few moments the secretary told Sydney to have a seat while they waited for Asher to wrap up his meeting. A few minutes later, Asher appeared out of one of the back doors. He wore his hair in a neat bun on top of his head, a black button-up shirt and jeans with his clear oval glasses. The sight of him made Sydney's heart flutter and she felt glued to the chair.

"Hey Syd... India," Asher said casually as she stuffed his

hands in his pockets.

"Mhm," India greeted. "I'll be here girl, go handle your business," she said, flipping through a magazine she had picked up from the coffee table.

"Hey Ash... can we talk?" Sydney asked, standing up.

"Yes. Follow me," he said.

As soon as Sydney entered Asher's office she felt it hard to suppress the smile that came across her face. Asher's office was every bit of him. From the Marvel posters of Iron Man on his walls, to the blueprints of skyscrapers that hung framed and even the smell of freshly burned incense that hung in the air.

"Welcome to Ash's world," Sydney said as she took a seat on a brown leather couch that sat in the corner of the room.

"Yeah, I guess you could say that. Can't really say that I had much say in the home décor of the house... so here is where I get to decorate myself. I don't get many guests," he said, letting out an awkward laugh as he sat tentatively on the corner of his desk facing her. "So to what do I owe this pleasure?"

Sydney picked up an Iron Man action figure off of a nearby table and played with it in her hand as she tried to muster up the courage to do what she was here for.

"How's Maverick?"

"He's... he's good," he said, unable to look her in the face.

"He's good? Ash, he nearly died; you have to give me more than that."

"Maverick has actually been hanging out at one of my coworkers for the last few weeks. Until I can find a more long-term option for him."

"Long-term? As in you're giving him away?"

"Yes... Well, no. I'm looking for the best home to put him in, which is hard considering..."

"Ash, he almost died. And now you're getting rid of him? What did she do to him? what did the vets say?" she felt herself beginning to get hot with anger.

"Syd, you don't have to keep repeating yourself; I was there too that night.We don't know what he could have gotten into... or how, but there was a high level of Ethylene glycol in his system."

"'Ethylene glycol'?"

"It's a chemical that is most commonly found in antifreeze and paint thinners," he said, clenching his jaw and still staring down at his feet.

"Ash..."

"Syd," he sighed as he removed his glasses and pinched the bridge of his nose with his eyes still closed, "I don't want to hear it. He's a dog, they get into stuff, this shit happens."

"Not with Maverick, not in that house. Where would he get into something like that? He also doesn't eat anything other than food, and you know that. Just stop it!" Sydney said, raising her voice.

"Sydney, what do you want?" he asked angrily.

"I want you Ash," she shot back before she could stop herself. "I want you, I want us, I want to not feel like I have to look over my shoulder every fuckin' minute. I want you to admit that Genevieve is psychotic and dangerous. She nearly killed him, Ash! How can you be okay with that?"

"Lower your voice, Syd!" he shot back, putting his glasses back on his face. "Besides, you don't know that."

"Yes, the fuck I do. Just as much as you do. You are delusional. You told me yourself that night about what Genevieve is capable of. How can you act like that didn't happen? What do you plan, to just get rid of Maverick the same way you got rid of me... or Rachael?"

Sydney heard her voice crack and got up to begin to pace the office trying to calm herself down, feeling herself on the brink of tears.

"That was low Syd," Asher said, wounded. "I didn't...I didn't get rid of you Sydney, it wasn't like that at all," he said, getting up and standing behind her. Asher gently placed his hand on her right shoulder and gave it a soft squeeze.

Feeling his touch made her feel a rush of feelings that led to her swinging around and digging her face into his chest while she cried. She could feel Asher soften up and hold her tight while he let her cry it out. After a few minutes, he returned stiff and cold and pushed her away.

"Syd, I hate to do this... but I really can't do this."

"Asher, I need help. She has ruined my life. I have no money, I am homeless, and I am just watching the door waiting for the day that her fuckin' lawyer finds me and serves me with papers telling me I'm getting sued," she yelled frantically. "Imagine what life is like for me?! I didn't want any of this Asher."

"And I did, Syd?! You really think this shit is sweet for me, like I don't— he cut himself off and walked further away from her, trying to calm himself down.

"Like you don't what?" Sydney asked with tears streaming down her face.

"You don't think I miss you? That I don't think about you every day? My heart dropped when I found out you were here. Syd, this hasn't been easy for me either. But she is my wife."

"And I was just the toy you two screwed for entertainment, right?"

"No, you are far beyond that. Your absence is felt, believe me. There hasn't been a night yet that I haven't gone to bed thinking about you. I know this situation we have you in is fucked up, but Syd, my hands are tied."

"Right... well I guess that is it then," Sydney said wiping her face and picking up her purse from the couch. "It's nice to know where I stand with you I guess."

"Syd... stop, wait," Asher said, grabbing Sydney's arm and stopping her from leaving. "There is one thing I can do. But it has to be the last thing I do. I will get G to break the contract, I'll have her rip it up and leave it be. You don't deserve this."

"Just like that?" Sydney asked, shocked and relieved.

"Just like that. Of course, it will take more than just ripping it up... but I will make sure that this is legally dead," he said, softening his tone. "Now this has nothing to do with the actual NDA. Syd, I know you are mad but there is nothing I can do if you break that."

"Got it, keep my mouth shut. I've been doing that for months, say less," she said eagerly. "Can you help me get my place back?"

"I can't do anything about the apartment, but I see you and India have made up, which makes me happy. Now I know you are safe," he said with a small smile on his face. "I assume that's India anyway, she looks just like how you described her."

"Yeah," she said reluctantly. "The only good thing to come out of this I guess."

"Let me give you some money—

"Ash, you don't have to."

"Yes, I do," he said running around his desk and grabbing a checkbook and scribbling on it, "This isn't much, but it is a start. And don't worry, it's from my personal account. G won't know anything about it."

"Thanks," Sydney said dryly as she stuffed the check into her purse, not bothering to look at it. "Is there just one more thing I can get before I leave you forever?"

"Anything," Asher said genuinely.

"Can I get a hug goodbye?"

Asher slowly strolled over to Sydney and outstretched his long arms and wrapped them around her tightly. Sydney breathed him in and hugged him tighter once she felt the tears bud in her eyes again. The two rocked and swayed in silence for minutes before Sydney finally let him go and walked out of his office without saying a word.

Chapter 23

Saturday, March 27th

A few weeks had passed since Sydney saw Asher in his office. Since then, she had developed a routine for herself that helped her get through her day-to-day and to think less of him or Genevieve. She set herself up in India's apartment and made the living room her new home where she spent every night on the couch. She and India seemed like two passing ships in the night as they took turns using the car and only seeing each other right before they both knocked out.

Sydney kicked her shoes off and peeled off her rain jacket as soon as she walked into the apartment. She was exhausted after working a full shift that night at Flamingo's. She sat down on the couch and pulled out her tip book that she had nestled into her coat. She counted her tips and smiled to herself when she saw she made nearly $300 that night. She was finally back in her groove at work and couldn't be happier.

"Girl, you home?" Sydney yelled down the hall towards India's closed bedroom door only to be greeted by silence. Sydney was surprised to see the light on under her door. She had also remembered that India told her she would need the car to go bar hopping with some of her new co-workers.

India finally found a job she liked as a paid intern at a physical therapist's office. Sydney on the other hand had scored herself a second job as an assistant manager at Gayle's, where she oversaw a small staff of five that included Angel. The irony of the situation had not fallen short on her. Sydney felt herself feeling hopeful and even opened a savings account and began to save her earnings. It was the first time she had ever saved in her life and with Asher's money in there, she felt a bit of security for her future. Sydney didn't know what was next in her life, but she was ready to find out. And though she had enough money to move off of India's couch, she still didn't feel ready to be alone again.

Asher's words about Genevieve's past still haunted her. Daily she would gasp after she thought she spotted Genevieve or Raphael's car somewhere. Twice, she thought she spotted her at Flamingo's during their lunch rush. The last time scared her so bad that she had a panic attack in the bathroom. Sydney knew that Genevieve would never allow her to get away so easily. Nowadays, she lived her life feeling as if she were always looking over her shoulder and bracing herself for the inevitable to happen. She just hoped that she wouldn't have the same fate as Rachael.

"Bitch, I know you're not sleep!" Sydney teased as she sluggishly stood to her feet and made her way slowly to India's room.

Sydney knocked on the door a few times before trying to open the door and finding it hard to open, as if something heavy lay in front of it.

"India? What is in front of the door? I can't open it," she said, now pushing it harder with more force. Suddenly, the hairs on the back of her neck began to stand and panic flooded her all over.

"India!" Sydney yelled as she stood back and kicked the door open with her still-toned leg. The door budged open just enough for Sydney to slide through and see India's slumped, bloody body on the floor. She had been what was blocking the door.

Chapter 24

Sunday, March 28th

Sydney stood shaking as she talked to the police at the New England Baptist Hospital. She stumbled over her words with her arms tightly folded as she recounted to them, again and again, what she walked into when she found India on the floor. Sydney was tired of repeating herself and looked down at her watch to see that it was three in the morning. This explained the pounding headache in her temples.

"I know it's been a long night, Ms. Mack, but please bear with me for one more second," the officer pleaded to Sydney as he noticed her getting agitated. "Are you positive that you do not know who is responsible for the attack on Ms. Carter last night?"

"I am positive, for the millionth time..." Sydney said, only half believing herself.

"Okay, well you have my card with both of my numbers on it," the cop said with his heavy Boston accent in tow. "Please do not hesitate to reach out to me. Is there, uh, anyone that we can call for you tonight? I promise to keep one of my guys here for today or however long she needs."

"Excuse me ma'am, you cannot go back there unless you are family, excuse me— "

Sydney spun around to see a nurse attempting to and failing at stopping Dij, who was pushing her way past random staff members in the hall.

"Syd!" Dij yelled when she spotted Sydney before rushing over to her. Dij looked disheveled as if she had just rolled out of bed.

"Ma'am I will call security if— "

"It's fine, she is family. She is her fiancé. Thanks for coming, Dij," Sydney turned to face the officers and stood up straight, "Officers I think we are all set here. I promise to be in contact and will stay near the phone. Now if you will excuse me," Sydney said, ushering Dij to the side.

"Syd, what happened, is she okay?" Dij was now panting, and Sydney could hear the quiver in her voice.

"Calm down Dij. I am sorry to call you like this in the middle of the night; I just didn't know who else to call. I couldn't get through to any of her family and—

"Syd, please... what happened?" Dij asked sternly.

Sydney recanted the evening's events to Dij and felt herself begin to cry again. Dij quickly pulled Sydney into a hug, just as Sydney's mother stepped out of India's room.

"How is she, Ma?" Sydney asked, pulling away from Dij and wiping the back of her nose with her hand.

"Oh, baby, here," Leah said, digging out some Kleenex out of her scrubs' front pocket and handing it to Syd. "Dij, it is nice to see you again. Listen, India is beat up pretty badly, but she is stable."

Dij let out a sigh of relief and placed her hands on her knees to catch her breath.

"She has a broken rib and jaw, but other than that everything else seems to be in order. She woke up for a second when she first got here and was screaming hysterically..." she said, shaking her head with concern.

"I'm just glad I was there with her once she woke up, I think it helped for her to see a familiar face. They have her on some heavy drugs for the pain and a little something to help her sleep tonight."

"Mommy, when I found her she was... naked on the floor. Did you have them..." Sydney couldn't dare to utter the words. The three women looked at each other silently, all waiting to hear if Sydney's suspicions were true.

"I checked myself, and no baby. She is fine," her mother said, rubbing Sydney's arm to comfort her. "At this time I do not believe she was sexually assaulted, but I do not know why she was unclothed. Maybe she was just out of the shower."

"Can I see her?" Dij asked.

"Yes, go ahead in. Y'all try to be lowkey tonight and I will make it so you both can stay here overnight, okay?"

"Thank you, Mrs. Mack," Dij said, breezing past her and going into India's hospital room.

Sydney woke up a few hours later to a tapping on her knee. She had fallen asleep on the bench that sat across from India's room. She decided to let Dij stay in the room with her while Sydney sat outside with the officer to keep him company. Sydney opened her eyes to see Asher standing over her.

*I must be dreaming,*she thought to herself as she rubbed her eyes and sat up. "Ash?"

"Hey Syd," Asher said, sitting down beside her with a bouquet of colorful flowers and a 'Get Well Soon' balloon. "How are you?"

"What are you doing here?" Sydney asked, confused.

"I... I uh," Asher looked across at the officer who sat beside India's door, snoozing away. "Can we talk in private?"

"Hey, can you find it possible to stay awake during your

shift," Sydney said, clapping the sleeping cop awake. "Sure. Let's go to the café for a coffee," Sydney said.

She was still surprised to see him there, especially since she hadn't called him. She hoped that the caffeine would help to make sense of the situation.

In the café, Sydney got a sausage, egg and cheese, a large coffee and a side of hash browns. She was starving and couldn't remember the last time she ate. The two sat down at the table and Asher sat silently as he watched Sydney eat.

"I forgot how much I enjoyed watching you demolish a meal. Careful Syd, the way you are eating those hash browns is starting to make me jealous," he said with the left corner of his mouth crawling up into a smirk. "By the way, I love the hair."

Sydney reached up and adjusted her braids that laid wildly over her shoulders. "Thanks. What are you doing here, Ash?" She asked, wanting to skip the small talk.

"Dij told me. I still, uh, cop from her from time to time. She and I were supposed to meet this morning for me to pick some up, but when I called her she told me what happened... Syd, I am so sorry you had to witness that."

"Well, thanks. I didn't witness it, but I saw the aftermath."

"It still must've been traumatizing for you... I know how important it is for you to feel safe and to find her like that is...tough."

He was right. Sydney felt a chill run down her spine from the memory of last night. After she saw India's lifeless body on the floor she immediately slammed the bedroom door shut and barricaded it with a dresser. She feared that they weren't alone. Whoever did that to India could still be in the apartment and could be ready to do the same to her. Sydney dialed 911 from India's phone since hers was still in the living room.

She had checked the closet while she told the operator the address. Once she secured the room, she went under India's mattress and pulled out her gun. She had imagined that India didn't have time to grab it before she was attacked. Sydney made sure that it was loaded and laid it by her side as she wrapped India's naked body in a blanket and held her while listening to her raspy breaths. Sydney waited like that until she heard the paramedics at the door.

"I just don't get what happened. I don't know who would want to hurt her this badly. Ash, they said that she was beaten so bad that she was near death and that they are sure it was more than one person. She'll have to have surgery on her jaw and everything," she said while briskly wiping the falling tears away. Sydney was so tired of crying.

"Syd, that is why I am here. I came to check in on you and India, but more importantly, I came to warn you. You are in danger. Has anyone been able to get a description of the attackers? I ask because ... I don't think those people were there for India. They were there for you."

Sydney felt her eyes bulge in surprise. Of course, the thought had crossed her mind a few times since last night. She wondered if this was finally the repercussion that Genevieve threatened would come once she left her. But to hear Asher confirm it sent another chill down her spine.

"How do you know that?" Sydney whispered to him. "Who would want to hurt me that badly that they settled for my friend?"

"Syd, we both know who... and before you start blaming yourself, this is all my fault," Asher said, dropping his eyes to his hands as he nervously unfolded and refolded them.

"You need to explain... I am so confused," she was beginning to get irritated.

"Okay, so it all started when Genevieve decided to break your lease a few months shy of it being over. She had instructed the landlord to trash all of your stuff and even told him she would pay him a hefty fee if he did it swiftly. I told her that that was unnecessary and that she should let you at least gather your things up. Needless to say, she didn't like how I was playing 'Captain save a hoe.'"

"'*Captain Save a Hoe*'?" Sydney repeated. Those words did not sound like Genevieve.

"I know," he said, reading her mind, "She got that from Vicky. She's been back hanging with her every day and going off to parties and doing God knows what, with God knows who. All we do is fight now. You know the other day she threw a Louboutin shoe at my fuckin' face?" Asher began to turn a shade of red but calmed himself down once he realized he was getting off track.

"Sorry Syd. Anyway, I convinced her to let me donate the stuff to charity, well at least I thought I convinced her. Instead, I bought a storage unit with my side account and I had all of your stuff moved, safely, into there. It's paid off for six months; I figured that would be enough time for you to get your own place with the money I gave you."

Sydney was touched. She hated herself for feeling that in this very moment, but she was. She felt the familiar flutter of butterfly wings somewhere deep within her.

"Well, G found out about the storage unit and the money I gave you. I don't know how she did—" he started to say before cutting himself off, "That's a lie. That woman has more eyes on me and control of my life than I ever want to admit. I should've known it would be a matter of time. When she found out, she flew all the way back from California to confront me. She had been there with... Finn."

"Of course," Sydney said, rolling her eyes, but still missing the point. "So how did this lead to India getting jumped?"

"Syd, I told you she is a psychopath. I have done my research, trust me, all the signs point to it being true. She's calculated, manipulative, shallow, and dangerous!"

"Yet, you've stayed with her for this long, so what does that make you?" Sydney shot back.

"When she confronted me, it all came out," he said, ignoring her dig. "How tired she was of me pouting over you leaving and how I still choose you over her, even with you out of the picture. She asked me about the check I wrote you and even the unit. She convinced herself that we were still having an affair and she ... lost it. She started swinging at me and throwing everything at arm's reach. Once she got tired of chasing me, she tried to strangle me when I refused to tell her where you were," Asher said with his eyes glossing over.

He unzipped the navy windbreaker he had on and pulled down the collar of his t-shirt to reveal the red scratches and bruises that still remained on his neck.

"Ash," Sydney gasped as she covered her mouth in shock. She felt her eyes water as Asher lowered his gaze in shame again. Despite everything, she still cared deeply for him.

"Did you go to the police?" she asked.

"What? No. What am I going to say? My wife is having another psychotic fit because she can't accept that her husband has fallen for her ex-lover?"

The two of them fell silent and looked each other square in the eyes. Sydney felt her lip tremble and her stomach do back-flips to hear Asher finally admit how he felt about her. Asher reached his hand across the table and gently picked up Sydney's.

"Syd, I know she did this to India. It all lines up. Once I refused to tell her where you were she kicked me out. I have been living at the W hotel for two days now. It is no coincidence that this has happened. I really fear what would have happened if it were you that was home instead of India."

"Oh my God," Sydney thought out loud, "What am I going to do? I have nowhere to go, Ash and neither does India... What about my mom?" Sydney began to panic, and then remembered her mother would be halfway across the world in Japan with her friends in less than 48 hours.

"I will protect her, I will protect you all, I promise," Asher said quickly.

"How, Ash? She has you on more of a lockdown than me; you can't sneeze without her getting notified. How the fuck can I trust you? I did that before and look where it got me," Sydney snapped as she snatched her hand back. It wasn't lost on her that Asher could be playing her and using that as some desperate, elaborate scheme to get back into Genevieve's good graces.

"You can trust me Sydney, I wouldn't hurt you—"

"Don't you dare lie to me again. You wouldn't hurt me? Ash, you hurt me the day you allowed me to run away from her — from you. The day you told me how evil your wife was, how she hurt your ex-girlfriend, how she hurt *Maverick*," Sydney said slamming her finger down on the table for emphasis, "You even feared *then* that she would hurt me. And then you turned your back on me, Ash. You let her treat me like trash. The only one who has hurt me so far, has been you."

Sydney felt it all pouring out of her. She tried her best to keep all these emotions bottled up, but she had reached her breaking point.

"Syd, I am done with her. I should've been done with her back when we were kids and she hurt Rachael. I should have been man enough to tell her I fell out of love with her the moment I laid eyes on you," Asher said, genuinely looking Sydney in the eyes. "I love you Syd. I love you and I want to be with just you. I will do anything in my power to make you love me back, but until then, I will keep you and your family safe."

"Why don't we just go to the police?" Sydney asked again. "Maybe they could help..."

"I am doubtful, Syd. G has some major connections. I know we have only been in Boston less than a year, but between her celebrity status and poly friends... G has connections all over this country. You'd be surprised how far people will go to protect their image," Asher said, shaking his head. "Those poly parties she would go to, but would never invite us to? They are filled with politicians, law enforcement and thugs. We don't stand a chance."

"So, what do we do? Just sit until she finally finds me and kills me? Or worse, my family and friends?" Sydney felt sick to her stomach as she realized there was a cop on India right now. For all she knew that could be one of her goons.

"Listen, I filed the papers with my lawyers for a divorce. I have also filed a restraining order against her. I suggest you do the same."

Sydney rolled her eyes, "You just said that we don't have the law on our side."

"We don't, but we need to create a paper trail of all of this, before it gets worse. I think she will get the message, Syd, and fall back. At least until I figure out something else for us to do," he said, grabbing his backpack and walking around the table to sit next to Sydney.

"Until then, I want you to take this," he said, handing her the bag and nodding for her to open it. "After my accounts were compromised, I withdrew all my money. I have it stashed in safe spots, but this is for you and India. I know your mom is leaving soon, but I have hired her security to watch her until then."

"But Ash," Sydney began.

"I got it Syd, he is unmarked and good. She'll never see him or have to know."

Sydney took a sigh of relief, "What about me and India?"

"I connected with an old Yale friend out here that I lost touch with after G and I hooked up... he owns a few Airbnbs across Massachusetts. He has a three-bedroom in Worcester for you guys; it's in a secured building with 24/7 watch. After I got off the phone with Dij, I figured that she wouldn't be leaving India's side, so I figured the extra bedroom would be nice."

"You thought of everything... thank you," Sydney opened

the bag and saw a stash of cash neatly tucked in an envelope and a small gun. She zipped the bag up quickly and looked over her shoulder. "Ash!"

"It's for your safety... listen I really don't know your stance on guns, but you need to be protected, Syd. I know Dij will be with you, but I won't be. And I need you safe," Asher said, wrapping an arm around her protectively.

Sydney sighed and did something she thought she would never be able to do again, she rested her head gently on his chest, closed her eyes and exhaled. Just by him being here, she already began to feel safe.

"What about you? What will you do? And for the record," Sydney said with a smile on her face, "don't sleep on your girl. I got one tucked in my purse as we speak."

Asher chuckled, kissed the top of her head and rested his on top of hers.

"You always find a way to surprise me, Syd. Just make sure you know how to use it, yeah?" he said, rubbing her arm gently. "You know how much of a klutz you are."

"Forget you, okay?" she said, playfully slapping him, "You forgot I have brothers in the army, I see?"

"Sydney, I haven't forgotten anything about you," he said, rubbing her arm gently. "I found a loft not far from you guys. I move in tomorrow... me and Maverick," Sydney could feel him smile while he rested on top of her head, "and then I figure out a way to permanently get us out of this mess for good."

"And what about us?" Sydney asked, knowing that the timing wasn't perfect, but it never was for them.

"I work on proving myself worthy of you, Sydney Mack, but before I do that, I keep you and all that you love safe and hidden."

Chapter 25

Monday, April 12th

Sydney finished lacing her brand-new platform Dr. Martens and stood back to admire her view. She wore her knotless braids in a high ponytail to show off the Africa-shaped wooden earrings that hung from her ears. She wore a simple fitted black jumpsuit that hugged her returned curves and exposed a humble amount of cleavage.

"Girl, what do you think?" Sydney asked India who she saw watching her through the mirror from the couch.

India banged her hand on the tray and rolled her eyes for a response. Sydney and Dij laughed at the bittersweet moment of watching India struggle to get out her opinions and comments. The three of them were in their Airbnb laying low and resting up while India recuperated from having her jaw wired shut from her corrective jaw surgery that she had had last Monday.

India banged on the TV tray that sat in front of her, trying to get Sydney's attention. She had only been home for a day and was already defying doctors' orders to rest and take it easy.

"Here babe, damn," Dij said, shaking her head as she grabbed the small dry erase board from across the room and handed it to India so she could write. "Your ass need to be laying down and relaxing and not worried about what we have going on out here."

India ignored her as she scribbled away on her board. She had a long recovery road ahead of her. Thanks to Sydney's mother, she was able to get surgery ASAP to work on her jaw that was damaged badly from the break-in. India's jaw had been shattered in three separate parts that the doctors assumed came from direct blows of a boot to her face, multiple times.

Sydney felt a jolt of guilt every time she looked at India's swollen and bruised face. As soon as Asher left the hospital that day, she ran to India's room and told both her and Dij everything. She felt it was only fair to be completely transparent with both of them when informing them how they all were in danger and would have to hide out for their safety.

"Shoes-No. Ash?" India wrote on the board as she shook her head disapprovingly.

"Yes, I'm getting ready for his work thing tonight. What's wrong with the shoes? I think they're cute."

"Umph," India grunted as she wiped down her board and began to write again.

"Goddamn, y'all about to be here all night fuckin' with her," Dij teased as she puffed up the pillows behind India and moved the TV tray out of the way so that she could prop India's legs up.

India's eyes warmed as she looked up at Dij lovingly as she took care of her. The two of them had not missed a beat, and by the time India woke up in the hospital and saw Dij by her side, all was forgiven.

India spun the board around and grunted for Sydney to read.

"Bitch, no. Wear my YSL pumps," Sydney read aloud, before rolling her eyes.

"Umph," India grunted.

"Mamas, let her wear what she wants. You can't dictate everything, remember?" Dij asked sweetly as she sat down next to India and gently wrapped her arm protectively around her.

"Damn, it's so good to see you two back together," Sydney gushed as she grabbed her purse and jacket. Asher should be arriving any minute now and she didn't want to make him wait.

"Besides," she continued, ignoring India's eye rolls, "I want Ash to see the real me. The me pre-Genevieve. I think he and I deserve that. Let's see how it goes; we're starting off from scratch."

"Man, fuck that bitch," Dij yelled as she began to flip through the channels on the large mounted TV that hung in their living room. "I still don't know why you don't just let me run up on that bitch and handle this. There's only so much amount of hiding and 'laying low' that I can do."

Sydney knew she was asking a lot for all of them to stop their lives to go into hiding. But after seeing what happened to India, she couldn't risk her getting hurt again. And she knew that Dij, being that hood baby that she was, would take matters into her own hands without Sydney's supervision.

"Don't start Dij. I mean, is this so bad? We got this nice ass apartment, bathrooms in every room, a full fridge and stocked bar—what more could we ask for?" Sydney asked her.

"Our sanity," Dij said before getting elbowed in the side by India. "Nah Syd, I know you just keeping us safe. And hell, I'm sure this way is smarter than what I had planned on doing to ole' girl."

"I'm sure," Sydney said, looking back over to India who had lazily placed her head on Dij's shoulder and was nodding off.

"But you look nice Syd, and despite it all, I hope it works out with you and my boy. Asher is a cool dude, but just be smart. He double-crossed you once, don't let him do it again, you feel me?"

"I feel you," Sydney said solemnly.

Later that night Asher and Sydney walked into the busy reserved bar that his job had rented out for an after-work party. Sydney felt like a nervous wreck as she held on tightly to Asher's arm as he navigated her up the stairs and to the coat check.

"You okay?" he leaned down and whispered in her ear as they waited in line to check her coat.

"Yeah, why do you ask?" Sydney asked as she looked around at the attendees and their attire and immediately regretted not taking India's advice. Women were in there in expensive suits, shoes and bags and screamed "Wealth."

"Well you're shaking and holding on to me like you are afraid I'm going to leave you," he said chuckling. "Not that I'm complaining. But let's say we make our way straight over to the bar, yeah?"

"Yeah," she said quickly as she handed her trench coat to the attendant.

It was their first outing as a "couple," though Sydney wasn't sure that was what they were quite yet. She was nervous and anxious and felt like she stuck out like a sore thumb. Sydney couldn't help but to feel like Genevieve would have been a better date than her tonight, but needless to say she put a big smile on her face and schmoozed and greeted every coworker that Asher introduced her to that night.

After a few glasses of wine that Asher's boss demanded Sydney try, Sydney felt loose and felt herself at ease nuzzled to Asher's side. After the first hour of the two being at the party, it became evident to Sydney that she wasn't the only one who was out of place at the junction. Asher didn't look or act like any of his fellow co-workers. They were all older white men in their late 50s-60s, balding, and making small talk over architecture designs and the new Keurig in the office. Sydney couldn't help but to wonder what they thought of Asher, who sported an impeccable man bun, rugged beard and had an office full of action figures.

"So, Sydney, I must thank you for getting Asher here out of the house and out to mingle with us for once. It's like pulling teeth trying to get this guy to come out for a drink with us," Rob, Asher's boss, said as he threw back another drink under his wife's disapproving eye.

"Thanks for having me. I'm having a great time," Sydney said truthfully as she snaked her arm around Asher's and looked up into his eyes. Asher seemed like a whole new person to her ever since that day at the hospital. He was lighter and happier and seemed to have a permanent smile on his face whenever Sydney was around.

"Well if you two will excuse me, I have to mingle with some of my other employees. Though Asher is my favorite," he whispered. "Sydney my dear, it was a pleasure and I look forward to seeing you at the company's BBQ this summer. Asher, keep up the good work and don't mess it up with this one. I like her, she has spunk," he winked while he and his wife walked over to another table.

"'*Spunk*'," Sydney whispered under her breath while trying to hold a laugh in.

"I feel like I'm in an episode of *Mad Men*," Asher said, chugging his beer back and placing his hand on the small of Sydney's back. "Thanks for coming. You know I hate parties," he said.

"Of course," Sydney said, feeling the warmth of Asher dancing on her skin as he pulled her in closer to him. "I didn't know you watched *Mad Men*."

"There's a lot you don't know about me Ms. Mack," he said while bending down and gently kissing her on the lips, instantly sending goosebumps all over her bare arms.

"Mhm, I guess that's the fun about starting over, huh?" Sydney said to him. "How about we recreate our own little

Mad Men scene now and you meet me in one of those single stall bathrooms we passed downstairs?"

"Yeah?" Asher asked mischievously as he looked around to make sure there were no bystanders eavesdropping.

"Yeah. We can pretend I'm the secretary and you just couldn't wait until the end of the workday to have me!" she said giggling.

"How about I play the secretary and you the boss? Sounds more accurate, don't you think?" Asher said.

Sydney didn't have a chance to answer before Asher was pulling her arm and leading her discreetly down the stairs to the bathrooms.

"You have to stay quiet, Syd. No screaming or we will get caught," Asher breathed into her ear once he locked the bathroom door behind them and began to loosen up the tie around his neck.

"Tell yourself that sir. Unzip me and make it fast, we have ten minutes before the next meeting," Sydney said, jumping into character before turning around so that he could free her from her jumpsuit. Sydney surprised herself sometime on how much she has changed from a few months ago. The old her was more reserved where this new her was like a dog in heat whenever around Asher. She was thrilled at the thought of feeling him inside of her again and could feel anticipatory shivers racing through her body.

Asher did as he was told and pulled her zipper down so roughly, she was sure that he broke her cheap jumpsuit. She then felt his kisses traveling from the nape of her neck, down her spine and finally to her butt. Asher pushed Sydney down onto the sink as he roughly yanked her panties to the side and parted her cheeks with his nose. He began to lick and slurp hungrily as he ate her out from behind and smacked her ass loudly while doing it.

Sydney covered her own mouth as she felt Asher's tongue

explore her completely and diligently as he continued to eat her out, while smacking as if he were eating a three-course meal. After she felt her knees begin to give he stopped and stood up and kissed her roughly as she reached behind her and began to unbuckle his belt.

"You better not make any noises," Sydney said sternly to his reflection in the mirror, "Or that's your job."

"Yes ma'am," he said as he tossed his tie over his shoulder before pulling his dick out and entering her swiftly from behind.

The two gasped together as he filled her up entirely. Sydney had almost forgotten how perfect he felt inside of her. She then began to feel him gently stroke her slowly, relishing in the feel of her. Asher began quickening his pace and bit Sydney lightly on her neck to suppress his own moans. He then snatched her hair tie out of her head, sending her braids to cascade all over the two of them as they watched themselves in the mirror.

"You like these?" Sydney asked as she tried to get a good grip on the sink to support her weight.

"I love them," he said before grabbing a handful and wrapping them around his hand and yanking them, causing her to arch her back more and be completely at his mercy.

"Hold on babe," he said as he began to pump harder. With each thrust, he sent shivers of ecstasy all over her body.

The sound of their wet bodies clapping and heavily panting filled the small bathroom and Sydney was sure that the two had an audience on just the other side of the door, but she didn't care. She felt herself begin to shake from the inevitable orgasm that was beginning to creep upon her. Being an expert in her body, Asher quickly grabbed his tie and stuffed it into Sydney's mouth just as she came, hard, and let out a muffled cry.

Chapter 26

Friday, April 30th

Asher

Asher cracked his car door window and let the crisp spring air fill the car. He breathed it in deeply as if the city-filled air was pure and fresh and not muddled with cigarette smoke, garbage and pollution. Asher sighed at the traffic and shook his head disapprovingly. He had been sitting in rush hour for nearly thirty minutes now and he was eager to get back home to Sydney. She had told him it was a bad idea to move into the city; he should have listened. Asher caught himself smiling at the thought of her, something he found himself doing lately.

He picked up his phone from his lap and tried to call Sydney for the second time since his trek home. And again, his Jeep filled with phone rings and was followed by Sydney's sweet voice mail of her promising to call the caller back as soon as possible. He thought that it was odd she wasn't answering for their usual after work call, but blew it off once he realized how nice it was outside. Knowing Sydney, he figured she probably left her phone in the loft again while taking Maverick for a walk.

I gotta get her out of that, he thought to himself as he secretly believed Sydney was still afraid to be attached to her phone due to Genevieve. He had expressed to Sydney numerous times how important it was for him to be able to reach her. He wanted her to feel safe with him and hated that she still held power over Sydney. And inadvertently, him as well.

It had been a quiet and peaceful month. Asher hadn't heard from Genevieve in a while, and he was beginning to feel at ease. He and Sydney were closer than ever, and he was madly in love with her. He couldn't believe how easily he almost lost her once, and vowed to never do it again. He planned on asking her to move in with him soon, and even though his divorce still had months before it was finalized, he was ready to ask her to marry him. There was no doubt in his mind who he wanted to be with, but he wasn't sure if there were any doubts for her.

Asher fiddled with the radio, trying to find a station Sydney had introduced him to a few days ago. He decided he might as well try to enjoy his ride as much as he could. He had only inched up a few feet and Asher knew he would not be home anytime soon.

"Aight let's get into this weather," the radio disc jockey said briskly on the air. "Hope y'all are out enjoying this beautiful day, because from tonight to tomorrow we got a mean storm coming our way!"

"How mean?" the co-host egged on as she giggled.

"All I'm saying is it's gonna be raining cats and dogs, men, ALL OF THAT, Kimmie. Hey, man, maybe you can finally find you a man?"

"Forget you, Trey, and your corny jokes!" Kimmie shot back.

"Nah folks, make sure you stay in. They're saying we are likely to get at LEAST five to seven inches of rain. They are expecting trees to be down, some areas to lose power and definitely some closures. This will definitely be another Nor'easter. So please people, stay home!" Trey yelled.

"I know right where I'll be tonight," Kimmie said.

"Yeah, in bed, alone. Aight, ya'll, back to these hits. Coming up next is that newest from my boy Blue, check it out..."

Another thirty minutes passed before Asher finally made it to his apartment. He parked his car in the garage and took the back stairs up to the apartment, skipping them two at a time. Asher walked to his apartment door and thought about the dinner reservations he would make for later tonight. All he wanted to do tonight was to wine and dine his lady and then to come back home and fuck each other senseless.

"Syd?" Asher called out as he walked in and turned the switch on his kitchen wall, sending lights to light up all around his loft.

"Maverick?" he yelled as he peeped around the corner.

Asher put his bags down and began to sort through his mail that laid on the kitchen island. He looked down and noticed Sydney's jogging sneakers missing from their usual random spot in the kitchen, at the same time he heard a scratch from the downstairs bathroom.

"Maverick?" he asked as he walked towards the noise. It didn't make sense; if he were scratching at the door, then where was Sydney and why were her shoes gone?

Maverick came barreling out of the bathroom and jumped anxiously all over Asher.

"Whoa, whoa, whoa, what's going on, boy? Calm down," Asher said gently to him as he rubbed his wild mane. "Where's Syd, huh?"

At the mention of her name Maverick's ears stood up and he froze before darting up the stairs. It was like her name triggered a memory for him, and Asher ran after him before stopping dead in his tracks at his bedroom door. Something was off.

He couldn't tell what, but he could feel it. For once, the room wasn't a mess. In fact, his room was always the messiest when Sydney was visiting. But today, the bed was made. All of the loose change on the floor was gathered and placed neatly on the newly cleared dresser. Sydney's bag with her clothes and things were also missing from the chair she usually left them on.

Asher dug in his pocket and pulled out his phone and called Sydney again. Meanwhile, Maverick strode past him and ran into the master bathroom. Maverick whined and sighed from the bathroom, causing Asher to follow him there. Asher walked into the bathroom and turned off the running shower that still ran hot and filled the room with mist. He then immediately spotted the blood all over the bathroom counter and floor. The blood still looked fresh as it ran down the side of the counter and lay on a puddle on the floor that Maverick sniffed and whined at.

He was now panicked at this point and already dialing 911, until he saw the handwritten note that sat on top of Sydney's vibrating phone. The note read, "Asher," in grand, black old-school cursive. He knew that handwriting anywhere. It was Genevieve's.

Chapter 27

Friday, April 30th

Genevieve

Genevieve sat patiently in the private garage of Asher's loft. She arrived earlier than scheduled and decided to sit and wait the extra twenty minutes to ensure that there would be no interruptions. She jumped out of her rented Maxima and grabbed the gym bag that sat on her passenger seat. Next, she walked to the back of the car and popped open the trunk. With precision and ease, she pulled out the heavy wheelchair that lay in the trunk.

Genevieve moved quickly as she unfolded the chair and set it in motion for the elevator. She walked with purpose as she pulled out the key card that Raphael had gotten her a few days ago. She waved the key in front of the elevator's fob and pulled her baseball cap lower on her head. She had been careful to disguise herself, as there were three hidden cameras near the elevator. Raphael had done her the favor of scouting them out a few days ago. Genevieve was pissed that she had to do this part of the plan by herself since he decided to grow a conscience so last minute.

After she found out about Asher's secret account and his

unwillingness to share his true feelings for Sydney with her, she decided to find out more answers for herself. Genevieve had become obsessed with finding out how Asher could leave her. She couldn't believe how her whole life came crashing down once Sydney entered the picture. She had herself to blame for it really. She should have known Asher was too weak to resist Sydney, and she couldn't blame him. Despite it all, she was still in love with Sydney, too. She missed her terribly and there were no new pets, toys or Finns who could add up to half of what she was. Genevieve still ached for her at night and missed her gentle spirit.

She stepped into the elevator and kept her head down as she stood beside a young couple riding the elevator up as they discussed what to cook for dinner tonight. She smiled to herself as she listened to them debate whether or not corn would suffice as a vegetable for dinner. They reminded her of she and Asher in their early years. She missed those times that felt like a lifetime ago. She believed they would get back to that eventually though, with the help of Sydney.

Genevieve had been very meticulous when planning today. Over the last few weeks, she had Raphael follow both Asher and Sydney. Raphael had their routine down pat. Sydney, on average, visited Asher at least five times a week and spent most of her time alone in his apartment with the dog while he was at work. Over the last few weeks, she slowly began to travel back to work at the restaurant and the mall. She only did light shifts during the day for both. Something new that had changed since India's apartment was broken into.

When she wasn't with him, she stayed in a secured apartment building with her two hoodlum friends in the city. There was no access point to that building, so they devised a plan around Asher's building instead.

Genevieve felt her heart beat harder in her chest the closer the elevator got to Asher's floor. Once they reached the fifth floor, the couple wished her a good evening and left her standing alone on the elevator. Genevieve took the moment to steady her nerves.

"Two more floors," she said to herself as she grabbed the key from her back pocket and held it in her shaky hand. Getting the key to Asher's loft proved a lot harder than she thought it would be, a vast difference from when she took over Sydney's place. In fact, Raphael had to reach out to some shady friends from his past to get the perfect duplicate made. Once he delivered it to Genevieve last night, he informed her that he couldn't go forward with the plan.

"You coward," Genevieve had yelled at him while he tried to explain to her how spooked he had felt the day before when he swore Sydney spotted him while on her way to work.

"I'm sorry Mrs. Cross, I can't. I can't harm her. Sydney is a great girl...a friend even. With all due respect, maybe this isn't a good idea. I was thinking, maybe we can go there and just scare her a bit? You know, smack her around a little so she gets the hint."

Genevieve fired him on the spot. She was outraged that he not only backed out on her last minute but made her feel guilty about her plan as well. He knew how important it was that everything went smoothly and how big of a role he had. She had made a conscious decision to take control of the situation fully for herself. Besides, she never had any intention of actually hurting her or Asher in this process, at least not at the moment. But if she needed to, she would, only as a last resort.

She called her goons to pay Raphael a visit though, the same way that they had done the night they visited India. But this time, they would have to finish the job. She couldn't afford any loose ends, even if that meant having to lose the best driver that she had ever had. This morning she received a message on her burner phone letting her know that the job was done and that her wire was received. Genevieve allowed herself one minute to let out a stifled cry for Raphael that happened behind her closed fist. Raphael had been a loyal employee of hers for the last few years, but like most good things, it always had to come to an end.

Genevieve allowed one tear to fall before quickly wiping it away and coming back to reality.

"Focus, G. We are in the present now," she said to herself, gaining back her composure. Over the last few days, she had had a hard time deciphering what was the present versus what was in the past. Lately the memories of old lovers and even her mother had been haunting her and causing her to lie awake at night. During her awake moments, she kept finding herself blacking out and coming to five to twenty minutes later, unsure of what had happened.

She was used to losing the people she loved, especially at her own hands. It was a familiar daunting task that she found herself doing a lot over her lifetime. The only thing different about now is that she was able to hire people to do it for her. A vision of her mother's face flashed in her head, and she quickly dismissed it once she reached her floor.

"Here we go," she said to herself as she pushed the wheelchair out of the elevator and walked down the hallway to Asher's apartment. Once she reached 7-B she took a deep breath and commenced the plan that Raphael was supposed to be doing. She put the wheelchair in park, tapped on the front door with her fingernails and placed her ear against the door. Right on cue, she heard Maverick's nails hitting the wood floor as he raced over to the front door. She looked under the door and saw his shadow as he feverishly sniffed. She imagined he thought it was Asher, and once he caught her smell she heard him let out a low whimper and growl.

She had been prepared for this and smiled to herself as she swung the gym bag on her shoulder and pulled out the bacon-flavored rawhide she bought just for Maverick. With a quick look over both her shoulders, she took a deep breath and placed the key into the door before hearing it unlock.

"Heyyyy Maverick," she whispered once it opened.

One hour later...

Genevieve beamed to herself as she eased onto the northbound side of the highway. She was just beside herself at how flawless her plan went. It was perfect and filled with excitement, anxiety and even love. Genevieve smiled to herself and turned the radio to one of Sydney's favorite radio stations. She remembered this station because Sydney would always force Raphael to turn to it every time the three of them were in the car. She hoped that hearing the familiar music would ease Sydney's nerves once she came to in the trunk of the Maxima.

That was one thing people never talked about, how you could hear the radio clear as day in the trunk of a car. Hell, depending on the make and model, the trunk could make you feel like you were in your own personal concert sometimes. The bass was strong, the lyrics were clear, and it was dark and close, close enough to make you feel as if you were in your own studio session. That's how she used to feel anyway in the back of her Mama's 1974 Red Mustang whenever her mother had a date.

Genevieve's mama would make her go into the trunk while she turned tricks in their car that doubled as their home. One time, a man tried to force her to join them since she couldn't stop "peeking." Her mother wouldn't be able to make money with Genevieve standing there gawking at her mother going down on old, white sweaty men.

Genevieve spent most of her awkward years locked in that trunk while her mother worked. She would be grateful when her mother turned the radio up to drown out the noise that would still reach back to her. She would allow for the music to take her away each time and would fantasize about a life and love as beautiful and rich as the lyrics that belted out to her.

Genevieve finally snatched the black baseball cap off her head, and then the designer frames that she had on. She combed her fingers through her bob that laid wild on top of her head. She checked her reflection in the rearview mirror and frowned at the bags that had formed under her eyes.

"I should've gotten a Mustang," she said aloud to no one in particular. She doubted that Sydney had woken up yet from the chloroform, but just in case she had, she wanted her to know that she was there with her and that she was safe.

"My mama used to drive a Mustang. We lived in that old beat-up car for most of my early teens," she continued as she accelerated on the highway while feeling that warm familiar feeling of her entering into another locked away dream.

"You know Sydney, as much as I hated that car, I loved it too," she said laughing to herself as she envisioned the many times she laid in the backseat curled up with a book as her mother ripped and ran all over the state of Maryland.

"It was my home; it was the only thing that kept me safe and was a constant in my life. That car kept me a hell of a lot safer than my mother did, especially once puberty hit. It seemed like overnight I developed a full bosom, hips and legs that went on for DAYS," Genevieve said with a twinkle in her eye.

"Wasn't too long before Mama had competition and she realized that making me hop in the trunk just wasn't going to do it anymore. Nope, wasn't good enough for Mama that her little girl was turning more heads than she ever could at just the age of 13," she said to no one in particular.

"Yup, Mama was a jealous bitch. Thirteen was the same age where she allowed that white man from the gas station to take me and take my virginity. Imagine little ole me sitting in the backseat of the car, nose deep in *The Bluest Eye,* while my mother stood outside smoking a cigarette and pumping gas. Then comes the greasiest, dirtiest man with an old oil rag in hand coming up to her offering to give her the gas for free if he could have ten minutes with me."

"Sydney, my head popped out of that book so fast!" Genevieve squealed as she laughed, "You know what she said to him? Do you know, Sydney? That heifer said, 'Throw in an extra $50 with that gas and you can have her'. Hmph, I just knew that I heard wrong. I mean who does that, Sydney? My mama, that's who; your mother would never."

Genevieve hear herself easily slip back into her Maryland accent as she reminisced on her damaged childhood. She felt another stray tear fall out of her eye. "Shit," she mumbled to herself as she wiped it with the back of her hand. She couldn't figure out why that kept happening lately.

"Needless to say, you know what happened in that dirty, dark gas station bathroom to me," she said letting out a dry laugh as she eased over to the fast lane and accelerated to 85 mph. "I fought like hell. Sydney, I did not let him take it easily. By the time we walked out that bathroom that man had red scratches all over his face and neck. And me? I had a black eye and blood in between my legs."

"I remember walking slowly through that store crying and rushing to get away from that man as soon as possible. He told me I could 'take anything that I wanted' from the store. I guess that was an appropriate tradeoff for my virginity. I remember grabbing a Coca-Cola, a pack of gum and an automobile magazine as I slowly walked outside to my mama, who sat waiting in the car."

"I hopped in the backseat and placed the cold soda against my eye and told my mama to drive. Three days later she was dead Sydney, her and that damn car. Somehow, she lost control with us in the car one night driving down a dark back road somewhere in Baltimore. I got lucky and was ejected from the car. The only injury I had was a messed-up knee that took the brunt of my escape from the car and a bruised eye from my rape.

Mama didn't make it though. I watched her and that car head into that river and listened while she screamed and cried for help. Once they finally pulled her and the car out of the water they said it looked like someone had tampered with the brakes, but they couldn't prove it since it was such an old car."

"I spent the next two months in rehab. I had countless knee surgeries and had to relearn how to walk. Since I was a minor, the state of Maryland had to reach out to my next of kin. I knew that that would mean me going into a foster home, but instead, they were able to locate my father. I never met the man; hell I didn't even think I had a father as simple as that sounds, Sydney, but I did. He lived in Richmond, a white man who had a wife and four kids. He didn't have time for me. His family didn't even know about me or his flair for hooking up with random prostitutes. We spoke on the phone a few times and it was then decided I would go away to boarding school."

Genevieve paused in her story once she thought she heard a small thump coming from her trunk. She turned the music down all the way and heard a faint moan coming from the back of the car. She smiled at the sound of her lover stirring, but she knew she would be incapable of moving for at least another two hours. And in case she did, Genevieve had her in restraints so she wouldn't be able to move too much.

Suddenly the car filled with the sounds of her ringing phone. She looked at the dashboard and saw "Hubby" flash on the screen.

"Oh, goody Asher, you're just in time!" she said, picking up the phone.

"Genevieve," he said calmly.

"Yes, my love?"

"Genevieve... what did you do? Where is she?"

Genevieve could tell he was trying to keep his composure,

which she found adorable. She knew that on the other side of this phone Asher's face was distorted into a hard frown with a quiver stuck deep in his throat.

"I guess you got my note? Guess where we are, Ash?"

"Where is she, Genevieve? Did you... hurt her? If you did—"

"If I did what? You better not call the police, remember the note honey," she teased.

"G... please, please just tell me she is okay," he said, trying to rationalize.

"Asher, I am shocked that you think I would want to hurt her or you. Why would I do that?"

"You did it to Rachael," he said flatly.

"Well, look who finally grew a set," she giggled. "Rachael deserved it. Actually, she deserved death, but the little bitch beat the odds and survived," she said dryly.

"I love Sydney and I love you," Genevieve said, snapping back to the present. " I love you both so much it hurts Ash, don't you get that? Neither one of you will listen to me, so I have to take matters into my own hands, as usual."

"G, please— "

"Ash, you are already not following the perfectly laid out directions that I left for you, hun. I packed a bag for you and left it on the foot of the bed. We are already about 90 minutes ahead of you, but if you get on the road now you can meet us by tonight. Before this nasty storm hits."

Asher took a long sigh, thinking about his next words.

"Why Rhode Island?"

"I thought you would feel more comfortable in your own stomping grounds. I thought it would also be a nice incentive to not go to the police because I am in such close proximity to your family. I don't think this is worth mentioning, but just in case, I have my gun too, Ash. And you know how much of an excellent shot I am."

"G... why?"

"Why? Because I love you, darling. I love us. The three of us belong together forever. You two cannot see it, but I will help you to. Listen, I am getting closer to the cabin, and I am not familiar with this town. I left the name of the cabin in the note. By the time you get there, Sydney and I will be waiting for you. We are going to have a fabulous weekend Ash. Just us three, in a secluded cabin, deep in the woods in the middle of a storm," Genevieve squealed from excitement.

"Okay, okay. I am grabbing the bag and I am on the way. Please G, please do not do anything until I get there so we can ...talk."

"No promises baby, just hurry up," she cooed into the phone.

"Okay, I am on my way."

"And Ash?"

"Yeah?"

"I love you baby, and I am glad we three are giving this another try..." Genevieve said, feeling the words tumble out of her mouth. She meant it.

"Yea, me too G... I love you too and will see you soon."

Chapter 28

Friday, April 30th

Sydney

Sydney swayed and wiggled as she heard music playing.

What was that? she thought to herself as she strained to catch the faint beat that played in the background. She knew this song; it was killing her to not be able to hear it clearer. Where was it coming from? Ash wouldn't usually play the radio in the morning before he left.

Ash, she thought as she tried to open her lazy eyes to see. The only problem was that they were so heavy. Why couldn't she wake up?

Suddenly the music stopped. A woman's voice began to drift to her and get louder and louder. The voice sounded both familiar and unfamiliar. Sydney felt a flutter in her chest, as she realized that the woman's voice was talking to her. The woman sounded muffled and barely audible; she couldn't make out what she was saying. Was she dreaming? And if so, why couldn't she wake up?

The sound of a ringing phone echoed all around Sydney, causing her heart to flutter more and to jolt her awake out of her sleep. Instinctively, she tried to reach for it to silence it, but she couldn't move her hands or her arms. Everything was just too heavy to move.

Sydney must've dozed back off because the next thing she heard was Asher's voice as it woke her back up. His voice sounded so strange and on edge. Again, she felt the flutter in her chest as she tried to force herself to fully wake up.

Something isn't right, Sydney thought to herself as she was finally able to open her left eye to see nothing but darkness. She tried to wipe the sleep out of her eye but couldn't feel her hands. Then, she remembered everything.

"Genevieve," she said aloud, raspy as her throat began to burn. The memories began to come flooding in.

Sydney remembered she was in the shower when she heard someone come into Asher's room. Though she was in the bathroom with the door shut, something told her that that wasn't Asher. Alarmed, she stepped out of the shower quietly, being sure to leave the water running so as to not spook the intruder. She threw a towel around her wet body as she desperately looked around the small bathroom for her phone. She had left it in the bedroom.

Sydney remembered trying to think fast about what to do. Her heart was jolting hard in her chest. Before she knew it, the bathroom door swung open and her worst nightmare appeared — cool, calm and collected in the doorway.

"Hi Sydney," Genevieve said with a twinkle in her eye.

The two stood there staring at each other, sizing each other up. Sydney knew if she moved fast enough, she would be able to get around Genevieve and out of the apartment where she could run. But as soon as she attempted to dart around her, Genevieve blocked her way and giggled as Sydney cowered away from her.

"Sydney, let's not make this difficult, hun. We just need to talk and sort through this. All of us."

"Genevieve, let me go," Sydney said, trying her best to sound brave.

"I can't let you do that Sydney," she said coldly as she stepped closer to her.

"He— " she tried to scream.

Sydney couldn't get the words out of her mouth before Genevieve took a lunge for her and covered her mouth. The two tussled for a while. Sydney was surprised at how strong Genevieve was. She was petite and dainty, and Sydney had at least a few inches on her in height. But at that moment, Genevieve moved like a deranged animal capable of murder.

Sydney was able to elbow Genevieve hard in the nose when trying to free herself from her grasp. The hit was so hard that it caused Genevieve's head to snap backwards as blood flew everywhere. In the process of Genevieve getting hit, Sydney's towel flew off, landed on the floor, and wrapped around her ankles and caused her to lose her balance as she fought from falling on the slippery bathroom tile. Clumsily, Sydney turned around and tried to make it to the door just as she got snatched backwards. Genevieve had grabbed Sydney's hair and yanked her back, causing her head to hit the sink. When she came back to, she was on the ground with her own blood pouring from the side of her head.

"Don't worry baby, I am here," Genevieve cooed as she kneeled down over Sydney with blood still pouring from her own nose.

Genevieve gently moved her braid out of Sydney's face and smiled, "God I missed you Sydney," she said before pulling a black handkerchief out of her pocket and placing it firmly over Sydney's mouth and nose.

Sydney tried to shake her face free, but Genevieve only held onto her neck and head tighter as she forced Sydney to breathe in the toxins that quickly turned her body numb. The last thing she remembered was Genevieve gently placing

Sydney's head back on the floor and then lightly kissing and sucking on her lips.

"I missed these lips baby. Stay here while I straighten up a bit and get you some clothes. I promise Sydney, everything will be fine."

Everything is not fine, Sydney thought to herself now in the present. She tried to rack her brain for a memory of what to do in a situation like this. In college, she and India had attended a women's safety seminar. One of the tips that the women gave was how to get out of a locked trunk when being kidnapped. Of course, in their scenarios they didn't prepare you for what to do when your psychopath ex-girlfriend drugs you, knocks you out unconscious and then proceeds to dress and tie you up before tossing you into the trunk of her car.

My feet, Sydney thought as she began to feel the hot burn that was coming from the left side of her skull. Maybe she would be able to kick the back taillight out and signal for help. She tried to move her heavy legs and feet but quickly realized they were tied down, too. She couldn't even defend herself if she tried.

Sydney began to let out a silent sob that shook her whole body. What was she going to do? Where was Genevieve taking her and what was her plan? Would she ever see her family again?

"Asher," she cried as she realized she may never see him again, either. But then she remembered hearing his voice in one of her hazy moments. That was him on the phone, was he in on this? Did he turn his back on her and play her again? What if this was just a sick game for the two and they decided they had had enough with their favorite toy.

Sydney felt a sharp pain from her skull and realized she was still bleeding and in pretty bad shape. She was sure she had a concussion, at minimum. Her head felt full as if it were swollen; she wondered if her head injury would be the demise of her, not Genevieve.

Suddenly, the car began to jump and shake as Sydney felt her body ease backwards. She could tell they were going down a graveled hill as she bounced all over the trunk, relieved to even feel the dull aches of her body bouncing against the heavy metal. She was gaining back feeling.

Once the car stopped, Sydney tried to calm herself down as she wiggled her fingers and then eventually her hands. She wanted to be ready for whatever may happen when that trunk opened. For all she knew, Genevieve could be getting ready to toss her ass off a cliff.

"Shit," Sydney squealed to herself as she tried to rip off the zip ties choking her wrists. She felt the car door slam and heard footsteps approaching her. Sydney froze.

She tried to think about what one of the instructors from the seminar talked about. Sydney remembered this woman in particular because she had a gorgeous tattooed sleeve on her left arm. In the seminar, the woman spoke to them about the importance of remaining as calm as possible as you took up as much information as you could.

Sydney focused on her five senses. She couldn't see shit but darkness. Even now, when she had both eyes fully open. She couldn't smell anything but her body wash and the smell of iron, her blood. She tasted metal, a sign of a bloody mouth and probably a concussion. She couldn't touch anything with her hands but felt the aches and trembles that shook all over her body. The drugs were wearing off. And finally, she could hear... birds. A lot of birds, chirping and singing in the distance. It had to be hundreds of them. Sydney closed her eyes and strained to hear more. She didn't hear other voices, cars or even music. Just birds and the sounds of nature. Faintly, she believed she even heard water, like from a nearby waterfall. Wherever they were, it was far from Boston.

Sydney began to wiggle her toes, thrilled to have feeling return to her feet. Maybe she would try to make a run for it. But how?

She didn't have much time to plot her next move before she heard a beep and the trunk began to slowly open, filling her small space with damp cool air and a drizzle of rain. It took Sydney's eyes a minute to refocus and adjust. When they did, the first thing she saw was a dark gray sky before seeing Genevieve's terrifying face below it.

Sydney hadn't been able to get a clear view of Genevieve before when she was fighting to get away from her. But now, she saw her more clearly. Genevieve was a mess. Her nose and lips were covered with dry blood from when Sydney hit her when trying to get away. Genevieve's hair, which looked like it hadn't been combed in days, was plaited all over her head and looked unwashed and unkept. Her eyes were beady, likely from sleep deprivation, and darted from side to side. Underneath them were dark and heavy bags.

Sydney was surprised to see this porcelain doll, now cracked. Genevieve was flawless from the moment she woke up to the moment she went to sleep, and now she looked like the monster she truly was.

"Rise and shine, baby, look who's awake!" Genevieve said as she gently rubbed Sydney's cheek with the back of her hand.

"Where are we?" Sydney asked hoarsely as she tried to snatch her face away from her reach.

"We, my darling, are on a much-needed couple's vacation. Or should I say a *throuple's* vacation?" she asked herself before laughing at her own joke.

"I got us a romantic cabin, deep, deep in the woods. So, if you scream, no one will hear you holler, Sydney," she said playfully tapping Sydney's nose, "Whether in ecstasy or otherwise. What do you think about that?"

Sydney responded with silence. She couldn't do anything but grit her teeth.

"Well, come on, let's get you out of the car and back into your wheelchair. We have to clean you up and tend to that wound you got yourself. Hopefully you'll be a good girl and I won't have to drug you again. What do you think?" she asked as if this were routine, as she locked the wheelchair in place and looked around.

Sydney looked up at Genevieve with a mix of disgust and terror.

"You are a sick, sick bitch Genevieve," she said painfully.

"Ouch. Save all that for when Ash gets here Syd, you know I only like dirty talk in the bedroom," she said winking as she hoisted her up out of the trunk.

Chapter 29

Friday, April 30th

A single tear rolled down Sydney's cheek as she heard the scissors snip away at her hair.

"Sydney, darling, you just look so much better with short hair, don't you think?" Genevieve asked as she stood over Sydney, cutting and yanking her braids wildly.

Sydney looked down at the fallen braids around her. She didn't know what Genevieve was doing to her head. There were no nearby mirrors for her to see the magnitude of the damage she had done. The only thing that was certain was that Sydney was sitting there helpless as this insane woman hacked her hair off , unevenly, with shears. Sydney didn't really care about her hair, the only thing she cared about was getting away and fast.

Once Genevieve dragged her into the wheelchair and out of the trunk, Sydney decided to act as if she still had no control of her arms or legs. Genevieve fell for it and fawned over Sydney as she helped her into the house and cleaned her up. Begrudgingly, Sydney acted limp when Genevieve gave her a sink bath and then put her into the pale-yellow short set that she had laid out on the California King bed in their cabin.

Genevieve wasn't completely fooled however; she still sat Sydney in the seat with her hands and ankles tied to either side of the wheelchair, trapping her in.

"Here, almost done. Oh!" Genevieve squealed as she ran over to stand in front of Sydney to admire her work, "I know what we are missing. I brought you something from your and Asher's place," she said, kneeling down in front of Sydney looking like a schoolgirl.

Sydney looked through her, trying to not give her the satisfaction of a reaction.

"Sydney, I know you can talk, honey, you're not fooling anyone," she said while rubbing Sydney's legs tenderly. "You should just give in and enjoy it babe. Asher will be here in a minute."

Sydney's eyes darted and looked directly into Genevieve's.

"Ahh ha, see I knew that would get your attention," she laughed teasingly. "Here let me go get it, I threw it in your bag," she said, hopping to her feet and running behind her out of the room.

Sydney took a moment to look around the cabin. It was a typical high-end small "glamping" cabin. The place was made of nothing but sturdy, durable wood, high ceilings and high-end furniture. It was right up Genevieve's lane. Sydney wiggled her hands in their restraints as she wondered which one of Genevieve's exclusive friends gave her this hook up and if they knew what she planned to do at this cabin.

Sydney tried to look around her to soak her surroundings in. She was still on high alert and wanted to map out any possible escape routes for when she was able to run. The front door was two rooms away from where she was, in the living room. But behind her was the master suite, where Genevieve was. She didn't see another back door and noted that there were not many windows, however there was one odd one in the bedroom that seemed reachable.

"Here, I know it's in here somewhere," Genevieve said, appearing out of the blue with a duffle bag in her hand.

Sydney gasped at the sight of the bag, causing her and Genevieve to freeze.

"What?" Genevieve asked, smiling looking back at her. "I saw your lipstick on the dresser, or at least I hope it was yours. Anyway," she said, quickly dismissing the notion that Asher could possibly have another woman, "I tossed it in the bag. Thought you would like— "

"I'd much rather wear yours, Genevieve," Sydney said, trying to mask the tremble in her voice. "You know that red YSL one you always carry on you. I know you have it babe," Sydney said steadily.

"Oh, you mean that *Rouge Pur Couture*," Genevieve said, lowering her voice and tossing the bag onto the nearby couch.

"Mhm," Sydney said, shaking her head as Genevieve ran to the bedroom.

Sydney took a sigh of relief before turning her eyes back to the duffle bag. Genevieve thought that bag was Sydney's, but it wasn't; it was Asher's. More importantly, was what was in it, tucked away in the pocket inside. The .22 caliber gun Asher had tried to give Sydney one afternoon last week.

Sydney had felt spooked when on her way to work the other day. She opted to hop off of the bus a few stops early so that she could walk the last two blocks to the restaurant. It was a beautiful spring day, and she wanted some fresh air; she was tired of being cooped up at both her and Asher's place. It hadn't been too long ago when Asher finally let her move around freely without him or hired protection. On that day, she felt paranoid during her walk. As if she were being watched and followed and even ran the last block to work. Right before she turned the final block before getting to her job, Sydney looked back and thought she saw a glimpse of Raphael's salt and pepper hair. She would've been surprised if he had really followed and kept up with her this long; but she swore it was him.

She told Asher what she saw as soon as he picked her up from work that night and he tried to tell her to take the gun. She told him no but compromised that they would keep it there for her. She tossed it in his bag for safekeeping and tucked it away, not trusting herself with it.This hadn't been like before when she had one after India was attacked. This time she not only knew her attacker, but she knew she may have to take a life to save her own. Sydney couldn't handle the thought.

Genevieve must've seen the bag tucked in the closet and thought it was Sydney's. Luckily for her, Sydney was a slob so her bright PINK bag was tucked underneath the bed and hidden from Genevieve's eyesight.

Sydney felt a flutter in her chest again, this time with hope. All she had to do was somehow manage to get the gun out of that bag, and she would be golden. But first, she had to keep Genevieve distracted and make sure that she kept her guard down.

"You were right, Sydney, I found a tube in my overnight bag. Now let me see those pretty lips," Genevieve said as she bent over to apply the ruby red lipstick carefully to Sydney's lips. "There...you're perfect, Sydney. Look."

Genevieve pulled her phone out of her back pocket and turned her camera on so that it could double as a mirror. It took everything out of Sydney to not cry once she saw her reflection. Her face was swollen and bruised. She had a knot on her forehead and could see the dark purple bruise forming around her left eye. Her hair was a hacked-up mess of scalp and chopped off braids. She looked like a black Cynthia doll from the Rugrats. The lipstick had been spread so wildly all over

Sydney's mouth and face as if she were a clown. She was unrecognizable.

"It's beautiful babe," Sydney said as she felt the tears burning her eyes.

"You're beautiful," Genevieve said, dropping back to her knees and sliding over to Sydney. "Since I saw you today, Sydney, all I could think about was how much I missed you. It hurt me so bad when you left me, Sydney. Why would you leave me like that, baby?" she asked as she rubbed Sydney's face gently with the back of her hand. For a moment there, Sydney thought Genevieve would shed a tear. Instead, she took her hand back and quickly slapped Sydney across her face, sending drool flying out of Sydney's mouth.

Sydney bit her lip to muffle a scream, though she felt the tears fall from her eyes. "I'm sorry Genevieve, but... hey I'm here now, right?"

"Yes, you are. And Asher should be here any minute," Genevieve said chipperly as she looked over her shoulder at the front door. "Hey I got an idea," she squealed.

"Oh yeah?" Sydney asked shakily, trying to regain a sense of composure even though her face was on fire.

"Yeah, how about a kiss. I should take advantage of this time I have you all to myself before Ash gets here," she said as she slowly stood on her feet before sitting down on Sydney's lap. She wrapped her arms around Sydney's neck, causing Sydney's nose to be assaulted with the smell of her body odor. Genevieve smelled and looked like she hadn't washed herself in days.

"How about you let me loose out of these ties so it can feel real?" Sydney asked softly, "I still don't have much feeling, but— "

"I missed those pretty, soft lips," Genevieve said softly as she cupped Sydney's fragile face in her hand before pulling her in for a kiss. Sydney held her breath as she felt Genevieve press her dry lips firmly against hers and moan. She closed her eyes and tried her best not to move away. Once she finally opened her eyes she saw Genevieve lost in her own world while she continued to kiss her.

"Umm, mhmm," Asher said, clearing his throat and appearing at the front door with a key in his hand.

"Oh, Ash," Genevieve said excitedly, gasping for air, "We missed you babe, come here," Genevieve said standing to her feet and wiping Sydney's lipstick from around her mouth.

Asher did as he was told and took a few steps over to them, never once taking his eyes off Sydney. Sydney sat in the chair gasping for the air that had been stolen from Genevieve's sloppy kiss. She took one look at Asher's concerned-etched face and cussed herself out for ever questioning him. It was clear he was here, without backup, because of his love for her.

"Looks like you guys got the party started without me G," he said now looking at her face and noting the smeared lipstick all over it.

"I mean look at her Ash, can you blame me? Here, I didn't forget about you either," she said standing on her tippy toes as she gave him a long dramatic kiss that included plenty of tongue and moaning.

While Genevieve happily sucked Asher's face off, she took the opportunity to pat his sides and butt, seemingly looking for a gun or weapon. Asher looked up at Sydney during this just in time to see her mouth "bag" as she pointed her head in the direction of his duffle bag. Sydney swore she saw a light glow in Asher's eyes once he realized what she was trying to show him.

"Whoa, whoa, there tiger. We have all night G," Asher said as Genevieve bit his bottom lip and held it captive between her teeth before he gently pushed her away.

"You're right babe, how about some wine to celebrate?"

"Sounds like a plan. Can we let Sydney out of these restraints though? I think they are a little excessive, don't you,

G?" he walked over closer to Sydney, only to be cut off by Genevieve who stood between them.

"Now, why would I do that?" Genevieve giggled as she reached behind her back to pull out a gun. "Do you know I had to actually tussle and drug this girl, Ash?" she chuckled as she pointed the gun in Sydney's direction.

"Easy there G," Asher said trying to lower her arm, "But there isn't a need for that now right? I mean look at her, look at us. Babe, we are here, we love you G," Asher said, grabbing her left hand and kissing the inside of her palm. "She is harmless, and you see I came weaponless like you asked."

"I love you too Asher... but no," she said, snatching her hand back and tucking the gun into her pants. "Let me get that wine for us. I'll be right back," she said, skipping off to the kitchen.

As soon as she was out of earshot, Asher made a beeline over to Sydney. He reached into his back pocket for his small pocketknife and began to cut off her right restraint.

"Ash, what are you doing, get the gun out of the bag," Sydney said under her breath as she looked over his shoulder to make sure Genevieve wasn't near.

"No Syd, I gotta get you out of here first. Once you are free, run. I want you to run south and do not stop!" he emphasized, "Do you hear me?"

"I'm not leaving without you," she said, beginning to cry as she felt her right wrist slowly become free.

"I will be right behind you. It's hella dark out and the storm has knocked a few trees down already. I want you to stay off the road as much as possible, so run through the woods but you have to be careful...there is mud everywhere. There is a gas station about two miles from here. Run there, call the police and tell them we are at the Shakes Luxury Cabin resort— "

"Ash, I am not leaving without you," Sydney snapped back.

"Syd, I am not asking you," he said curtly as he freed her

right hand."I have to stay back to make sure she doesn't go after you or my family. She knew what she was doing; this place is only 15 fucking minutes away from my mother's. I will be right behind you."

"What are you going to do?" Sydney asked, not wanting to hear the answer. "And what about Raphael? I'm sure he's lurking around here somewhere. This just confirms it was him that I thought I saw the other day, Ash!" Sydney said, raising her voice slightly.

"Shh," he said as he began to work on her left wrist, "We don't have to worry about him, Syd."

"Why not?"

"Because he is dead." He paused as he looked at her. For the first time, Sydney could see fear etched all over his face.

"How do you know?"

"His sister called me on the way in... she said it looked like a home invasion."

"Yeah, that sounds familiar," Sydney whispered. "Ash, what are you going to do?"

"Something I should have done years ago," he said as he cut her other wrist free and looked up at her. "I love you Syd, we are going to be alright, I promise. This is all my fault and I will make it right. Aww babe... look what she did to your face," he breathed as he touched her forehead lightly before his eyes softened.

"Ashhh," Genevieve sang from the kitchen, "You guys are too quiet in there. You better not have gotten started without me."

"Here," Asher said, closing the knife and putting it in her free hand, "Finish this quickly and get out as fast as you can," he said before pulling out his gun from an ankle holster and placing it in between her legs.

"I'm right behind you, I promise. Lock the door and escape out of the bathroom or something," he said as he kissed her on the forehead before rolling her backwards into the bedroom and closing the door. "I'll get the other gun from the bag. We're going to be fine I promise, Syd."

As soon as the door closed behind Ash, Sydney leaped forward in her chair and locked it. Shakily, she then fumbled to open the switchblade and began cutting the zip ties around her ankles. Ash hadn't had a chance to scope the place out like Sydney did. If he had, he would know that there wasn't a window in the bathroom to escape from, not one that actually opened anyway. By him wheeling her into this room, he basically trapped her in a cage.

"Where is Sydney?" Genevieve asked stiffly, returning to the room.

"I thought you and I could talk... just us two," Asher said calmly.

"No, no, no, we don't do this anymore Ash!" Genevieve yelled as Sydney heard the sound of glass shattering.

Sydney began to work faster and heard the beautiful snap of her restraint pop on her right leg. She moved over to the left while keeping an eye trained on the door, ready to shoot if need be.

"G, just calm down!" Asher yelled.

"No, Asher, I will not. Things got messed up when this trio decided to just be two, don't you remember? Don't you, Ash? It's just like Rachael all over again. This time, I will give you Sydney; you see I am letting her live, right...? Well for now."

"For now?" Asher said, sounding closer. Sydney could tell he stood blocking the door to the bedroom.

"Yes, for now. I wanted to tell you this when all three of us are here. But I figured it out, Ash. I knew it would only be a matter of time before my brilliant mind figured it all out, per usual. You, Sydney and I? This is for life, baby. I've come up with a plan to keep all three of us together forever."

"G... you're scaring me; what are you saying?"

"I'm saying," Genevieve paused theatrically, "that this is it for us. This is where our story both ends and begins."

"Genevieve, put the gun down," Asher said calmly.

"I planned a romantic evening for us three. We will make love in that big bed in there. All three of us, just like how we used to. Don't you remember that, Ash?" she asked with tears clouding her voice, "Don't you remember how happy we were? I know it was only for a short spell... but we were happy Ash."

"Yea G, I remember. I remember the jealousy and fights that came with it too," Asher said sharply.

Sydney cut her last leg loose and stood up, allowing blood to rush back to her weak legs. She didn't know why Asher was getting so combative with a gun in his face. Then she remembered the small gun she left in the wheelchair and the other in his gym bag. She wanted to know what Genevieve had planned for them and hoped it wasn't what it sounded like. Asher was too close to the bedroom, moving farther and farther away from the bag. What was he doing?

She tried to grab the gun quietly as she scanned the room to find any shoes for her. Sydney knew that Ash was buying her time to get out, but she couldn't leave him. Not like this.

"G... put the gun down," Asher said slowly, as if talking to a wild animal.

"What? This? No Ash, I will not," she laughed. "Don't be scared, hun. I promise it will be quick."

Sydney froze in her tracks and gripped the gun tighter in her hand.

I should just go out there and shoot this bitch, she thought to herself as she realized what was happening.

"What will be quick, Genevieve?" Asher said coarsely, his words ripping through the air.

"Hmph," Genevieve chuckled, "It will be the best murder-suicide in history. Just think about it Ash, I will be immortalized forever. I can see it now, all the headlines will say '*World famous Author Genevieve Cross, murdered alongside her husband by her obsessed former assistant,'"* she said crying and laughing at the same time.

Genevieve sounded hysterical and Sydney didn't know how much longer Asher would be able to hold her off. Fear reset in Sydney as she ran over to a small window that sat above a dresser in the room. Sydney instantly had a flashback of her hazy ride in the trunk of Genevieve's car. She remembered hearing Genevieve talk about her mother. More importantly, she remembered hearing her confess to killing her as well. Sydney placed the gun down on the dresser that sat in front of her, and slowly hoisted her body on top of it so that she was eye level with the window.

She slowly unlatched the lock on the window and slid it open to a wired screen. She unsuccessfully tried to open the wire screen to realize that it was sealed close. She wouldn't be able to get through it like this. Sydney quickly reached into her pocket and pulled out Asher's switchblade and pierced a hole through the screen that stood as a barrier between her and the outside. She struggled to stay quiet as she stood on her tippy toes, trying to cut through the tough and wet wire silently. She began to dig hard at the small opening that she had created. This window was just big enough for her to get through. She had to hurry up if she wanted to save them both.

"G... no. We don't have to die; we can figure this out. Just you and me— "

"Just you and me? Just you and me!?" she yelled louder. "Where were 'you and me' when you were fuckin' the help behind my back, Asher? Answer me that, darling."

Asher was silent.

"You see, you have that same look on your face that you had when I tried to get rid of Rachael. The same look you had on your face the night you came running after me into Sydney's room. You're pathetic Ash, honestly," she laughed dryly. "A part of me was delighted to see you go. I could finally live the life of my dreams. I could come and go as I pleased. Fuck who I please and actually be around people who were actually *interesting*. People who could hold both an enlightened conversation about the politics of the world while simultaneously divulging the importance of having nonstop non-monogamous sex for the rest of our lives."

"So why don't you just let me go Genevieve? If I am so fuckin' beneath you and boring, let me go," he shouted back.

Genevieve continued her deep throaty laugh before finally answering him, "I said only a part of me, Ash. The other part quickly remembered who the fuck I am."

"So now you plan to just kill me? If you were so fuckin' better off without me— why this?"

"Because your love is mine and mind alone! You are *my* husband Ash, don't you get it?" she asked with her voice cracking in pain. "If you won't have me, then who will, Ash?" she screamed back.

"When will it stop G? First Rachael, India, then Raphael... now us," he shouted, this time with fear in his voice. "You can have anyone and everyone you ever want. I give you that! I sat here for years with my balls in my hands for years! The moment I find true happiness... you take it. When does it just fuckin' end?"

"Tonight, my love, it ends tonight," Genevieve answered back. "Move out of my way Asher."

"G—"

"No, let me rephrase this. I have the gun, you have nothing. Now move out of my fuckin' way," she shouted hysterically.

"Genevieve this is between you and me. Look, I do not want to hurt you. Please just let her go— "

"Go? She's in a wheelchair, how can she *go?* You and her both *go* and *do* what I say Ash," she said laughing again. "I can't fathom why you, the idiot without a gun, and her, the girl strapped into a wheelchair, have the audacity to think—"

Abruptly, Sydney heard a scuffle in front of the bedroom door. She began to cut harder only to have the knife get caught in the wire. She couldn't get it to move or even take it out of the tangled wired mess.

"Fuck," Sydney cried to herself as she painfully began to tear at the wired screen window with her bare hands, desperate to get out to safety. The screen began to bend and tear apart as her bloody,shredded hands shook while she tried to rip it quickly and quietly.

"G, no!"

Sydney heard the rupture of a bullet in the air and froze in terror.

Asher, she thought to herself, feeling the hairs on her arms raise. She came back to her senses once she saw the gun that lay beside her on the dresser. She instantly tossed it through the open window and onto the wet yard outside.

Sydney stuck both arms out of the window and pulled her sore body through the small opening. She bit her lip in pain as she felt the wild wire cut through the flesh on her side and thighs as she crawled out on her elbows.

"Ugh," Sydney groaned as she turned onto her back and pulled herself out the rest of the way. "I made it, I made it," she said, reassuring herself as she grabbed the gun and tried to stand barefoot on the wet grass.

Sydney got her bearings together just in time to hear another gunshot from inside the cabin. Her heart sank.

I should go back, he may need help, Sydney thought to herself as she looked down at the gun in her hand.

Just as she began to raise the gun to head into the now quiet cabin, Sydney heard the sound of another shot, this time through the bedroom door.

"Sydney!" Genevieve screamed wildly as she began kicking and beating on the door.

Sydney took off running south. She knew that Asher was dead and as much as it killed her, she had to leave him. There was no point in waiting. She must do what he told her to do.

Sydney made wide strides barefoot through the hilly grass that led to the trees. She knew that she had to get out of Genevieve's sight as soon as possible and it would be best if she stayed off of the roads. It didn't help that she was in a bright yellow romper that would be easily spotted even at night. Sydney ran into the woods, feeling branches, leaves and rain slap her in the face with every step. Every stride on her bare feet felt like hot whips as she ran blindly through the woods over slippery twigs, roots and sharp rocks.

Sydney tried to stay focused on her run and tried to pretend it was no different than her daily runs that she did through the city. She kept her mouth closed and legs swift as she fearlessly ran as fast as she could towards help.

Sydney had to be running for a few minutes when she finally ducked off behind the trunk of a large tree. She panted silently as she strained to hear if she were being followed. Sydney shakily grabbed at the earth around her feet and rubbed it all over her body. She wanted to blend into the dark forest as best as possible and as long as she was in this yellow, she would stick out like a sore thumb.

"Breathe Syd, breathe," she said quietly to herself as she tried to regulate her breathing and nerves. Her hands were shaking so hard that Sydney didn't know if it was from the cold or fear.

Asher's face suddenly appeared in Sydney's mind, and she felt a crushing sense of sorrow come all over her body. Suddenly her whole body convulsed and she bit her lip to suppress the scream that was forming in her throat.

"Asher's dead." Her initial shock had worn off. "He died

trying to save me," she yelled as she wrapped her arms around herself and sobbed.

Sydney knew she didn't have time for this breakdown, but she couldn't help it. She was scared, hurt and alone. The only person in this world who knew where she was had been killed and she was sure to follow. Sydney slumped back further into the tree as she allowed the grief to consume her.

"I promise, if you come back with me now, it will all be okay, Sydney."

Sydney instantly grabbed the gun that laid at her feet and held her breath. It was Genevieve, and she was close, very close. Sydney put her back directly on the tree as she slowly rose to her feet and strained to hear where Genevieve was. She couldn't believe she had caught up to her. Sydney had easily run a mile. What was a quick warm up for her would have exhausted the average non runner.

"Darling," Genevieve said eerily as the gun's safety went off, "Come out and all will be fine."

Sydney stood frozen behind the tree. She weighed out her options of making a run for it. Through the darkness and rain, she could see a small opening only a few feet in front of her. If she made it through that, she should be able to lose her quickly.

"You know, he said your name just as he died, Sydney. '*Sydney... Sydney*'," Genevieve said, mocking him. "Sounded rather pathetic if you ask me, him begging for you— to his wife — " Genevieve spat bitterly, with her voice sounding even closer in the dark.

Sydney ran around the tree and began to shoot the gun off wildly in the air out of anger.

"Ugh," she screamed as she shot off into the darkness, praying that one of the bullets would penetrate Genevieve's cold heart.

Sydney only released the trigger once she realized there were no longer any bullets flying out. She threw the gun down and turned around to take off running. Sydney ran with vengeance through the woods, this time barely feeling any of the branches that scratched at her skin, leaving her even more bloody.

"You stupid bitch!"

Sydney could hear Genevieve gaining on her from behind her as she panted and stomped through the thick mud. She hadn't shot her at all.

"Fuck," Sydney screamed as her left foot got caught under a root, sending her entire body falling frontward into mud.

"Sydney! Help!" Genevieve screamed in pain, "My knee! Sydney please, please I think it blew!"

Sydney tried to stand up on her feet only to wince in pain from the shooting pain that came from her own broken ankle. She bit her lip more as she laid down and listened to try to figure out where Genevieve was, which was hard as the rain was pounding the ground around them.

"Sydney! Babe, please help me, please," Genevieve screamed somewhere in the darkness.

To Sydney, she only sounded a few feet away. She was way too close to her, and Sydney cursed herself out for wasting time by breaking down at the tree.

Sydney looked behind her and couldn't see anything more than the dark sky and pouring rain. She was no fool and damn sure wasn't going back to help her. Her bum knee proved to be a blessing in this moment. This gave Sydney a distraction to get away from Genevieve, who she imagined laid out somewhere near unable to move.

Sydney looked over her shoulder as she tried to keep the weight off her left leg as she pulled herself up onto a nearby tree. Ahead, she could see the lights of the gas station that couldn't be more than forty yards away. Sydney happily started to hop towards it only to lose her balance and fall back to her knees exhaustedly.

Stubbornly, she slid up onto all fours and began to crawl to the station. She would make it there by any means necessary. She pushed through and ignored all the agony of pain that she felt all over her body as she crawled clumsily through the slick, thick mud and darkness. It was no wonder that she and Genevieve hurt themselves out here, these woods were like a deathtrap in this storm. Asher was right.

"You stupid, ungrateful little bitch," Genevieve growled behind Sydney as she grabbed Sydney's jagged braid and turned her towards her.

"You were about to just leave me out here to die; you're a stupid, stupid little girl," she spat in her face as she shoved the gun under Sydney's chin.

Sydney swung back at her wearily to only have Genevieve shove the gun harder into her throat as she pulled Sydney closer to her face. Sydney wrapped her hands around Genevieve's arms in hopes of moving the gun from her windpipe.

"You hear me crying for help and you ignored me? Maybe I'll just kill your worthless ass out here instead and be sure to pin it all on Asher. How would you like that, huh?" Genevieve stood lopsided, supporting her weight with her right leg.

"Fuck you Genevieve," Sydney choked as tears ran out her eyes and mixed in with the rain.

"Oh Sydney, oh darling, you have fucked me in more ways than you will ever know. Sydney, you were my favorite. I adored you, you were my protégé, babe. Why have you forced us to do this? Why would you want to ruin what the three of us had?! Answer me!"

"G!"

"Huh?" Genevieve said as she turned around just in time for the bullet to rip through her chest, forcing her to fall lifelessly on top of Sydney.

Chapter 30

One year later...

Sydney scrolled aimlessly on her phone as Cai talked to her in the background. They were on their way home from a long Saturday shift at Flamingo's. Sydney stretched her legs and sighed as she thought about how tired she was. Lately, she had been burning the candle at both ends while working and taking her classes.

Thanks to the nudge of her mother and Maverick, Sydney had finally figured out what to do with her life. She decided to go back to school to be a veterinarian.

"And then I told him, 'Don't you know you have to take me somewhere nice?' I mean is it too much to ask that we don't go to Boston Market for every date night? Right? Helloooo," Cai asked agitatedly as she swatted at Sydney's thigh.

"Sorry girl," Sydney said, yawning and continuing to swipe before landing on the profile of a twenty-something man in New Jersey.

"I'm giving you a ride Sydney; the least you can do is listen to me bitch about my dating life," Cai teased.

"You're right Cai, my bad," Sydney said half-heartedly as her eyes remained glued to the screen.

"What you looking at anyway?" Cai said, peeking into Sydney's phone once they reached a light.

"Nothing," Sydney said, locking her phone screen.

"Sure didn't look like nothin'," Cai squealed. "So India was right!"

"Right about what? Didn't I tell you that you guys are not allowed to talk or be friends unless I am around?" Sydney asked sarcastically.

"She told me she saw you on a dating site! I didn't believe her, but now look," Cai said, gliding the car through the light and entering Sydney's neighborhood.

"It's nothing, Cai, you and India are just nosey! And why is she up there anyway?"

"She and Dij broke up again, but don't try to change the subject and don't tell her I told you. Did you not learn from last time? I mean honestly, Sydney, you almost died!" Cai yelled as she parked sharply in front of Sydney's building.

"Damn, thanks for the ride with a side of whiplash Cai," Sydney joked as she rubbed the back of her neck and looked over at an agitated Cai.

She knew she was bound to get this response from her family and friends. That's why she didn't inform any of them that she had ventured back on to the dating scene. Last year was really rough for Sydney and everyone close in her life. But nothing was rougher than when she had to tell her mom the truth about her relationship with Genevieve and Asher.

"Cai, I promise. I know last year was rough, but that was then, and this is now."

"And what about him? Is he okay with this?" Cai asked, pointing her chin to the apartment building behind her.

Sydney sighed and faced the window.

"Asher doesn't know. After all that we've been through, the last thing on his mind is sharing me with anyone."

"I don't blame him, that lady was sick. That whole lifestyle—"

"Hey," Sydney said sharply as she raised her hand to stop Cai, "As I said before. Genevieve... Genevieve was a psychopath. Her ideas, her ways and her insanity had nothing to do with the polyamory lifestyle. It had everything to do with Genevieve."

Sydney had become so used to defending this, she almost had her speech memorized from when she explained it to her mother and Asher.

"I believe in the polyamory lifestyle. I love Asher with every fiber of my being and things are great! But I would be lying if I said something wasn't missing. I miss having that third person," Sydney said quietly.

She wasn't lying. Genevieve was a narcissist. She was a control freak with a mental illness and degrees to match. Everything that Sydney went through was to be blamed on Genevieve and not polyamory. It wasn't all bad though. Sydney hated to admit it, but at times she missed the trio. She missed waking up to the two of them, the deep conversations they would have that they all would add their unique perspective to. She missed the balance of having a third person, and to be honest, she missed the sex.

A few hours later, Sydney had successfully taken a shower, walked Maverick and was nose-deep in a textbook in their bedroom when Asher finally got home. Per usual, she heard Maverick bark and pant with excitement at the sight of Asher to only follow it with a low growl.

"Ash?" Sydney asked, her heart beginning to race.

After their intrusion last year, they got Maverick some security training in order to protect the household. The growl that he let out was one of warning.

"Yeah babe, it's me," Asher yelled up the stairs to Sydney's relief. "Can you come down for a sec? We have company."

Sydney could hear how off-putting Asher's tone was and she immediately got up and headed down the stairs.

"Hey my love," Asher said, brushing the braids out of Sydney's face and kissing her on the lips. "This is Vic, my lawyer."

"Yes, we met during the trial. Nice to see you again Vic," Sydney said, shaking his hand.

"You too, Ms. Mack," Vic said as he shook her hand eagerly.

"That's right, sorry, how about we all have a seat?" Asher asked as he swooped his hair off of his shoulders and into a loose bun at the top of his head.

Uh oh, Sydney thought to herself.

Sydney did as she was told and followed Asher to the loveseat before placing her hand on his knee.

"What's wrong?"

"Syd, I don't know how to say this or where even to start," Asher said, dropping his eyes to his feet and clenching his jaw.

"How about I step in Asher? If I may," Vic said, clearing his throat.

"Please," Asher said, removing his glasses and pinching the bridge of his nose.

"Well, I'm going to keep it real simple and not sugar-coat anything for you, Ms. Mack," Vic began, "This afternoon, my office received word that Asher was being sued by Genevieve's estate."

Sydney let out a harsh laugh. She must've heard wrong.

"Why would they be suing him? She tried to kill us, remember? The only reason either one of us are here right now is because Asher shot her to save me."

"Syd, let him finish," Ash said quietly as he cupped her hand into his.

Sydney bit her trembling lip and took a deep breath. She

instantly had a flashback of that night, seeing Genevieve getting shot and desperately trying to move her body from off top of her before the shooter got her next. By the time she pushed her off of her, she saw Asher holding himself up on a tree clenching his bloody side with one hand while holding a gun in his other hand. He fell to the ground once he saw Sydney was alive. Sydney had crawled over to him and held him in her arms until the police came.

Vic cleared his throat again, "Well, seems like Genevieve's estate is suing Asher for child support—"

"Child support?!" Sydney yelled looking at Ash for validation.

"Yes, as you know, Genevieve was found guilty for attempted manslaughter and kidnapping. Though we didn't get the result we wanted of life in prison, it was decided that she would be condemned to the psychiatric hospital."

"Of course, so tell me where the child support comes in?" Sydney said sharply, wanting him to get to the point. An attribute she learned from Genevieve.

"Well it seems during the trial, before she was sentenced obviously, Mrs. Cross got her hands on some old semen samples that the couple had stored a few years ago. She successfully underwent in vitro and was already almost in her second trimester when she finally got sentenced."

"How is this possible," Sydney gasped as she snatched her hand from Asher. "Or legal?"

"Syd, this isn't my fault. I promise I didn't know. A few years back, we started to talk about maybe having kids. We both had some work done, froze what needed to be frozen, and I honestly hadn't thought about it since. I promise, I knew nothing about this until this afternoon."

"Ms. Mack, as you know Mrs. Cross—"

"Look, I know the divorce isn't final yet, but she is not his wife."

"My apologies, she was just very adamant during the trial that she was not giving the last name up and I—"

"Vic, just wrap it man," Asher said exhaustedly.

"Right, well, as you know Ms. Cross," he stressed while sympathetically looking at Sydney, "lost everything from this. All her business deals, book deals and sponsors dropped her once this broke. She is even having a trial start soon with her former publishing company for the bad press her name has brought them. To be blunt, she is broke."

After all of the drama had settled, it was confirmed that book number five was just a figment in Genevieve's twisted mind. Once the publishing company officially sued Genevieve, they tried to at least get back pay from what was to be her final book. Unbeknownst to everyone, the book that Genevieve had been working on for months was nonexistent. There were pages written, but nothing that was comprehensible. The book was full of gibberish and love notes about Sydney and Asher. Uncovering this information only aided Genevieve's lawyers in proving how much of a nutcase she was. It did little to nothing for Asher and Sydney proving why she needed to be jailed and not hospitalized.

"How is that our problem? The bitch tried to kill us! Do I have to keep reminding everyone, because I still have the scars to prove it," Sydney said looking down at the keloid scar that ran from her kneecap to her upper thigh.

"Because a child is involved. He is three months old and at the institution with her for now."

"He?" Sydney asked, feeling her stomach turn.

"Asher Jr.," Asher said dazed.

"How is that even safe or legal?" Sydney asked again. She just couldn't understand.

"It's safe. The two of them are kept away from the other patients. And I assure you, it will remain that way until they leave," Vic said looking at Asher. "As far as legal, my team is looking into it. Clearly the procedure with Asher's sperm was done without his knowledge."

"Leave?" Sydney's heart dropped. This had to be a horrible nightmare.

"Yes, looks like even though she's dead broke, she has some friends willing to help her out. They hired some big shots, and her new attorneys are digging into her past. They are blaming all of this on PTSD from her rape as a girl. It's looking likely that she may be a free woman after all of this."

"And Rachael, India, Raphael... her mom? What about all of them?"

"No evidence, no case," Vic said nonchalantly. "Here's what it is, folks. Ms. Cross and baby will be out in a few weeks, and she will be put on house arrest for now. I will figure out the terms of that. We will make sure to take out an updated restraining order for you both if you would like. In the meantime, she and her attorneys will be coming for you for everything you got," he said to Asher. "They are already preparing for a custody battle."

Sydney put her head into her hands. Just as things were beginning to look up, here Genevieve came ruining it all again. Asher had just begun his own small architecture practice and the two were toying with the idea of moving back into the mansion once the divorce and legalities were finalized.

Sydney remembered the weight of Genevieve's body on her once she was shot. Sydney remembered wishing she was dead as the paramedics revived her on the scene. Sydney spat on her as they wheeled her past her on the gurney when the cops were questioning her.

"What do we do now?" Sydney asked. "She's gonna kill us Ash, I just know it."

"We fight Syd, we fight and we don't stop," Asher said, pulling her into his arms.

MAJOR KEY PUBLISHING
LASHAYE
Ryder
HAYNES
THE LIES THAT BIND
NEW NEW NEW NEW NEW
HAVE YOU READ THIS YET?
FREE W/KINDLE UNLIMITED!
amazon.com
FOLLOW US
@MAJORKEYPUB

READER'S GROUP

JOIN NOW!!

https://www.facebook.com/groups/everythingmajor

BE THE FIRST TO FIND OUT
ABOUT GIVEAWAYS,
CONTESTS &
NEW RELEASES!

www.majorkeypublishing.com

Be sure to check out our other releases:
www.majorkeypublishing.com/novels

To submit a manuscript to be considered, email us at
submissions@majorkeypublishing.com

Be sure to LIKE our Major Key Publishing page on Facebook!

Made in the USA
Middletown, DE
14 September 2023